Gracie Taylor grew up in rural West Yorkshire. After university she spent time in several different cities, but eventually returned to settle in the Dales. Gracie Taylor is a pen name for Lisa Firth, who also writes award-winning contemporary romantic comedies as Mary Jayne Baker and uplifting women's fiction as Lisa Swift. *Edie's Home for Strays* is her first historical novel.

Edie's Home for Strays

Gracie Taylor

avon.

Published by AVON
A division of HarperCollins*Publishers* Ltd
1 London Bridge Street
London SE1 9GF

www.harpercollins.co.uk

HarperCollins*Publishers*
1st Floor, Watermarque Building, Ringsend Road
Dublin 4, Ireland

A Paperback Original 2021

First published in Great Britain by HarperCollins*Publishers* 2021

Copyright © HarperCollins*Publishers* 2021

Gracie Taylor asserts the moral right
to be identified as the author of this work.

A catalogue copy of this book is available from the British Library.

ISBN: 978-0-00-840759-9

Typeset in Minion Pro by
Palimpsest Book Production Limited, Falkirk, Stirlingshire
Printed and bound in the UK using 100% renewable electricity at CPI Group (UK) Ltd

MIX
Paper from
responsible sources
FSC™ C007454

For my own Home Front hero:
my grandad, Eric Firth.

Chapter 1

January 1941

Edie Cartwright had been staring into her cup of tea for nearly half an hour when Susan arrived to meet her at The Sparrow Café. The brew had long since grown tepid, but Edie kept her hands wrapped around it, trying to absorb the last bit of heat. It was so hard to get warm these days, with coal in such short supply.

'Well, how do I look?' Susan asked, twirling for her.

She was kitted out in her new uniform: the khaki skirt and jacket of the ATS, with the brass badge on her cap polished to a high shine. It wasn't the most fetching of the women's auxiliary services uniforms, but the tightly belted jacket clung flatteringly to Susan's Hedy Lamarr curves and Edie reflected that her best friend would manage to look like a film star even dressed in an old potato sack. Whereas her own scrawny frame bore so much resemblance to a bag of bones, it was a wonder no one had tried to claim her for salvage.

'Like the Third Reich's worst nightmare,' she said, summoning a smile. 'Old Adolf won't know what's hit him.'

Susan laughed as she took a seat. 'Edie, I'm going to

1

work as a despatch rider in Hull; I'm not getting dropped in the heart of Germany.' She watched as her friend absently stirred her now undrinkable tea. 'Are you all right? You look unhappy.'

'Not unhappy exactly. Just . . . reflective. I can't help dwelling on the fact that after Alfie ships out tomorrow, you and I will be the last of our little set left. And in a few more weeks I'll be losing you too. That's one of the worst things about this war – I mean, apart from all the fighting. The way it breaks up families.' Edie flushed. 'I've always felt we were family, you know. At any rate, the closest I have to one.'

'I always hoped I might have you for a real-life sister one day,' Susan said with a small smile.

'Well, and so you do, in love if not in law.' Edie reached out to squeeze her hand. 'I'll miss you to blazes, Sue.'

'I'll write you all the time. Twice every week, I cross my heart.'

'You better had. I only wish I was coming with you.'

'When are you going for your examination with Dr Grant?'

'Tomorrow.' Edie held up her crossed fingers. 'Wish me luck.'

'All the luck in the world, darling.' Susan frowned as Edie took out her handkerchief to cover her mouth while she let out a hollow cough. 'But do take care, won't you? Don't push yourself to do more than you're capable of.'

'It's just the dust. All these damn raids.' The bell over the café door jingled and Edie waved to the young soldier who entered. 'Aha, here he is. The man who's going to have this thing all sewn up by Easter.'

The two women got to their feet. Susan saluted as Edie mimed playing 'Hail the Conquering Hero' on an invisible trombone.

Alfie laughed as he tossed his cap on to the table. 'At ease, ladies.'

He greeted them both with a kiss and took a seat.

'Well, Alfie, what will you have for your goodbye supper?' Susan asked. 'Anything you want, our treat. At least, anything as long as it's fish and chips because that's all they've got.'

'Fish and chips it is then,' he said, smiling. 'You know, Sue, you never offered to buy your big brother fish and chips before he was going to war. What would you call this, the condemned man's last meal?'

Edie shuddered. 'Alf, I wish you wouldn't joke about that. It's bad luck.'

'Oh, don't worry about me, sweetheart. It'll take more than that Charlie Chaplin impersonator in Berlin to beat this soldier.'

'Three cod and chips, please,' Susan said to the waitress who approached their table.

The woman shook her head. 'No cod here, darlin', nor nowhere else in London at the moment, neither. We got snoek fishcakes, rock salmon or the door.'

Edie pulled a face. 'Snoek and chips. Doesn't sound right, does it?'

Alfie shrugged. 'Well, there's war for you. No one ever said it was going to be tasty.' He shot the waitress a smile. 'That's fine, love. Three lots of fishcakes and chips.'

'On leave?' the waitress asked him as she scribbled their order in her notepad.

'Yes, embarkation leave. I'm being posted overseas.'

'Where to?'

'Oughtn't to say really, ought I? Careless talk and all that.' He smiled at the woman's raised eyebrows. 'Let's just say it's somewhere hot.'

She looked interested. 'My old man was in the Suez.'

'Oh, really? Is he still there?'

'No, my Stan ain't nowhere much these days.' She bowed her head. 'I mean, nowhere on this earth.'

Alfie looked up at the woman with sympathy in his green eyes – and, Edie thought, a hint of fear too.

'I'm sorry,' he said quietly.

'Never mind about that. Just you watch out for yourself, that's all, sonny.' She called over her shoulder to a woman who could be seen frying fish through the kitchen hatch, a cigarette balanced expertly on the edge of her lips while she hummed along with Reggie Dixon on the wireless. 'Ethel! Three snoek and chips. No charge for this young gent's.' With a brief nod to Alfie, she bustled off in a businesslike ruffle of starch.

Edie shook her head at Susan. 'Oh, to be a boy in uniform. Flash a woman a smile and you're up to your ears in free chips.'

Alfie took Edie's hand and pressed it to his lips. 'You know you only have to say the word, Edie Cartwright, and my endearing young charms can be yours alone.'

'Now, don't start all that nonsense. I'm not sure I can bring myself to turn you down in khaki.'

'Did you ever consider that perhaps that was my plan all along?' he said, grinning.

His playful teasing was interrupted by the too-familiar wail of the air-raid sirens piercing through the other sounds of the bustling city street outside.

Alfie groaned. 'The blighter never lets up, does he?'

'For goodness' sake, not again,' Susan muttered. 'I'm starved.'

'If my chips go cold then Hitler's really going to be for

4

it.' Alfie got to his feet. 'Come along, girls. Piccadilly's nearest. We'll shelter there until Jerry goes back to bed.'

'Wait there a second,' Ethel called through the kitchen hatch. 'Let me wrap these up and you can take them down with you. Gawd knows but it might be morning by the time we get the all-clear.'

When they each had a newspaper-wrapped packet of fishcake and chips tucked into their pockets, Alfie offered an arm to each of the women and they made their way through the plumes of blushing smoke to the nearest Underground station. After months of constant bombing raids, walking calmly through hell had become second nature to Edie and her fellow Londoners.

The ash that hung in the air got into Edie's lungs, making her cough. An incendiary bomb must have dropped somewhere nearby. White-hot flames licked the air in the distance, and the bark of efficient voices echoed along the street as a couple of ARP wardens with sandbags in their arms organised a chain to extinguish the fire. The skies vibrated with the moan of the sirens and the ack-ack of the anti-aircraft guns; and, above it all, the terrifying hum of the German planes.

Edie slipped her hand into her pocket, finding the soft, warm mass of her chips – slightly damp where the vinegar had soaked into the paper – oddly comforting. Fish and chips were such an ordinary, everyday thing; almost a promise that the world would, one day, be calm and peaceful once again.

'Don't fret too much about me when I'm gone, will you, Edie?' Alfie whispered as they joined a queue of people heading in the same direction.

'I can't help it, Alf.'

'Oh, I'll be all right. But, sweetheart . . . remember me in your prayers, eh?'

*

'I'm sorry, Edie,' Dr Grant said when he'd finished examining her in his rooms the following afternoon. 'I'm unable to tell you anything different from what I said before: it just isn't possible.'

'I can't accept that. I won't.'

'My dear, you don't have any choice,' he said firmly. 'If you go before the WRNS assessment panel they'll give you exactly the same answer, I'm afraid. In your state of health, it isn't safe for you to be in active service.'

'Dr Grant, please! I can do this. I'm as fit and healthy as you are.'

The old man gave a hoarse laugh. 'Oh, you're not in such poor shape as that, I hope.'

'I'm really so much better; better than I ever have been,' Edie said, a note of desperation creeping into her voice. 'I hardly cough at all any more, honestly I don't.'

Dr Grant sighed and took a seat opposite her.

'Edie, please don't lie to me. I may be an old man but I'm not quite a dotard yet.'

'Well, there is still a little coughing, perhaps,' she admitted. 'But that's only from all this dust and smoke. Outside of London, I'd be perfectly all right.'

'Now, that's the most sensible thing I've heard you say.' He leaned forward to take her hands. 'You get out of London, my girl. Join your aunt in the country. That's the best thing you could do for those poor scarred lungs of yours, and I must confess, I'd feel better for knowing you were out of Herr Hitler's reach.'

The unmarried aunt who had brought Edie up after her father's death, Aunt Caroline, had taken herself off to family in the Cotswolds in the early days of the war, but Edie had resisted the invitation to join her, opting to stay behind in the small terraced house the two of them shared. She hadn't wanted to leave her friends, or her job teaching the infant class at Brick Street School, and anyhow, the war had seemed so very far away, then. In those first few months, it hadn't really felt like there was a war on at all. Life had gone on much as it had before for those on the Home Front – with a few new hardships, true, but as autumn became winter and then melted into spring, the days had passed in exactly the same quiet, safe, familiar way they always had.

But that was before the Luftwaffe started paying their nightly visits to the capital, and the life Edie knew had ended for good. Before the nights spent underground in cold, damp shelters; before rubble and fires and bombed-out skeletons that hours earlier had been comfortable family homes. Before the high-explosive bombs that brought destruction and chaos wherever they landed, and the constant, mournful wail of the sirens. Before friends and neighbours who'd lost their health, their homes and in some cases their lives to the nightly horror of Hitler's Blitzkrieg.

Now Edie's few friends had all been stolen away by this evil thing: the boys called up into the armed forces, the girls doing various forms of war work around the country. Brick Street School was closed, its premises requisitioned by the ARP, and Edie's former pupils evacuated to the safety of the countryside. Only she remained: desperate to do her bit for the war effort but thwarted at every turn by lungs weakened through the consumption that had blighted her early childhood.

'I just want to help win this blasted thing, the same as everyone else,' she told Dr Grant. 'All my friends are doing something important. There are men out there getting shot at, people being blown to pieces, and I'm sitting at home knitting comforts for the troops like some elderly spinster.

Please, you were my father's dearest friend. You served in the trenches together. There must be something you can do.'

'I am sorry, Edie,' Dr Grant said in a gentle voice. 'I understand, of course, but I really can't in good conscience recommend you for service – either as your doctor or as an old family friend. You may feel healthy, and I hope and believe you have a long, happy life ahead of you, but your lungs will never be as strong as those of other people. That, I'm afraid, is just an inconvenient medical fact.'

'Don't tell me what I can't do, tell me what I *can* do! There must be something you think it's safe for me to volunteer for. If I can't join the auxiliary services then there's the ARP, or the Women's Voluntary Service . . .'

'Fresh air and open spaces are what you need – somewhere out of London, as I keep telling you.'

The cough Edie had been desperately trying to suppress throughout her examination now forced itself out and she hid her face in her handkerchief, feeling the sting of tears brought on by a combination of pain and mortification. Dr Grant waited patiently until the fit had subsided.

'There must be something I can do,' she repeated weakly.

'Well . . .' The doctor looked thoughtful. 'If you absolutely refuse to evacuate for your own sake, then you might consider the Women's Land Army.'

Edie blinked. 'Farm work? You think I could do that?'

'Certainly. Eyes, ears and heart are all sound, and the country air would do all manner of good for those poor lungs of yours. Life in the countryside could be just the ticket, away from the soot and ash. And besides, you'd be safe there.'

'I don't care about being safe,' Edie said, sticking out her chin. 'Why should I be safe, when everyone else is fighting?'

'Perhaps because you've lost so much already,' Dr Grant said quietly. 'As your family doctor, I can declare you physically fit for the Land Army without the need for a panel assessment. And they do good work – vital work. Think about it, Edie.'

Chapter 2

March 1941

It was early afternoon on an unseasonably balmy Saturday in mid-March and Edie was waiting for the most important train of her life: the train that would take her away from London towards a new existence.

A smell of roasted chestnuts drifted to her from somewhere nearby, the scent blending in her nostrils with fresh-blooming lilacs, cigarette smoke, hot bodies. It was the sort of incongruous but oddly delicious mix you could only find in the big city. She'd miss that, when she was gone.

All was serene. It was hard to believe that tonight the air would be thick with smoke and sirens as the German planes returned for yet another assault on the capital, bathing the London skyline in fire. After six months of continuous bombing raids, the Luftwaffe were showing no signs of getting bored. But for now the city was quiet, only the barrage balloons dotting the sky serving to remind Edie that this coming spring would not be like any that had gone before.

A dog – a stray, judging by his protruding ribs and

mangy fur – had approached to sniff at one of her suitcases. Edie bent down to give the poor fellow a stroke.

'Hungry?' she whispered. The dog looked up at her with sad brown eyes and Edie rummaged among her possessions for some food.

'Here you are,' she said, slipping the dog an arrowroot biscuit from the meal she'd packed. 'Make it last, now. There's not a lot of it around at the moment.'

The train pulled in, spewing out steam like a huge, angry teakettle, and Edie watched the dog slink off with his bounty.

'You shouldn't feed it, you know,' a young sailor who was lounging nearby observed, blowing a lazy smoke ring from his cigarette. 'We're hard pushed to feed people these days, let alone disease-ridden vermin like that. Better to starve 'em out.'

Edie kept her face fixed, trying not to let her irritation show.

'I can't accept it's ever wrong to help someone – or something – worse off than you are,' she said. 'That's why we're fighting, isn't it?'

'You have to think about the greater good, love. We all want to get through this thing alive if we can.'

'Well, doesn't that apply to animals other than human beings?'

The man shrugged. 'It's a matter of being cruel to be kind, by my reckoning. My dad had our old lurcher put to sleep the week war broke out – best way, he said, spare her worse to come.'

He wasn't the only one. Edie knew of dozens of friends and neighbours who'd chosen to have their pets humanely killed rather than subject them to the unknown horrors that might be lying ahead. It had near broken her heart, seeing people trudging home clutching a bag containing the remains of the family's much-loved dog or cat for burial in the back garden. Thank God, her own beloved Tessie – Aunt Caroline's ancient Siamese – had accompanied her mistress to the safety of the Cotswolds.

Edie wondered to whom the stray dog she'd fed had belonged. Had his owners evacuated and left him? Died in a raid? She'd never seen so many scavenging strays on the streets of London as she had since the nightly blitzes began six months ago.

Poor, lost little souls. How awful it was to see animals suffer: that heartbreaking bewilderment in their eyes because they couldn't understand where their world had suddenly disappeared to. She'd give them all a home if she could.

The sailor watched Edie struggling with her heavy luggage for a moment before straightening up. 'You need a hand with that?'

'I can cope, thank you.' She forced a smile. 'I'm about to start work as a Land Girl, it won't hurt me to build some brawn.'

'Suit yourself.' He stamped his cigarette out and walked off to find his carriage.

Once Edie had loaded her luggage on to the overhead rack in her compartment, she claimed a seat and took out the papers telling her everything the local War Agricultural Committee felt she needed to know about her new home. Which apparently wasn't a lot.

She was headed for the village of Applefield in Cumberland, not far from Kirkton: the town where her father had been born, although she'd never been there herself. There she'd be billeted on a local estate, Applefield Manor, managed by a lone widow – Prudence Hewitt – and her staff.

There was scant information about the estate itself; however, its grounds covered several acres and their upkeep had obviously been deemed vital to the war effort by somebody at the War Ag, so Edie guessed it must be rather grand. Her responsibilities were to assist the gardener there in the orchard and kitchen gardens for three days a week, and for the other two and a half she would be working at the romantic-sounding Larkstone Farm nearby.

There was nothing about how many girls would be billeted at Applefield Manor along with her. Edie just hoped they wouldn't be too stuck up. Susan and Alfie were good correspondents, but a letter wasn't the same as a flesh-and-blood friend. There would be nothing worse than starting a new life among strangers who'd already made up their minds they didn't want her there. And Northerners could be uncommonly close, couldn't they? Suspicious of outsiders. Edie wasn't quite an outsider – half the blood in her veins belonged to that part of the world – but she had a feeling that was unlikely to help her case a great deal.

She sighed as she packed her papers away again. Edie didn't question that the Land Army did valuable work, ensuring there was food enough to fill hungry bellies for the months, perhaps even years, it could take for the war to be settled one way or another. But on the training course she'd attended – learning how to load a threshing machine; the correct way to apply udder cream; how to plant a potato – the work had seemed so . . . ordinary. So small.

Before her medical assessment, Edie had dreamed of joining the Wrens and applying for overseas posting. Saving lives, seeing the world, helping in a very real, tangible way to win this bloody war; it was everything she wanted. But then Dr Grant had delivered the bad news about her health, and . . . well, here she was on a train to the very back of

13

the back of beyond, preparing to do her bit for the war effort not through helping to plan key naval operations but by trimming some old lady's box hedges.

She cast an envious look at the woman who had taken a seat opposite, her smart navy-blue jacket and peaked cap clearly marking her out as a Wren.

'Good afternoon,' the Wren said, smiling cheerily. 'Rather a scorcher for the time of year. Far to go?'

Edie nodded. 'Cumberland. I'm taking up a posting there.'

'Crumbs, as far as that! Which service?'

'The Land Army.'

'Oh, really? Well, good for you.' Edie couldn't help noticing the slight sneer on the woman's lips. 'Still, rather you than me, dearie. Terribly ugly uniform, isn't it? Every little helps though.'

Having discovered Edie was only a lowly Land Girl and not a member of the Forces, the woman's attention drifted away and Edie was left alone with her thoughts for the rest of the journey up north.

The journey to her new home was a feat in itself. The train from Euston ought to have taken Edie directly to Kirkton, but bomb damage to the line meant it was diverted to Oxford, where Edie transferred to the Wolverhampton train, and from there she went on to Crewe. There followed a cold night spent shivering on the platform while she waited for the train to Kirkton – as the Land Army were not a fighting force she was denied entry to the NAAFI tearoom there, which felt rather hard when she, too, was about to take up valuable war work. After an uncomfortable night Edie was tired enough to get a little sleep on the Kirkton train, and from there she caught the bus to Applefield.

By the time she reached the stop where her directions instructed her she should alight, Edie had been travelling for the best part of two days in hot, dark, crowded vehicles and was utterly exhausted. Frequent stops for air raids and roadblocks, with hours spent shunted into sidings, and diversions due to damage on the railway lines had extended the journey significantly, and it was after nine o'clock at night when she finally stepped off the bus.

The last leg of the journey was equally gruelling, although it was only a mile and a half. Edie was met at the bus stop in Applefield by the local coalman and driven in his rickety horse-drawn cart over dark, narrow roads to her new home of Applefield Manor. Her poor old bones felt like they'd been fed through the threshing machine she'd spent so many long, cold days learning to use during her four-week Land Army training course.

In pitch darkness and with every cottage window blacked out, it was hard to properly get a feel for her surroundings as they drove. She could just make out the ominous shadows of the fells all around them, rising black against the star-flecked sky. The sky that felt so disconcertingly empty and quiet when in London the moan of sirens and the sinister bumblebee drone of the bombers had become such a part of everyday life. Here, the only sound was the occasional bleat of a sheep.

Edie had expected to feel a certain freedom out in the countryside. That was what one was supposed to feel, wasn't it? But in reality, the impassable giants all around her, the tightly packed little settlements, the narrow, frightening roads, all served to make her feel more hemmed in than she ever had in the city. Here, it seemed, was a place with no escape route. While Edie couldn't deny she felt relieved – as well as a little guilty – at having broken free from the terror of the Blitz, homesickness began to gnaw. She fumbled for the little silver watch she always wore around her neck, pressing it with her fingers as they pushed on into the darkness.

Applefield Manor, too, was shrouded in velvet darkness when they arrived, although Edie could tell it was built on quite a scale. She wondered how many others were billeted there, and if she'd have a roommate.

When the old man driving the cart had unloaded her suitcases and driven off, Edie pulled the bell rope that hung by the large front door, before immediately wondering if she ought to have looked for some sort of tradesman's entrance.

It was answered by a woman Edie assumed must be the housekeeper. She was dressed in a plain black frock and stiff white collar, her hair pulled back into a bun so severe it looked almost painful. The harsh hairstyle, stern expression and Quaker-like attire made her look older than she was, although Edie would have estimated her real age at no more than fifty.

'Um. Good evening.' Edie faltered in the face of the woman's hard stare. 'Edith Cartwright; Mrs Hewitt is expecting me. Could you tell her I've arrived, please?'

'I can, very easily indeed.' Edie thought she could detect the faintest flicker of amusement in the woman's face. 'Come in.'

Edie blushed at her mistake. 'I'm so sorry. You're Mrs Hewitt?' She'd been expecting somebody rather older, and, well, grander than the plain, bird-like woman before her.

'I am the lady of the house, yes,' Mrs Hewitt said in a clipped voice. 'And perfectly capable of managing the household myself, despite what must seem to you my very advanced years.'

16

It was a strange accent she had. Cautious and considered, each vowel carefully rounded, like the woman was unconsciously trying to cover up her native Cumberland tones. 'Gives herself airs, that one,' Edie could imagine her Aunt Caroline muttering with a disapproving sniff. But Edie sensed it stemmed more from a learned sense of shame, a fear of being somehow 'found out', than from any delusions of grandeur.

'Well, you'll be tired, I expect,' Mrs Hewitt said in an offhand tone. 'I'll give you a quick tour, then my cook will provide you with a bite of supper before bed. Leave your luggage and gas mask in the hall for now.'

Edie left her cases at the foot of the stairs and followed Mrs Hewitt as she made her way with purposeful strides down the oak-panelled hallway.

'Are we far from Larkstone Farm here?' Edie asked.

'Not very far. Some two miles.'

'Who is it run by? A family, or . . .'

'Samuel Nicholson manages their flock of Herdwicks alone now, since his uncle passed on,' Mrs Hewitt said. 'I daresay he'll be grateful for another pair of hands during lambing season. I've arranged with him that you won't start work there until Thursday next, to give you a little time to settle in here. When you're not working for him then you'll be under orders from Mr Graham, my gardener.' Mrs Hewitt gestured in the direction of what must be the gardens, although any view of them was blocked by the heavy blackout curtains covering all the windows. 'We're aiming to plant potatoes on some of our unused land, and there's the greenhouses to tend to, the kitchen garden, and the apples from the orchard to get in if you're still with us when the season comes around. Our gardens provide fruit and vegetables for the whole village, not merely ourselves.

Jack – Mr Graham – will give you your itinerary tomorrow.' She fixed Edie with a stern look. 'And mind, Edith, the staff here are used to hard work. We've little time for shirkers in this part of the world.'

Oh yes, all very well when you were the lady of the manor, eating grapes and fanning yourself while you watched the lower orders do the work. But Edie just smiled politely.

'That's fine,' she said. 'I've come prepared to get my hands dirty. Dig for victory and all that – stuff.'

Edie had stopped herself just in time. 'All that rot,' she'd been about to say, but that would have sounded mocking and disrespectful. She wasn't with her friends now, laughing at it all like some big joke to hide the fact that deep down, they were bloody terrified. Terrified of losing someone they loved. Terrified of dying themselves. And more than all that, terrified of losing the war – and of what might come after if they did. But that was defeatist talk, and even with Susan, her oldest, closest friend, Edie would never dare give voice to such an idea.

'Well, let's hope you still feel that way after a week or two of graft,' Mrs Hewitt was saying when Edie tuned back in to the here and now. She looked Edie up and down, taking in her skinny five-foot-two frame and pale, freckled complexion. 'I must say, I was hoping they'd send me someone rather more . . . a strong, sturdy country girl was what I asked for.'

Edie suppressed a wave of annoyance. Why did everyone insist upon treating her like some puny weakling? She might be small, but she was determined.

'I'm stronger than I look,' she said. Mrs Hewitt, however, looked far from convinced.

'Hmm. Well, for your sake I hope so. And, Edith, do

make sure you wear a hat when you're out in the sun. With your fair skin and red hair, you must burn terribly. Now follow me.'

She led Edie into a room and gestured around it with little interest. 'Sitting room. I never spend time in here, but you're welcome to do so if you wish. I've a wireless set in the library I can have moved in for you. For myself, I mostly keep to my room of an evening and read. I've grown used to my own company since my son Bertie joined up.'

The room was large, but somewhat neglected. Carpets and furnishings that must once have been grand had grown shabby, fraying at the edges, and a glass chandelier was missing much of its crystal. Furniture was covered by old cotton sheets.

'That's very kind,' Edie said. 'The other girls, do they sit in here?'

'Other girls?'

'I assumed you must have other Land Girls billeted with you. Don't you?'

'I told the county committee I only required one, to help Jack now the boy we used to have has been called up. I don't care to have strangers in the house unless it's absolutely necessary.'

'Yes, but when you have all this space . . . there must be some way it can be used to help the war effort. It seems such a waste otherwise.'

Mrs Hewitt frowned. 'Young lady, I believe you're forgetting yourself. What I do with my home is my business.'

Edie flushed. 'I'm sorry, I didn't mean to be impertinent. I simply thought . . .'

'Not all thoughts need to be uttered. Some are far better off remaining in our heads.' With a stern look that reminded

Edie of Aunt Caroline in her terrifying, maiden-aunt prime, Mrs Hewitt beckoned for her to follow.

'This is the dining room,' she said, pushing open a door. 'Dinner is served at 6 p.m., but as you'll be working long hours during the lambing season, I've instructed Matilda, the cook, to be prepared with cold provisions on the days you're at the farm.'

'Thank you.'

'Now for the other rules, there are to be absolutely no gentlemen callers, or visitors of any kind without my prior consent. Curfew is 9 p.m. on weekdays, but on Saturdays you may stay out as late as 10 p.m. Monday to Wednesday you'll be working here with Mr Graham, and from next week, Thursdays, Fridays and Saturday mornings will be spent at Larkstone Farm. Saturday afternoons are your own. Sundays we go to church, then you can spend the rest of the day how you wish. Are you church or chapel?' Mrs Hewitt paused, then, when Edie didn't answer immediately, carried on. 'Because if you're chapel, we've none in Applefield. You'll have to bicycle to the next village. If you're Catholic, there's a makeshift place of worship in one of the Nicholsons' old barns for the Italian prisoners of war – they live mostly at the farm during lambing. That's if you don't mind sharing with them, but after all, we're all God's children.'

'Um, I'm Church of England,' Edie said, feeling a little dazed by the barrage of information delivered in Mrs Hewitt's staccato, no-nonsense manner. She wasn't a regular churchgoer at home – not since her aunt had left for the country, anyhow – but she could see that her new landlady believed Sunday mornings ought to be spent on your knees or not at all.

Mrs Hewitt nodded her approval. 'Then you may come to St Mark's with me and the rest of the household. There are only the four of us: you, Mr Graham, Matilda and myself.'

'Yes. Thank you.'

Edie's eyes were drawn to a couple of photographs in matching silver frames sitting on an oak dresser: two young men, one in army and one in navy uniform. They were very alike in build and features, although their outfits and the quality of the photographs showed them to be serving in different wars.

'Your husband?' she asked, nodding to the man in the army uniform.

'Yes.' Mrs Hewitt followed Edie's gaze, and for the first time her expression softened. 'Albert. He was a captain in the last war.'

'Did he come home?'

Edie bit her lip almost as soon as she'd asked the question. What a thing to ask of a widow, and a stranger to boot! But Mrs Hewitt didn't seem to have noticed, gazing at the photograph with a little smile playing at the corner of her mouth.

'He was one of the lucky ones, I suppose, if you can call any of the men who lived through the horror of the trenches lucky. Yes, he came home.' She sighed. 'But he's gone now.'

'Your boy looks a lot like him.'

'He does, and like him in character too,' Mrs Hewitt said, with another brief flicker of a smile. 'Scapegraces, the pair of them, always finding their way into trouble when they were lads. Young Bertie is a midshipman on the *Majestic*.' Mrs Hewitt turned to look at her. 'Do you have family in the Forces?'

'Friends, yes, but no family. I don't have any close relatives, besides an elderly aunt. My mother died giving birth to me, and I never had brothers or sisters.'

'I'm sorry to hear that.' Mrs Hewitt's voice sounded ever so slightly gentler, and although her face was as stern as ever, there was pity in her eyes. In these days of loss upon loss, when everyone was encouraged to bury their grief under a song, a smile and a stiff upper lip, those telltale signs of compassion meant a lot.

'What about your father?' Mrs Hewitt asked.

'He . . .' Edie swallowed. 'He's dead too.'

'The war?'

Not the war. Me. I killed him.

Edie turned her face away while she blinked back a tear. 'No, tuberculosis. When I was six.' She forced a smile and turned back. 'I'm sorry, but would you mind awfully showing me to my room now? I've had a very long journey.'

Chapter 3

Edie was woken by the welcome smell of frying bacon, and a numbness in her bare toes where they'd slipped from under the covers. She turned on the bedside lamp, looked at the alarm clock and groaned.

Nearly 5.30 a.m., which meant the alarm would start ringing at any moment. And on the days she was working at Larkstone Farm, she'd need to get up even earlier. Edie knew the working day began at cock-crow out in the countryside, but it was still a shock to the system. She reached for the clock and turned off the alarm before the deafening ringing pierced the air.

Still, the early start was worth it if that was the price of spending the night in an actual bed, in an actual room, rather than shivering in the damp of the Anderson shelter dug into a pit in Aunt Caroline's back garden. A hot water bottle and an eiderdown quilt too! Unimaginable luxury. The hot water bottle had long since grown cold, but the eiderdown was wonderful to wake up to. Edie pulled it over her face and rubbed her cheeks into it, savouring the downy softness.

The bedroom she'd been shown to by Mrs Hewitt the evening before was spartan apart from the indulgence of her fluffy eiderdown, containing little more than an iron bedstead, dressing table, wardrobe and chair. Edie's uniform – the green woollen pullover and corduroy breeches of the Women's Land Army – were laid out over the chair ready for her first day of work.

Edie poked a toe out from under the bedclothes again to test the air. It was cold: so, so cold compared to the crammed city full of warm human bodies. Edie twitched aside one corner of the heavy blackout curtain and noticed that ice crystals had tessellated prettily inside the thick panes of the mullioned windows. She drew her toe back under the quilt, trying to muster the will to get out of bed before Mrs Hewitt came to make sure she was awake.

Prudence Hewitt: now there was an odd one. Edie couldn't decide how she felt about her new landlady. She seemed so closed off, so inexpressive. During the whole of their conversation the previous evening, Mrs Hewitt's features had scarcely flickered – except perhaps when she'd talked of her husband and son.

To Edie's romantic imagination, Prudence Hewitt seemed almost a Miss Havisham figure, alone in this huge house with only a couple of servants for company. Yet she didn't seem lonely – if anything, Edie sensed Prudence was irritated by the intrusion of an outsider into her solitude, although she herself had been the one to request assistance from the Land Army.

Unpatriotic, Aunt Caroline would have called it. From Wolf Cubs to white-haired matriarchs, everyone was doing their bit for the war effort in one way or another, and yet here was this snooty widow acting as though the conflict currently threatening their freedom was everyone's problem but hers.

It made Edie angry. Edie, who had been so desperate to serve that she'd happily have risked her fragile health to do so; and she was far from the only one willing to make that sacrifice. Whereas Mrs Hewitt had rooms and land at her disposal that she'd rather see decay than used to help win this thing.

Other houses the size of Applefield Manor had been turned into hospitals and convalescent homes, or given over to the army as billets for soldiers doing basic training. Every country dweller with a spare room had an evacuee or two staying with them. During her tour of the house last night, Edie had counted at least six empty bedrooms – did Mrs Hewitt really care so little about the plight of her fellow man that she couldn't turn a few of them over to those who needed them? There were sick and injured in need of beds, children desperate to escape the bombs . . .

And yet . . . Edie inhaled the freshly laundered scent of her eiderdown. There were few touches of luxury at crumbling, austere Applefield Manor. The fact Mrs Hewitt had shown enough concern for Edie's comfort to procure this for her was an act of unwarranted kindness that indicated she couldn't be devoid of softer emotions.

Then there was her accent, the one she took so much trouble to try to hide – hardly the crystal tones of landed gentry. Exactly what was Prudence's story? Yes, the lady of the manor was an enigma all right.

With an effort, Edie eased herself into a sitting position and peeped through the blackout curtains to get a better look at her new home. But it was still dark, and she could only make out the same shadows as when she'd arrived the evening before.

There was a knock at the door. Edie let the curtain drop.

'Yes?' she called.

'You'd best show a leg,' a gruff male voice with a strong Cumberland accent said. 'Work to be done.'

'Yes, I'm coming. Thank you.'

The voice hadn't felt it necessary to introduce itself, but Edie guessed it must belong to the gardener, Jack. She got up, dressed carefully in her uniform and went downstairs to the kitchen.

Prue watched from the shadows as the girl descended, looking rather childlike in the too-large breeches and jersey of her Land Girl uniform. Such a little thing . . .

Her smallness triggered a protective feeling in Prue. Cursing herself for her weakness, she banished it to the depths.

It did no good to get close. The girl was a tool, nothing more.

Prue didn't much care for this, lurking in doorways as if she were a stranger in her own home. Still, she was a necessary evil, this Land Girl; Prue was aware of that. Jack was fifty years old – he couldn't manage the gardens all alone, and this nasty business in foreign parts had taken most of the able-bodied lads from the village. Not to mention that Jack was . . . well, there was the other issue to consider. He was a good man – an old friend – and after a lifetime of service, she owed it to him to ensure he didn't struggle.

The girl – Edith, wasn't that her name? – had been something of a disappointment. Pale, little, and far too delicate for hard work; not at all what Prue had asked for. The bony thing looked as though she'd never seen a good meal. Prue had decided to give the child a fortnight, then if Edith wasn't up to the work she'd see if she couldn't trade her in for a more suitable replacement. Prue needed someone who could ease the burden Jack was currently shouldering alone, not add to it. If the girl had come to her with the sort of weak, sickly disposition that would require constant care . . . well, this wasn't a hospital.

Rather sure of herself for such a tiny thing, Prue thought as she watched Edith march into the kitchen. Polite enough, perhaps, but over-confident; not afraid to speak her mind. It wouldn't have done in Prue's day, certainly it wouldn't – she could just picture the back of her mother's hand heading her way if Mam had caught her only daughter swaggering about, taking her betters to task.

But Prue had been raised in the days when the old queen was still alive, and children seen but not heard – and ideally not seen an awful lot either. These young bits now just didn't seem to care what people thought of them, Prue reflected with a touch of reluctant admiration. That was the way of things, she supposed. People changed, the world changed, and the human race was lucky if it could survive from one generation to the next.

Well, the world could do as it wished, but this was Prue's home – her world – and war or no war, at Applefield Manor she made the rules.

She turned when she felt a heavy hand on her shoulder.

'You eaten, Cheggy?'

'Jack.' Her face lit with a smile. 'No, I'm going to wait until the girl's finished. I don't like to go in while she's there.'

'You'll eat now,' he said firmly. 'If you don't, you won't. I know you.'

'You mollycoddle like a mother hen, Jack Graham. I'm a grown woman, you know. An old woman.'

He smiled. 'To me you'll always be that same little thing with her skirts full of horse chestnuts and her face full of brazen cheek.' He pinched one of her cheeks, as if to make his point. 'Come on. I'm going to see you served myself. You're getting scrawny as a plucked pigeon, lass.'

'Jack, I don't like this,' she muttered, her gaze turning in the direction of the kitchen. 'This . . . this damned invasion.'

'You asked for her, Cheg.'

'I asked for her through necessity. That doesn't mean I have to be happy about it.'

'I told you, there's no necessity for owt. I can manage well enough. This business'll be over by the autumn, trust me, and the boys will be home.'

'That's what they said the last time,' Prue muttered. 'It'll all be over by Christmas – do you remember? Four years later, millions slaughtered . . .'

'That was different.'

'Was it? There are still boys out there fighting. Losing their lives, or worse, their wits –'

Jack flinched heavily, and Prue cursed herself.

'Oh, Jack, I'm sorry,' she said gently. 'I shouldn't have said that.'

He was silent for a moment, staring down at the carpet.

'This is different,' he repeated when he finally looked up. 'The Kaiser was a clever customer. This Hitler's a madman. He'll never hold out another year – less if we can get the Yanks to come in with us. You didn't ought to have stuck your oar in, Cheg. I'm just fine on my own.'

Prue looked up into his face, brown as a nut from outdoor work, somewhat lined now around the eyes and mouth, and rough with a grizzled half-beard. Heavy purple bags nestled under his eyes, and there was a greyish tinge to the deep tan.

'"Just fine" my Aunt Fanny, old man.' She softened her voice. 'The dreams have been bothering you again. Haven't they?'

'Nay, not lately. Not so much.' He turned away. 'Bad night's sleep, that's all. Birthing yow on one of the farms bleating her lungs out half the night.'

'Jack, come on.' She tapped his arm. 'You can't kid me, I've known you too long.'

'Well, it don't matter. Let's eat, shall we? I want to get the measure of this new girl of ours.'

Chapter 4

'Good morning,' Tilly said when Edie had followed her nose – and her grumbling stomach – into the kitchen. It felt like a long time since the hunk of bread and cheese she'd had for supper the night before. Edie had never been a big eater, but the country air had obviously stimulated her appetite.

Edie had met Tilly the previous evening, and been struck by how little the woman resembled her idea of a cook in a country house. For a start, she didn't look much older than Edie herself – she surely couldn't be more than twenty-three. Secondly, she was tall and willowy – or at least, she would have been willowy some months previously – with vibrant copper hair Edie felt sure had come out of a bottle, and arms and legs as thin as twigs.

Once when she was small, Edie had overheard her Aunt Caroline tell a friend that you should never trust either a skinny cook or a fat footman. She hadn't understood what that meant at the time, but the meaning had dawned on her once she was grown up. A fat footman is likely to have his fingers in the butter, and it must follow that a skinny cook is a rather poor one.

Nevertheless, Edie trusted Matilda Liddell the instant

Mrs Hewitt had introduced them; she couldn't help it. Tilly might not have the chubby limbs and mop of white curls that cooks always had in picture books, but the blooming cheeks and wide smile certainly fitted. And any doubt the cook might not be doing her job properly was instantly assuaged by the scent now emanating from the cooker.

'Morning.' Edie inhaled deeply as she took a seat at the kitchen table. 'Golly, that smells good. You certainly eat well here, don't you? You'd hardly know there was a war on at all.'

'Perk of country living, love. There's always a bit of extra fat to skim off the land,' Tilly said as she piled a plate high with bacon, toast and mushrooms.

Edie eyed the plate warily. 'Not the black market?'

'Oh no, nothing underhand. But there's plenty of game about, and a little extra from the farms when all's divvied up . . . you know, enough to keep us off the tripe.' She gave Edie's cheek a sisterly pinch as she placed her breakfast in front of her, and Edie noticed an unusual ring she was wearing: thick silver, crudely wrought. 'Anyway, it looks like we need to fatten you up.'

'I'm not going to try to talk you out of it,' Edie said with a smile.

'If you give me your book, I'll pick up your rations with the rest of the household's.' Tilly cast her eyes over Edie's uniform. 'Now that brings back memories. You'll never see it that clean again, I promise you.'

Edie blinked. 'You were a Land Girl?'

'Before I invalided myself out,' Tilly said, placing one hand on her swollen belly. 'I was your predecessor up at Larkstone, with a couple of girls from the WLA hostel in Kirkton.'

'How did you like it?'

31

'Hard work, but I adored every second. Mind you, I'm born and bred in Applefield. Farming's in our blood.' She took in Edie's skinny frame. 'I hope you won't find it too much.'

For goodness' sake, not this again . . .

'I'm stronger than I look,' Edie muttered while she dug into her food.

'Oh, please don't be offended,' Tilly said, resting a hand on her shoulder. 'I'd hate for you to push yourself too hard, that's all. Just promise me you won't let Sam bully you.'

Edie frowned. 'The farmer? Why, is he likely to try?'

'He's not a cruel man, but he can be a hard one to read – and to like, until you understand him. Not a great talker, and exacting with his workers.' Tilly turned down the heat on the gas cooker. 'Sam tends to forget that not everyone is used to twelve-hour days chasing errant sheep over the fells. But he'll play fair with you, and if you stand up to him once, you'll have his respect forever.'

'Right.' Edie was starting to build a picture of this gruff old farmer: grizzled, set in his ways, suspicious of outsiders. But as nervous as she was, she was determined to hold her own when the time came to meet him. 'Well, thanks for the advice.'

'My pleasure.' Tilly arched her back, one hand on her stomach. 'Oof,' she said, wincing. 'It gets more difficult every day, this lark.'

'How many months left?'

'Three or four, I think. I'm not sure of the exact date, to be honest.'

'Which service is your husband in?'

'None of them. I haven't got one.'

'Oh, I'm sorry. You're a widow?'

'No. Not a widow.'

'Oh. Oh!' Edie said as the penny dropped. 'So he left you. You poor thing, what rotten luck.'

'Nothing so romantic, I'm afraid.' Tilly turned back to the cooker. 'No, the father was one of the Brylcreem boys from the airbase. Charlie. There was a dance and . . . well, you know how these flyers are. Talking girls out of their knickers must be part of RAF basic training. One minute he's waltzing you over the floor, all handsome in his uniform, whispering in husky tones that Veronica Lake isn't a patch on you and asking if you've ever thought of going into films.' She sighed. 'The next thing you know, you've missed a monthly, he's hopped it to goodness knows where and you're seriously up the creek. You know?'

Edie knew. All her friends knew to be on their guard against *those* men: the ones who pressed the idea that it was a girl's patriotic duty to give them 'something to remember her by' before they shipped out – with the unlucky girls finding themselves left with something to remember him by too.

'Does he know about the baby?' she asked.

Tilly nodded.

'And he won't do the decent thing?'

'That's the problem, he already did. I found out after I was expecting that he already had a wife down in Somerset. Serves me right, I suppose.' She glanced up from the cooker when Edie remained silent. 'Sorry, I didn't shock you, did I?'

'No,' Edie said quickly. 'No, of course you didn't. Why should I be shocked?'

She laughed. 'Sweetheart, your eyes are as round as plates. And I mean the big ones we use for company.'

'I'm sorry. I mean, I know how it all works and everything,

but I've never met anyone before who . . .' Edie broke off. 'Perhaps I have led rather a sheltered life. I was raised by a maiden aunt and she was excessively stuffy about those sorts of things. But I don't . . . *think* anything about it, honestly. I try never to judge anyone. Why should I? I've got no right to.'

'Well, I wish I could say the same about the old guard down in the village,' Tilly said with a wry half-smile. 'I suspect they'd get on rather well with your aunty. Things err on the traditional side here.'

'Are your parents in Applefield?'

'Not any more. Couldn't stand the looks in church of a Sunday. I've got an aunt who won't speak to me and that's it.'

'So you've got no one to help you?'

'I wouldn't quite say that.' Tilly turned to face her. 'How did you find Prue? Did you like her?'

'Not exactly. And not exactly not. She seems . . . odd.' Edie mopped up her bacon fat with a chunk of Tilly's home-baked bread, so much lighter than the tough wedges of National Loaf she'd been surviving on back in London. 'Sort of cold.'

'I know what you mean.' Tilly took the empty plate and put it in the sink. 'I've known her all my life. Me and my cousins used to dare each other to steal fruit from her greenhouses, and get a clip round the ear for our trouble if she caught us. She was always . . . formidable, shall we say. But when it felt like everyone in the village had turned their back on me, Prue was the one who offered me a home and situation.' Tilly eased herself into a seat across the table. 'I owe her a lot.'

Edie pondered this, tracing shapes on the old oak table. 'Why do you think she keeps the house empty like this?'

she said. 'It seems a shame it's not being used to help the war effort.'

'She doesn't care much for outsiders. It's my opinion she closed herself off after her husband Albert died in '32. Then when Bertie joined up, she withdrew even further. I believe they were the only people she ever really loved in her life, Albert and Bertie – and perhaps one other.'

'Yet she offered you a place.'

'She did, although she'd managed without a cook for years. She used to do all that herself, and still could if she was minded, I imagine.' Tilly poured Edie a cup of tea from the pot that sat snug in its knitted cosy between them. 'If you ask me, Prue has a weakness for lost causes. Not that you'll ever hear her admit it.'

'Are you a lost cause?'

'We all are, here. I think it's safe to say that the world's given up on each of us, one way or another.'

'Then I ought to fit in perfectly,' Edie said with a smile.

'You as well?'

'I'm afraid so.'

'You'll have to tell me about it sometime.' Tilly glanced towards the door, where there were sounds of movement, and lowered her voice. 'If you really want to get the measure of Prudence Hewitt, Edie, then watch her with Jack.'

Edie frowned. 'The gardener?'

'Not only the gardener.' Tilly put a finger to her lips as the door opened. 'Just watch.'

'Good morning, girls,' Mrs Hewitt said. 'I hope you won't mind if we join you.'

Tilly smiled at Edie. 'I think we can allow that, don't you? Since it is Prue's house.'

Edie smiled back, a little uncertainly, and drew her legs under her chair to make room for them at the small table.

Mrs Hewitt took the seat Tilly had previously occupied, and the huge, silent mountain of gardener sat down beside her. His beetling brows looked like they were joined in the middle as he directed a fierce glare at Edie. She summoned a friendly smile, but he didn't change his expression.

'I generally eat in here with the staff,' Mrs Hewitt said to Edie. 'It seems foolish to set the dining table when we're so few. But now we have an additional member of the household, perhaps we might make more of an effort to dine formally on the days when you're working in the gardens.'

Edie was surprised to hear that it was customary for the staff and the lady of the house to eat together, but she bit her tongue.

She watched as Tilly placed a plate of food in front of her mistress, only for Jack to shake his head and hand it back again.

'Another rasher and four or five more of those mushrooms for Missus,' he said firmly. 'She can't live on that.'

Prue smiled. 'Now, Jack. There's a war on, don't forget. We all have to tighten our belts.'

'You can have my share. I've no appetite this morning.'

'No, I won't have that. What have I got to do with myself but potter about in the house? You'll be turning soil most of the day, you need a full belly.'

For the first time, Edie saw Jack's brow ease and his lips relax in a smile. 'Cheggy, we'll be trying to feed each other all morning at this rate. Just do as you're told, lass. I really couldn't eat yet.'

'There's the remains of last night's hunt pie in the pantry,' Tilly said. 'You can have it as an early lunch, Jack.'

'There, you see? I'm all provided for,' Jack said, nudging Prue.

She smiled. 'You're a hard man to say no to, Jack Graham. Between me and that damn bird of yours, I believe you'd give all your food away if I let you.'

Jack flashed her a full grin, the triumph of knowing he'd won glowing through as Tilly placed a piled plate in front of Prue.

'Edie, as I'm sure you've gathered, this is Jack – Mr Graham,' Tilly said. 'I suppose I might as well do the introductions if no one else is going to.'

'How do you do?' Edie said politely, holding out her hand.

Jack eyed it suspiciously.

'We work hard here,' he told her.

Edie could feel a cough trying to force its way to her throat and fought to stifle it. She could sense Jack was trying to get the measure of her, and she didn't want to show any weakness.

'So I've been informed,' she said stiffly.

'I don't know what you're used to down in London, but we've little truck with shirkers in the north. Their sorts don't tend to last long here, any road. If it's an easy time you're after then you'd best go back where you've come from.'

Edie sat up straighter. 'What makes you think that's what I want?'

His eyes skimmed her body. 'You weren't built for graft, child.'

The cough forced itself out, but after a moment's painful wheezing, Edie was able to force it back under control.

'Maybe not, but I'm reliably informed there's a war on,' she said hoarsely.

'Mappen there is,' Jack said. 'If you did nowt but read the papers and listen to the wireless, you'd think there was nothing mattered but the bloody war. But my concern's not with wars, it's with this potato crop I want to get in the ground by end of April. And while you're working this estate with me, so's yours.'

Edie bristled. 'No, my concern is helping to win the war. The Women's Land Army isn't cheap labour for your vegetable patch, Mr Graham.'

Jack shot Prue a look of surprise, but his mistress just quirked an eyebrow while she tackled her bacon and mushrooms.

'Edie, don't listen to him,' Tilly said, shaking her head at Jack. 'We're not growing spuds for our own amusement. We want to reclaim some waste ground to grow potatoes we can sell down in the village. We're also planning to invest in a chicken coop and some hens so we'll have eggs to sell as well.'

'Hens?'

'That's right. Just a couple to begin with, then once we've got the hang of it we'll get more. So you see, we are doing our bit to keep people fed.'

Jack nodded. 'Aye, we do our share. Maybe it's not glamorous, Miss whatever your name is –'

'Cartwright.'

'Maybe it's not glamorous, Miss Cartwright, but I'm sure you've heard the saying that an army marches on its stomach. You can't win a war with a grumbling belly.'

'I'm well aware of that, Mr Graham. I'd hardly be here if I wasn't.'

Jack's face creased in a grin. He grasped her tiny hand in a bear-like fist and gave it a firm shake. 'Well, you might not have much brawn but you've got guts. And a fair cheek on you too.' He glanced at Prue. 'I knew another little lass like you once. Let's see how you get along, shall we?'

Edie laughed as he released her hand, flexing it to bring some feeling back into her fingers. 'You mean you're going to be testing me.'

'Summat o' that.'

'What will we be working on today?'

'I need to be getting on with clearing the ground for the potatoes. You can do the light work, tending to the green-houses and such.'

'I'd rather help you,' Edie said with unfeigned eagerness. She was keen to prove she meant it when she said she planned to work hard.

'Nay, it's man's work. You'd be dead by teatime.'

'I can handle it.'

Jack smiled. 'All right, since you're so mustard-keen then you can give me a hand for a spell. Just mind you do as you're told.' He stood up. 'I'm going to get to it. Come find me when you're done with your cuppa.'

He clapped Prudence on the back and left without further ceremony.

Edie glanced out of the window, watching him as he strode across the lawn in the thin light of morning.

It wasn't just the wasted rooms on the inside of the house: there was a lot of unused space outside too. Yes, there were the kitchen gardens, which grew vegetables for the house and village, and the greenhouses and orchard. But there were also the landscaped gardens. Pretty enough, with well-tended hedges and a large fountain in the centre, but they seemed excessive as a pleasure ground for one middle-aged widow who really didn't seem to be taking much pleasure in them. Slowly, an idea started to form.

'Do you have any sort of summer event here?' Edie asked Mrs Hewitt.

'We used to,' Mrs Hewitt said. 'An agricultural show, over

in Kirkton. I expect they'll bring it back once the war's over.'

'I actually meant something smaller, like a fete. Does Applefield have one?'

'Not any more,' Tilly told her as she cleared away Mrs Hewitt's plate.

'Because of the war?'

'No, it just died out. I'm not sure why. We had a smashing one when I was a girl, when old Mr Hewitt was alive. He and his wife used to organise it as a treat for the Sunday School children, but the whole village attended. When he died, they kept it going for a while, but . . . I don't know, it seemed to have lost its heart.' Tilly sighed. 'It's a shame. I used to love treat day.'

'Has anyone ever tried to bring it back?'

'We've no time for thinking about nonsense like that,' Mrs Hewitt said, standing up. She'd seemed more relaxed in Jack's presence – warmer, and younger too, somehow – but now he was gone, the brisk, businesslike woman of the evening before had reappeared. 'As you're so fond of reminding us, Edith, there's a war on. And what that means in practical terms is that there's work to be done.'

Chapter 5

The sight that greeted Edie when she emerged from the house stole her breath away for a moment. Last night, although all had been shrouded in darkness, she could tell the giants that surrounded Applefield were something impressive. But in daylight . . . gosh.

To the east was a towering beast with a long, knobbled back, its flank just transforming from beige to green as spring staked a tentative claim on the landscape. It probably had a name – a descriptive, adventurous name, Edie hoped, like . . . Old Man Mountain, or something of that nature.

By its side was a smaller peak – smaller but no less impressive. Its snow-dusted top reminded her of an old print of the Alps that her Aunt Caroline had owned. A glittering blue-diamond lake nestled between the monsters, like a painting on a picture-postcard.

An involuntary gasp escaped her lips. Incredible that two days' travel was all it took to reach somewhere as alien and strange as another country – another world! And yet this was her home, in a sense. This was where her father had been born; spent his boyhood; grown into a man. It was part of him, and, as frightening as it seemed, it must be a little part of Edie too.

She shook her head to bring herself out of the reverie, smiling at her foolishness. Jack was waiting, and it wouldn't do to dawdle on her first day. She spied a figure in the distance and started striding in its direction.

The grounds looked smaller now she was actually in them. Still, they were pretty big, from what she could see. Her friend Alfie, a Charlton Athletic supporter, had a tendency to use football pitches as a unit of measurement, and Edie would guess the grounds of Applefield Manor could host two or three concurrent matches easily. Perhaps that wasn't really all that big for a country estate, but Edie was a born-and-bred Londoner. It felt like more grass than she'd ever seen outside of Hyde Park.

A lot of the ground seemed unloved, much like the old house itself. The small area directly to the front was neat and trim, with its carefully sculpted topiary and well-kept lawn, but the space around it had grown ragged – increasingly so the further one got from the house. It had a wild, forsaken look: a gradual melting of civilisation into wilderness. The grounds were a lot for one man to cope with on his own, Edie supposed. And for all that he looked to be a sturdy, well-built man, Jack Graham wasn't exactly young.

She could see the gardener clearly now, working on some ground behind the dirty greenhouses. He'd removed his shirt and vest, braces hanging down by his thick thighs, and he was laying the full weight of his bare chest against the shovel as he pushed it into the stubborn earth.

Occasionally he stopped and slumped over the handle, his chin sagging. But the pauses were only momentary: after a few seconds Jack would return to his work with renewed vigour, turning over huge, peaty mounds of earth as if they weighed nothing at all.

No, he wasn't young, but he was strong and virile – and handsome for someone of his years, in a rough, country sort of way. He and Prudence Hewitt couldn't have seemed any more different, in their appearance and their demeanour. And yet they were a similar age. They must have been young together, once upon a time . . .

Edie recalled their playful behaviour at the breakfast table when Jack had insisted Prudence eat his portion of the meal: the gruff gardener and the stern matron in that moment, as their faces broke into smiles, looking like young people in the throes of a first love affair. And the nickname he'd given her – Cheggy. Gardeners didn't speak to their mistresses that way. There was more to their relationship, but what? Old friends? Perhaps. Old lovers? Possibly. None of her business? Definitely. But the mystery-loving part of Edie's brain couldn't help being intrigued.

When she had nearly reached Jack, Edie turned to get a proper look at the house.

Unlike the gardens, Applefield Manor looked bigger when you weren't inside it. Two rows of mullioned windows, five above and four below, were flanked by a couple of turrets that gave the otherwise austere sandstone block an air of fairytale grandeur which didn't suit it, somehow. The golden stone was bright where the rising sun hit it, but the climbing ivy was beige-tinged and unkempt; most of the windows dark, covered by blackout curtains no one had bothered to draw back. The house, the whole estate, had an air of going to seed that made Edie think of her favourite childhood fairytale, *Sleeping Beauty*. All it needed was a princess to awaken.

She thought of Prudence Hewitt, and her determination to shut out the world and everyone in it – even the war itself. Well, maybe there was someone at Applefield Manor who needed waking up.

Jack had obviously been too deep in his work to notice her approaching, and he started visibly when she hailed him. The look he flashed her frightened Edie for an instant. It was a wild, hunted look, filled with fear and a sort of desperation. But the impression passed quickly, and within a second he had arranged his face into a smile.

'Well, so you're here, are you?' He snatched his vest from the ground and pulled it on. 'Suppose I'd better keep my clothes on if we're going to have young ladies springing up all over the place.'

'Where would you like me to start?' Edie asked, eager to prove her salt.

'I'd best show you around the place first.'

She followed him as he led her to the greenhouses.

'We've six of these,' he told her. 'We grow all sorts in 'em – tomatoes, plums, rhubarb, cabbage, or whatever's good for the time of year. I've got celery and cucumbers ready for sowing, and the last of the sprouts to harvest when you've had enough of clearing land.'

'I told you I can –'

He laughed. 'Aye, I know, you're as strong as an ox and you could turn soil from now until sunset. But them sprouts need getting in all the same.'

He moved away from the greenhouses and gestured to a plot of herb beds.

'Parsley, horseradish, sage, rosemary and so on,' he said. 'The rosemary has a habit of taking over if it's not looked to so that'll need trimming down regular as we come into the warmer weather.'

Next he showed her the vegetable patches and the little apple orchard, the trees stark and bare now, although it wouldn't be long before they'd be snow-white with blossom.

'Apples'll be ready for picking backend, if you're still with us – that's autumn to you,' he told her. 'Come on, I'll show you the stables.'

'Oh, do you keep horses?' Edie asked as she followed him. Prudence Hewitt hadn't looked like a horsey sort, but then again, this was the countryside. A lot of people probably got about on horseback here.

'Nay, not now. The late squire's father kept racehorses before his marriage, but they're long gone.'

'How does Mrs Hewitt travel then?'

'She doesn't.'

The stable was large, if rather dilapidated. It must once have housed quite a number of horses. Jack pushed open the door and Edie followed him inside.

It was divided into two rows of stalls, enough for a dozen animals. Although it was a long time since the place had last contained a horse, there was a definite horsey smell lingering: manure, saddle leather, hoof polish. Edie breathed in deeply.

Apart from the cobwebs that hung thickly in every corner, all that seemed to occupy the stable now was rubbish: old flowerpots; empty paint tins; an ancient washboard propped against one wall.

'Not used for much these days,' Jack told her as he took out a tin of tobacco and started stuffing his pipe. 'It'll do for storing the potatoes when we've got them in. For now it just sits empty, apart from one long-standing resident.'

Edie frowned. Resident? Was there a horse after all, or –

She shrieked and covered her head as something swooped past.

'Good heavens, bats!'

Jack laughed. 'No, it's just old Pepper. Say hello, Pep.'

'Hello!' a harsh, grating voice observed.

Edie peeped out from between her fingers to see a huge black crow sitting on Jack's shoulder, its head cocked as it fixed her in a beady-eyed stare.

'Hello,' she greeted it cautiously.

'Hello!'

Jack took out a match. Edie couldn't help noticing how his hand trembled while he lit his pipe.

'That's all she can say for now, though I'm trying to teach her more,' he said. 'I did worry she might pick up a few choice words from Matty, the boy who worked here before. I wasn't at all surprised when he went into the Merchant Navy. He certainly had the vocabulary for it.'

Edie took a step forward and cocked her head at the inquisitive bird. It almost seemed to smile at her mimicry.

'Go ahead, stroke her,' Jack said. 'She's a soft old thing.'

Edie ran a tentative finger over the bird's head, and Pepper gave a soft caw.

'Is she a pet?' Edie asked.

'She's a wild animal. But I suppose you could say we have an understanding.' Jack cast a fond look at the crow sitting parrot-like on his shoulder. 'I found her under the oak tree outside one morning when she was a chick. Fell out of her nest, I suppose. I waited a while to see if Mam would come back for her, but that evening she was still there. She'd have died if I'd left her overnight so I took her back to the house to nurse. When she was old enough I made her a little nest in here.' He stroked Pepper's head. 'That was a year ago. I never expected her to make it.'

'How long will she . . .'

Edie trailed off. The bird was still looking at her with those piercing eyes, and it struck her that what she'd been about to ask was rather personal. But Jack knew what she meant.

'In the wild they live ten or fifteen years, usually,' he said. 'Pepper might manage longer, with me to look after her.' He reached into his pocket for a handful of seeds and held them up to her. 'Here you are, Pep. If you're a good lass and eat it all up, I'll bring you some nice wriggly maggots for your tea.'

Pepper didn't need telling twice. She wolfed down the seeds and gave Jack's ear an affectionate nibble by way of thanks. Then, deciding she could no longer tolerate the thick blue pipe smoke wreathing the air around her master now there was no more food on offer, she spread her wings and soared back to her perch in the rafters.

Jack hadn't been lying when he'd said turning soil took brawn. Edie struggled on manfully for the first hour, but eventually she was forced to admit defeat and Jack set her to chopping brambles and clearing away rocks and stones so he could dig in with his shovel. That was easier but it was still hard work, and by the time she settled down to picking Brussels sprouts in the greenhouses, Edie's body was aching all over. She'd been bent double for so long that when she finally came to straighten her back, she howled with pain. Not to mention that every living thing on God's green earth, flora and fauna, had taken it upon itself to bite or sting any exposed area of her flesh.

'Two more days of this!' she said to Tilly as she drank her cocoa in the kitchen that evening.

'There's some liniment in the bathroom cupboard. You're welcome to help yourself.' Tilly wrinkled her nose. 'Just the smell of it's enough to make me feel ill. My bedroom stank of the stuff when I was with the Land Army.'

Edie flinched as she tried to cross her legs and a spasm of pain shot through her knee. 'Thank goodness I'll have a few days to recover before I start at the farm next week.'

'I don't envy you farm work at this time of year. Not to frighten you, but if you think you're tired now, just wait until you start lambing.'

'Is it that bad?'

'Wicked. Mornings so cold you feel like just stamping your feet will break a bone. Fingers cracked and red-raw. Aching in every muscle, working from dawn until dark . . .'

Edie groaned. 'Did you have to tell me?'

'Oh, it's not all bad,' Tilly said, smiling. 'There's nothing like seeing a new lamb bond with its mother for the very first time. And you'll sleep like a baby at the end of each day.'

'If I can still bend to lie down,' Edie muttered.

Chapter 6

Edie's first day at Larkstone Farm came all too quickly.

She'd been looking forward to a four-day holiday after her first few days working on the estate, with nothing to do but explore the local area, rest and read. She had all sorts of plans for visiting the lake and the village, and perhaps seeing if Tilly would accompany her to the cinema in Kirkton. The two women had quickly become good friends.

But after three days of country air and hard work, Edie managed to do very little on her days off other than sleep. She felt far too sore for walks or bicycle rides – her only trip outside was to attend church. Before she knew it, it was Monday and she was once again clearing brambles with Jack on the estate.

'It will get easier,' Tilly promised her as they sat together in the kitchen. 'It just takes a little time for your body to adjust.'

Edie groaned, rubbing her aching hip. 'Easy for you to say; you're used to this way of living. I never felt more like a townie than I do now. And tomorrow's my first day at the farm. I don't suppose I'll be able to walk by the time Saturday comes around.'

*

Edie started work at Larkstone Farm at 6 a.m., which meant she was woken by her alarm at the ungodly hour of 4.30 a.m. By the time she'd dressed and had a bite of breakfast, it was half past five and she needed to be on her way.

The Land Army had seen to it that she was provided with a sturdy black bicycle – luckily she had learnt to ride one as a child, taking turns with Susan on an old boneshaker Alfie had discovered among someone's rubbish and fixed up for the three of them. So then the only challenge was going to be finding her way to the farm along winding, unfamiliar country roads that were, since they were all taken down the previous year, completely absent of any road signs that might point her in the right direction. Still, it was only two miles from Applefield Manor to Larkstone Farm: ten or fifteen minutes' ride. How hard could it be?

'Damn it!' Edie muttered as she braked in front of a five-bar gate.

She was sure Larkstone Farm was meant to be at the bottom of this road. A man she'd asked for directions the last time she'd taken a wrong turn had said first left after the whitewashed cottage. But this couldn't be it. There was nothing in any direction but fields and hills – no farmhouse, no workers, no sign of life at all other than the sheep. There seemed to be a hundred times as many sheep as people in this godforsaken part of the world.

Edie glared at the one currently staring at her through the gate.

'All right, you, where have you hidden the farm?' she demanded.

The sheep blinked at her, urinated noisily, then wandered off.

She was now fifteen minutes late for work. Not a very auspicious start to her first day. Edie propped her bicycle against a drystone wall, cursed as she stepped in a very fresh-looking pat of sheep muck, and fumbled in her breeches pocket for her directions.

Straight on past Robin Cottage, third left . . .

Third left. Not first. That must have been what the villager said. Had she really forgotten her father's voice so thoroughly that the local accent should sound so alien?

She touched a guilty finger to her watch chain, then mounted her bike and retraced her route.

Finally Edie arrived at the track flanked by fields that matched the description on her directions. She hadn't even started work and she was already tired, irritated and up to her knees in mud – not to mention other, less savoury types of countryside dirt. She dismounted, looked around at the placid Herdwick sheep and their lambs grazing in the shadow of the fells, and wondered where she was supposed to report for duty.

No sign of the farmer, but there was a farmhouse with some outbuildings at the end of the track and a few barns dotted across the fields. She was just hesitating, trying to decide where this Samuel Nicholson was most likely to be found, when a voice hailed her.

'Good day to you! The new girl, yes?'

Edie looked around to see who had spoken and found herself face to face with a lean man in his mid-twenties, protected from the intermittent drizzle by a long macintosh made of what looked like barrage balloon panels. His skin was deeply tanned, with curling, jet-black hair and slumberous dark eyes that twinkled merrily.

He crushed underfoot the cigarette he'd been smoking and held out a hand.

51

'Yes,' she said in answer to his question, shaking the proffered hand. 'I'm the new girl. Edie Cartwright.'

His mouth flickered as he took in her bedraggled appearance. 'You look as though you have been hard at work already, Edie Cartwright.'

'I, er, had a bumpy ride over. Are you the farmer?'

He laughed. 'Most certainly not. My name is Luca. Just a skivvy, the same as you.'

His English was very good but there was a strange formality in the grammar, and the distinct lilt of a foreign accent. European, maybe Free French or . . .

'Oh!' Edie said, suddenly remembering what Mrs Hewitt had told her about the Catholic church Mr Nicholson had set up for his Italian POW labourers. 'So you're . . .'

'The enemy,' Luca said, grinning. 'I'm afraid so.'

Edie tried not to stare. She'd never met an enemy alien before. She glanced behind her, wondering if anyone had seen them shake hands, then quickly back again before Luca noticed.

'Ah, Miss Cartwright,' he said, still smiling broadly. 'No need to be frightened. We're not so different from anyone else.'

'I'm sorry, I didn't mean to be ill-mannered. It's just I've never, um . . . I don't travel a great deal,' she finished lamely.

'I'm nothing more nor less than a man, Miss Cartwright. A doctor, in my own country – a far better doctor than I am an airman. I was shot down on my first mission.' He sighed dramatically. 'It was highly embarrassing. My mother had much to say on the subject when she wrote to me.'

'Um, yes. I suppose it would be . . . embarrassing,' Edie said, feeling a little dazed. She was finding it hard to read Luca's expression. He looked amused, but also sort of . . .

52

sad? Haunted? Angry? She couldn't tell. Perhaps it was because he was a foreigner. Maybe they didn't show their feelings in the same way English people did.

'Well, it does no good to cry over spilled milk, as they say,' he said. 'God never intended me to be a warrior; only a healer. I'll take you to Sam. He posted me here to peel my eyes for you.'

'How many of you are there here?' she enquired as she wheeled her bicycle along the dirt track behind him.

'What "you" are you meaning? Other workers? Or other prisoners?'

'Er, workers.' Was that what she'd meant? Edie wasn't sure, but it sounded the politer question.

'Six, and now you make it seven. Two more Land Girls, a young man from the village, Sam – the farmer – and Marco and I from the camp.'

'Are there a lot of your men working on farms?' Edie had never heard of prisoners of war doing work outside their camps before.

'No. Marco and I are among the few,' Luca said. 'There has been a terrible shortage of labour here. Most of the young men have gone to war, and these country villages have so small populations. So, a handful of us who are considered politically benign are sometimes loaned out as agricultural workers, or to work in the mines and quarries.'

'Don't you have a guard or . . .'

'At first when we worked here, they would send a few soldiers from the Kirkton Home Guard to watch us. Now the men seem to have decided they have more important things to do than play nursemaid. They know we would not try to escape.'

'Oh.'

He glanced over his shoulder. 'Try not to be afraid of

us, Miss Cartwright. We are not fascists. Just people who want an end to this so we can go home to those we left behind.'

'Yes. Yes, I know that.'

'Ah, but do you? When I first arrived here, I was forced to open my mind to the idea that these so-called enemies my government had made monsters of were men and women no different than ourselves. You may find now that you have to do the same.' He stepped forward to knock at the farmhouse door.

'I'm not prejudiced, honestly,' Edie said. 'I suppose I might be a little naive. I've not been out in the world much.'

He looked at her for a moment, then smiled. 'Well in that case, Edie Cartwright, I'm glad to make a new friend.'

She returned his smile. 'So am I.'

'How is the other young lady?' he asked while they waited for Sam Nicholson to answer the door.

'Young lady?'

'You are lodged at Applefield Manor?'

'That's right,' she said, frowning. Young lady – he couldn't mean Prudence?

'The cook,' he explained.

'Oh, of course. Tilly worked here too, didn't she?'

'Miss Liddell, yes. She was a good worker, we were sorry to lose her. Does the baby grow healthily?'

Luca asked the question quite casually. It seemed that not everyone around here found Tilly's pregnancy to be so very scandalous. Perhaps in Italy, where people were said to be more passionate than the buttoned-up English, such things weren't considered shocking at all.

'As far as I know,' Edie said. 'She certainly looks blooming and glowing and all that.'

'I am very glad to hear it.'

'Did you know her well?'

'We were good friends, yes.' He put his hand into his pocket and slipped a soft disc wrapped in brown paper into Edie's hand. 'Here, give this to her when you return home. Only a little goat's cheese I was able to trade for at my camp, but I believe it will do her and the baby some good. And that is on the orders of her Dr Bianchi, be sure to tell her. She must eat it all herself and not share even a bite.'

'Thank you,' Edie said, putting the cheese in the covered basket on the front of her bicycle. 'I'm sure she'll appreciate that.'

'Ah, here's the boss,' Luca said in a low voice as they heard the door being unlatched. 'Now you mustn't mind him, Miss Cartwright. He can sometimes be a little *asciutto* – oh, what is the English? – a little . . . curt, but he is a good man in his heart.' The door opened, and he smiled at his employer. 'Here is your new girl, Sam, with shining morning face.'

Sam Nicholson didn't say anything, but he ran his eyes over Edie's slight frame and let out a 'humph' of irritation.

Luca glanced between them. 'Well, if I am not needed then I shall go help Marco feed the *pecora* in the pens.'

'Yes, go,' the farmer said. 'Thank you, Luca.'

Luca disappeared, leaving Edie staring up at the looming, glowering figure who now filled the door of the farmhouse. Instinctively, she took a step back.

'Um, it's Miss Cartwright,' she faltered. 'I'm . . . new. That is to say, I'm your new girl. The new Land Girl, I mean.'

The man stared at her for a moment before deigning to speak.

'Aye, so you are,' he said in a deep, harsh voice. 'What kept you? We've been at work half an hour.'

'I, um . . . I got lost.'

Sam Nicholson wasn't what Edie had expected, and yet in some ways he was everything she'd thought he would be.

He certainly didn't *look* like she'd expected him to. Edie had been picturing someone in his sixties, a typical northern farmer: craggy-faced, patched red from the sun and purple from the rain, probably in a cloth cap with a sheepdog at his heels. Sam Nicholson had none of those things, except perhaps a dog, judging by a doggy sort of smell that seemed to hang around him.

For a start, he wasn't sixty. Neither the rough, sandy stubble that covered his jaw and chin nor the frown on his brow was enough to disguise his youth. He couldn't be much over thirty years old – perhaps less.

His face wasn't purple either, or craggy. It was actually rather a fine face, weathered from outdoor work but nevertheless high-cheekboned and delicately featured. The eyes that peeped from under his furrowed brow were clear, intelligent and a deep, piercing blue. He reminded Edie of an illustration in a copy of *Robinson Crusoe* she'd owned as a child.

No, he didn't look as Edie had pictured him, but in another sense he was exactly what she'd been expecting. Sullen, suspicious, unfriendly – like so many of the people she'd met here. She wished Luca had stayed with them. The warmth and wry humour exuded by the young Italian were a tonic compared to the Sams and Jacks and Prudences of her new life.

Sam made her think of the mountains that dominated the local landscape. Beautiful in a terrifying sort of way, but forbidding, dangerous – and definitely not to be approached.

'We won't tolerate tardiness here,' he growled. 'Since it's your first day I'll let it pass, but next time it comes out of your wages.'

'It won't happen again. As I said, I got lost.'

'Where've you come from then?'

'Applefield Manor. I know it's not far, but, um, I got some bad directions and –'

'I meant, where do you come from in the country?' he said, with a roll of his eyes that told Edie he clearly believed he had an idiot on his hands.

She flushed. 'Oh, I see. London.'

'Aye, I thought as much.'

'My father was from Kirkton though,' she added quickly. 'Originally, I mean. He's dead now.'

She wasn't sure why she'd told him that. Why should she care whether this surly farmer thought she had a right to be here or not? Her blush deepened, and she let out a small cough. Nerves made her throat feel tight.

'We work hard here,' Sam informed her. 'We're used to graft in this part of the world.'

'Yes, I have been told.' Three times since she'd arrived a week and a half ago, in fact. Did she really look like such a loafer?

She coughed again, more deeply this time, and took out a handkerchief to cover her mouth.

'Not sick, are you, London?' Sam asked.

'No. Just hay fever,' she said hoarsely. She pulled herself up to her full height, recalling what Tilly had said about not letting Sam bully her. 'Pardon me, but is there a reason people around here keep telling me what hard workers they all are?'

His mouth twitched. 'Perhaps we worry your sort haven't got what it takes to keep up with us.'

'Townies, you mean.'

'Women.' He pointed out a distant field, where several human figures were mingling with the resident sheep. 'You're up there clipping out this morning. The others will show you what to do. Tell Ava Gardner to finish what she's doing and come back here. I need her help moving the yows in top field.'

'Right.' Edie thought it was probably wisest to work out which of her fellow Land Girls might answer to the name Ava Gardner when she got to the field. She certainly didn't want to spend any more time with Sam, or the enormous chip he seemed to have on his shoulder.

'Off you go then,' Sam said.

She flushed. 'Um, sorry, but have you got a – anywhere I could powder my nose?'

'Christ almighty, you're already half an hour late for work. Can't you at least manage to piss in your own time?' Sam took in her shocked expression and sighed. 'Outhouse is round the back. Then I want you up at that field earning your wage.'

Chapter 7

Edie took in the topography of the farm as she climbed over stiles, heading for the field Sam had directed her to. Some of the fields had been divided into makeshift pens using bales of straw, where those of Sam's flock who had recently given birth were ensconced with their lambs. She could see Luca and another man weaving in and out of them, checking water supplies and giving the animals their morning feed. The other fields remained free-range, dotted over with ewes in various stages of pregnancy and those with older lambs.

When she arrived at the field where she was to be working, two Land Girls and a young, skinny lad were already there. The boy and one of the women were hard at work, each holding a sheep on its back while they cut away clumps of excrement from their rear ends. The second Land Girl sat on a stile nearby, smoking a cigarette. The women looked a few years older than Edie, and each had a stripe on her uniform denoting one year's service with the Land Army.

Edie didn't need to stretch her deductive powers to work out which one of her new co-workers might answer to the nickname Ava Gardner. The girl on the wall was in the same corduroy breeches and green pullover as she was herself, but Edie only wished she had the curves to fill them the same way. The woman's pristine make-up and dark pin curls, tied up in a pink chiffon scarf, gave her an air of glamour that no amount of dirt could cover up.

'Hullo. New blood,' she said as Edie approached. She had a light Liverpudlian accent with a fun, teasing edge. The other two stopped what they were doing to look up at the addition to their numbers.

'Um, hello,' Edie said, bashful at the sudden attention from three pairs of eyes. 'Sorry I'm late. I, er . . . I got lost.'

The girl on the wall laughed as the others left off what they were doing and came to join them. 'Sam gave you a ticking off for that, I bet.'

'Yes.' Edie shook her head, scowling. 'Honestly, he's the rudest man! Does he talk to everyone that way?'

The blonde Land Girl, who was solid, ruddy and jolly-looking, nodded. 'Don't worry, you get used to him. I'm Vinnie, by the way.' She nodded to her friend. 'That's Barbara on the wall, having one of her infamous two-hour fag breaks.'

Barbara shot her a look. 'Ten minutes' sit-down, is that too much to ask? I've been clipping sheep shit since the break of day.'

'Well, give us one then, if we're all having a rest.'

Barbara produced a packet of Player's and shook out a couple for Vinnie and the boy.

She grinned when she noticed Edie's awed gaze fixed on her carefully styled hair. 'Beauty is duty, love. There's more than one way to do your bit for the boys.' She offered her the cigarette packet. 'You want one?'

'No, thanks. They, er, don't agree with me.' Edie shook hands with each of the women. 'Edie. Nice to meet you both.'

'You too.' Barbara gestured to the boy, who was scuffing at the ground, his cheeks bright pink now he found himself in the presence of so many females at once. 'This is Davy. He won't be with us much longer, he's just waiting for his chance to get out there and give the enemy a good hiding. Isn't that right, Davy?'

The boy nodded shyly.

'Which service do you want?' Edie asked him.

'Army,' the boy mumbled, not making eye contact. 'I was worried brass might try to make out I was reserved occupation 'cause I work on a farm, but my dad wrote and told them I'm only working here till I'm old enough to fight and there were plenty of wops at the camp could take my place. So they said I could be called up, once I'd turned eighteen. That was last month so I could be called for my medical any day now.'

He looked up at last, glowing with pride at the prospect of serving his country, and Edie smiled. But she felt a tug in her belly, all the same. The boy looked so . . . young. So small, still. He could easily have passed for two or even three years younger than his eighteen years.

'Oh.' Edie turned to Barbara on the wall. 'Mr Nicholson wants you. At least, I assume he meant you.'

'Heh. Ava Gardner?'

'Yes, that's who he asked for.'

'We all get called by nicknames here. I'm Ava, Vinnie is Prop Forward –'

'Because of my broad shoulders,' Vinnie said, grinning as she flexed them. 'Very nice, I'm sure.'

'– and Davy just answers to "lad",' Barbara finished. 'How about you?'

Edie scoffed. 'I'm "London", apparently. Is he not able to remember people's names?'

'He can when he wants to,' Vinnie said. 'I think that's just his sense of humour.'

'What about the Italians, what do they get called?'

'The POWs don't get nicknames,' Barbara said. 'Don't ask me why. He treats them with more respect than the rest of us.'

'And us being ladies too,' Vinnie said, tilting her nose in mock offence.

'Why's that?' Edie asked.

'Who knows why he does anything? He's a queer fish, Sam Nicholson.'

'Best to just get on with your work, collect your money and not ask questions, Edie,' Barbara remarked coolly, finishing her cigarette. 'He isn't a bad boss. Better than some we've had, anyhow.'

'You've worked on other farms?'

'We go where we get sent,' Vinnie said. 'Barb and I are billeted at the Land Girls' hostel in Kirkton. They just pack a gang of us into a Tilly every morning and drop us where we're needed. We've been with Sam for six months now though. It's a good job, we've been glad to hang on to it.'

'There are far worse people to work for, believe me,' Barbara told Edie. 'Farmers who won't pay what you're due, or try to get from you what they're not getting from their wives, if you know what I mean. Sam pays us on time, serves up decent grub and doesn't try to cheat us. Keeps his hands to himself for the most part. Appreciates what he's got, with us and the POWs working for him, which is more than some do.'

'What has he got?'

Barbara scoffed. 'Cheaper labour than he had before, that's what. If we were blokes we'd be on another six bob a week. The Italians don't get the full rate either, despite working all the hours God sends.'

'Where's their camp?' Edie asked.

'Just north of Kirkton. The two here don't go back to camp much at the moment though. They've been given special permission to bed down in one of the outbuildings during lambing so they can help with overnight births.' Barbara jumped down from the wall. 'I'd better go to Sam, before he gets into one of his moods. Bye, girls. Davy.'

Davy cast a resentful look at the farmhouse as Barbara strode off, whistling to herself. He'd sidled closer to Edie as they'd been talking, as if he could sense the protectiveness she couldn't help feeling towards him.

'My dad don't like me working here,' he told her confidentially.

'Why not?'

'He don't like Sam. Nobody likes him round here, 'cepting the wops –' He stopped when he caught Edie's disapproving look. 'Sorry, Miss, I know that's not polite to say with ladies. The Italians, I mean. Them're the enemy and he's nicer to them than us. Even made 'em a church. Why's he not in uniform? That's what our dad wants to know.'

Vinnie shrugged. 'Reserved occupation, isn't it? Someone has to keep the farms running.'

''Most everyone else has gone,' Davy said stubbornly. 'He could hire a manager, someone who couldn't fight. Not right able-bodied men should scrimshank their way out of fighting, hiding out in some safe country funk hole while others are getting bombed and shot at. You know what I heard?'

Vinnie shook her head. 'You oughtn't to spread rumours, Davy. You could lose your job if he hears you.'

'Who cares about that? I'll be off soon any road.'

Nevertheless, Davy lowered his voice. 'I heard old Pete Nicholson wouldn't fight neither when his turn come round.' He looked at Edie. 'That was Sam's great-uncle who had the farm before. Dodged the column in the last war. My dad heard he was a conchie.'

'Lots of people are conscientious objectors for religious reasons, aren't they?' Edie said. 'Quakers and people like that.'

'What do you think about that?' Vinnie asked her.

Edie hesitated. 'I've not really thought about it much. I suppose I can understand that, not wanting to take a life.'

'We'd be in a nice mess if everyone were to feel that way though.'

'If they did, there'd be no war.'

'Well, everyone on our side then. Other men have to go risk their lives. Why should COs get to pick and choose their battles?'

'That's all very well for us to say though, isn't it?' Edie said. 'No one's ever going to ask it of us.'

'True. You're wise beyond your years, Edie.' Vinnie finished her cigarette and stamped it out. 'Could you?'

'I . . . don't know.' Edie tried to imagine a scenario where she might be asked to take a human life, and gave an involuntary shudder. 'No. To be honest, I'm not sure I could.'

'I suppose I'd do what I had to, if I was a man. Otherwise Hitler would have the world by the throat. But I don't like to think of it.'

'But us men have to,' Davy said, lifting his chin as he claimed his right to be considered a man and not a boy. 'And Pete Nicholson weren't no Quaker. Cowardice probably runs in the family, that's what my dad says. And where's the rest of them? Where's Sam's people, where'd he come from? Maybe he's not even one of us. Maybe he's one of them.'

Vinnie laughed. 'Don't be daft.'

'He's not Applefield,' Davy said with a dark look at the farmhouse, from which Sam and Barbara were emerging with a couple of border collies at their heels. 'He turned up here with nobody, 'cept just one great-uncle who had this farm, and he weren't born here neither. You can't trust folk with no people. They could be anyone.' With that, he picked up his shears and strode off.

'Don't mind him,' Vinnie said to Edie when they were alone. 'There's a lot of paranoia round these parts about fifth columnists, Nazi sympathisers and the like. It's fear, that's all. Hard to blame people with everything that's going on.'

'No, I suppose not.' But Edie had something else on her mind, something she hadn't wanted to mention while the boy was present. 'Vinnie – when Barbara said Mr Nicholson keeps his hands to himself for the most part. What does that mean, for the *most* part?'

Vinnie gave a wry half-smile. 'It means that when there's a lusty tup on the loose, a girl needs to watch herself. Keep her knees together.'

'I don't understand.'

Vinnie studied her for a moment. 'You don't, do you? How old are you, Edie?'

'Twenty-one. Why, what has that to do with it?'

'Plenty,' Vinnie said, laughing. 'Well, never mind, Barb and I will keep an eye out for you.' She clapped Edie on the back. 'All right, roll up your sleeves and I'll show you how we do the clipping out.'

Edie took off her greatcoat and watched as Vinnie made a grab for one of the silver-fleeced Herdwicks. It tried to

65

escape, but the Land Girl was faster. She caught hold of its fleece and guided it towards Edie, then wrestled it expertly into a semi-reclining position on its back. This didn't seem to cause the sheep any discomfort, although it did look rather surprised.

'So,' Vinnie said. 'It's not the pleasantest job, I'm afraid. Actually, I wouldn't put it past Sam to have started you on this as a test, see if you're willing to get your hands dirty.'

'Why, what is clipping out?'

'Cleaning their bottoms up, basically,' Vinnie said with a grin. 'Not much fun but it is important. If the muck's left clinging to their fleeces then maggots will burrow in and start eating their flesh, the poor loves. We need to cut away any dirty sections around the tail before they're due to lamb.' She raised one eyebrow. 'Think you can handle that?'.

'Of course,' Edie said, a little too quickly. If this was a test, she didn't want to show any hesitation.

'You'll be able to do it by yourself with a bit of practice, but I think as you're new to it, we'd better work as a pair this morning. I'll hold her while you clip.'

Edie nodded and seized the clippers Barbara had left. She knelt by the sheep, wincing slightly at the pain of sinking to her poor stiff knees.

Edie hadn't expected to enjoy the dirty job she'd been assigned, but actually clipping out was rather relaxing once you got used to the smell. She took a strange pride in seeing the expectant ewes all clean, knowing she'd helped to make them a little more comfortable. They were a placid bunch, the Herdwicks – or Herdies, as the locals called them – and sort of adorable, with their little white faces that always seemed to be smiling.

Vinnie kept up a constant flow of chatter while they worked, telling Edie all about life at the Land Girls' hostel, her parents at home in Southport, and her friendship with Barbara, who Edie was surprised to learn wasn't someone Vinnie had become acquainted with in the hostel but was a friend from schooldays. Vinnie also told her all she knew about the business of sheep farming here in the north country.

By the time two hours had passed, Edie had learned a lot. She knew that a tup was a male breeding sheep, while a yow was the local word for a ewe: a female that had given birth. A wether, or wedder in the dialect of the region, was a castrated male, and a shearling an animal yet to have its first shearing. A gimmer, Vinnie informed her, meant a female sheep – thus a gimmer shearling was a female sheep aged less than two years, while a gimmer hogg was a female lamb that had finished weaning. A bell wedder was an aged sheep kept to help heft the flock to its territory.

Edie shook her spinning head. 'How will I ever remember all of this? I never knew there were so many different words for sheep!'

'Wait until you get to the counting. Yan, tahn, teddera, meddera, pimp . . .' Vinnie laughed at Edie's bemused expression. 'Well, first things first. Let's work on your clipping out today and by summer I promise we'll have you counting sheep like a native.'

Edie finished trimming the sheep she'd been attending to. She rubbed it down with antiseptic, then Vinnie let it get to its feet and it trotted back to its friends, none the worse for the experience.

Vinnie took hold of another nearby ewe and wrestled it on to its back. 'Hey, are you busy on Saturday night? We're having a little dance at the hostel. Some of the boys from the airbase are coming over, if you're interested in that sort of thing.'

Edie frowned. 'The airbase?'

'Well, if you're not one for mixed dancing don't worry, nor am I,' Vinnie said, catching her wary expression. 'We have wizard teas though, and the girls are a lot of fun. Our roommate Potty Dotty's got a bottle of gin stashed away that we can pass around. Come along, we'd love to have you there. You are one of us, after all.'

'I've got a curfew,' Edie said, pulling a face. 'My landlady insists I'm home by ten.'

'Not on Saturday nights, surely.'

'That's the Saturday curfew. It's nine on a weekday.'

'Crikey. She's strict.'

'I know, and a bit scary too. I wish I could stay with you at the hostel.' Vinnie's tales of the japes and tricks the girls got up to had made hostel life sound like those boarding school stories in the *Girl's Own* paper that Edie had devoured as a child.

'Well, living conditions are rather on the spartan side. We're four to a room, bedding down on straw-stuffed palli-asses with just a couple of army blankets each. Bloody freezing.' Vinnie shuddered at the memory. 'We have a lark though. What are your digs like in the posh house?'

'I can't complain. Mrs Hewitt's strict but she's made me cosy enough,' Edie said, thinking of her fluffy eiderdown.

'Anyway, you can still come to the party for a little while. It won't take more than half an hour on your bike, and we'll pile you back into the saddle at half past nine before you get into trouble. How does that sound?'

'Lovely,' Edie said, although she was certain that by Saturday night all she'd really want to do would be to fall into bed. But Vinnie seemed genuinely keen to have her attend, and she wouldn't like to hurt her new friend's feelings. 'Thank you, I'd love to come.'

Vinnie frowned. 'Hullo.' She let go of her sheep, which took immediate advantage of its liberty to jump to its feet and trot off. Vinnie hardly seemed to notice, shielding her eyes as she peered into the distance.

'What is it?' Edie asked, standing up.

Vinnie nodded to the corner of the field, where Edie could just make out a little black dot. 'Early arrival, it looks like.'

Her eyes widened. 'A lamb?'

'That's right. Come on.'

Edie dropped her shears and jogged to keep up with Vinnie as they headed to where the lamb was nestled in the grass, being given a thorough licking by its mum.

When they got there, Edie knelt down beside it. She tried not to simper – she wasn't going to get far as a Land Girl if she swooned at the sight of every baby animal she laid eyes on – but as a born lover of all things fluffy and four-legged, she couldn't help it. The lamb was so tiny, its mother glowing with the sheep equivalent of pride as she cleaned it up.

'What do we do?' Edie whispered to Vinnie. She'd been dreading this part. There hadn't been a great deal about lambing in her Land Girl training, which had a definite bias in favour of dairy and arable farming. But Vinnie seemed strong and capable, so if Edie just followed her lead then hopefully she could learn all about it without exposing her ignorance on the subject to that grumpy farmer.

'Hmm. She's being very rough with him,' Vinnie said as she watched the new mum. 'She's going to mother him to death if she's not careful.'

'Can that happen?'

'Sometimes. Lambs are smothered in their sleep, or their

69

tails chewed off while Mam's cleaning them up . . .' She stepped forward and deftly picked up the lamb by its front legs. The tiny thing instantly went limp, swinging from her hand like a child's toy. 'Let's get mother and baby to the infirmary,' she said, nodding in the direction of the large barn in the next field. 'I spotted Marco and Luca heading that way. They can keep an eye on them.'

Chapter 8

'Luca! Marco! Are you there?' Vinnie called when she marched into the barn. 'We've one here who might need some looking out for.'

The building was divided into fourteen pens, seven at each side. About ten were currently occupied. Some contained new mothers, with either one or two lambs apiece, while a few contained lambs only. These parentless infants kept up a shrill, urgent wailing that very quickly became part of the unnoticed background noise.

'Pet lambs,' Vinnie told Edie. 'Orphans, or rejected by the mothers, so they need to be fed by hand.'

Edie peered at something half hidden by the straw on the floor, and her eyes widened.

A dead lamb!

She approached and prodded it lightly with her wellington. No, not a lamb. Or not a whole lamb. Just the skin, freshly cut from the body. She put her hand over her mouth to stifle a wave of nausea.

She knew why. They'd been told about this during training. When a ewe rejected her baby, or when she died giving birth, the lamb would be wrapped in the hide of another sheep's dead offspring – still covered in embryonic juices from the birth – so it could be adopted by a foster mother. That was the way lives were saved. Still, Edie shuddered as she stepped away from the bloody fleece.

There was no sign of Luca, but a face belonging to an older man who she presumed must be the second prisoner, Marco, popped up from one of the pens.

'Let me see him.' He approached Vinnie to examine the lamb and prodded it in a few places. 'He seems healthy, for an early arrival. Is there some problem, Lavinia?'

'A bit of over-mothering going on. I think we'd better keep an eye on them for a day or two.' Vinnie looked around. 'Where's Luca?'

'What do you English say? He has gone to spend some pennies?' he said, grinning. He turned to Edie. 'And who is this?'

'Edie Cartwright.' This time Edie held out her hand without hesitation. 'Nice to meet you, sir.'

Marco pressed her fingers to his lips with chivalry obviously too ingrained to care how filthy they were. 'Marco Pia. It is my honour.'

Vinnie settled the lamb in one of the pens while they were making their introductions. Its anxious mother immediately joined it, casting a resentful look at Vinnie before she started washing the little thing again. Coming to life at its parent's touch, the lamb bleated softly.

Vinnie watched them for a moment before approaching a large piece of slate mounted by the door and adding a chalk mark to one of three tally columns.

'The left is for single lambs, the centre for twins,' she told Edie.

'What about the third one?'

'That's deaths.' She turned to Edie. 'Look, why don't you stay here a while? You've done your share of the dirty work.'

'But Mr Nicholson told me I was to –'

'Oh, bugger Mr Nicholson. It'll be helpful for you to learn how we care for the little ones.' She clapped Marco on the shoulder. 'Come on, old lad. You can help me with the clipping out.'

Marco rolled his eyes at Edie. 'Can you believe she asks this clipping out of me? You know, at home in Tuscany I was the mayor of my town.'

'You kept an inn,' Vinnie said, her lips twitching.

'This is God's truth: I did keep an inn, and shall again, I hope, if my wife does not burn the place to the ground before the war ends. Miss Cartwright, mine is the finest inn in Tuscany – no, in all Italy. They say –'

'They say Pope Leo himself once stayed there,' Vinnie finished, laughing now. 'I know, Marco, you've told us a thousand times.'

'And when this is all over you shall visit me there, Lavinia, and see my inn for yourself.' He waved a lavish hand towards Edie. 'The two of you shall visit, and Sam and Barbara also. We shall eat olives and oranges and sing all the evening. My Lotta and I should make you most welcome.'

'And the wine will flow, I'm sure. It's a nice dream for another day, Marco,' Vinnie said with a smile. 'But this is the present, and those sheep's arses aren't going to clean themselves.'

'You see what I must put up with?' Marco whispered to Edie with a melodramatic sigh, and she laughed as he followed Vinnie out of the barn.

When they were gone, Edie knelt down beside the mother sheep and her new lamb. Mum had left off washing him now and was resting her head on his downy fleece while he suckled.

He was so small. Vinnie had told her the ewes they'd

73

been clipping today weren't due to give birth for a week or more.

'Well, little chap, I hope you make it,' she whispered to the lamb. She glanced at the empty fleeces littering the floor. 'You're jolly lucky to be here, really.'

The sky had been glowering all morning, and a low rumble of thunder now filled the air, making Edie flinch.

'We're all jolly lucky to be here,' she muttered to herself.

'You shudder, Miss Cartwright. Surely a big girl like you is not afraid of the thunder?'

She looked up to discover that Luca had come in. He'd removed his long coat and was in a shabby grey uniform with a large red circle on the back, identical to the one she'd just seen his countryman wearing.

'You'd shudder too if you'd come from where I have,' she said as she got to her feet. 'It isn't thunder that shakes the skies in London.'

'I know it,' he said quietly.

She looked up to meet his eyes, which had that same pinched, haunted expression behind their warmth that she'd noticed earlier.

'Sorry,' she said in a softer voice. 'I didn't mean to be abrupt. It must have been hellish, actually being up there.'

'Not so hellish as the landing.' He turned away. 'Come, Miss Cartwright.'

'Please, call me Edie.'

'Come, Edie. Let me show you something.'

He led her to the door so they could look out at the mountains. The rain was falling now, although lightly. The heart of the storm was still some distance away.

A group of Hurricanes from the nearby airbase flew overhead, trailing white smoke. Edie wondered what they were flying into, and if they'd be coming back. Luca watched them too, until they became mere specks on the horizon.

'It has a beauty, this place,' he said, breathing in. 'Not like the beauty of Naples, where I come from, but a wild one all of its own.'

She followed his gaze to the two mountains.

'Yes,' she said quietly. 'Yes, it does.' She turned to him. 'Would you stay if they let you? After the war, I mean.'

'I . . . do not know.'

'Oh, I'm sorry. Do you have a family to go back to?'

'No family. No children. No wife.'

He spoke with a quiet sadness that made Edie feel she ought not to have asked. Minding her own business was never a virtue of hers. She liked to know about people, and she forgot, sometimes, that not all people cared to be known about.

'I'm sorry,' she said again.

'It is no matter.' Luca summoned a smile. 'When we are even greater friends than we are now, then I promise I will tell you all about myself. But not at this moment.' He nodded to the foot of the mountains. 'In the summer we shall let our sheep and their lambs wander the fells. And you, Edie, shall be a shepherdess. Summer will be a happy time for us here.'

'What are they called, the mountains?'

'To the east is High Kirk Crag. To the west, Broad Fell.'

'Oh.'

He laughed. 'You were hoping for something more romantic?'

'Perhaps a little,' Edie admitted.

'In time, when this begins to feel like home, you can give them names of your own invention.'

A rough voice cut through Luca's soft musings. 'What's this, a bloody tea dance?'

Sam appeared from behind the barn, scowling as usual, with a lively but rather fat border collie bouncing at his heels.

Luca cleared his throat. 'Sorry, Sam.'

'What are you two doing standing about idle?' He glared at Edie. 'You can court in your own time, London.'

'Luca was just telling me what happens in the summer,' Edie said, flushing.

'Aye, well, summer's summer. This is spring,' Sam told her shortly. He turned to her companion. 'Luca, I want the girls to drive into the village for the feed. You'll go with them and help load the truck, please. I can take over here.'

'You're the boss, boss,' Luca said with a mock salute.

'And spare them the sodding poetry, can you?'

He shrugged. 'Hey, I'm Italian.'

Sam allowed himself to smile. He gave Luca a friendly slap on the back, and the POW, looking relieved there were no hard feelings, went to seek out Barbara and Vinnie.

Sam jerked his head towards the inside of the barn. 'London, with me.'

Edie stood aside to let him in then followed as he strode to the nearest pen. She wasn't relishing the idea of working alongside Sam instead of the much friendlier Luca, but apparently she didn't have a choice.

'Thought I put you on clipping out,' Sam muttered as he dropped to his knees.

'I traded jobs with Marco. Vinnie thought it would do me good to –'

'Well, Vinnie's not in charge here. Next time, see if you can manage to do as you're damn well told.'

'Um, all right,' she mumbled as she knelt down beside him. 'Sorry.'

The lamb Sam was examining gave a bleat of protest as

76

he eased it away from its mother and pulled it between his knees. He felt its tiny stomach with firm, gentle hands – surprisingly gentle, Edie thought, considering both the size and roughness of the hands and the surly disposition of their owner.

'Is it sick?' she asked.

'No, but its mam isn't all she ought to be. His belly's empty, which means she's still got no milk. I'd hoped she might by this morning.'

'So will he die?' Edie whispered.

He turned to frown at her. 'Hellfire, London! If you're going to be blinking saucer eyes at me like a schoolgirl in love then you can go help Davy.'

'I beg your pardon?'

'We don't have room for sentimentality here,' he said, reaching beyond her to feel the mother sheep's udder. 'Animals get sick. They die. If you can't cope with that, I wonder you decided to join the Land Army.'

Edie got to her feet.

'Do you always have to be so jolly rude?' she demanded.

His eyes skimmed her petite frame as she glared down at him, hands on her hips, and his lips twitched.

'In the north we call it bluntness,' he told her.

'No, in the north you call it rudeness. My father came from this part of the world and he never spoke to women the way you do.' She touched a finger to the watch chain at her throat. 'Do you know why? Because he was a gentleman. And you, Sam bloody Nicholson, are no bloody gentleman.'

For the first time in her company, the farmer's scowl relaxed.

'You ought to watch your language,' he said, gesturing to the pens. 'There's children present.'

'And *you* might want to learn how to show people a little

respect. Even Marco and Luca know how to treat a lady, and they're . . .' She faltered. 'Well, they're . . .'

'They're what?' Sam asked quietly.

'They're . . . I mean, they're not Englishmen, are they? I'd have thought you'd be ashamed to have foreigners show you how you ought to behave.'

'You're a bit of a prig, London, do you know that?'

'I'm a . . . how dare . . .' Edie exhaled through her teeth. 'You . . . you complete and utter . . .'

He grinned. 'Cat got your tongue, lass? Or can you just not think of anything dire enough to call me?'

'You . . .' Edie racked her brains for something bad enough to really shock him; a word that would have her Aunt Caroline clutching her pearls in horror. 'You absolute . . . you absolute *arse.*'

'Ouch!' He put a hand to his heart. 'London, that hurts.'

Then, to Edie's immense surprise, Sam started to laugh: a deep, throaty chuckle that crinkled the corners of his eyes. She scowled at him for a second, but soon, unable to resist the infectious absurdity of the situation, she broke into laughter too.

'All right, Miss Cartwright, you can stand down,' Sam said, patting the straw. 'I'm sorry I was rude and I'm sorry I called you a prig. There.'

'Well, in that case I suppose I'm sorry I called you a – the thing I called you.' Edie hesitated, then sank back down beside him.

'You're right, I'm no gentleman,' he said quietly. 'I'm a rough country farmer who's not had a deal to do with women and has no idea how to talk to them with all the right high-society bustles and bows. My labourers do the work of men, so I talk to them like men. It's too late for me to change my ways now.'

'Fine. Just show me what I need to do. I'm here to work, aren't I?'

He clapped her on the back. 'Good man.'

Sam leaned across her body, and Edie tensed. What had Barbara said? *Keeps his hands to himself . . . for the most part.* Just how far did Sam Nicholson really treat his women workers like men?

They'd been warned about such things by the forthright lady who ran the Land Army training course. Farmers who thought the young girls they were supplied with were there to satisfy more than the needs of the farm; lusty farmhands who couldn't keep their minds – and their hands – on the job. 'When in trouble, girls, remember that your best friend is a sharp knee,' Edie recalled the instructor telling them. But Sam only picked up a bottle with a rubber teat attached and handed it to her.

'This little one's hollow,' he said, nodding to the lamb. 'Me and you need to give him his feed.'

Edie glanced over her shoulder at the grotesque skinned fleeces on the floor. 'Wouldn't you usually pair them with other ewes when the mothers can't make milk?'

'If they're orphaned, or the yow rejects them, we'll always try to pair with a foster mother. Keeps the lamb alive and stops the yow pining for her dead bairn. But if it's a case of no milk, we feed by hand and let the mother provide the rest of the nursing. Lamb stands a better chance that way.' Sam took the bottle from her and got to his feet. 'I'll fill this, then you can see how it's done.'

He returned fifteen minutes later with a full bottle.

'Milk, egg, sugar and cod liver oil, warmed to body temperature,' he told her as he pulled the lamb between his knees again. The mother gave a low *baa* of protest, but Sam ignored her. 'Half a pint every four hours for newborns.

We've this little lad to do, then eight more.' He brought his thighs closer together until the lamb was forced to get up on its wobbly, knock-kneed little legs. 'Needs to be standing or it might go into his lungs. Hold his head up for me, can you, London?'

Edie did as she was told, gently tilting the lamb's head upwards while Sam held the bottle above it and let the milk mixture drip into its open mouth. After a few seconds, the lamb was lapping eagerly and Edie was able to draw her hand away as he took the teat for himself. His little tail wagged with appreciative speed while he filled his belly, with Sam taking short breaks every now and again to ensure the lamb didn't finish its meal too quickly.

'Right, that's enough,' Sam said after ten minutes. He patted the anxious mother as he restored her offspring. 'Sorry to upset you, old lady, but you'll thank me for it when he grows up big and strong. Might even be tup material, this lad.' He gave the lamb a pat as well. 'Now there's a life to dream of, eh, little one?'

'How can you tell?' Edie asked.

'Hmm?'

'How can you tell which ones ought to be tups?'

'All in the undercarriage,' he muttered.

She flushed. 'Oh.'

Sam glanced up, his mouth curving. 'We'll save the lessons on breeding for another day, eh?'

Edie turned her overheated face away, suddenly very aware of Sam's thigh against hers. 'Um, yes.'

They moved on to the next animal, and this time Sam kept the lamb's head steady while Edie administered the milk. She couldn't help flashing him a look of delight when the lamb reared up to take the teat.

'Well, lass, perhaps we'll make a sheep farmer of you

yet,' Sam said when they were done with the feeding some time later, clapping her on the shoulder.

Edie glowed with pride.

'What should I do now?' She felt like she was really getting into her stride and was eager for the next task.

'Heyup, Sadie!' Sam patted his leg, and the portly sheepdog trotted to his heel. 'We'll go back to the farmhouse. Did you bring your dinner?'

'Yes.' The jam sandwiches and slice of fruitcake that Tilly had put in a tin for her were in the basket of her bike.

'Marco will have some soup ready too. I want you with me in lower field after dinner. Gimmers in there are due any day. You might get to see a few births this afternoon.'

'You mean you want me to help with the actual lambing?' Edie said.

'Yes, why?'

'I thought . . . won't I be working with Vinnie and Barbara?'

'Not frightened, are you?'

'No, but . . . they didn't really teach us a lot about birthing animals during the training.'

'Then you'd better learn right quick, hadn't you? Given that's what you're here for.'

'I'd rather learn with the girls.'

He frowned. 'It wasn't a request, London. It's not me you're afraid of, is it?'

Edie dropped her eyes. The truth was, she was a little afraid of him – or at least, afraid of being alone with him for long spells. While she didn't give any credence to Davy's fanciful theory that Sam might be some sort of undercover Nazi agent, she couldn't help dwelling on Barbara's enigmatic comment earlier. What did she mean when she'd said he kept his hands to himself – *for the most part*? Had he made advances to one of the other women? Was he likely to try anything with her? Edie knew she was nothing to write home about – certainly not compared to the pretty, curvaceous Barbara – but Sam did seem keen on keeping her by his side. And men weren't always particular when it came to casual affairs, were they?

She thought of Tilly, and the married lover who hadn't cared a jot about the situation he was leaving her in. No, men weren't particular – so long as they got what they wanted.

'Of course not,' she said, trying to sound like she meant it. 'I'm just worried about looking an idiot.'

'I'll be gentle with you,' Sam said, with a grin that did nothing to alleviate her fears. 'Come on, let's get ourselves some fodder.'

Edie needn't have worried. It would be untrue to say Sam was the perfect gentleman while they worked alongside each other all through that cold, drizzly afternoon, since he continued just as abrupt and unchivalrous as ever, but he certainly seemed to have little interest in her as anything other than a hard and obedient worker.

Edie got to witness her first few births too, watching as Sam eased each lamb from its mother with front legs outstretched like a woolly little diver. Again, she was struck by the tenderness he displayed when caring for the animals.

At the end of a long, exhausting but satisfying day, Edie felt reassured that she was safe enough with Sam Nicholson, whatever liberties he might have taken with the other girls on the farm. Obviously she just wasn't his cup of tea, which suited her perfectly. She didn't have enough vanity about her appeal to the opposite sex for it to wound her much.

What was more, she felt that her willingness to work,

her eagerness to perform whatever task was set for her, had earned Sam's professional admiration. Unlike his amorous interest, his respect as a farmer was something she valued more than she cared to admit.

'You did well today, London,' Sam said as she reclaimed her bicycle and prepared to heave her aching limbs back home. 'Well done.'

She beamed, her cheeks flushed with pride. 'Thank you.'

He gave a gruff nod, dropping his eyes as if her evident pleasure at the compliment embarrassed him. 'Aye, well, I'll see you in the morning then. Bright and early, don't forget. I'm expecting you to make up for the time you missed today.'

'Fine,' Edie said, although she'd already worked more than her allotted hours.

As she prepared to mount her bike, she spotted something in the distance. Something small, black . . .

'Mr Nicholson –'

'Sam, for God's sake. I can't abide being Mr Nicholson, it makes me sound like a schoolmaster.'

'Look,' she said, pointing. 'Over there. I think it's a lamb. And . . . oh gracious. It's not moving.'

He looked to where she was pointing and frowned. 'You're right. Look sharp then.'

She left the bicycle and followed as Sam ran to where the lamb was lying motionless.

The farmer was faster than her, strong enough to vault the stiles without climbing them, so it took Edie a minute or two longer to reach the new lamb. When she got there Sam was already kneeling beside it, looking it over with concerned eyes.

'Is it –' She stopped to cough, but managed to recover herself. 'Is it dead?'

The tiny lamb was lying full length, eyes shut.

'Not yet,' Sam muttered, running his hand gently over its body. Its little chest rose and fell almost imperceptibly. 'Cold as death though, and breathing's very shallow. Where's the mother wandered off to? These girls weren't due yet.'

Edie looked around her. 'This field . . . we found another lamb near here. Vinnie thought the mother was being too rough with him so we took them to the infirmary.'

Sam had picked the lamb up and was rubbing it between his hands, trying to impart some warmth. 'Just the one lamb?'

'We thought so, but . . . could it have been a twin? This one might've been hidden by something.'

'Hmm. Very likely. Vinnie should know better than to not check the area.' He picked up the motionless lamb and got to his feet. 'You'd better go home. I'll take care of this.'

Edie didn't like the ominous sound of those words.

'You don't mean you'll . . . you're not going to kill it?' she whispered.

'Good God, you really think I'm a brute, don't you? No, of course I'm not going to kill it.' He glanced at the lamb. 'But it'll be dead by morning, all the same.'

'You'll try though? You'll try to save it?'

'This is the problem with employing women,' he muttered. 'Too soft-hearted to get the work done.' He gave her a stern look. 'London, this is a mutton flock. Most of these animals are destined for the butcher's block. You do understand that, don't you?'

'Yes, but . . .' Edie cast a helpless look at the lamb. 'It's so small.'

'I'll do what I can for it. Just don't start blubbering on me if it's bad news tomorrow.' He strode off towards the farmhouse with the lamb dangling from one fist.

Chapter 9

It was early Friday evening and Prue was on her knees, scrubbing the marble fireplace in the dining room.

She hadn't been able to forget Edith's expression when she'd shown her around the house on her arrival – the distaste in the child's eyes when she'd caught sight of the dustsheets and grubby furniture – and somewhere in her soul, Prue had felt ashamed.

Yes, it was true that she didn't keep the house as smart as she had when dear Albert was alive. It seemed foolish, that was all, spending time scrubbing every room when they used only a handful between the three of them. Matilda attended to the kitchen, cooking and laundry, Jack saw to the gardens, and Prue made sure the hallway, bathroom, occupied bedrooms and the library, where she received her few visitors, were fit to be seen.

But it did no harm to give the old place a spring clean once in a while, she'd told herself, and this morning she had rolled up her sleeves and made a start.

Prue had spent the morning dusting and polishing the sitting room, where she'd also moved the wireless set, so the two girls could make it a common room of sorts if they wished. They seemed to like each other's company, and it was good for Matilda to have a friend her own age. If the new girl was to be staying, of course. Prue still hadn't made up her mind on that point, although Jack had given a strong report of her first two weeks' work. But of course the old fool warmed to anybody who was kind to that mangy bird of his, Prue reflected with a fond smile.

After she'd finished in the sitting room, she had moved on to the dining room. She thought that perhaps they might use it this Sunday after church, now they were four, and have a proper roast dinner – or as close as one could come to a full dinner these days, at any rate. Matilda was clever with the rations though, and she could make a small joint go a long way.

Yes, Prue believed she would like that: a Sunday dinner just like they used to have. It had been a long time since the family had sat down together at the table – not since Bertie had last been home on leave. Perhaps they could invite those two Italians from Samuel Nicholson's farm too. The pair of them had often come in for a spot of tea in the kitchen when dropping off eggs, but they'd never been invited for a meal. God knew it couldn't be easy for them, poor souls, far away in a foreign land. Prue hoped that if her Bertie was ever a prisoner, someone would show him the same kindness.

Prue smiled at herself. The family, had she called them before? Well, she supposed they were a family of sorts. A mismatched bunch, but they suited one another: her, and Jack, and Bertie, and Matilda. They understood each other, and they liked each other's company. Prue never had felt it necessary to make the distinction between mistress and servant at Applefield Manor.

If only she could keep it to just the four of them – or the five of them, when the bairn arrived. But the war would

86

encroach on her life, no matter how hard Prue tried to shut it out. Bertie was gone and instead there was Edith, almost as if heaven had intended her to take his place. As if he might not be coming back. The thought made Prue shudder.

'Superstitious old biddy,' she muttered to herself. 'Don't be such an ass, Prudence Hewitt.'

Jack and Matilda seemed to have taken to her – Edith – but there was something about the girl that unsettled Prue. The way she'd looked at the house, making Prue feel she was failing in her duty to it. All her talk of reviving the village treat, and doing their bit for the war, giving rise to an unwelcome spike of guilt that needled Prue in the belly. Prue didn't like change, and she certainly didn't want any young bits bringing it here to Applefield Manor. All she wanted was her Bertie home again, and the war to be over so life could go back to how it had been before.

She cursed when the bell for the front door rang out. Had Edith forgotten her key? She went to answer it.

'Oh,' she said when she opened it. Her lips hardened. 'Patricia.'

A tall, sharp-featured woman in a tweed twinset was on the doorstep, with a watery-eyed boy of about six clinging to her skirts.

'Prue.' Patricia took in her appearance, her bare arms mottled with ash. 'My dear, you look like a charlady. Whatever have you been doing?'

'Deep sea fishing, of course,' Prue said, wiping dirty hands on her apron. Patricia looked puzzled, and Prue willed herself not to smile. 'I've been cleaning out the dining room grate, Patty. Do come in.'

'Why not have Matilda do that?' Patricia asked as she followed Prue to the library. 'I don't see the point in having servants if you're going to do all their work for them. It's like keeping a dog only to bark yourself.'

Patricia paused, as if she expected to be congratulated on what she obviously thought was a highly pithy and original observation, but Prue just indicated two leather armchairs placed either side of a coffee table.

'Matilda has her work and I have mine,' she said shortly when they were both seated. 'She is also in a rather delicate condition, in case you've forgotten. I won't have her risking her own health and the baby's by taking on more than she can manage.'

Patricia turned to the little boy.

'Edgar, there are some lovely picture books of birds and animals on the shelf over there,' she said, pointing out a mahogany bookcase. 'I'm sure Mrs Hewitt won't mind if you take a look at them.'

'Hmm,' Prue muttered. 'Hands, Edgar.'

The boy submitted them for inspection without a whimper. Satisfied they were clean, Prue nodded and Edgar wandered away to look at the books.

'Prue, you behave like a common drudge,' Patricia continued in a lower voice. 'You really ought to hire a maid if your current staff are unable to cope. It's not fitting for the lady of the house to clean for herself like some sort of . . . topsy-turvy Cinderella.'

'And what would I do all day while this Mrs Mopp sticks her nose in where it isn't wanted?' Prue demanded. 'Settle myself on the chaise longue with a pug and a boxful of chocolates until I'd bored myself into an early grave? No thank you.'

'But in your position . . .'

Prue flicked a hand. 'Oh, pooh to my position, Patricia Featherstone. Don't forget it was my mother's job to keep this house for over a decade. If she could manage, so can I.'

Patricia flinched. 'I wonder you can talk of it so coolly.'

'Why shouldn't I? I'm not ashamed of where I came from, despite the best efforts of people in this village to make me feel I ought to be.' Prue patted her hair, which was coming free from its bun. 'Now is this a social call? If it is I'll fetch us some tea.'

'Partially,' Patricia said, sitting up straighter. 'But I am also here in my WVS capacity. I've been assigned the job of checking on local Land Girls in private billets. Where is –' She stopped to consult a piece of paper. 'Where is Edith? Did she arrive as expected?'

'Yes, she arrived last Monday. She's at work at the moment, over at Larkstone.'

Patricia frowned. 'Is she now? Mr Nicholson must have her working well over her allotted hours.'

'In lambing season everyone works over their hours, Patricia. You ought to know that.'

'Hmm. I suppose they do. Well, how is she settling in? Does she seem . . . happy and all that?' Patricia asked, fumbling for a suitable word.

'It's not really for me to say. I suspect I'd be rather home-sick if I were in her place, but she's confided nothing to me. She and Matilda seem to have become firm friends, however.' Prue regarded Patricia with one eye narrowed. 'Perhaps you might like to see her while you're here.'

'Yes, that was my intention. I don't suppose it will be too long until she returns from work.'

'Not Edith, Patty. Matilda. She is your niece.'

Patricia drew herself up. 'You know my views on that. Matilda receives an allowance from Andrew and me, and I'm happy to send clothes for the baby or anything else she

89

might need. I'm a Christian, after all.' She cast a look at Edgar. 'But I can't have her near my grandson.'

'Mercy's sake, Patty. Illegitimacy isn't a disease, you know. It isn't *catching*.' Prue followed Patricia's gaze to Edgar, who was sitting cross-legged on the floor, looking through Bertie's childhood copy of *Princess Mary's Gift Book*. 'Besides, she wouldn't be the first young woman who'd been caught the wrong side of what's considered right, would she?'

'Keep your voice down,' Patricia hissed. 'Edgar was six weeks early. I told you that.'

'Or your Martha's wedding was six weeks late,' Prue muttered.

'At least Thomas is a respectable man, a man who knows his duty. If Matilda hadn't given herself to that – that *person* . . .' Patricia spat the word as if it was the vilest insult she could summon. 'Assuming he even is the father, of course,' she observed with a sneer. 'I suspect there may be more than one candidate for that particular honour. It's a disgrace how the younger generation are using the war as an excuse for all sorts of wanton behaviour.'

Prue scoffed. 'You know, Patricia, for a Christian woman you pick a great deal of specks out of a great deal of *other* people's eyes.'

'Prudence, you'd better be careful how you –'

They were interrupted by the sound of the front door being opened, and weary steps trudging upstairs.

'The girl,' Prue said in an undertone. 'Let her change her clothes and have a rest before you start haranguing her, Patty. I'll go fetch us some tea and we'll try to keep civil tongues in our heads for half an hour, shall we?'

*

When Edie reached her room, she struggled out of her soaked woollen socks and filthy breeches and fell back on the bed in just her jersey and knickers, groaning.

Today had been her second day on the farm. She'd started out feeding the ewes in the bale pens with Vinnie and Barbara, but in the afternoon Sam had commandeered her services again. This time he'd really seemed to be testing her, and she had actually delivered two tiny lambs with her own hands.

It was a business that benefited from a high tolerance for pain, as you felt around inside the sheep trying to work out which limb belonged to which lamb so you could help guide them out. Each birthing contraction pressed your arm painfully between the sheep's insides and the huddle of lamb. But when the ewe finally saw her baby and let out a low, laughing bleat of joy . . . Edie was convinced there was no more satisfying job in the world. And now, at the end of her second day as a sheep farmer's assistant, she felt happy, exhausted, and like her body had been run over by a tank.

She'd been relieved to learn that the tiny lamb she'd discovered on her first day was still clinging to life, although Sam had told her it was far from being out of danger. It had been left alone too long for the mother to know it as hers, which meant it would have to be bottle-fed, but it was in a poor way.

Edie supposed she should have sought out Mrs Hewitt and let her know she was home, but she was covered in dirt and smelled like a combination of sheep excrement and wet border collie. She couldn't possibly present herself to another human being in this state.

The eiderdown quilt felt very welcoming after her long day. Edie pulled it over her face and breathed it in. She could just fall asleep now, if she wasn't so jolly hungry.

The bathroom was three doors along. After lying still for a moment to give her sore limbs a rest, Edie eased herself painfully to her feet, wrapped her dressing gown around her and made her way there.

Edie's mother and her mother's older sister, Caroline, had grown up in a comfortable middle-class family in the Cotswolds, but Edie's spinster aunt hadn't been a wealthy woman in later life and the two of them had lived in genteel but straitened conditions in Pimlico. The two-up-two-down terraced house Edie and Aunt Caroline had occupied boasted few modern conveniences, so the sight of an indoor bath – and what was more, an indoor lavvie – had filled Edie with a sense of wonder the first time she'd ventured into Applefield Manor's bathroom. Imagine just being able to turn on the taps and watch the tub fill with steaming water, whenever you felt like it! At home it took forever to heat enough water on the cooker to half-fill their old tin bath.

Edie sighed as she examined the olive-green tub. A hot bath would be wonderful, but even at Applefield Manor there was a war on and baths were restricted to one a week. Unfortunately Edie had already used up her allowance.

Instead she approached the sink. There was a bar of red toilet soap and a bottle of Yardley's Lavender Water above it, and she had her own flannel and sponge. She could clean up here before seeking out Tilly in the kitchen in the hope of some food.

When Edie had washed, changed into her civvies and made her way downstairs, Tilly was arranging slices of seed cake on a pretty floral plate.

'Tilly, if you tell me some of that is for me, I'll love you forever,' Edie said.

'I'm afraid not.' Tilly pulled a face. 'The Wicked Witch of the West is paying a visit. I've been ordered to provide tea, cake and any winged monkeys we happen to have hiding in the pantry.'

Edie laughed. 'Who is it? A friend of Mrs Hewitt's?'

'It's my Aunt Patricia. She and Prue have been friends for years, so naturally they can't stand one another.'

'The aunt who won't speak to you?'

'Yes, my dad's sister,' Tilly said, grimacing. 'She's the most frightful snob.'

'Don't you see her at all?'

'Rarely. I think she'd quite like to pretend I didn't exist, except I'm a little too visible around here for her to get away with it. So she sends me a few bob once a month and calls that doing her duty. I'm a terrific embarrassment to someone in her position.'

'What is her position?'

'Professional busybody. She's married to our vicar, as well as being chairwoman of the Women's Institute and a WVS organiser. Aunt Patricia volunteers for every good cause going, just so long as she knows people can see her doing it.' Tilly glanced up to take in her friend's appearance. 'Edie, my love, you look all in.'

Edie groaned as she eased herself stiffly into a chair. 'It's been a long day.'

Tilly slipped one of the slices of seed cake on to a plate and handed it to her. 'There you are. I'll fetch you something more substantial when I've seen to milady's tea.'

'Tilly, you're an angel,' Edie said, falling on the cake with relish. 'I mean it, you're an actual heaven-sent angel.'

The door opened and Mrs Hewitt peered in. 'Are the refreshments ready, Matilda?'

'Yes, all here,' Tilly said, adding the plate of seed cake to a tray bearing a silver teapot with matching strainer and two delicate china cups. 'I'll bring it in to you.'

'No need for that, you're not a parlourmaid. I can take it.'

Tilly gave a wry smile. 'You mean Aunt would prefer not to see me. Well, the feeling's mutual.'

'Yes, I thought it might be.' Mrs Hewitt glanced at Edie as she took the tray. 'Mrs Featherstone does want to see you though, Edith. It's part of her work for the Women's Voluntary Service to see how you're settling in, apparently.'

'She wants to see me now?' Edie said, hastily brushing illicit seed cake crumbs from her mouth.

'No, no, have your cup of tea first. She knows you've only just come home, and she's perfectly capable of waiting for half an hour. Just come along to the library when you're ready.' She picked up the tea tray. 'And don't worry, I won't let her pick on you.'

Chapter 10

'You see, she's not such a mean old stick,' Tilly said when Prudence had disappeared.

'After Sam Nicholson, she seems positively delightful,' Edie muttered.

Tilly made a pot of tea and took a seat while she waited for it to brew. 'You don't like him?'

'I'm . . . not sure. At first I couldn't stand him – rude man! But after we'd worked together for a couple of days . . .'

Tilly smiled softly. 'Yes, he has got a certain charm.'

Edie snorted. 'I wouldn't go that far. He's hardly Ty Power.' She followed the ribbons of steam coming from the teapot's spout. 'Tilly, do you think I'm a prig?'

Tilly laughed. 'Where did that question come from?'

'Do you though?'

'Of course not. I might say you seem like something of an innocent, but that's nothing to be ashamed of, Edie.' She smiled. 'So Sam called you a prig, did he? The cheeky sod.'

'Yes. But I called him an arse so I suppose that makes it even.'

'You never did!'

'I did, I promise you. I even surprised myself.'

She laughed. 'Edie Cartwright, you little minx.'

'Did you like working for him?'

'I did. And what's more I liked him as a man, once I got to know him,' Tilly said. 'Although at first I thought he was rude and ill-bred, just like you did. I got the shock of my life when I found out he had a good heart underneath.'

'He is very gentle with the animals,' Edie said, absently picking at the crumbs of her devoured seed cake.

'Animals he likes. It's people he's not so keen on.'

'You mean apart from the POWs. He was very chummy with them, please-ing and thankyou-ing and calling them by their proper names. The boy who works there thinks he's a fifth columnist.'

'Sam? What rubbish.'

'I can see why people might gossip though. Do you know why he isn't in uniform?'

Tilly shrugged. 'Farming's a reserved occupation. They wouldn't let him join up even if he wanted to.'

'Unless he hired a manager to run Larkstone in his place.'

'Well, yes, I suppose he could do that,' she admitted. 'He'd have to trust whoever it was to run it properly and not cheat him though. That's a lot to ask.'

'Tilly . . . Barbara, one of the other Land Girls, made a comment yesterday. About Sam. I hoped you might be able to tell me what she meant.'

'So Vinnie and Barb are still there, are they?' Tilly said. 'You don't want to listen to those two, Edie. They're nice girls but they could gossip for England.'

'But gossip has to come from somewhere, doesn't it? Barbara said . . . she said Sam only kept his hands to himself *for the most part*. And then Vinnie made this joke about tups which I didn't understand at the time, but that's a breeding ram, isn't it? I think she was talking about Sam.

Do you suppose he might have . . . you know, interfered with one of them?'

'Ignore them, love. It's just tittle-tattle. In small villages, you can't escape it.'

'Yes, but surely it must –'

'He didn't try anything with you, I suppose?'

'Well, no, he didn't, but –'

'There you are then.' Tilly stood up. 'Tea's mashed. I'll pour us a cup.'

Edie watched Tilly strain the tea, wondering why she seemed so anxious to change the subject. What was all this mystery for? And why did no one want to tell her what was going on?

'Oh, I almost forgot,' Tilly said, pulling Edie out of her musings. 'A letter arrived for you.'

She took a green military envelope from her apron pocket, and Edie smiled at the spidery writing on the front.

'It's from my soldier friend, Alfie,' she said as she took it. 'He must've planned for it to arrive soon after I did. I expect he thought I'd be homesick. Thoughtful boy.'

'Your sweetheart?'

'No, an old friend. I've known him and his sister Susan since we were knee-high.'

Tilly raised an eyebrow. 'The green envelopes are only used for *especially* private communications though, aren't they?'

Edie shook her head, smiling. 'Now, there's no use making that face. I told you, it's nothing like that. At least, not if you don't count the fifty or so proposals over the years.'

'Proposals!'

'Oh, not real ones. We're like family, Alfie and Susan and I. He just enjoys teasing me, that's all.'

'If you say so,' Tilly said, placing a cup of tea in front of her.

'That reminds me.' Edie tucked the letter away to read by herself later. 'I had something to give you too: did you find it? You were in bed when I came home last night so I left it on the slab in the pantry.'

'The goat's cheese? I wondered where that had appeared from. Where did you get it?'

'One of the prisoners at the farm gave it to me for you – Luca, the younger one. He said he'd traded for it at their camp.'

'The fool,' Tilly said, smiling. 'He'll be going without his cigarettes now.'

'He said it would be good for you and the baby. And he says you're to eat it all up and not share a bite: doctor's orders.'

'He is a dear. Be sure to thank him for me, won't you?'

'I will.'

'How did you like him? I thought he was rather a sweetheart.'

Edie sighed. 'Honestly? I don't know what to think about him, or Marco either. I was turning it over in my head all last night.'

Tilly frowned. 'You mean because they're foreigners?'

'No,' Edie said in a low voice. 'Because . . . because they're the enemy, aren't they? Luca was talking yesterday about how frightening it felt to be in the skies, and I did feel for him, but . . .' She looked up at Tilly. 'Till, if you'd lived through the Blitz . . . people were dying every day, people I knew. They still are, back in London – I don't know what I'll find when I go home. Who'll be dead and who'll be alive, which buildings will still be standing. In Pimlico, where I lived, you could go down into the shelter and come out to find half your street missing. Your neighbours home-less, or killed . . . you lived your life in constant terror that you might be next. The people who did that were Luca's comrades and allies. As nice as he seems, it's not an easy thing for me to just put to one side.'

'I know how you must feel.' Tilly sat down again with her cup of tea. 'But this isn't Cowboys and Indians, where the heroes are all brave and selfless and the villains are after our scalps. Hitler, Mussolini, all of them – evil, evil men, but we can't judge every person who fights for them that way. It isn't that simple.'

'But when those people have killed British men, maybe even someone you knew –'

'And Luca and Marco felt the same way about us, no doubt,' Tilly said quietly. 'People do their duty as they see it, which-ever side they fight for. Women have to say goodbye to their men in Germany and Italy, just as we do, and weep for them when we kill them.' Edie was surprised to see there were tears in Tilly's eyes. 'Marco and Luca have lost people too.'

'Have they?'

'Hasn't everyone nowadays?' Tilly reached across the table to take Edie's hand. 'Edie, Luca Bianchi was shot down over France with four other men. They were above high ground and couldn't gain enough height to bail out. It was six hours before he was eventually captured by Allied troops. Six hours. All that time, he was trapped in the wreckage with the corpses of his friends – the only survivor.'

'My God!'

'It's easy to forget that war brings grief to us all, allies and enemies alike.' Tilly stood up. 'You'd better go to the library. I'll warm you a bowl of hotpot for when you're done.'

*

The door to Applefield Manor's library was ajar, and Edie could hear raised voices coming from behind it. She hesitated outside, wondering whether she ought to interrupt what sounded like a blazing argument.

'I tell you, Patricia, I won't have it!' she could hear Prudence Hewitt saying. 'I've done my bit. I let them take my boy, didn't I?'

'Your "boy" is a grown man. It wasn't as though you had a choice in the matter,' another female voice observed.

Edie peeped around the door. Prudence was wearing a filthy checked apron, as if she'd been surprised in the middle of cleaning. She was on her feet while her tweedy friend, who in profile looked not dissimilar to an eagle, was sitting calmly in an armchair. A pale little boy watched them from a corner, his eyes round. Edie recognised the woman from church on Sunday, sitting stiffly erect in the front pew with the same little boy at her side.

'I supply half of this village with food from my gardens,' Prudence said. Edie couldn't help noticing how much broader her Cumberland accent sounded when she was too provoked to take that calculated care over her vowel sounds. 'I even offered accommodation to the Land Girl so we could increase our production, although Lord knows I never wanted her here. What more do you want from me?'

'I want you to do what people with far fewer resources than you have readily agreed to do. We're trying to get a quart into a pint pot, the nation over, evacuating children out of the blitzed cities, Prue. With all these empty rooms at your disposal, I wonder you can be so selfish.'

'Selfish! How dare you.' Prudence gave a hard laugh. 'Yes, you're selfless enough when the eyes of everyone are on you, aren't you, Patty? But not when the cause is a little closer to home. You should be ashamed to see your niece going into service just to keep a roof above her head.'

'I don't know why you took the little trollop in. You'll open this place up to any young hussy with no one but herself to blame for getting into trouble, yet you'd rather see innocent children bombed than offer them a home, wouldn't you?'

'You will not refer to Matilda that way in my presence,' Prudence said stiffly. 'I'm warning you, Patricia. Any more of that language and you can leave my house.'

'You mind your business and I'll mind mine, Prudence Hewitt,' Patricia said in a low voice. 'But I expect you to take in those two evacuees or, old friend or not, I won't hesitate to –'

Clearing her throat, Edie gave a light knock on the door. There was silence for a moment, then she heard Prudence call, 'Come in!'

She entered, fixing her face into a bright smile that she hoped would hide the fact she'd overheard their argument. 'Um, good evening. You wanted to see me, Mrs Hewitt?'

'Edith.' Prudence looked flustered. 'This is Mrs Featherstone from the WVS. She came to see how you were settling.'

'Yes. Thank you, Prudence,' Patricia said coldly. She directed an appraising look at Edie. 'Sit down, dear. I'm sure Mrs Hewitt won't object to leaving us alone for a moment.'

Prudence frowned. 'Is that necessary?'

'I think Edith will feel more comfortable discussing her living arrangements without you present.'

'Hmm.' Prudence cast a look at Edie. 'Ten minutes. And don't you bully her, Patricia.'

Edie took the seat opposite Patricia, feeling

self-conscious. The atmosphere hung in the air like lead. Patricia kept her eyes fixed on Prudence until she'd left the room, closing the door behind her.

'Pay her no mind, my dear,' she said, flashing a smile that didn't extend to her eyes. 'I'm here to check your needs are being attended to, that's all. Prudence seems to think I'm planning to have you for my dinner.' She trilled a laugh, a tinkling sound that didn't suit her eagle face at all.

'What do you want to know?' Edie asked.

'You will be visited by the local Land Army representative in due course, who will make a full welfare report, but in the meantime I've been asked to ensure you have everything you require.' Patricia took out a notebook and pencil. 'Is your room comfortable?'

'Yes, very,' Edie said, feeling defensive on Mrs Hewitt's behalf. 'Much nicer than at home. I spent nearly every night there in the shelter.'

Patricia frowned. 'Every night? How odd.'

Edie stifled a wave of annoyance. 'Not if you wanted to stay attached to your limbs, Mrs Featherstone. The Luftwaffe have been very keen on trying to separate us from them these past six months.'

Patricia looked up from her notepad to give Edie a hard stare. 'There's no need for irony, young lady. I'm well aware of what's been happening. We have our problems here too, you know.'

Such as what, Edie wondered? Not being able to get fresh onions for ready money? Having to take your meat ration in corned beef? She bit her tongue before she made a comment she'd regret.

'Sorry,' she said. 'It's been a difficult time for us in the capital.'

102

'I'm sure,' Patricia said with an uninterested air. 'Now, your food. Are you being adequately provisioned?'

'Yes, I've been very well fed. Your niece is a tremendous cook.'

'Hm.' Patricia looked embarrassed at the mention of Tilly. 'You haven't been asked to assist with the household chores, I hope? Other Land Girls have complained of being put upon in that way. You have your own daily work to do; you oughtn't to be expected to cook and clean on top of that.'

'I haven't, but I'd be happy to pitch in.'

Patricia turned to a new page of her notebook. 'How are you finding your work?'

'Hard, but I enjoy it. Sam – that is, Mr Nicholson – seems a firm but fair employer.'

'Yes, well, the least said about that young man, the better,' Patricia said, pursing her lips as if she were sucking on something sour. 'Besides, dear, I really meant your work here on the estate.'

'I enjoy that too. Mr Graham ensures I perform a range of tasks so it isn't all hard physical labour, and Mrs Hewitt is exacting when it comes to making sure I don't do any more than my allotted hours. I'm very satisfied with my situation both here and at Larkstone.'

'You must be lonely, with no girls your own age to talk to.'

'Oh, but I have. Your niece and I have become good friends.'

The invisible lemon in Patricia's mouth seemed to grow even sharper. 'Hm. Yes.'

Edie wondered why Patricia should be more interested in her work on the estate than at the farm. Oughtn't she to monitor her working conditions in both locations, make sure she wasn't being exploited by either of her employers? Edie couldn't help feeling this was more about catching out Prudence than it was about her welfare.

'So no complaints at all?' Patricia asked hopefully. 'I promise grievances will be attended to with the utmost delicacy.'

Edie shook her head. 'Not one. I'm very happy here.'

'Well, I'm glad to hear it,' Patricia said, although she sounded disappointed. She put her notepad away and stood up. 'Edgar, here.'

The little boy trotted obediently to her side in a way that reminded Edie of Sam calling for his sheepdog, Sadie.

'If there's anything you need, you can telephone me at the vicarage.' Patricia took a card from her pocket and held it out. 'Here is my number, and the address should you need it.'

'Thank you.'

Edie pocketed the card and followed Patricia and her grandson from the room. Prudence was in the hall, waiting for them to finish.

'Is everything above board then, Patty?' she asked.

'It would seem so.'

'Oh dear. Well, never mind, perhaps next time.'

'What about you, Prue?' Patricia asked, ignoring that comment. 'Are you happy with Miss Cartwright?'

Patricia cast a glance at Edie, and Edie thought she noticed a tiny twinkle in her eye. 'Yes, I believe I am.'

'Good, then we're all happy, aren't we?' Patricia said with a tight, cheerless smile. She pushed open the front door. 'Prue, I'll be here on Sunday at a quarter past eleven to bring you James and Agnes.'

'What? No! Patty, I told you I wouldn't –'

'I'll be here with them on Sunday,' Patricia repeated

firmly. 'If you try to fight this, Prudence, I will take it to a higher authority. I wouldn't be surprised if you then found the whole place requisitioned.'

'They couldn't do that,' Prue said in a low voice.

'They certainly could. Quite allowable under the Emergency Powers Act. For your sake, I'd advise you to keep your head down and do your duty.' With that, she snatched up Edgar's hand and swept out.

'Insufferable woman,' Prue muttered. 'I wonder how her husband stands her. If I were him, I'd have asked the Almighty for a stray lightning bolt in her direction years ago.'

'Everything all right, Mrs Hewitt?' Edie asked.

'Oh, do call me Prue,' she said absently, pushing distracted fingers into her hair. 'Evacuees, here. Children! Whatever am I supposed to do with two children at my time of life?'

'I can help.'

Prue blinked. 'You? What are you going to do, plant them?'

Edie laughed. 'Only if they really misbehave. No, I'm a schoolmistress. That is to say, I was – my school closed when the bombings began.' She rested a hand on Prue's shoulder. 'Don't worry. Between us we can deal with this.'

Chapter 11

That evening was the pleasantest Edie had spent at Applefield Manor so far. She soon polished off the Lancashire hotpot Tilly heated for her dinner, then while Prudence and Jack kept to their bedrooms, the girls settled themselves in the sitting room.

Edie hadn't liked to sit in there before in spite of Prue's invitation, with the sheets everywhere making it look as though it was waiting to be decorated, but this evening the room had been made quite homely. The sheets were gone, the furniture polished and floor swept, and a blazing fire roared in the hearth.

'I hope you didn't do this,' she said to Tilly, eyeing her friend's swollen tummy. She couldn't imagine trying to sweep out a grate while being roughly the size of a small house.

Tilly shook her head. 'I never lifted a finger. Prue did it all.'

'Not for my benefit, I hope.'

'Perhaps. She hardly ever cleans in here unless Bertie's due to visit.' She turned on the Philips radio and started fiddling with the tuning knob. 'Well, shall we have the Forces Programme or the Home Service?'

'Oh, either,' Edie said as she took out her knitting. 'You can choose.'

'Let's have *Belinda Lou, Lady Investigator* on the Forces Programme then. I hardly ever listen to the Home Service if I can help it. It's so bloody worthy, don't you think? All those organ recitals.'

Edie didn't answer, being overtaken by a sudden fit of coughing.

'Are you all right?' Tilly asked, sounding concerned. 'You seem to have these coughing episodes quite often.'

'It's nothing,' Edie said breathlessly. 'Just hay fever.'

'Are you sure? I get hay fever too but it never makes me cough like that.'

'Yes, but you've lived in the countryside all your life. My constitution's still adjusting.'

Tilly didn't look convinced. 'That's really all it is? It sounds very bad, Edie.'

Edie glanced over her shoulder to check the door was closed.

'If I tell you, do you promise you won't say anything to Prue or Jack?' she said in a low voice.

'Anything about what?'

'My lungs . . . they're fine, for the most part. Not so bad they stop me doing my work or anything. But they're not . . . strong. Not as strong as most other people's.'

'Why not?'

'I had consumption as a little girl and it left some permanent damage.'

'Consumption!'

'Yes.' Edie put away her handkerchief and massaged her throat, which felt sandpaper-sore after this latest fit. 'That's why I ended up in the Land Army. I wanted to join the

107

Wrens but they wouldn't have me. My doctor thought work in the countryside might do me good.'

'Edie, whyever didn't you say anything?'

'I was afraid,' Edie said quietly. 'Afraid they wouldn't want me here, or at the farm. I really want to help the war effort, and if this is all I can do . . . You won't tell on me, will you?'

'Not if you don't want me to. But, sweetheart, you mustn't push yourself too hard, really you mustn't. You'll make yourself ill.'

'I'll be fine, honestly. Just don't tell Prue, please.'

'I promise.'

'Thank you.'

Tilly scrutinised her. 'You said when you arrived that you were one more lost cause to add to the others here. Is that why?'

Edie flushed. 'Oh. No. Well, partially. I suppose I'm not so much lost as alone.'

'No family?' Tilly said softly.

'Only the aunt who raised me, and she had me left on her hands – she never wanted me, although she was always kind in her stern way. I don't think she really understood children.'

'And your parents . . .'

'Dead. My mother died having me, and my father . . .' She swallowed. 'When I was six. Consumption.'

'Like you had?'

'Yes. He . . . I suppose it was in the air,' Edie muttered.

'No brothers and sisters?'

'No. I sometimes feel like my friends Susan and Alfie are the only family I ever had.'

Tilly reached out to squeeze her hand. 'Well, you've got us now. We are like a family at Applefield Manor, in a funny sort of way.'

Edie smiled. 'Thanks. I'm not sure Prue feels the same though. It's obvious she'd rather not have me here – in fact I heard her say as much to your aunt.'

'Oh, she'll warm up. She's always suspicious of strangers, but once she thaws you'll be surprised by her. She is growing fond of you, I can tell.'

'Do you think so?'

'I do. She can probably sense you belong here,' Tilly said, smiling. 'I told you: we're all lost souls in one way or another here, even that perishing crow of Jack's. It's why we fit together so well.' She laughed. 'Sometimes I feel this is more like a sanctuary for refugees than a country house.'

The girls spent a happy hour and a half in front of the fire, Edie knitting a pair of socks and Tilly sewing a baby blanket from scraps of old clothes. At half past eight, Tilly prepared to take herself to bed.

'Not to sound too much like your mother, but you really ought to do the same,' she told Edie. 'It's an early start for you at the farm.'

'I won't be long. I just want to listen to the news.'

'All right, I'll see you tomorrow.' Tilly smiled as she picked up the bits and pieces of her blanket. 'I'm glad you came, Edie. It's pleasant to have young company in the evening. I don't see any of my old friends here since . . . well, you know.'

'I've enjoyed it too,' Edie said, returning her smile.

'So, same time again tomorrow?'

Edie was about to agree when she remembered she already had plans.

'I can't, sorry,' she said with a grimace. 'I said I'd go to a dance at the Land Girls' hostel. I'd rather not, but Vinnie insisted.'

'Oh. Well, you ought to. It sounds like fun.'

'I wish you could come too.'

Tilly laughed, laying a hand on her belly. 'I'm not really at my waltzing weight at the moment. No, you go, have a good time. Have a dance and a drink for me, and a kiss if he's worth it.'

'Thanks, Tilly. Goodnight.'

Edie was glad of some time to herself so she could read Alfie's letter. As soon as Tilly had gone upstairs, she took it out.

Like all of Alfie's communications, it was energetic, jolly and borderline illegible. Edie was used to his scrawl by now, however, and didn't find it too hard to decipher.

Hullo Edie! How's my best girl? it began. *Did you plough your first field yet? I hope you've not been turning all those young farmers' heads in your uniform or I'll be horribly broken-hearted and waste away to nothing before I've even seen any action. And how guilty will you feel then?*

All continues well here, except that it's devilish hot but you can't complain about that, I suppose. The locals have to put up with it all year round, poor souls, but then they're used to it. I'm as brown as a sparrow: you won't recognise me, Ede.

Sergeant Major is as much of a you-know-what as ever. Young Bixenby had a run-in with him last week after a heavy night on the beer. We were drilling in the morning and of course he had an almighty hangover and couldn't keep in step. Tried to give out he had sunstroke but SM's no fool. Anyhow, I suppose SM could've had Bix on a fizzer but he managed to dodge the glasshouse and get away with extra kitchen duty, which I think was fair at the end of the day. Oh, and Sue's in love again, of course. It's no use asking her about it because she'll deny it to the hilt, but he's an ack-ack gunner called Clarence. Told her that as the man of the

110

family I absolutely forbade her to walk out with a Clarence, which of course only made her all the more determined to do it. Be sure and tease her about it properly, Ede: that's your duty to me, you know. Love you as ever and counting the days till I see you. Save me a kiss, remember.

Your favourite sweetheart, Alfie.

Edie smiled as she read it. Alfie's letters were always the same, just a whirlwind of fun and nonsense. It was safe to say that her friend was the complete opposite of the sort of stoical, taciturn people she'd met here – Sam Nicholson and his ilk.

She never understood above half of Alfie's letters, which rushed with dizzying speed from one thing to the next and were always scattered liberally with military slang, but she wouldn't have them any other way. He wrote so much like himself, it felt like he was here with her. She hoped there'd be a letter from Susan soon too, with more information about her latest beau. Although Gunner Clarence might already be yesterday's news – Alfie's letters were always weeks behind his sister's, and Sue went through boyfriends at a rate of knots.

The door opened, and Edie hastily tucked the letter away.

'Oh,' Prue said. 'I'm sorry. I thought everyone had gone to their rooms.'

'I was just waiting for the news bulletin.'

'Then I'll join you. I don't listen very often – I have a gramophone in my room – but I do like to hear the news before bed.' Prue glanced at the wireless. 'Is this the Forces Programme?'

'That's right.'

'I never listen to it myself. The programming always strikes me as rather frivolous,' Prue said as she sat down.

111

'Still, I expect it's morale-boosting for the troops. Bertie tells me he enjoys the comedians.'

'Would you like me to retune it?'

'No, no, leave it as it is. There isn't long until nine o'clock.' She looked at Edie's knitting. 'Continue what you were doing, please. Don't mind me.'

Edie picked up her needles, feeling awkward.

'What are you making?' Prue asked.

'Socks for soldiers,' Edie said, smiling. 'Or for one soldier in particular. My friend Alfie.' She looked at the sock on her needles. 'I wish I'd known when I began that he'd be posted to Africa. I don't suppose he'll be needing woolly socks for a long while.'

'But he'll be very grateful to have them when he comes home on leave, I'm sure,' Prue said. 'Rather a shock to the system, the English weather after all that heat, I'd have thought.'

'Yes, that's true.'

'So are you and this Alfie . . .'

'Just good friends.'

'Ah.'

Edie put her knitting down again. 'Mrs Hewitt – Prue.'

'Yes?' The woman looked wary, as if she was half afraid of what Edie might be about to say.

'I'm so sorry, but I couldn't help overhearing earlier. Your . . . discussion with Mrs Featherstone.'

Prue had shrunk back in her chair now, crossing her arms over her chest as if to place a barrier between them.

'You had no right to listen to that.'

'I didn't intend to eavesdrop. I just felt awkward, walking in on an argument.'

'Well, then why bring it up?' Prue said, frowning. 'It

112

seems to me that you struggle with knowing when to hold your tongue, Edith.'

'Perhaps. Nevertheless, I wanted to say . . .' Edie took a deep breath. 'I just wanted to say that it was jolly decent of you, defending Tilly when her aunt called her those horrid names. I wouldn't have the nerve to stand up to her that way.'

'Oh.' Prue didn't seem to know what to say to that, but she uncrossed her arms.

'And I know you don't want evacuees intruding into your home, any more than you really wanted me, but I think it will be a very kind act to let them stay here and to . . . to keep them safe and everything. I'll help with them all I can and you'll hardly know they're here, I promise.'

'You certainly set a lot of store by your opinions, young lady.'

'When I know I'm right I do, yes,' Edie said stoutly. 'If you knew what it was like to sleep in a shelter every night and hear the bombs falling around you, wondering if your house would still be there when you came out, if your friends would still be alive . . . Prue, if you only knew that, I don't think you could ever send them away. The poor little souls must be terrified, every day. You won't send them away, will you?'

Prue was silent for a long moment. Then she stood and turned up the volume on the wireless.

'Hush now,' she said. 'The news is starting.'

'They're here, the bastards! They've come for us!'

The shout rang through the air, jerking Edie from her dreams. She sat up with a jolt.

Was there a raid? The shelter . . . she had to . . .

Slowly her sleep-addled brain caught up. No. Not

London. She was at Applefield Manor, and the voice she'd heard wasn't an ARP warden alerting her to another air raid but one of her fellow residents.

It was a male voice she'd heard – Jack Graham's voice. Edie could hear the furious stomp of his bare feet outside in the hallway. What in heaven's name was going on?

'Wagstaff!' the voice shouted. 'For Christ's sake, lad, get down!'

Edie shivered, pulling the bedclothes up around her.

If she hadn't known there was only one man in the house, she never would have matched the voice with Applefield Manor's stolid, gentle gardener. This voice was cracked and shrill, filled with raw terror. It made the hair on the back of Edie's neck stand on end.

For a moment she considered burying her face in her quilt and hoping it would all go away. Jack Graham was a powerful man, and if his mind had become unhinged after some sort of night terror . . .

Then she berated herself for her cowardice. Hadn't she slept in the shelter every night with the sound of bombs falling around her? Come face to face with the Luftwaffe? There might be danger, and Tilly and Prue would need her help.

Edie's dressing gown was lying over the chair. She pulled it on over her nightdress, squared her shoulders and went to find out what the commotion was.

When she opened the door she immediately took a step back, gasping at the scene that met her.

Jack was in his pyjamas, backed against the wall with one of the plates that usually lived in the hall dresser raised above his head like a weapon. Edie couldn't tell if he was asleep or awake. His eyes were open – engorged, wild and restless – but they seemed to look straight through her.

114

Jack looked as he had that first morning she'd worked on the estate, when he'd turned eyes on her that for a split second had flashed with pure terror.

'I said, get *down*!' he screamed. 'They'll blow your damn brains out, you young fool!'

He wasn't talking to Edie. His head had jerked to his left, as if someone invisible was standing beside him.

Tilly appeared at the door of her room and, seeing her friend, she darted to her side. Edie reached for her hand.

'Edie, what the hell's going on?'

'I think Jack's sleepwalking,' Edie whispered. 'He's been raving like a madman, talking to someone called Wagstaff.'

'God help us, not again,' Tilly muttered.

Edie blinked. 'What, has this happened before?'

'Every once in a while, he . . . It's not usually as severe as this. He has nightmares. About the last war. He was sent home with shellshock after he lost most of his section at the Somme.'

'You mean his wits are touched?'

'He's as sane as you or me, for the most part. But sometimes . . . well, sometimes there's an incident like this.' Tilly pressed her hand. 'He saw horrors, Edie. Men – friends – blown to bits in front of him.'

'Good God,' Edie whispered. 'The poor man.'

Jack's eyes darted from side to side. Then he hurled his plate at the wall, where it smashed to smithereens. Tilly and Edie shrank back into the doorway of her room.

'What should we do?' Edie whispered. 'They say it's dangerous to wake a sleepwalker, don't they?'

'We need to get Prue. She'll know what to do for him.'

Jack had thrown himself flat on his face now. He was holding his elbows over his ears, shuddering, muttering through choked sobs. It was a heart-rending sight, that giant of a man crying like a frightened child. Edie cast a worried look along the hallway.

'We can't get to her room without passing him.' Her eyes drifted to the shards of the broken plate. 'Tilly . . . might he be dangerous?'

'I honestly don't know. When he's awake he wouldn't hurt a fly, but if he believes he's back in the trenches . . .'

Edie squeezed Tilly's hand and let it drop. 'I'll go.'

'Edie, no! Let me. He's known me longer.'

'You can't risk it. You've got the baby to think of.' She lifted her chin. 'It's all right. I'm not afraid.'

Tilly opened her mouth to remonstrate, but at that moment Prue saved them further discussion by appearing at the door of her room. Her dark hair flowed over her nightgown, and Edie couldn't help noticing how much younger she looked without the harsh bun she usually wore.

'Girls, don't move!' she called in a reassuringly no-nonsense voice. 'Stay right where you are.'

'What are you going to do?' Edie asked. 'Ought we to telephone for a policeman or . . . or a doctor or something?'

'Oh, nonsense, we don't need any of that. It's only Jack.'

She approached and crouched down beside him, resting a gentle hand on his shoulder. Jack jerked as if he'd been shot, his strong, powerful body trembling all over.

'My God, Prue, please be careful,' Tilly muttered.

'They're here,' Jack said, fixing wild eyes on Prue. 'They're here, they're . . . they're bloody everywhere! We'll never get out, Wagstaff.'

'It's me, Jack,' she said softly, massaging his shoulder. 'It's Cheggy. You're safe, my love.'

'Cheggy . . .' His eyes unclouded slightly, and he fixed them on her. 'They're . . . Do you see them too?'

'I only see Jack Graham in his pyjamas, and two very

frightened young ladies. Not to mention the remains of Albert's mother's second-best dinner service.'

'Wagstaff and the other boys . . . did they make it?'

'No,' she said, bowing her head. 'But that was a long time ago. You were dreaming, Jack. We're at Applefield Manor. The war – that war – is over.'

'Then it's . . . it's really you.' He seemed to be coming out of the trance now. 'Cheggy . . .' He laughed: a hollow, desperate sound. 'I used to think I saw you. Used to dream . . . dream of home. And you. I thought when it was all over, I could come home and I'd be safe again.'

'You are home. You are safe.'

He looked behind him, straight at Edie, and she instinctively recoiled when she met his eyes. The look of raw, brutish pain in them was unbearable. Like an animal caught in a trap, its eyes begging for the relief of death.

'No,' he whispered to Prue, bringing his lips close to her ear. 'I brought the horrors back with me.'

'We'll face our horrors together, as we did when we were children.' She stretched out a hand to him. 'I'll keep you safe.'

He looked up to meet her eyes, his lips forming a tremulous smile as with childlike trust he put his huge hand into her little one.

'Go back to bed now,' she said softly. 'I'll sit by you until you're calm again.'

'Yes. Yes. Sorry, Cheg.' The dream had fled completely now, and he looked at the two girls as Prue helped him to his feet. 'Sorry, ladies.'

Edie exchanged a look with Tilly. 'Um, don't mention it,' was all she could think of to say. They watched as Prue took Jack by the arm and guided the stooped, broken figure to his room.

Chapter 12

Tilly was making porridge when Edie rose next morning, although usually she left a cold breakfast ready on the days Edie worked at the farm.

'You're up early,' Edie said.

'Yes, I couldn't get back to sleep after Jack woke us up. In the end I thought I might as well get up and do something useful.' She watched Edie rubbing her eyes. 'You look like I feel, love.'

'Thank goodness it's Saturday and I've got the afternoon off,' Edie said with a yawn. 'I'm not sure I could manage another twelve-hour day clipping out the wedder gimmers, or whatever one of the million terms they have for sheep around here is the correct one.'

Tilly laughed. 'Well, it's not that one. If there was such a thing as a wedder gimmer, it would be a castrated female. Which I'm sure even an unworldly soul like you must realise is somewhat impossible, Edie.'

'Oh.'

'How were you thinking of spending your free afternoon?'

'I had planned to go into Applefield and look around, but the way I feel this morning, I may just go back to bed.'

'Why not come help me spend the housekeeping? It'll be nice to have someone to keep me company in the queues, and I can show you what little there is to see in the village. You'll still have plenty of time to get ready for your dance.'

Edie groaned. 'I'd forgotten the dance. I wish I could think of an excuse not to go.'

'Oh, you'll have buckets of fun.' Tilly came over with a bowl of porridge. 'There you are, that'll warm your bones.'

'Are Jack and Prue up yet?' Edie asked as she added a spoonful of treacle.

'I don't think so.' Tilly took a seat and poured Edie and herself a mug of tea from the pot. 'You won't say anything to him, will you? He'll be so humiliated if you mention it.'

'I wouldn't dream of it. The poor man, it must be horrific having to relive it over and over.' Edie thought back to the evening before: the wild, helpless look in Jack's eyes, and the way Prue had calmed him with a maternal tenderness Edie would never have expected in her. 'Why does he call her Cheggy, Till?'

'No idea. He has done for as long as I've known the two of them – all my life, in other words. I've always wondered but I never liked to ask.'

'What is their story? She doesn't treat him like he's just the gardener.'

'Because he isn't just the gardener,' Tilly said, reaching for the milk jug. 'Prue and Jack have known each other since they were children.'

'Did they both live in the village?'

'They lived right here at Applefield Manor. Jack's father was the gardener before him, and Prue's mam was the housekeeper. A real dragon, from what I've heard. I don't think Prue has many happy memories of her. Free with her hands – and her fists.'

'So they grew up together?'

'That's right, alongside Albert Hewitt: the young master, as it were. The three of them were the bosomest of pals. All of an age and thick as thieves, with parents who didn't care enough to mind where in the grounds their children were so long as they never had to set eyes on them – well, apart from old Mr Graham, perhaps. Jack always speaks fondly of him.' She paused to sip her tea. 'From what Jack's told me, I think Prue might have been rather wild when her mother wasn't around to check her. Hard to imagine, isn't it?'

'And Albert and Prue fell in love?'

'Yes.' Tilly laughed. 'That's the price his toffee-nosed parents paid for letting him fraternise with the domestics' children. They were mortified when he announced he was going to marry the housekeeper's daughter. I think they'd have liked to cut him off with nothing, but there was some legal reason they weren't allowed. Albert and Prue married as soon as they were of age, and eventually Applefield Manor became theirs.'

'Gosh. It's like a fairytale,' Edie said in a half-whisper.

Tilly smiled. 'I hate to shatter your girlish faith in the power of true love, Edie, but the real world rarely works the way it does in a storybook.'

'You mean they weren't happy?'

'Oh yes, they loved each other deeply. I think if Prue hadn't adored Albert quite so much then by now Jack might've –' She stopped herself. 'But it's not my business to talk about that. What I mean is, a happily-ever-after nearly always comes at a price.'

'What price?'

'Suspicion. Judgement. Applefield is good at that, I can testify to it myself. Prue had married outside her class, and

120

people don't like it when they see others not keeping to their place. It makes a mockery of what they see as The Rules.'

'But if she loved him . . .'

'She did. Anyone who saw them together could tell that Prudence and Albert Hewitt thought the world of each other, but it didn't stop the gossip. Whispers that she was a fortune-hunter, that she and her mother had concocted the plan to "trap" Albert when Prue was just a child. All sorts of nonsense. Then after her marriage Prue found she was neither one thing nor the other: despised by the class she was born into for thinking she was above it, sneered at by the one she married into because she wasn't truly one of them. I imagine Cinderella had a very similar experience.'

'Is that why Prue closes herself off the way she does? Why she hates to have strangers in the house?'

'I believe that's part of it,' Tilly said. 'She finds it very hard to let people in. Prue loves and trusts only two people in the world now Albert's gone: Bertie, her son, and Jack, her oldest friend. And I think she's come to trust me in the five months I've worked for her – I hope so.'

'So you and Jack are her two lost causes then?' Edie said, smiling.

'That's what I've always thought. Jack with his little problem, me with mine.' She rested a hand on her stomach. 'Outcasts, like her. People who don't fit any more.'

'People who are alone,' Edie murmured. 'Like me.' She roused herself. 'I'd better go to work. Tell Prue and Jack I said good morning.'

'Wait,' Tilly said before Edie could leave.

'What is it?'

'Can you take a note up to the farm? It'll save me the price of a stamp.'

'Of course.'

Tilly took a pretty lilac envelope from under the trivet. It was sealed, but there was no name or address on it. Edie took it, noting that it was scented with lavender water.

'Pass it on to Sam, he'll know what it's for,' Tilly said.

'What is it for?'

'Nothing important. Just business.'

Edie raised an eyebrow. 'That sounds mysterious.'

Tilly laughed. 'It isn't, I promise. If you must know, Sam goes rabbit-shooting on Saturday afternoons and I'm hoping to sweet-talk him into selling me one for our pot. Can you give it to him?'

'Oh. Yes, of course. Bye then.'

Edie knew the route to Larkstone Farm now, and she arrived at work with time to spare. She didn't want to give Sam any reason to withdraw the good opinion – or at least the tolerant opinion – he'd formed of her on her first couple of days. The workers were in the farmhouse when she arrived, being assigned their daily jobs, and Edie took her place among them.

On the stone-flagged floor, beside a roaring fire, was a wooden crate containing a tiny sleeping lamb. Its little chest rose and fell with a weak but steady rhythm, and Sadie and the other sheepdog, Shep, kept watchful eyes on it from their station under a big oak table.

A paraffin lamp sat on the table, set beside a tin mug half-filled with cold cocoa and what must have been Sam's suppertime reading: a copy of *The Farmer and Stock-Breeder* sprawling incongruously beside a well-thumbed edition of Mr Orwell's *The Road to Wigan Pier*. A couple of pheasants and a hare were strung from the rafters alongside pans and copper kettles, and a long shelf filled with home remedies for a variety of sheep ailments ran the circumference of the room. Although there was no electricity in the farmhouse, there was a battered Bakelite wireless sitting in one corner, the type powered by a rechargeable accumulator. That and a well-stuffed bookshelf were the only luxuries in this otherwise spartan example of rustic living.

'You two, infirmary, do the morning feeds,' Sam was saying to Vinnie and Barbara, with his customary lack of courtesy.

'Yes, Sam.'

Sam was as sullen as ever, but Edie couldn't help noticing that he seemed a lot less fresh than he had on the previous two days. His face was haggard, and his eyes bagged with purple. She wondered if it had been an unsettled night for some of the in-lamb Herdies.

'Luca, Marco, I'd like you doing the feeds up at the pens please, then you can help the girls fettle the infirmary,' Sam said to the two Italians. 'Take the boy.'

Luca saluted. 'Yes, boss.'

Davy shot a scowl of deep suspicion at the two prisoners and opened his mouth to object, but Sam raised a hand to silence him. 'I know what you're going to say. Do as you're told or you're out, lad. I won't brook surliness, or workers who can't be fashed getting their hands dirty.'

'I don't mind getting my hands dirty,' Davy muttered.

'Well, then is it obeying orders you object to? You might find that's a problem for you in the army.'

'What would you know about it?' Davy mumbled, only half under his breath. Sam shot him a sharp look.

'Son, this is your last warning: belt up or you can bugger off. This is my place. If you don't like the terms of your employment here, you're welcome to find somewhere else.'

Davy looked like he had a retort on the tip of his tongue,

but something in the farmer's expression seemed to stop him.

'Fine,' he said. 'Whatever you like.'

'That's better. And mind what Luca and Marco tell you; they're in charge.' Sam finally turned to look at Edie. 'London, you're with me.'

'All right.'

Hmm. So they were to be alone again. Edie had been convinced that Sam had no romantic interest in her, but he did seem fond of singling her out as his working companion. She could see her fellow Land Girls exchanging raised eyebrows.

Sam clapped his hands. 'Sharp as you like then. Sadie, Shep, here! I'll be needing you two this morning.'

So they'd at least have the dogs as chaperones. Edie wasn't sure they'd be much help in the event of any unwanted attention from her boss, but it was better than nothing.

The two sheepdogs came trotting to Sam's heels. He strode to the door, and Edie was about to follow when Vinnie plucked her elbow.

'You're still coming to our beano tonight, aren't you?' she asked.

'Of course.'

Vinnie slapped her on the back. 'Good girl. I can't wait to introduce you to the others.'

Edie's eyes flickered to the door. 'Do you two know what's the matter with Sam? He looks worn out.'

Vinnie nodded to the lamb by the fire. 'He was up till God knows what hour with this little chap. It was at death's door yesterday evening; he spent most of the night trying to get it out of the woods. Marco says he found him with it cuddled in his arms by the fire this morning, sleeping like a cherub. Do not tell Sam I told you that.'

Barbara, standing at Vinnie's side with one arm resting on her friend's shoulder, quirked a knowing eyebrow. 'You certainly seem to have gained yourself an admirer, Edie.'

Edie flushed. 'Don't be silly.'

'Am I? You've only worked here two days and already Sam won't let you out of his sight. It's been a while since he had a favourite.'

'Nothing happened between you two yesterday, did it?' Vinnie asked.

'Such as?'

'Come on, Edie. You can't be as green as all that.'

Edie felt her cheeks burning again and faked a cough so she had an excuse to cover her face with her handkerchief.

'It isn't like that,' she said. 'I've got the most to learn, that's all. I expect Sam wants to make sure I'm getting all the training I need.'

Barbara shot a look at the door and lowered her voice. 'Just be careful, love. Things didn't turn out too well for Sam's last pet.'

'What do you –'

'London!' a voice boomed from outside. 'You coming, lass? Less laik, more work.'

Barbara patted her arm. 'TTFN, darling. We'll see you tonight.'

'Yes. OK.'

With a worried look over her shoulder at the two women, Edie hurried to the door.

'Sorry,' she said to Sam, who was waiting outside for her.

'Never mind sorry, don't do it. I don't pay you to chat.' He pointed towards one of the outbuildings. 'Job for us in the henhouse. Nest of rats to flush out.'

Edie brightened. Now this had been covered in her

training. Finally, something she could do without embarrassing herself!

'That lamb by the fire, was that the one from Thursday?' she asked as she half walked, half skipped to keep up with his long strides. 'The one I found, I mean?'

'Aye, that's him. Still clinging on to life, just.'

She looked up to examine Sam's profile, noting again the bags under his eyes. 'Did you have a bad night with him?'

'A long one. I'm used to it. Lambing season, you're lucky if you get to bed at all for six or seven weeks. When you do, you keep your boots on.'

'It was kind of you to try to save him.'

He grunted. 'Nowt of the sort. Don't want to lose my investment, that's all.'

Sadie had waddled up to Edie's leg. Edie reached down to tickle her ears, and the portly dog wagged her tail appreciatively.

'I thought sheepdogs were supposed to be lithe and sinewy,' Edie observed.

'So they are, when they're not full of more sheepdog.'

'Pardon?'

'Pups. Four or five, by my reckoning.' He nodded to the other sheepdog. 'Shep here's a devil. Can't leave her alone when she's on heat.'

'Oh.' Edie found herself blushing again, and cursed her stupid cheeks. 'Will you keep them all?'

'Nay, I've no call for five dogs. Plenty of farms round here with good homes for them though.' He patted Sadie's rump. 'She's not a deal of good for shepherding work when she's this far gone, but she likes to feel she's helping.'

'Oh! I nearly forgot.' Edie reached into her pocket and took out the lilac envelope. 'From Tilly. She asked me to give it to you.'

He took it from her, frowning. 'Tilly?'

'Tilly Liddell. She used to work for you, didn't she?'

'Oh. Yes.'

He stuffed the note in his pocket and carried on walking.

'Aren't you going to read it?' Edie asked.

'Not now.'

'Do you know what it's about?'

That was definitely far too forward, but Edie couldn't help wanting to know more. She was sure Tilly hadn't been telling the complete truth when she told her that story about wanting to buy a rabbit. Who wrote letters about game purchases on scented purple notepaper?

'Yes,' Sam said. 'I know.'

And without another word he strode off ahead, leaving Edie and the sheepdogs bringing up the rear.

Edie watched him as he made for the henhouse: broad and erect; firm muscles, forged through a lifetime of hard work, shifting under his clothes; shirt sleeves rolled up to the elbows to expose a pair of powerful forearms lightly dusted with fair hair. Tilly had called him charming. Edie didn't know about that, but he was certainly strong and vigorous, and not unpleasant to look at either, especially when his scowl lifted. Sam Nicholson was hardly what you'd call a ladies' man, but some women preferred that sort, didn't they – the strong, silent type? Yes, Edie could see how Sam might have the capacity to charm. She could imagine a woman susceptible to that charm even finding herself falling in love with him.

Her brow furrowed in a frown. An idea had started to form, and it wasn't one she cared for at all.

Chapter 13

The henhouse was a small barn with a fenced paddock to the back. There were around a dozen fat brown biddies and one very cocky cockerel strutting around it when Edie and Sam arrived.

'How many hens do you keep?' she asked.

'Twenty, plus the cock. I'd like more – plenty of demand for eggs, and meat too – but I don't have time to tend to them and the sheep.'

Edie noticed how he became more animated when he discussed his work, and his seemingly immovable frown lifted. Farm life was hard, but it was obvious he loved it.

'Prue Hewitt is in the market for some hens,' Edie said. 'She wants to sell fresh eggs down in the village.'

'I wouldn't mind the competition. There's more demand in Applefield than I can supply. Tell her I'll put by a couple of chicks for her from the next lot, no charge, and she can see how she gets along with them.'

'Thank you, she'll appreciate that.'

All the time he was talking his eyes were roving over the hens, counting them.

'Fourteen,' he said. 'Let's check inside.'

In the henhouse, five hens sat roosting in their hen boxes. The sixth, though, lay on the floor in a mess of blood and feathers, stone dead. Edie hastily averted her eyes.

Sam shook his head, scowling.

'That's rats, that is,' he muttered. 'I knew they were in here. I've been finding broken eggs for weeks.'

'Do they eat them?'

'Aye, suck out the insides. I emptied the traps of three of the little buggers last week, but it's taken more than a few to do this. There's a nest somewhere.'

He picked the dead hen up by the neck, its lifeless head lolling pathetically, and threw it on to a shelf.

'You can take that home if you want, boil the giblets for soup,' Sam said. 'Wouldn't eat the flesh if I were you though, not after the vermin have had their teeth in it.'

Edie didn't particularly relish the idea of cycling home with the victim of a brutal poultrycide in her bike basket, but waste not, want not, she supposed. Plus it was off the ration, a little extra to supplement their meagre meat allowance. Chicken wasn't rationed but it was scarce, and when you could find it you could expect to pay a king's ransom for it.

Sam was feeling generous to the residents of Applefield Manor today. Fleetingly, Edie wondered why. Guilty conscience perhaps?

'Thank you.' She glanced around the dimly lit barn and gave a slight shudder. 'I suppose we ought to get looking for the rats.'

'Let's get these girls outside first.' Sam felt under the roosting hens to check for eggs. 'Nothing again today, thanks to our scurrying friends putting them off laying. All right, ladies, wake up. Shoo, shoo, go on! Out in the run.'

When the henhouse was empty, Sam closed the hatch leading outside and opened the door for Shep and Sadie.

'Rats can get anywhere,' Sam told Edie. 'In the rafters, under the straw. They're devious little sods. The dogs should be able to sniff them out though. See where these two go, then have a dig around. Here.' He tossed Edie a pair of heavy leather gloves and started pulling on a pair of his own. 'You don't want to get bit.'

Sam bent down to tuck his trousers into his socks as Edie pulled on the gloves.

'Stops the buggers running up the legs,' he explained when he noticed her watching. 'Don't want them digging their teeth into anything tender up there, do I?'

Edie found herself blushing again. She crouched down to make sure her own breeches were tightly secured inside her standard-issue Land Army socks, glad of an excuse to hide her face. That earthy northern bluntness was going to take a bit of getting used to where some things were concerned.

The dogs began digging around in the straw, looking for the bloodthirsty intruders. Humans and canines had been searching for a good half-hour when Edie pulled out one of the nest boxes and clamped her hand over her mouth to suppress a squeal. A pair of big black eyes stared up at her, before the enormous rat bared its teeth and scurried away in a flash of brown.

'Shep! Sadie! Go to it!' Sam commanded, grabbing Edie's arm to pull her back. Unconsciously she sagged against him, dizzy from the shock.

The dogs didn't need telling twice. With a delighted yelp, Shep leaped into the shadows. A second later he had the rat in his mouth, growling as he shook the life out of it. The thing was dead almost as soon as the dog's jaws closed on its throat, and its plump body fell, lifeless, to the floor.

'Sam, there's a nest, like you said,' Edie whispered. 'Under the boxes. Loads of them . . . babies. That must've been the mother.'

'Best thing is to turn them out, let the dogs deal with them. Sounds cruel, I know, but it's more humane than gas or poison.'

'Is it –'

She stopped herself. 'Is it really necessary?', she'd been about to ask, but of course she knew it was. And yet the little things had looked so helpless, even though they were vermin. She wished there was another way.

Her friend Alfie had had a pet rat when he was a boy, a little white chap with pink eyes named Merlin. He'd been tame enough to carry in Alfie's pocket, and clever as anything. Alfie had taught him to do tricks: to roll on his back, and beg for his food just like a dog. It had broken his heart when Merlin had finally died at the age of three.

Edie turned her face away from the dead rat on the floor, trying not to think about Merlin. How had she thought she was prepared for this? To learn about it in theory was one thing; in practice it was quite another.

'Are you all right, London? You've gone very pale.'

There was a softer note to Sam's voice than she'd heard there before. Edie realised she was still resting her weight against him, and he'd placed one hand on her hip for support. Hastily she moved away.

'I'll be OK,' she said. 'It was a shock, that was all.'

'Hmm.' He looked into her face. 'Perhaps you ought to go outside. You're right, it's a nasty business. I don't like it myself, but . . .'

'But it has to be done. I know.' She pulled herself up straight. 'No. I want to see it through. It's my job.'

'I won't think any less of you, Edie.'

She looked down at the rat on the floor and closed her eyes.

'Let's just get it over with,' she said.

After the rats had been dealt with, Edie and Sam took the bodies to the midden where all the farm's rubbish was dumped, then they mucked out and sluiced down the henhouse before setting baited traps for any vermin who might have escaped the bloodbath. At quarter to twelve Sam told her she was free to go.

'You've been quiet this morning,' he observed as he walked back with her to the farmhouse. 'Normally I can't shut you up.'

It was true. After the upsetting incident with Jack Graham last night, and then the massacre in the henhouse, Edie hadn't felt much like chatting.

But it wasn't only that. The idea that had formed this morning was still there, getting stronger and more fleshed out as she remembered the hints and whispers she'd been hearing both at the farm and Applefield Manor. She couldn't put it out of her mind.

'Sorry,' she said to Sam. 'I didn't sleep too well last night either.'

'Hmm. Well, be sure you're fresh when you're back here next Thursday. I want to –'

He broke off, scowling at something white on the farmhouse door.

'What is it?' Edie asked, but Sam didn't answer.

He strode off ahead, and as they got closer Edie saw that it was an envelope, pinned to the wood. There was no name, no address: just one word scrawled on the front in a childlike hand.

COWARD.

'Where could it have come from?' Edie asked as he tore it open.

'Some kind-hearted neighbour,' Sam muttered. 'Must've heard my eiderdown needs restuffing.'

He tossed it to her so she could take a look too. Inside were three white feathers.

'What does it mean, Sam?'

'It means Applefield still isn't ready to award me that gallantry medal.' He frowned as angry shouts came from the big barn they called the infirmary. 'What the hell is going on in there?'

Too curious not to find out what the fuss was about, Edie stuffed the envelope into her breeches pocket and followed Sam to the barn.

It was quite a sight that met their eyes when he flung open the door. Davy was bent double, struggling to get out of a headlock Luca was holding him in. Marco had the boy's hands pinned behind his back, but as they watched he managed to get one free and started raining punches into Luca's side. The young Italian, Edie noticed, had a very sore-looking black eye. Barbara and Vinnie stood by, looking bewildered.

Edie went to join her fellow Land Girls.

'What happened?' she whispered.

'Davy started it,' Barbara said. 'He just flew into a rage.'

Vinnie bowed her head. 'It's his brother. The family got the telegram last night – MIA. Poor lad's been primed to go off all day.'

'What the devil is going on here?' Sam thundered,

133

marching into the fray. 'Good God, Luca, let him go! You'll strangle him to death, man.'

Panting, Luca released Davy from the headlock. The boy made to lunge at him again, but Sam grabbed him and pinned him against the wall by his shoulders.

'Does somebody want to tell me how this started?' he demanded.

Davy made another bid for freedom, but Sam held him firmly.

Luca shook his head. 'I cannot understand it. There was nothing. We were cleaning out the pens, and I began to sing an old air from back home. Marco joined me, and the next thing the boy had flown at me. I tried to restrain him without hurting him.' He touched his bruised eye gingerly. 'I was not very successful preventing him from hurting me, as you can see. That's a good strong punch you have, Davy.'

'If you calm down and keep those fists to yourself I'll let you go,' Sam told Davy.

The boy glowered for a moment, then, seeing he wasn't going to be allowed his freedom unless he agreed, gave a reluctant nod. Sam released him.

'Why did you attack him?' he demanded.

'There's a war on, isn't there?' Davy muttered. 'I'm on one side and he's on the other. *You* might not think that's how it is, but it is.'

'The war isn't happening on this farm. We're all on the same side here.'

'You would say that, you bloody . . . wop-lover,' Davy shot back angrily. 'If we lost you wouldn't give a damn. Hell, I bet you want us to lose.' He glared at Luca and spat on the ground. 'Our people are disappearing and dying every damn day, we're losing the bloody war, and he's here mocking us with his filthy foreign songs like it's a game.' He sneered. 'Let's all have a singsong, eh, Luca? Why not?'

'I don't want to be your enemy, Davy,' Luca said quietly.

'But I want to be yours. Swaggering around acting like we're all friends, making love to our women, like your people and mine aren't out there killing each other.' He swallowed hard. 'I'm glad I blacked your eye,' he said in a choked voice. 'I'll do worse when they let me out there, just bloody wait and see if I don't.'

The boy was white with grief and impotent rage. His hands, thrust into his pockets now, were still balled into fists.

'Right. I told you this morning that this was your last chance,' Sam said in a low voice. 'Come to the farmhouse and get your week's pay, lad. You're not coming back.'

'Hey,' Luca said, resting a hand on Sam's shoulder. 'There's no need for that, Sam.'

'And the envelope on the door, that was you as well, wasn't it?' Sam demanded, ignoring Luca.

'What envelope?' Davy said.

'I doubt you need me to answer that.' He cast a look over his shoulder. 'Luca, let me settle up with young Mr Braithwaite here then we'll get a bit of something on that shiner. I haven't got any steak so you'll have to make do with liver. Davy, since you can't stay off politics, you can fetch your money and go. I'll pay you for the full day, but I won't have bad blood on my farm.'

Edie went to fetch her bicycle, following a little way behind Sam and Davy as they headed to the farmhouse. She swung one leg over the crossbar, paused, then dismounted again.

Eventually she heard the door click open and peered around the wall. As she'd hoped it was Davy, alone. He had his hands stuck in his pockets and his face was flushed, like a child struggling to suppress tears. Knowing how embarrassed he'd be if he knew she'd seen him blub, Edie called out to him.

'Are you all right?' she asked when she'd approached him.

'Fine. I didn't want to work in this rotten place any road.' He tossed a filthy glance in the direction of the infirmary. 'Don't like the company you have to keep.'

'You shouldn't have done that, Davy. Luca didn't mean any harm. The Italians always sing while they work.'

'He's one of them. Course he means harm. How many of ours did he kill before he got shot down? You ever thought of asking him that?'

'Do you really think everyone who fights for the other side is a monster?'

He stared at the ground. 'All I know is, our Geordie's gone and they're to blame. Them and all their kind.'

Edie felt for the boy. Being eighteen was hard enough whenever it happened to you, and now Davy had the war to contend with on top of everything that went with growing from a child to a man. All the propaganda, the fear of losing loved ones and of ultimately losing the war, and knowing that any moment King and Country would be calling to tell you your childhood was over no matter how unready you felt to leave it behind. And now his older brother was missing in action. No wonder the lad had been smouldering like a primed grenade.

Edie laid a hand on his shoulder. 'I'm sorry about Geordie.'

He shrugged, not meeting her eye. 'It happens. Happens to lots of people.'

'But it never happened to you before, did it?' She gave his shoulder a squeeze. 'It's OK to feel angry,' she said softly.

'But you didn't have to take it out on Luca. He's lost people too.'

'Not our people.'

'No, his people. You think that doesn't hurt, because he isn't English? I know it's war, but it doesn't have to be personal.'

'What, so you think I should say sorry? To *him*?'

'Why not? I'm sure he'd put a good word in with Sam. He never wanted you to be sacked.'

'I'm not crawling to any damn wop. Let him say sorry.'

Edie sighed and removed her hand, sensing she was fighting a losing battle. The prejudice Davy had been exposed to at home had done its work, and nothing she could say was going to undo that.

'Hey,' she said as he made to go. 'Was it you?'

'What?'

She took out the envelope with the feathers in it and held it up so he could see that word, *COWARD*, on the front. 'Sam found it pinned to the farmhouse door.'

Davy shook his head. 'Never seen it before. What's it say?'

She frowned. 'Can't you read it?'

'Some words I can read, the ones I need. My name and that. Don't know that one.'

So Davy was illiterate. Then it couldn't have been him who . . .

'What's it say, Miss?' he asked.

'Oh . . . nothing. Nothing important.' She put the envelope away again. 'Think about that apology, Davy. This doesn't have to cost you your job.'

'Who cares about the job? I'd not have been here much longer. Sam only hired me for the lambing, and I'll probably be called up before that's done anyhow.'

'You don't know that. Some lads end up waiting months and months for their call-up. You want to stay in work while you're waiting, don't you? I suppose you need money to live on, the same as we all do. Go on, Davy, apologise.'

'I tell you, I *won't*!' he said with boyish belligerence, digging his fists further into his pockets. 'Not to him.'

He slouched off, eyes wet with unshed tears.

Chapter 14

'I felt so sorry for him,' Edie told Tilly as they walked into Applefield that afternoon. Each of the girls had a shopping basket hooked over one arm, with their free arms linked together like old friends. 'I don't think he's a bad kid. Just angry at the way things are.'

'I know the Braithwaites,' Tilly said. 'Davy's dad Fred is our village butcher. His eldest Geordie is my age.'

'What's Fred like?'

'Hard, very hard. A real bully-boy, if you want the truth. He took the two lads out of school when their mum died; that's where Davy's problems started. Fred said his boys had no need of book-learning for good, honest work.' Tilly curled her lip. 'That's the sort of thing he likes to say. Makes him feel like a man.'

'That's why Davy can't read.'

'Yes. He worships Fred though.' She sighed. 'He won't half get a whipping when his dad finds out he's been sacked.'

'Davy certainly seems to have picked up some views about foreigners from him.'

'Poor Luca. He'd never fight anyone if he had the choice; he's ever so soft-hearted. Was he badly hurt?'

'Just a black eye,' Edie said. 'After what happened to his

brother, you can understand why Davy lashed out. Do you think Luca could talk Sam into giving him his job back?'

'Perhaps.'

The footpath they were following widened, leading to a packhorse bridge that crossed a little chattering beck.

'Or maybe you could have a word,' Edie said, studying her friend's face. 'You know Sam well, don't you?'

Tilly looked like she was only half paying attention, absently turning the strange silver ring she always wore around her finger as she walked. 'I doubt he'd listen to me.'

'Why?'

'He never does,' Tilly said with a half-smile. She appeared to rouse herself. 'But I might pay a call on him. I do need to thank him for the chicken. The stock ought to keep us in soups and stews for a few days.'

'You can call on him when you pick up the rabbit.'

'Pardon?'

'The rabbit. Wasn't that what the note you asked me to pass on was about?'

'Oh. Yes.'

Edie had been watching her carefully, trying to detect anything that would give weight to the idea she'd been pondering. She felt it would be a liberty to ask Tilly directly if she was right. They were still very new acquaintances, after all, although in some ways it felt like they'd known each other for years. And if her friend had lied, she must have a reason for doing so.

Instead, Edie turned the conversation to the party at the WLA hostel that evening.

'Is there anywhere in the village I could buy a lipstick?' she asked. 'I only brought one colour, and it won't go at all with the blue silk I was planning to wear.'

Tilly laughed. 'This isn't London, Edie. If you need to buy a ball of string or a quarter of acid drops or a tin of mustard powder, Applefield's the place to go. Anything more exotic and you'd need to make a journey into town.' She squeezed her arm. 'But never mind about that, I've got plenty of everything you can borrow.'

'Are you sure?'

'Of course. And mind, you must let me make you all pretty before you go out. It's the nearest to fun I'm likely to get for a little while. Is it only girls?'

'Vinnie said there'd be some boys from the RAF base.'

Edie watched Tilly's expression, but there was no sign this information brought back unhappy memories of her own experience.

'Then we'd better make sure you're the belle of the ball, hadn't we?' she said. 'Who knows but that there might not be a future Mr Edie Cartwright there tonight.'

Edie flushed. 'Don't be silly.'

'Well, and why not? You want to get married, don't you?'

'War's no time to be thinking about that.'

'Of course it is. There's nothing like an uncertain future to turn the mind to thoughts of love. Eat, drink and be merry, Edie, my dear, for tomorrow we die.' Tilly rubbed her stomach, wincing as the baby gave her a kick. 'But I'm the last person you should let talk philosophy to you. Look at the pickle that sort of thinking got me into.'

When they reached Applefield's main street, Edie started to see exactly what Tilly had meant about the pervading atmosphere of judgement and suspicion. Her friend had a cheerful greeting for everyone they met, and while some of the villagers responded in kind, just as many gave only a curt nod, or cut her dead. Some even crossed the road

141

to avoid her, pulling their children close as if worrying unwed motherhood might be infectious.

Edie noticed a few suspicious looks in her direction too. She wasn't certain if she was attracting them because she was a newcomer, because she was evidently a bosom pal of the village's official fallen woman, or a bit of both.

'Sorry,' Tilly whispered. 'I hope I'm not ruining your reputation by association.'

'They can't intimidate me,' Edie whispered back. 'I've faced the Luftwaffe.'

'Oh, the Luftwaffe have got nothing on Applefield.' Tilly gestured along the main street. 'Well, Edie, welcome to hell. There's the village shop, purveyor of anything and everything: butter, kippers, Oxo cubes, soap flakes – whatever you like as long as it's solid and boring. The Golden Fleece pub, Braithwaite the butcher, Jowett's greengrocer's, post office, tobacconist's, village institute, and a little further up is St Mark's Church. And that's it. We're the very definition of what in the Westerns they call a one-horse town.'

'It's very pretty,' Edie said, casting an appreciative eye over the pink sandstone cottages, the whitewashed pub and the village green, where old men were enjoying a game of bowls.

Applefield seemed to Edie to be the epitome of a snug, civilised country village: a real slice of old England. This was somewhere the pace of life had remained the same for centuries; such a contrast with the grime and bustle of London.

She inhaled deeply. Dr Grant had been right: she could feel the fresh air doing her good as it filled her body.

Tilly scoffed. 'You wouldn't say that if you'd been born here. I'm convinced there's no duller place in the world. I think some of us younger folk were almost glad the war came along to shake things up a little.' She caught the look on Edie's face. 'Oh, now, you know I'm only joking. Come on, we'll join the queue for Jowett's. If you see an onion, grab it before anyone else gets their hands on it.'

But there were no onions, as there hadn't been anywhere for months, so they came away with five pounds of potatoes, a cabbage and a few beetroots, with their other needs supplied by Applefield Manor's gardens. In the village shop they bought tea, sugar, flour and other necessities, then they visited the butcher's.

'I can't give you a joint so it's no good asking,' the brawny, sallow-faced man behind the counter told them gruffly when, after half an hour, they reached the front of the queue.

'What can you give us?' Tilly asked. 'Anything off the ration? I'd love a couple of sausages if you've got any under the counter.'

'No sausages, no kidneys, no rabbit. I've liver, oxtail and tongue not on coupons, plus braising steak and a few chops if you've got the coupons for 'em.'

'Lamb chops?' Edie asked.

'Pork.'

'Oh. Good.' She lowered her voice to talk to Tilly. 'I'm not so keen on lamb all of a sudden.'

'That's fine, thank you, Fred,' Tilly said. 'We'll take a pound of liver, an oxtail and six chops, and you can make up the rest in corned beef.' She nodded to Edie. 'We've got coupons for four of us now.'

'Aye, I heard. Up at Nicholson's with our lad, isn't she?'

'Yes,' Edie said, even though the question hadn't been addressed to her. It didn't seem as though Davy had been home yet to tell his father what had happened that morning.

'Davy's a fine young man. You ought to be very proud of him, Mr Braithwaite.'

'Huh. Wouldn't know about that. The boy's half simple if you ask me.' He wiped his hands on his bloody apron and weighed out the meat. 'Five and tenpence for that lot.'

Tilly cast a glum look at the meagre amount of meat on the chops as Fred took them from the scales.

'Not a lot between us, is it?' she said in an undertone to Edie. 'Goodness knows how we'll manage when they cut the ration to a bob each next week. I swear, if I eat a single carrot more I'll turn into one. Thank heavens for Sam's giblets.'

But Edie wasn't thinking about the recent announcement of yet another cut to the meat ration. She was watching Fred Braithwaite's beefy, calloused hands as he wrapped their order, hoping Tilly had been wrong when she'd said Davy would have a beating waiting for him.

Fred turned to spit over his shoulder. 'I wouldn't work for that dirty bastard Nicholson for any money. Thinks more of those pet Eyeties of his than he does of honest English folk. The whole thing stinks like that bloody garlic they're always eating.'

'Just the chops, please, Fred,' Tilly said calmly. 'We don't have the coupons for opinions.'

Fred snorted. 'Surprised *you've* got a good word to say for him. He's done you no favours.' He put the parcel of meat on the counter and leered at her over it. 'But perhaps you like it that way, eh, love?'

'I did say *just* the chops,' she repeated firmly, handing over their four ration books and a ten-shilling note. 'I wouldn't like to have to register us elsewhere, Geordie being such an old friend.'

With a grunt he stamped their books and handed them back with the change.

At the door, Tilly stopped and turned back.

'I was sorry to hear about Geordie,' she said in a softer voice.

Fred's face was a hard, knotty mass of anger and hurt.

'That's the problem with this war,' he muttered. 'It took the wrong bloody son.'

'Well?' Tilly said when they were outside. 'What do you think?'

Edie shook her head in disgust. '*That's* the father Davy idolises? Whatever for? He's a pig!'

'Because that was all he had, all he ever knew,' Tilly said quietly.

'Simple! The boy's as bright as a button,' Edie snapped, every maternal hackle raised on Davy's behalf. 'If he can't read, whose fault is that?'

'Fred always favoured Geordie, and he made sure he reminded Davy of it every chance he got. All Davy ever wanted was to impress him.'

'That's why he's so desperate to get into the army?'

'Yes, like his brother. You should have seen Fred bursting with pride when Geordie was home on leave in his uniform.' She sighed. 'It'll only get worse for Davy now.'

They walked on in sober silence.

All her life Edie had felt alone; the outsider. She hadn't had what her friend Susan had had: a cosy home, two loving parents and a brother who thought the world of her. Just an aunt whose affections were lukewarm at best, and a house she lived in as a charity child. She supposed that was why she'd always felt a kinship with the stray animals she used to see on the streets of London, and the children in her class who were orphans like her.

What Edie hadn't realised was how many others were alone in their own ways. Tilly Liddell, rejected by her

145

family and sneered at by her community for one mistake that had cost her her reputation. Prudence Hewitt, beaten and neglected by her mother, rejected by the upper-class family she married into as not of their breed. Jack Graham, still tortured by visions of the young men he'd watched die. Davy Braithwaite, bullied by a domineering father who'd filled his child with hate. Luca and Marco, aliens in a land where they were regarded with fear and suspicion. And Sam Nicholson . . . Edie didn't know what his story was, but she could tell he was another such lost cause, as Tilly called them. She hadn't realised, until she came to Applefield, just how many of them were around.

The whole village had a flavour of loneliness, now she opened her eyes. Edie had thought Applefield seemed the perfect country village, but when you delved below the surface, the place thrummed with hostility and fear. Too many people seemed keen to stay away from their neighbours, avoiding eye contact as if they were strangers. In London, the war had brought people together; communities, facing nightly attacks on their homes and lives, were knit more tightly than they ever had been. But here . . . no wonder people were so ready to believe their fellow villagers might be spies and collaborators, when they scarcely spoke to them.

'The treat days you used to have, what were they like?' she asked Tilly.

Tilly's eyes clouded with nostalgia. 'Oh, they were wonderful fun. Old Mr Hewitt, Prue's father-in-law – he was an awful toffee-nose but he knew how to throw a party. It all happened in the gardens at Applefield Manor. We used to have swingboats and games: hoop-tossing, lucky dip, coconut shy and so on. The adults ate cake and drank beer, and us children were allowed to eat sweet things until we made ourselves sick. Other than Christmas, it was my favourite day of the year.'

'Didn't Prue and Albert want to keep it going?'

'I don't think it was that. The treats just changed, somehow. The atmosphere changed.' She looked thoughtful. 'Perhaps the problem was that Prue's heart wasn't in it. She never really forgave the village for its attitude to her marriage.'

'Might she consider bringing it back? I think it would be a first-class way to bring people together. It could raise money for the Spitfire Fund.'

'Well, it'll be a braver person than me who asks her.' Tilly groaned as she spotted a couple approaching them from the church. 'Oh Lord. It's my aunt and uncle.'

'Shall we cross the road?'

'No.' Tilly drew herself up. 'Let her cross if she doesn't want to see me. This is my home too.'

She lifted her chin as Patricia and Andrew – Patricia in her bottle-green WVS uniform, her husband in his clerical shirt and dog collar – strolled towards them.

'Good afternoon, Aunt,' she said when they met. 'And Uncle Andrew. I hope the day finds you both well.'

Patricia managed to ignore Tilly's greeting completely – quite an achievement when its deliverer was standing less than a yard from her nose. She turned away and pretended to be examining a little patch of daffodils by the churchyard wall. Her husband, however, removed his hat and smiled.

'Good afternoon, Matilda,' he said. 'We're doing well, thank you, very well indeed. And yourself?'

'I'm fine, thank you. The baby's started to kick quite often now though, which keeps me awake at night.' She laughed.

'I think there might be a future can-can dancer joining the family.'

Patricia looked appalled that Tilly had dared refer to her condition so openly. Even Andrew looked a little embarrassed, but he bore up manfully.

'I'm pleased to hear the Lord has blessed you with a healthy child,' he said.

Patricia scoffed. 'Blessed,' Edie heard her mutter. 'There's a joke.'

Ignoring Tilly completely, she turned her attention to Edie.

'Good afternoon, Edith,' she said with exaggerated politeness, as if to make a distinction between her and her niece. 'I hope work at the farm hasn't been too much for you in your first week there?'

'Yes, thanks. I mean, yes, it hasn't been too much for me. Or, no.' Edie grimaced. 'That is to say, I'm enjoying it.'

'I'm glad to hear it. Do give Prudence my regards, and remind her I'll be there tomorrow with Agnes and James.'

Once again acting as though Tilly were invisible, Patricia hooked her arm through Andrew's and swept past without a word.

'Are you all right?' Edie whispered, squeezing Tilly's arm.

'Oh, don't worry about me, I'm used to her. To be honest, I enjoy seeing how red I can make her ears turn when we bump into each other.'

Their shopping completed, the girls carried on in the direction of Applefield Manor. They'd been walking for less than a minute when Tilly's Uncle Andrew came jogging up behind them.

'Matilda,' he panted. 'Before you go home.' He pressed a ten-shilling note into her hand. 'Take this. From your aunt and me.'

Tilly shook her head. 'Uncle, you don't need to do that. I have my wages.'

'Please, take this as a little extra. Buy something for the baby, a present from me. I mean, from us, of course.' He glanced warily over his shoulder. 'I'd better go back. I told your aunt I would wait for her outside Mr Braithwaite's. I'll see you in church tomorrow, young ladies.'

Tilly smiled as she put the note away in her purse.

'He's a sweetheart, Uncle Andrew,' she told Edie. 'He often slips me a few bob when she isn't looking. She knows nothing about it, of course, although he always claims it's a gift from the pair of them. I sometimes wonder why he married her, unless it was because she was prime vicar's-wife material.'

'They don't seem very well matched.'

'No. It's a funny thing really. He's only an uncle by marriage, and a man of God too: he'd be within his rights to want nothing more to do with me. Instead it's the blood relation who casts me off and the Reverend Uncle Andrew is the only family member I've got who still admits to being kin to me.'

'One decent relative is better than none, I suppose. It's a shame he can't preach a sermon or two about Christian charity to his wife.'

'Isn't it?' Tilly shook her head. 'Evacuees at Applefield Manor, can you believe it? I'm amazed Aunt got Prue to agree.'

'I don't think she left her a choice,' Edie said. 'I wonder what they'll be like. How old, and where they lived before.'

'I hope they're small ones. I could do with some practice before . . . well, you know.'

'Oh, there's nothing to it,' Edie said, smiling. 'Children

are just like small, drunk men. Trust me, I'm a school-teacher.'

Tilly laughed. 'Are you? That explains a lot.' She squeezed Edie's arm. 'Let's go home. We have to get you ready for a party.'

Chapter 15

When the girls arrived back at Applefield Manor, Tilly set about her task with a relish, dragging Edie into her bedroom as soon as the shopping had been put away.

'You really don't have to do this.' Edie was anxious enough about the dance as it was without having her scrawny, curveless little body dolled up in a way she knew couldn't possibly suit her. 'Don't you have to cook dinner for Prue and Jack?'

But Tilly wasn't to be put off.

'Don't worry, I made a steak and potato pie this morning. It only needs heating through.' She held Edie at arm's length. 'Hmm. Did you say you were planning to wear a blue silk?'

'I don't have much choice. It's the only posh frock I brought.'

'Then today is your lucky day, Edie Cartwright, because I've got a range of lovely dresses I'm sadly now too huge to wear. I think we must be about the same size.' She looked down at her protruding tummy. 'Well, once upon a time.'

She went to her wardrobe and started rifling through.

'Not that I'm sure your blue silk isn't lovely, but green is really your colour, with all that gorgeous auburn hair.'

151

Tilly cast it an envious look. 'You don't know how lucky you are, Edie.'

Edie reached up to touch her hair. 'You mean it?'

'Certainly. I'd kill for a lovely rich colour like that. Thank goodness for dye, eh?'

'I hated being a redhead when I was a kid,' Edie confided. 'The other children called me Carrot. It got me into a lot of trouble once.'

'Can hair get you into trouble?'

'Mine can,' Edie said, laughing. 'When I was fourteen I dreamed of being a platinum blonde, like Jean Harlow. One day my friend Susan tried some of the dye her mum used on me. Only it didn't make me a platinum blonde so much as a platinum . . . green. My aunt was livid when I came home looking like someone's prize-winning leek.'

Tilly laughed. 'I wish I'd been there to see that.'

'Well, at least it meant the end of Carrot. After that I was Edie Cabbagehead until the end of school.'

'Children pick on anyone different. That doesn't mean it's not beautiful. The red hair, I mean, not the green.' Tilly produced an emerald-green dress with a sweetheart neckline from her cupboard. 'Speaking of which, this is the frock for you.'

Edie shook her head. 'Oh, no. I couldn't wear anything like that.'

'Why not?'

'I haven't got the figure to fill it. I'll look like a little girl who's raided her mum's wardrobe.'

Tilly laid the dress down and rested her hand on Edie's shoulder. 'Nonsense. You'll look beautiful, because you are beautiful.'

'Don't be daft.'

'You are, Edie. I wish you could see yourself as others

152

do.' Tilly sat beside her on the bed. 'Will you promise to do something for me?'

'What is it?'

'Promise first, then I'll tell you.'

Edie laughed. 'That hardly seems fair.'

'You trust me, don't you?'

'All right, if you're going to cheat. I promise.'

'Then wear this dress tonight, and your hair and make-up just how I tell you. Call it an experiment.'

'What's the experiment for?'

'You'll see. Just wear it, as a favour to me.'

'Well . . .'

'Edie. You did promise,' Tilly said, raising an eyebrow. 'You're not the sort of friend who goes back on a promise, are you?'

Edie shook her head, smiling. 'You're wicked.'

'Then we're agreed.' Tilly picked up the dress and laid it over Edie's knees. 'Put it on, then we'll do your make-up.'

There was a knock at Tilly's door just as she was putting the final touches to Edie's pencilled brows.

'Who is it?' she called.

'It's Prue. Can I come in?'

'Yes, please do.'

The door opened and Prue entered. Edie blushed at being seen in all her borrowed finery. She had an idea Prue would probably disapprove of parties and sweetheart necklines, but her landlady didn't look shocked to see her dressed up; only surprised.

'Well!' she said, raising her eyebrows. 'Edith, I wouldn't have known you. Are you going out?'

'Yes, there's a dance at the WLA hostel. Um, if that's OK. Sorry, I should have asked first.'

'Don't be silly. You can't miss the chance to have fun. Just be sure and get home by ten.'

'I will.'

Prue turned to Tilly. 'I was going to ask if I ought to set the dining table, but it seems Edith won't be joining us for dinner. Never mind, we can eat in the kitchen.'

'We'll all be here for Sunday dinner tomorrow though,' Tilly said.

'Oh! That's right, I meant to tell you,' Prue said, pressing a hand to her forehead. 'I've invited the Italians to join us. I hope that won't be a problem.'

'Luca's coming? And Marco?'

'Yes, I thought it would be a nice gesture. It must be hard, being so far from home.'

'That was a kind thought.' Tilly reached out to press Prue's arm. 'Thank you.'

'Will there be enough food though, with the evacuees to feed as well?' Edie asked. 'We only have rations for four.'

Prue's brow darkened. 'The evacuees. Yes. I'd forgotten about them.' She turned to Tilly. 'Will there be enough?'

'Thanks to Sam's chicken, I believe we can make it stretch,' Tilly said. 'I can do cock-a-leekie soup with barley to start, then hopefully no one will mind that the main course is a bit smaller than usual.' She finished applying Edie's mascara and stood back to survey her handiwork. 'What do you think, Prue? Isn't she a beauty?'

'She's certainly immensely improved by a fortnight's country living,' Prue said. 'Already there's more colour in her cheeks. Or is that rouge?'

'No, it's embarrassment,' Edie said, blushing furiously. 'I don't think I'm a rouge sort of person.'

Prue nodded. 'Very wise. A fair complexion like yours is best left as nature intended.'

'What ought I to do with her hair?' Tilly asked Prue.

'Mercy, dear, it's no use asking me. I stopped keeping up with the new fashions decades ago. Or centuries ago, it sometimes feels like.' Prue tilted her head to appraise Edie, who was surprised to note that her eyes had kindled with interest in much the same way Tilly's had. 'I do like the way Miss Hayworth wears hers though, swept to one side in that sophisticated way.'

'Oh, yes! Perfect,' Tilly said, clapping her hands. 'Just the thing for Edie's face shape, and we won't need to set it either.'

'Well, I'll leave you two to get on,' Prue said, a note of regret in her voice. 'You don't want an old lady like me interfering. I'll see you for dinner, Matilda.'

Tilly raised an eyebrow at Edie, who took the hint.

'No, stay, please,' Edie said. 'I'd love a second opinion. Tilly wants to doll me up a bit more than will suit me, I think.'

'Well . . .'

'Please. As a favour to me.'

'If you really believe it would be helpful,' Prue said, looking pleased. 'I can certainly spare the time. Yes, I will stay.'

When Tilly and Prue had finished getting her ready, Edie completed her chic party outfit with the rather incongruous additions of her Land Army greatcoat and wellingtons, to ensure she didn't get splashed with mud cycling over to the large farmhouse where her fellow Land Girls were lodging.

The weather was fine that evening, the sun illuminating the countryside with a mellow golden glow. Spring was evident everywhere: in the scent of bud and blossom, the

155

creeping green and new life. Every field Edie passed seemed to contain mothers with their lambs, the parents grazing contentedly while their boisterous offspring sprang into the air in that curious way they have, heads tossing while they kicked their back feet in a joyous celebration of being alive. With a lighter heart than she'd had in a long time, Edie realised she had scarcely had a coughing fit all day.

She didn't have too much trouble locating the hostel, arriving just after six, when the girls would be sitting down to their evening meal. Edie hesitated at the door, wondering whether she ought to just march in, when a voice called to her.

She looked around to see Vinnie's smiling face poking out of a window. 'There you are, Edie! Come in and get some grub in your tum. We've been looking out for you this quarter of an hour.'

Edie did as she was told. The front door opened into a hallway, where she removed her coat and wellies and slipped on the satin pumps Tilly had lent her, then went through the open door to the dining room.

'Sweetheart. So glad you could make it,' Vinnie said, coming forward to embrace her. She held her at arm's length. 'Bloody hell, Edie. You scrub up, don't you?'

'She's not wrong,' Barbara said as she kissed Edie on each cheek. 'None of us will get a look all night once the boys arrive.'

Edie blushed at the unfamiliar sensation of being compli-mented, and the proud, if slightly frightening, knowledge that for once in her life the flattery might actually be deserved.

There was a mirror on one of the walls, and Edie could see a strange girl – no, woman – in a glamorous green dress with sophisticated side-swept hair looking back at her. She'd never have recognised the figure as herself, if it hadn't matched the reflection presented to her by the mirror in Tilly's bedroom before she left.

On those occasions she'd let Alfie escort her to their local dance hall so they could make up a foursome with Susan and her boyfriend of the month, Edie had always been very much the wallflower. She preferred it that way, hiding behind her friends, hoping not to be noticed. Alfie always claimed her for every dance beforehand anyhow, so even if one of the other young men should, out of politeness, ask her to stand up with them, she had the perfect excuse to demur.

But there was no Alfie to look after her tonight. What would she do if one of the RAF boys asked for a dance? Did she dare stand up? It was all new territory and she had no idea how to navigate it.

'Come park your little bottom over here,' Vinnie said, taking her hand to guide her to the dining table where around a dozen other girls were tucking into their evening meal. 'You picked a good day to visit. It's toad in the hole tonight.'

'With actual toad and everything – two whole sausages each,' Barbara said. 'And spotted dick for pud. We always eat well here.'

Edie settled in the seat they pressed her into, between her two friends, and Barbara went to the kitchen hatch to get her her meal.

'Let me introduce you to everyone.' Before Edie could protest Vinnie was banging her fork against her water glass, and the noise level dropped as all eyes turned towards her. 'Ladies, may I present Edie Cartwright, our comrade in arms. Best damn sheep-shit-shearer this side of Windermere.'

There was a loud cheer and a few of the girls clinked their glasses together in a toast, making Edie laugh.

'I won't introduce all these reprobates now,' Vinnie said to her. 'You'll never remember names if I just reel them off. Besides, you'll get to know everyone in time. This won't be your only visit, I hope.'

A girl in round spectacles seated on the other side of Barbara's empty chair leaned across to Edie.

'Here you are, rookie,' she whispered, taking a Thermos flask from under the table. 'Have a little gin to wet your whistle.'

'Thank you, but I'd better not.'

'Methodist, are you?'

'No. It's just that I've never really, um . . .' Edie trailed off. She was embarrassed to admit that her experience with alcohol was limited to an occasional glass of tonic wine, administered by Aunt Caroline when she felt faint.

'A drop won't hurt,' the woman said, tipping a generous measure into Edie's empty water glass. 'It'll help take the edge off your nerves before the lads arrive – I can see you're a shy one.'

Maybe Sam had been right, Edie reflected. Maybe she was a prig. There was certainly a lot in life she hadn't experienced. With a grateful nod to the woman, she took a sip of the gin.

Golly, it was strong! She tried not to cough. Wouldn't you normally mix something in with it? But all the other girls seemed to be drinking theirs neat, and Edie didn't want them thinking she was a prig too.

The woman with the Thermos introduced herself as Dotty, Barbara and Vinnie's roommate. She kept up a lively flow of conversation, so that Edie was feeling a little windswept by the time Barbara returned with a generous plate of toad in the hole, gravy and mashed potatoes.

'Thanks, Barbara,' she said. 'Do I need to pay or anything?'

'Certainly not. You're our guest so there's nothing for you to do tonight but enjoy yourself.'

Edie jumped as something soft brushed against her legs. She leaned down to look under the table, and a single green eye blinked lazily back at her.

'A cat! Does it live here?'

Vinnie laughed. 'Sorry, I should've warned you there'd be competition for your toad. This is Princess, our unofficial mascot. The building's owners keep a couple of moggies around to deal with mice, but Princess is the only one clever enough to have worked out we're too soft to deny her a few scraps at feeding time.'

Edie tickled Princess's ears, then slipped her a bit of sausage from her toad in the hole. The cat purred, pressing her nose against Edie's hand. She seemed a friendly soul, although her missing eye made her look a bit of a rogue.

'What happened to her eye?' Edie asked.

'Who knows?' Barbara said. 'Got on the wrong side of a particularly nasty mouse, I expect. Come on, eat up. The menfolk will be arriving in less than an hour and we need to push the table back to make room for dancing.'

The men turned up around half past seven. With eight strapping RAF lads and nearly twice as many buxom Land Girls, it was a tight squeeze to get everyone in, but none of the young people complained about the press of hot bodies. In fact, they seemed to like it. The men were hardly through the door before they'd been commandeered as partners and dragged on to the makeshift dancefloor, while the hostel warden – a jolly middle-aged soul who seemed to enjoy watching her boisterous charges having fun – struck up a lively dance tune on a piano in the corner of the room.

Edie, feeling suddenly shy, retreated to a small table. Vinnie joined her, and the two of them watched Barbara as she swung her shapely hips around an awestruck-looking flying officer.

'The lucky sod doesn't know what's hit him,' Vinnie said. 'It must be nice to be beautiful. Not that I need to tell you, of course.'

Edie felt she should say something complimentary in return, but couldn't think of anything that didn't sound like flattery. So instead she asked, 'Does Barbara have a lot of boyfriends?'

'Is she fast, do you mean?'

'Oh no, I didn't –'

Vinnie laughed. 'I'm teasing, Edie.' She shrugged. 'She has a lot of boys keen on her, naturally. No steady though, and no casual flings. She likes the compliment of being admired, but romances aren't something that appeal to her. To either of us.'

Edie sipped at her gin, the harsh, burning sensation in her throat making her cough. Being unused to it, she was already feeling a little light-headed.

'What did the two of you do before you joined the Land Army?' she asked Vinnie.

'Barb was a shorthand typist. I was behind the counter at Woolworth's.' She smiled as she watched Barbara energetically kicking her legs while she danced, almost like one of the gambolling lambs outside. 'I never knew there could be work like this, out in the open air surrounded by all this beauty. I couldn't go back to the other kind now.'

'Will there still be farm work though, after the war?' Edie wondered. 'For us, I mean. When the men come home they won't need us any more.'

'Barb and I have got a plan,' Vinnie confided. 'We're

160

going to try for a place of our own, with some savings we've put aside. Just a small cottage, and a little plot of land. A few chickens, vegetables, a cow – enough to be self-sufficient, with some produce to sell so we can pay our way. The war's an evil business, but we can at least be grateful for this: it taught us a trade that allows us to keep ourselves. Thanks to the Land Army, we needn't ever be dependent on anyone else to support us.'

'You want to marry though, surely?'

Vinnie shrugged. 'No. Why should we? Men . . . I suppose I like them well enough, the ones I count as friends. But when it comes to all the rest of it, Barb and I are happy enough with just our two selves.'

'Yes, but to be an old maid,' Edie said, shuddering as she thought of the unappealing vision of spinsterhood exemplified by her Aunt Caroline. 'As a life it just seems so . . . I don't know, lonely.'

'We won't be lonely while we have each other,' Vinnie said, smiling slightly. 'I don't see why marriage should be served up as the only aim of a woman's life. Besides, there's no bloke whose company we'd ever prefer to one another's, and neither of us want children. I know it's not very orthodox, but it's all we want out of life.'

Chapter 16

One of the RAF chaps, who had held off dancing so far to
help the old girl on piano turn her music, now approached
Edie and Vinnie's table.

'Rob.' Vinnie stood up to greet him with a chummy
punch on the shoulder. 'Nice to see you, feller. Not dancing
tonight?'

'There didn't seem any point while you were keeping the
prettiest girl in the room all to yourself.' He took off his
cap and nodded to Edie. 'Can I get an introduction to your
charming friend, Vin?'

'If you like. Edie, this is Flight Lieutenant Robert Gill,
an old pal. He's been coming to our little hops here for
absolute donkey's. Rob, this is Edie Cartwright, the new
girl at Larkstone Farm. And she's under mine and Barb's
protection so be a gent.'

'Aren't I always?' He smiled at Edie. 'How do you do,
Miss Cartwright? It is Miss, I hope.'

She smiled back. 'It is, but Edie will do just fine.'

Edie stood to offer a hand, which Rob chose to press to
his lips rather than shake.

'So now we're such old, old friends, how about a dance?'
he asked with an ingratiating grin.

'Oh, no, I don't really,' Edie said, feeling that familiar heat colouring her cheeks. 'You and Vinnie go.'

'But I'm not asking Vinnie – no offence, old girl,' he said, giving Vinnie's back a hearty slap. 'I'm asking you. Come on, Edie, what do you say? I promise on my honour as a pilot not to tread on your toes.'

Tilly was right, the RAF boys looked almost indecently handsome in their uniforms. Rob was a strapping lad, six feet tall, spruce in brass buttons and slate-blue blazer, his dark hair slick and styled in the fashion that had earned them their 'Brylcreem boys' nickname. He also had a lovely warm smile, not to mention appealing chocolate-brown eyes. Edie could appreciate all that, but the uniform also served as a reminder – and a warning. Charm wasn't always all that it seemed, and trouble could follow if you lowered your guard . . .

Rob, deciding that Edie's hesitation was tantamount to a yes, had already seized her hand and was leading her towards the dancefloor. She cast a helpless look back at Vinnie, but her friend just smiled and raised her gin glass in a toast.

'I'm really not very good,' Edie told Rob.

'Don't worry about that,' he said as the warden struck up a new tune. 'This is a slow one, it's easy. All you need to do is get nice and close then wobble about a bit.'

She stiffened as he pulled her against him, one arm snaking around her waist while with the other he clasped her hand to his chest.

'Edie, relax,' he whispered as he began rocking her in time to the music. 'Sweetheart, it's only a dance.'

Edie watched from the corner of her eye as five other couples swayed around them, lost in each other, their eyes gazing into their partner's as their bodies pressed close. No, she didn't want that! She tried to remain erect, allowing only the minimum of bodily contact, although she could feel Rob's hips insinuating with a polite but insistent urgency against hers. How had she allowed herself to be surprised by a slow dance – had Rob bribed his friend on piano? And how could Vinnie be so cruel as not to rescue her?

Alfie never held her this way when they danced. In fact they usually sat out the slow dances, which her friend found boring, and waited for something a bit livelier. That had felt innocent, a sort of play that still belonged to childhood, but this . . .

She and Rob were fully clothed, in the middle of a crowd of people, dancing as men and women had been doing since the dawn of time. Yet somehow, as Rob's fingertips slowly caressed the curves of Edie's waist and hip, this felt more like a seduction than a waltz.

'I've been watching you all night,' he whispered as he swayed her.

'Um, have you?'

'Ever since I walked through the door. You don't know the torment I've endured because of you, Edie. Why do you think I wasn't dancing?'

Right. This was flirting, wasn't it? She'd never really got the hang of flirting. She should probably give a careless laugh, then say something witty that was at the same time teasingly aloof. But even with the sideswept hair falling over one eye, Edie was well aware that she was no Rita Hayworth.

'Well, I thought you might be a bit worn out,' was the best she could manage. 'I expect it's tiring, flying and all that.'

Rob laughed: a deep, pleasant sound. Edie could feel it rumble through his chest as it pressed against her bosom.

'You little comedian,' he purred in her ear.

'Sorry.'

'Don't apologise. Beautiful girls ought to be funny. For me that's the perfect combination.'

Honeyed words. Seductive words. Edie's aunt had warned her about words like that, whispered by boys who let their hands wander too far and too freely while they danced; the sort of boys who went conveniently deaf when a girl said 'no'. And yet Edie could feel her body starting to relax in Rob's arms as the soft music and her own instincts overruled every lesson she'd ever been given. Sensing her surrender, Rob pressed her closer.

'I didn't dance before because I didn't want to dance with anyone but you,' he murmured, his lips close to her ear. 'It took me ages to get up the nerve to talk to you. I was terrified some other chap was going to sweep you away before I made it, but clearly they're all as dumbstruck by the stunning new girl as I am.'

'That's . . . nice of you to say.' Edie inhaled against his chest. He smelled good, sort of masculine and clean . . . soap and cigars . . .

'I know you're thinking I probably say that to all the girls I dance with.' He tilted her chin so he could look into her face. 'I promise that isn't true. I know what people think, but we're not all wolves in the RAF.'

'I didn't think anything of the kind,' Edie murmured, looking up into his eyes.

His face was drawing closer, his hot, slightly ragged breath on her cheek. It was intoxicating, this new world of handsome, gallant officers who smelled good and paid you compliments and let their fingers trail over your body with tantalising softness while they danced. Edie could feel her heart thundering as Rob's lips moved closer to hers, her power to resist almost gone . . .

He turned her in time to the music, and it was then that she noticed someone watching them through the kitchen hatch. Not one of the girls, but a male someone – a someone she knew.

Sam Nicholson! What was he doing here? Hastily Edie struggled out of Rob's arms, but when she turned to look again, Sam had disappeared.

Rob frowned. 'Edie? Is something wrong?'

'No, I . . .' She held a hand to her forehead. 'I just feel a little light-headed, that's all. I need to go out for some air.'

'Shall I fetch you some water?' he asked, looking concerned. 'You ought to drink something if you're faint.'

'Please, Rob. Just . . . let me alone a moment. I need to be on my own. Sorry.'

She hurried for the door, leaving a puzzled Rob staring after her. Outside in the moonlight, she sagged against the hostel wall and inhaled deeply.

How did she feel? Angry? Disappointed? Relieved? Something had been about to happen, on the dancefloor with Rob – with a stranger, for heaven's sake! And what was more, she'd wanted it to. If it hadn't been for Sam . . .

Edie stood still for a moment, waiting for her heartbeat to slow. When she was calm she looked inside herself and realised that her dominant feeling was, after all, relief. She had been about to lose her head. If Rob had kissed her, she knew she wouldn't have resisted. That was definitely a very, very bad idea. Really, she owed Sam a debt of gratitude for appearing when he had.

What on earth had come over her tonight? She wasn't acting at all like herself and she didn't like it one bit. She didn't like the feeling of not being in control; of being someone else, a new Edie who danced and flirted and . . . kissed. Kissed men she scarcely knew, at that. It had taken the familiar, earthy sight of her boss in his work clothes to snap her back to reality.

Gin was a wicked affair, she decided. Clearly it turned perfectly sensible young women into the sort of blithering idiots who swooned at a few compliments from a good-looking man. Edie made a mental note to stay away from the stuff in future.

'Having a nice evening, are we?' a gruff voice demanded.

She started. 'Bloody hell, Sam. I thought you'd gone.'

He stepped out of the shadows. 'Clearly not. What's the matter, London? You didn't look right happy to see me just now.'

'I . . . what are you doing here, anyhow?'

'Dropping off some eggs. I supply the kitchens here. Didn't realise you ladies were having a soirée or I'd have put on my top hat and tails.' He leaned down to look into her face. 'Had a drink?'

'A little gin.' She pulled a face. 'I didn't care for it much. It tasted like your sheep dip smells.'

He didn't smile. 'Who was the toff you were gazing besottedly at before?'

She could tell him it was none of his business. She had every right to. But for some reason, she didn't.

'Rob Gill. He's a flight lieutenant in the RAF. Friend of Vinnie and Barbara's.'

'And yours too, I'm guessing. You certainly looked . . . close.'

'We just met tonight. He asked me to dance with him so I did.' She met his eye defiantly. 'That's all right, isn't it? Dancing, at a dance? I mean, I didn't realise I had to get my boss's permission.'

'You can do as you please,' he said with a careless shrug. 'Just surprised you'd go for a bloke like that, that's all. They think a deal too well of themselves, those johnnies in uniform, and they've got a line for every woman they meet. Wouldn't have thought that would impress an upstanding young lady like yourself.'

Edie bristled at the obvious mockery in his tone. 'I'd say they're entitled to think well of themselves. They're serving their country, aren't they?'

Sam frowned. 'And just what do you mean by that, lass?'

'I mean that if a man's risking his life for all our good, it's only right he feels proud.'

'Didn't know you felt that way,' he muttered, turning away. 'I'd best get back to the farm.'

Edie flinched. 'Sam – wait.'

He turned back. 'What now?'

'Sorry. I'm sorry. What I said about the men serving their country, that wasn't aimed at you.'

'Huh. If you say so.'

'Honestly. If it sounded that way then I apologise.'

'Well, all right. Let's forget about it.'

'Look . . . would you do me a favour?'

He frowned. 'Favour?'

'Yes. I wondered if . . . Would you talk to Davy?' she blurted out. 'I'm sure he must be sorry by now about what happened this morning. He was upset, that was all.'

Sam shook his head, scowling. 'That boy's been nowt but trouble since I took him on. He's got a chip on his shoulder a foot high. Hates me, hates the POWs, hates the world. Davy Braithwaite's a rum lad and as far as I'm concerned I'm well rid of him. Why the devil should I go begging the little sod to take his job back?'

'He'd had some bad news,' Edie said quietly. 'His brother's missing in action. The family just found out yesterday.'

Sam's frown lifted slightly.

'I didn't know that,' he said in a softer voice. 'Well, I'm sorry for it. Still, one bad apple can spoil the barrel. I don't need discontented workers around my place.'

'It wasn't Davy who pinned the feathers to your door, you know.'

'And how would you know that?'

'He's illiterate. So he couldn't have written on the envelope.'

Sam frowned. 'Is he?'

'I'm surprised you didn't know. You'll be acquainted with his father, I expect?'

'Aye, more's the pity,' he said in a low voice. 'Nasty piece of work, Fred Braithwaite. A bully, and a bigot to boot.'

'Tilly told me he beats his son, and it's obvious Fred relishes keeping him in ignorance while he fills him up with hateful ideas. Davy's young. His dad's the only male figure he's had to look up to and he doesn't know any better than to admire him.' She latched her gaze on to Sam's. 'Think about it, Sam, please. The farm's the one place he can get away from the poison he's being served up at home.'

'Important to you, this, isn't it?'

'Yes, it is.'

'What for? You didn't know Davy Braithwaite from Adam's brother this time last week.'

'I just think life's dealt him a pretty rotten hand, that's all.' She held his gaze. 'Will you think about it?'

'Hmm. We'll see.' He turned to go. 'Enjoy your dance, Miss Cartwright, and your pretty flight lieutenant. I'll see you on Thursday.'

He was about to walk off when he stopped.

'That's a nice dress, by the way,' he said, without turning around.

Edie flushed. 'Oh. Thanks. Tilly lent it to me.'

'Looks better on you,' he said quietly. 'Matches your eyes. Night then.'

When he'd gone, she leant back against the wall and exhaled.

What was it about that man? Why should he make her feel ashamed for doing the most natural thing a twenty-one-year-old woman could do: dance with a handsome young man? She'd felt as guilty while he was cross-examining her as if he'd walked in on her and Rob . . . well, doing something a lot more intimate than they had been doing.

And yet Sam hadn't really said anything to accuse her, other than showing some natural male jealousy of the RAF boys and their reputation for being successful with women. Just the fact of him being there, looking at her with judgement in his eyes, had been enough to make her feel she was doing something wrong.

She scowled as confusion gave way to anger. Sam *bloody* Nicholson! Just who did that man think he was, demanding explanations from her? She'd only known him for three days and he'd managed to infuriate her more in that time than any man she'd ever met. Then he'd had the cheek to pay her a compliment – a genuine, honest, understated one that had sounded more sincere than any of the flattery Rob had whispered in her ear.

And then there was her nagging worry that maybe there was more to Sam than just being infuriating. Maybe, just maybe, he was also . . .

Edie strode back into the hostel and sought out Vinnie and Barbara.

Chapter 17

Inside, Rob had returned to the piano. It looked for a moment as though he might approach Edie to claim a second dance, but something in her expression obviously told him it was unwise.

'Oh. Edie,' Vinnie said, looking up from an absorbing conversation with Barbara. 'What happened to Rob?'

'He's by the piano.'

'Did you like him?' Barbara asked. 'He's a good laugh. We've known him for ages.'

'Handsome too,' Vinnie said, watching her face.

'He's . . . I don't know,' Edie said, sitting down. 'Charming, but . . . maybe a little too well-practised at saying the right thing.'

Vinnie shook her head. 'Rob's not a playboy. A flirt, yes. If I hadn't trusted him to behave, Edie, I promise I would have rescued you.' She looked at Rob, who'd fallen into conversation with one of his comrades. 'Anyhow, he's keen on you. He hasn't asked anyone else to dance all night. He's a bit of a catch, you know.'

'I thought you didn't approve of marriage.'

'I said I didn't want to enter the blessed estate,' Vinnie

said with a shrug. 'That's not the same as disapproval. We're all different, aren't we?'

'Oh, *marriage*,' Barbara scoffed. 'Whyever do girls have to ruin a perfectly good bit of fun by bringing marriage into it? Go on, go dance with Rob. He can't take his eyes off you.'

'Forget Rob for a minute.' Edie lowered her voice. 'Guess who was just here.'

'Who?' Vinnie asked.

'Sam Nicholson, that's who.'

'Yes, he usually brings us fresh eggs on a Saturday.' Vinnie frowned, catching her expression. 'What's the matter? Did he try it on?'

'No. Just made me feel like a naughty schoolgirl caught with her hand in the biscuit barrel.' Edie looked from one woman to the other. 'You two have been hinting at something ever since I got here, all this talk of lusty tups and wandering hands. Just what is it about Sam that you know and I don't?'

Barbara glanced at Vinnie. 'We wanted to put you on your guard, that's all. Sam does favour you, and you're so . . . well, you seem rather naive about these things, if you don't mind me saying.'

'You think he's the father of Tilly's baby. Don't you?'

Vinnie nodded. 'We know he is.'

'How?'

'She was his favourite when she worked at the farm. It was always her he picked to work alone with – just like he's started doing with you.'

'Is that all there is to it?'

'No,' Barbara said. 'There were other things. She still comes up to the farm every fortnight or so for a private interview with him, and writes to him. We thought perhaps they were making arrangements about the baby, for him to pay for its support.'

'She did give me a letter for him this morning,' Edie murmured, half to herself. 'Told me it was something about buying a rabbit, but she seemed evasive. And it was on this fancy scented paper, like . . . almost like a love letter.'

'Has she confided anything to you?' Barbara asked.

'Not about Sam.' Edie glanced at Rob talking to his friend. 'She told me the father was a pilot from the airbase. Why would she lie?'

'Who knows? Embarrassment, perhaps, that she's still got her cap set at Sam even after he broke it off.'

'She did say she thought Sam was charming. And she changed the subject when I asked if she knew what you meant about him having wandering hands.'

'It's no secret around the village that he's the dad,' Vinnie said. 'Not that the gossip bothers Sam. He wasn't well liked in Applefield before and he doesn't seem to care if folk have one more thing to hate him for.'

'Has he tried anything with either of you?'

'Not with us, no,' Barbara said. 'It's one of the reasons we've clung on to the job. Some of the farmers round here are like bloody octopuses.'

'Octopi, my dear,' Vinnie said in a superior voice.

Barbara nudged her affectionately. 'All right, clever clogs.'

'Have you asked him about it?' Edie asked, determined not to drop the subject until she had the full story.

Barbara shook her head. 'I wouldn't have the nerve. Vin did though.'

Vinnie nodded. 'I didn't ask him outright, but I was feeling brave one day when we were mucking out the hens so I asked if there was a sweetheart anywhere. Asked if he thought he might have a fat farmer's wife and a couple of ruddy-cheeked children to help him run the place one day. He must've heard the gossip around the village – at least, he knew right away what I was getting at. That was when he admitted it.'

Edie frowned. 'Surely not.'

'He bloody did. He told me I'd do well to keep my nose out of his business and said he and Tilly had an understanding – mentioned her by name. I'd only half believed it before that.'

Edie couldn't help feeling disappointed. She'd come to respect Sam over the three days they'd worked together, and, yes, to like him a little now she understood his character. Although she'd been pondering her theory about the paternity of Tilly's baby all day, a part of her had secretly hoped she'd be proven wrong.

'But if it's his, why doesn't he marry her?' she asked.

'He's a man,' Vinnie said, shrugging. 'At least it looks like he's going to support the poor brat. More than a lot of them do.'

'There but for the grace of God, ladies.' Barbara rested a hand on Edie's shoulder. 'You'd better be careful, Edie. It looks as though he could have his eye on you next.'

The watch that always hung around Edie's neck told her it wasn't quite half past nine when she arrived home, well before her curfew. She put her bike away and dragged her tired body into the house.

She was glad she'd gone to the dance but she wouldn't exactly describe it as a good time. She hadn't been able to recover her equilibrium after Sam had surprised her, and once Vinnie and Barbara had confirmed her fears about the paternity of Tilly's baby, she'd spent the rest of her evening sitting alone, lost in thought.

Edie had eventually agreed to dance with Rob again after repeated entreaties, but her mind was elsewhere, and the spell he'd cast earlier broken entirely. Four other men had asked her to stand up as well, but she'd politely turned them down. The only individual she'd got to know well in the latter part of the evening was Princess the cat, who had weaved herself contentedly around Edie's legs while the others threw themselves about to Glenn Miller records and played gin rummy for cigarettes. Eventually, unable to get into the party mood, Edie had pleaded a headache and set off home.

When she'd tiptoed up the darkened stairs to her bedroom, she found Tilly in there, sitting on the bed in her voluminous nightie.

'Well?' she demanded eagerly.

Edie took off her headscarf and tossed it on to the dressing table. 'Well what?'

'Well, how was the dance? I've been waiting up so I could get all the news. Did you make any new friends? Dance with the boys? Did everyone admire my dress?'

Edie sank down next to her friend with a groan of pain. There wasn't a part of her that didn't hurt now, including her poor little bottom, which was horribly tender after days bouncing down rutted lanes on the rock-hard bicycle saddle.

'I made friends with a very nice cat,' she said. 'Her name's Princess. She lost her eye in a vicious mouse battle.'

Tilly shook her head. 'Edie Cartwright, you just better have some good gossip for me. Never mind cats: tell me about the men.'

Edie's brain was full of unsettled thoughts. All she really wanted was to go to sleep, but Tilly seemed so excited on her behalf that she didn't have the heart to ask to be left alone.

'Well, it was all very jolly and gay,' she said, forcing a smile. 'The warden played the piano for us. Eight men came over from the airbase: some handsome, all smart, and very good dancers.'

'How many of them did you dance with?'

'Just one.'

Tilly tutted. 'Oh, Edie. I bet every single one of them asked you, didn't they? They must have done, the way you looked tonight.'

'Quite a few asked,' Edie admitted. 'Only . . . I had a little gin and it didn't agree with me, so I sat down after two dances. Headache.'

'What was he like, the man you danced with?'

'He was a flight lieutenant, Rob Gill. Good-looking, tall, dark hair and eyes, very suave . . .'

This was obviously the stuff to give the troops, and Tilly's eyes sparkled as she conjured up a picture of her friend's beau.

'Did he make a date with you?'

'He asked, but . . . I don't know. I did like him but I don't think he really suited me, somehow.'

Actually, Edie wasn't sure why she'd turned down Rob's invitation to go to the Palais dance hall with him the following weekend. He was handsome, charming and pleasant, and Vinnie and Barbara had assured her he wasn't one of *those* boys, the sort to grab what they could. He just didn't feel like a good match for shy, awkward little Edie Cartwright. He was too . . . polished. Too artificial, somehow, like a schoolgirl's vision of her dream man.

Tilly looked disappointed. 'You had a nice time though?'

Edie forced a smile. 'Yes, I enjoyed myself,' she said, not wanting to hurt Tilly's feelings. 'The girls are a super bunch, and it was nice to be admired, even if I was too nervous to dance much.' She leaned over to give her friend a kiss. 'Thanks for making me pretty, Till.'

'My pleasure. Although nature did the hard work, of course.' Tilly pushed herself to her feet. 'Any time you need my services, Edie, just ask.'

Edie looked up at her. 'Tilly . . .'

'Hmm?'

'Your dress did get one compliment tonight.'

'Who from?'

'Sam Nicholson.'

Tilly's eyebrows lifted. 'Sam was at the dance?'

'Not as a guest. He came to bring some eggs for the kitchen.'

'Oh. So he . . . You didn't dance then, the two of you?'

Edie laughed. 'Dance with Sam? Of course not.'

'Is it as absurd an idea as all that?'

'I suppose I just can't picture Sam on a dancefloor.' She met Tilly's eyes. 'Can you?'

'Of course, why not? Not that I've ever seen him at any sort of social, but I should imagine he looks rather handsome in his best bib and tucker.'

Edie fell into a thoughtful silence.

'Well, goodnight then,' Tilly said, taking this as her cue to leave.

'Tilly . . . wait.'

'What is it?'

'We're friends, aren't we?'

'Of course.'

'So you know that if you ever needed to tell me anything . . . I mean, if you were upset or worried . . .'

Tilly looked blank. Edie tried again.

'I just mean that if you ever need a friend to confide in,

177

I'll be right here. Troubles shared are troubles halved and all that.'

Tilly blinked. 'All right. Thank you.'

'So, um . . . is there anything?'

'Not that I'm aware of. But thanks for your concern, Edie.'

Chapter 18

Patricia arrived at quarter past eleven exactly. She was always perfectly punctual; in fact, she prided herself on it. That was just the sort of petty achievement she would pride herself on, Prue reflected bitterly. The woman's self-worth was entirely based on her feeling of superiority over others.

Prue heard the doorbell chime as she was arranging flowers in the dining room. The girls were in the kitchen preparing dinner, while Jack was outside feeding that damn bird of his. He would insist on going to the stables to see it, even in his best Sunday suit, and always came back reeking of horse and tobacco.

She accepted, now, that she had no choice about taking in these evacuees, but the idea still unsettled her.

It wasn't so much having them in her home, although opening Applefield Manor up to two children was frightening to say the least. Still, if it was just a case of giving them lodgings for a little while then she could probably cope with that. What Edith had said about the horror of the bombing raids had been preying on her mind, and she didn't doubt, too, that Patricia could make life difficult for her – maybe even force her to give up the whole house to the war effort. Taking in the children was definitely the lesser of two evils if the alternative was having troops charging about the place, using her topiary for bayonet practice.

What was really troubling was the idea that she would have to be *in loco parentis* to children who were neither kith nor kin to her – strangers from an unfamiliar part of the country. She would hate them to be unhappy, but how did she even begin to give them what they needed?

She'd never been good with children in that way some women naturally were. Even with Bertie, although she'd adored the boy from the moment he was put into her arms, she had worried she wasn't innately maternal enough to raise him properly. And if Prue had struggled with her own son, how on earth would she manage with the two little aliens about to burst into her life? Thank goodness for Edith and her expertise with young ones.

Actually, she'd grown to rather like that girl. Prue had discovered in her a strength of character that she'd never have expected in one so young. Edith's willingness to work, the way she'd stood so calm and unruffled when Jack had been having one of his episodes, and her solid common sense about her appearance as she'd got ready for her dance had all impressed Prue.

She had been flattered, too, when the child had asked for her advice about her costume – and, although she was half embarrassed to admit it, she'd enjoyed helping. Seeing the girls' excitement had reminded her of her own youth, getting ready to receive Albert when he'd taken those first bashful steps towards courting her – when, with blushing surprise, Prue had realised what a fine young man the friend of her girlhood had become.

Yes, Edith was a good girl. Perhaps she might fit into their strange little household after all.

Straightening her collar, Prue took a deep breath and went to answer the door.

Any last lingering thought of turning the two evacuees away vanished as soon as she saw them, labels around their necks like a pair of lost parcels. Prue had never been so shocked at a child's appearance.

The little boy, who Prue guessed must be around five or six, was ashen-faced and seemed absolutely terrified, gripping his sister's hand; the girl, some years older, looked positively fierce. Each held a case in one hand and a pair of shoes, tied together by the laces, dangled over their arms. Their little feet were stockingless, bare toes wriggling against the hard ground, and they were both so gaunt that their cheekbones stood out. Modern clothes aside, they could have come straight from the pages of *Oliver Twist*.

'Prue,' Patricia said with a curt nod. 'I'd like to introduce James and Agnes Cawthra, from London. Children, this is Mrs Hewitt. She will be taking care of you from now on. Can you say good morning to her?'

Neither of the children spoke. The boy just blinked wide, frightened eyes at Prue, while the girl fixed her with a defiant stare. Prue had never before encountered such an angry-looking child.

'Hello, children,' Prue said in her best *Children's Hour* voice, smiling warmly. She cast a quick glance at Patricia, who was watching her with eyebrows raised, waiting to see if she was going to object to their arrival. 'Welcome to Applefield Manor. I hope you will both be very happy during your stay here.'

The girl scoffed. 'Fat chance of that, Missus.'

Prue blinked, taken aback.

'Well, we shall do our best, I hope,' she said. 'Come in, please.'

'I'll leave you to get know one another,' Patricia said, with the smug smirk of one who felt she'd won this round. 'Do call if you have any trouble with them, won't you, Prue?'

Prue knew what that meant. This was a test, one her 'friend' was hoping she'd fail.

'No need to worry about us,' she said cheerfully. 'I'm sure we'll become great friends. Goodbye, Patty.'

She ushered the children into the hall. The youngest, James, was already casting awestruck glances around the big house. His sister just stared determinedly at the carpet.

'Well, let's introduce ourselves properly, shall we?' Prue said, feeling more uncomfortable by the second. She wished she could fetch Edith, but she was up to her elbows in flour, making rhubarb crumble in the kitchen. 'My name is Mrs Hewitt. What do you like to be called?'

'Aggie,' the girl muttered. 'This is Jimmy. He's my brother.'

The child's ferocious undertone seemed to be expecting some sort of challenge, but Prue only nodded.

'And what age are you both?' she asked.

'Ten, me. Jimmy's seven last birthday.'

'Seven! You're very little for your age, Jimmy.'

'What of it?' Aggie demanded.

'Merely an observation.' Prue frowned at the child, irritated by her aggressive manner. 'Perhaps, Aggie, you might like to let your brother speak for himself.'

'Nah, he don't.'

'He don't– he doesn't what?'

'He don't speak. Not to people he don't know. I talk for us.'

Prue glanced down at their bare feet, and the shabby shoes dangling from their arms. 'Why don't you wear your shoes? You'll catch cold going about barefoot.'

'We've only got these pair each. If we don't wear 'em much they'll last us longer, Bet says. Saves money, see.'

'Bet is your . . . stepmother?' Prue hazarded, trying to remember what Patricia had told her of the children's situation.

Aggie snorted. 'Stepmother, that's a laugh. Bet was Dad's bit of stuff, before he died of a bomb. She keeps me and Jim around for the extra rations, only we don't see 'em unless we can swipe a bit while she's out cold.'

'Out cold?'

'From the whisky. She drinks it in ladles.'

'That's, er . . . does she indeed? In ladles? Well well well,' Prue said faintly. What a child this was! 'Now, would you like to go to your room and rest a little before dinner?'

Aggie shrugged, which Prue decided must mean yes.

'Bring your cases and follow me,' she said.

The children trudged behind her on their dirty feet and she showed them into the bedroom she'd prepared. It hadn't been used in years, but there were twin beds: she'd anticipated that the siblings would feel less homesick if they shared. Prue had also brought in some children's books and a few of Bertie's old toys.

For the first time since they'd arrived, Prue saw Aggie's scowl lift as she caught sight of the shelf of books.

'These ain't for us, are they, Missus?' she asked in a hushed voice.

'Certainly. Do you like to read?'

'When I can get 'em.' Aggie took a book from the shelf and regarded the cover reverently. It was an old *Greyfriars Holiday Annual*, with a colourful illustration on the front, of Billy Bunter and his chums taking part in their school sports day. The little girl held it up to show her brother. 'Here, Jimmy, these're a bit posh.'

183

'I'm sorry that they're more for boys,' Prue said. 'They were my son Bertie's.'

'I don't mind boys' stuff.' Aggie looked up from the book with interest. 'Is Bertie bigger or littler than us?'

'Oh, a lot bigger. He's a man now, away fighting in the war,' Prue said. 'But he was no bigger than you are when those were his favourite stories. What do you read at home, Aggie?'

'I can't get books much. Bet don't read so there's only Dad's old ones, and I've read all them loads. Sometimes I nick a couple from the library if I can sneak 'em out without getting caught.'

Prue raised her eyebrows. 'You don't mean you steal them?'

Aggie shrugged. 'Have to, don't I? They won't let me have a card, snooty beggars, and I can't keep reading Dad's over again. I've read *Tales of Terror* a hundred times already.'

'That doesn't sound like it's a storybook for little girls.'

'It's all there is.' Aggie drew herself up. 'Anyhow, I don't want no little girl storybooks.'

Jimmy was examining Bertie's old toy fort with its painted soldiers, an expression of wonder on his dirty little face. He reached out and touched one of the faded redcoats with the tip of his finger, as if worried it was a mirage that might soon disappear.

Prue crouched down to bring herself level with him.

'Do you like to read too, Jimmy?' she asked gently.

The little boy shook his head, then looked at his sister in mute appeal.

'Told you, he don't talk,' Aggie said shortly. 'He can't read yet, Missus, he's only seven. I read to him sometimes, when Bet's asleep and I know I won't get a smack.'

'Seven's big enough to read a little.'

184

'He don't know his letters. Our old teacher picked on him about it, said he was simple.' She cast Prue a look of challenge, as if defying her to make a comment. 'He ain't though. He's bright as I am. Bright as you.'

'I don't doubt it.'

'Jimmy likes to invent stuff. He can fix 'most any machine just on his own. That's brains, that is.' Aggie turned back to the books, and her eyes sparkled. 'Here, can I really have all these?'

'I told you, Aggie, they're yours if you'd like them.' Prue got to her feet. 'I'll leave you to rest for a little while. Dinner will be in an hour: do make sure you wash before you come down.'

Edie was rubbing together fat and flour for a crumble when Prue came in and sank into a chair at the table.

'Oh my goodness!' She rested her forehead on her palms.

'What is it, Prue?' Tilly asked. 'Are the children here?'

'Are they! I honestly don't know,' Prue murmured. 'The oldest one's ten but she's cynical enough for forty-five, and the boy seems to be some sort of deaf-mute. Whatever has your aunt sent me, Matilda?'

Edie felt a twinge of guilt. She had meant to greet the evacuees with Prue, but she'd become so absorbed in her baking that she'd lost track of the morning.

'I'm sorry, it was my fault,' she said. 'I promised I'd help with them.'

'Oh, never mind apologising. If I thought I couldn't manage, I'd have fetched you.' Prue rubbed her eyes. 'I ought to be able to manage. I did raise a child once. Mercy, I even used to be one. But these children! Can they go into Borstal at ten? I'm sure Aggie must have done some time.'

'Is she that bad?' Tilly asked.

'Tough as old shoe leather. I've never met a child so convinced the world is out to get her. And really, I'm hardly surprised. This common-law stepmother they live with sounds like a monster.'

Edie frowned. 'Really?'

Prue nodded. 'A violent drunk, apparently, and it's obvious she barely feeds the little mites.'

'Where are their parents?'

'I understand from Patricia that the mother died when the boy was a baby. The father was killed when a bomb fell on his factory last year.'

Edie felt a surge of fellow-feeling. Orphans, thrust on an unenthusiastic relative: she could sympathise with that. Still, at least Aunt Caroline had always been kind in her way. Edie could only imagine the misery of a childhood with a parent figure who neglected and abused when they ought to nurture.

'The stepmother takes all their rations for herself, Aggie says, and I believe her,' Prue continued. 'Both of them are smaller than they ought to be and evidently malnourished – there's barely enough flesh on them to keep body and soul together. And Jimmy looked at Bertie's shabby old fort as if he'd never had anything of his own to play with.'

'Oh, the poor dear,' Edie whispered. It broke her heart to think of a child without love or toys.

'The girl likes to read but she's been surviving on stolen library books and the worst sort of penny dreadfuls. The boy doesn't know his letters and refuses to speak a word.' Prue sighed. 'Poor wretches. However are we going to get on with them?'

'It sounds like they need some looking after.'

'Yes, I rather think they do.'

When Prue had gone to set the table, Edie cast a glance at Tilly.

'So,' she said in a low voice. 'Prue seems to have found herself a couple more lost causes. They ought to fit right in, wouldn't you say?'

Chapter 19

At half past twelve the doorbell chimed to announce the arrival of the dinner guests, and some minutes later Luca appeared in the kitchen. He looked out of place at Applefield Manor somehow, in his shabby uniform with his suntanned face and nasty-looking black eye, and he blushed furiously as he gripped his cap in both hands.

'Luca.' Tilly turned to him with a smile. 'It's good to see you.'

'Hello, my old friend. It has felt too long.' He took her hand and kissed it, then greeted Edie in the same way. 'I see we will be spoiled with charming young ladies at our dinner table today.' He pulled a face. 'Usually we have only the boss to look at.'

Tilly laughed. 'Rather hard on Sam but I'm glad you feel we're an improvement.' She stepped forward to examine his face. 'Luca, your eye looks awful.'

He touched his finger to the tender area and winced. 'It is not so painful as it was.' He glanced at Edie. 'Who knew the boy had such a swing on him, yes?'

'Has Sam said anything to you about giving him his job back?' Edie asked.

'No. It seems he is not to be swayed.' Luca sighed. 'Poor

Davy. He is so young, and that father of his . . . if he leaves the farm, he will be at the man's mercy. A man who hates all that he sees; all that is different.'

'And poor Luca too,' Tilly said, still looking at the swollen eye. 'Have you had anything on it, love?'

'Only liver.'

'I've got some cream for bruising in the bathroom, let me fetch it.'

He took her elbow as she passed him. 'Let Edie go, *cara*. In your condition you ought not to be running up and down flights of stairs. Trust your Dr Bianchi.'

'Oh, nonsense,' Tilly said, flicking a hand. 'I've still got two legs, haven't I?'

When she'd disappeared Luca shook his head at Edie, smiling. 'I never knew a girl like her for wilfulness.'

'Please, sit down,' Edie asked. 'Where's Marco?'

Luca helped himself to a chair. 'Mrs Hewitt has him looking at her broken gramophone player. Marco is good with these things.'

'And you came to the kitchen to . . .'

'Oh! Yes.' He took an envelope from his pocket. 'To deliver this to your friend Miss Liddell. It accompanies the gift of a leg of mutton.'

Edie frowned. 'From Sam?'

'That's right.'

Before Edie could make further enquiries, Tilly returned with a tube of cream.

'Thank you, Matilda,' Luca said earnestly. 'You are too kind, always.'

'Close your eye and let me put some on for you then,' Tilly said.

Smiling, he closed his sore eye and submitted to having the cream applied.

'Your friend forgets who is the doctor,' he observed to Edie while Tilly worked in the cream with gentle finger-tips.

'Well, even doctors sometimes have to be patients,' Tilly said. 'No, don't move your head. It'll sting to blazes if it goes in your eye.'

'Yes, Nurse.' He caught sight of the crude silver ring on her finger. 'You still wear this old thing, I see.'

'Always.' Her fingers moved dextrously over the sore flesh. 'Young Davy really gave you quite a sock, didn't he?'

'He sure did. I don't know whether to be angry or impressed. Mainly I think I am just embarrassed that such a little boy got the best of me.'

'I heard some news of him this morning,' Tilly said with a sideways glance at Edie. 'Sally Constance from the dairy farm always brings me the gossip with the milk.'

'About his job?' Edie asked.

Tilly shook her head. 'No, his brother. The family had another telegram to say Geordie was reported captured. He's being held in a prisoner of war camp in Italy.'

Luca nodded with satisfaction. 'This is good. He will be safe there until he can come home.'

Tilly finished tending to his eye and screwed the cap back on the tube. 'There, all better. Take the cream with you and apply it every day, then in a week you'll be just as handsome as ever.' She went to wash her hands.

Luca blinked a few times and stood up. 'And how is the health of my first and favourite patient on English soil? Does the baby give her any trouble?'

Tilly laughed. 'He does today, little sod. He's never stopped kicking me all morning.' She glanced up from the sink. 'Come and feel for yourself. He's at it now.'

Luca looked pleased. 'May I?'

'Certainly, I'm sure Baby Liddell would be honoured to give you a boot in the knuckles. He's a real brawler.'

'Ah, so he takes after his mother,' Luca said with a grin.

She rolled her eyes at Edie. 'So much for this famed Italian chivalry, eh?'

Luca went to rest a hand on her swollen stomach, and looked up in delight when he felt the baby give a vigorous kick.

'A strong one, by God!'

'Don't I know it? My insides must be as bruised as your eye,' Tilly said. 'You'd better go into the dining room, Luca. We'll be eating shortly.'

'Just a moment. I came in here on an errand, before you began your nursemaiding.' He handed her the envelope he'd brought. 'There is a leg of mutton as well, in your porch. A gift from Sam. He has slaughtered a sheep for his workers this week, to reward our hard work during lambing, and he insisted Applefield Manor share the bounty.'

Tilly gave a nod that seemed more than a little conspiratorial to Edie's watchful eye.

'Please thank him for me,' she said earnestly. 'I do appreciate it. More than I can say.'

As Prue rang the old bell in the dining room to summon the household, she realised she had gone from looking forward to this dinner to dreading it.

The evacuees' upbringing had obviously left a lot to be desired, and she had no idea how they would behave over their meal. Could they even use a knife and fork? Goodness knew what her guests would think of these two feral little animals slurping soup in their midst. Italians always seemed so refined and well-bred. Prue

191

could almost hear the click of her mother's tongue, telling her she'd failed in her duties as hostess – as she did at all things.

She was relieved, at least, to see the children arrive in the dining room with their feet, legs and faces washed, although they were still barefoot. The way they constantly scratched worried her though. Might they have lice? She shuddered as she thought about what other horrors they might be harbouring in their little bodies – ringworm, impetigo and goodness knew what. She must speak to Dr MacKenzie about checking them over.

Edith, who was already in her seat, smiled at the pair and beckoned for them to sit by her. Prue was sitting opposite, between Marco and Jack.

Luca took Bertie's place at the head of the table, next to Tilly's empty chair. He had been anxious to stay close to the kitchen hatch so he could help bring in the food, which was typical of the considerate young man. Prue had grown quite attached to the two Italians on the occasions she'd been in their company. They were always so anxious to be helpful, and with such impeccable manners, that it was a delight to have them as guests.

The little girl, Aggie, looked rather more cheerful than she had when she'd arrived. The gift of the books seemed to have taken some of the edge off her hostility. Jimmy, however, looked the same as before: pale and frightened, huddling close to his sister.

'Hello,' Edith greeted the children brightly. 'Jimmy and Aggie, isn't it? I'm Edie, I live here too.'

Aggie turned to examine her curiously.

'Is that posh lady your mum then, Miss?' She nodded at Prue, who pretended she hadn't heard.

'No, I'm a Land Girl,' Edith told them. 'That means the

people in charge of the war sent me here to help grow food. I haven't been here very long yet: not much more than a fortnight.'

But Aggie's thoughts were elsewhere.

'Here, do you know what they got in this place?' she asked Edith in a very audible whisper. 'Only a bloody privy. In the house! You pull a chain and all the water swirls out of it.'

Well, Prue thought, that accounted for the four or five flushes she'd heard while she was in her room with Marco, trying to repair the gramophone. She must have a word with the children about wasting water – not to mention their language and choice of conversation while at the table.

'It's terrific, isn't it?' Edith said, smiling at the little girl's excitement. 'We never had an indoor one either. I'm from London too, like you.'

Prue had to admire the way Edith was so quickly able to develop a rapport with the children. She spoke to them in such a cheerful, relaxed way that they couldn't help but warm to her. Why couldn't Prue do the same? Already Aggie was opening like a daisy, inclining towards Edith like an old friend.

'Where in London you from then?' Aggie asked Edith.

'Pimlico. How about you?'

'Bethnal Green. We got a lot of bombs there.' The girl lowered her eyes. 'One of them killed our dad.'

'I know, sweetheart. Some of my friends died too. But we'll be safe here.'

'Till they send us away,' Aggie muttered.

Edith frowned. 'Why do you say that, Aggie?'

'We're always getting sent away. We been in two houses afore this one, and they both slung us out. First one reckoned she had heart trouble and couldn't keep us, but she never. The last lady says we was "uncoof" and she didn't want us near her kids.'

Aggie primped her little finger and lifted her nose in a comical impersonation of her previous landlady, and Edith laughed. Prue, talking to Marco at the other side of the table but watching and listening all the while, felt a smile twitching on her lips too.

This was new information though. Patty hadn't mentioned anything about the pair having been evacuated before.

'Well, no one will send you away this time,' Prue heard Edith tell them.

'You promise, do you, Miss?'

'I certainly do.'

'Ain't your house though, is it?'

'No, but if you behave yourselves then I don't see why anyone would want to send you home again.'

Prue realised Marco was talking to her and turned her attention to him.

'I'm sorry, Mr Pia, what were you saying?'

'I only apologise that I could not fix your gramophone, Mrs Hewitt,' he told her earnestly.

'Oh, please don't worry about that. It was very good of you to try.'

'And when you have been so good as to have us into your beautiful home.' The poor man looked genuinely mortified. 'I am so sorry.'

'That's the least I can do,' Prue said, giving his hand a heartfelt pat. 'I'm sure your people wouldn't hesitate to do the same for our men who are prisoners in Italy.'

'Of course, they shall be taken good care of until we can all go home again.' He sighed. 'I wish I had been able to do more. For your gramophone, I mean. It appears the motor is broken, but I cannot see where the problem lies.'

Prue became aware that Aggie was observing them. It came as no surprise that the child had never been taught it was poor manners to eavesdrop on your elders.

'Yes, Aggie? Did you want to say something?' Prue said, lifting her eyebrows.

'Here, you're a wop, ain't you?' the child said to Marco.

Marco looked taken aback, and Prue frowned at the girl. 'Aggie, we don't use that word in this house. Say sorry to Mr Pia at once or you may eat your dinner in the kitchen.'

'Say sorry for what?' The child turned a puzzled look on Edith. 'What did I say wrong, Miss? Ain't that the right word?'

'It's not a very polite word,' Edith said, sending Prue a worried look. 'When people use it, they're usually . . . well, they're usually not being very nice. But you didn't mean it in that way, did you, Aggie?'

'That's just what our dad said. I thought that's what they were called, people like him.'

Prue felt Jack nudge her under the table.

'Softly, Cheggy,' he muttered. 'Little lass don't know any better.'

'In polite company we say Italian, if we find we need to say anything,' Prue told Aggie in a gentler voice. 'But as you didn't know that then I shan't be angry with you. Just remember for next time.'

The damage had been done, however, and the child's surly frown returned. Marco tried to ease the situation.

'Where there is no intent to hurt then there is no hurt,' he said with a warm smile. 'Give it no further thought, Aggie.'

'Didn't mean nothing by it,' the girl muttered.

'I know that. We are all learning new things, every day.

You know, I have a little girl of my own just your age back in Italy.'

But Aggie wasn't to be won over and she retreated behind her protective armour as Luca brought over a tureen of cock-a-leekie soup from the kitchen hatch.

'Bet we definitely get sent away now,' Prue heard her whisper to her brother.

Prue stood to serve the soup, overcome with guilt for being so quick to snap. As usual, Jack had played the voice of conscience in her ear and she realised she had badly misjudged the situation. Of course Aggie didn't know any better. Why should she, when she'd never been taught otherwise?

Dinner seemed to have a positive effect on the children, however. There wasn't much meat with the main course, but there were plenty of mashed potatoes to go with it and as much boiled vegetables and gravy as each of them could manage. Both evacuees had second helpings, and Prue was pleased to see they had at least a rudimentary knowledge of how to use a knife and fork. By the time pudding was served Aggie had stopped frowning, while Jimmy's face was wreathed in smiles. Mash, boiled cabbage and liver was hardly what you'd call a banquet fit for a king, but Prue suspected the little chap had never eaten so well.

She offered to serve the pudding herself, and while bringing Aggie a bowl of rhubarb crumble she crouched down by her.

'Aggie, I owe you an apology,' she said quietly. 'It was wrong of me to embarrass you in front of everyone at the table. None of us know the bad words from the good until someone tells us, and as no one told you until today I had no right to threaten to punish you. I was a foolish old lady and I ought to say I'm sorry.'

Aggie looked up at her, her eyes wide. 'You're saying sorry to me, Missus?'

'That's right. When people are wrong they ought to say sorry, you know – even adults.'

'So . . . you mean you ain't going to send us away?'

'I am certainly not going to send you away. You were brought here to keep you safe.' She glanced at Edith. 'I promise.'

Edith smiled. 'Well done,' she mouthed.

'Anyhow, I was only listening to you and the – to the Italian man 'cause I wanted to say something,' Aggie said. ''Bout your record player.'

'What did you want to say?'

'Wanted to say that our Jimmy can fix it.' She swelled with pride. 'He can fix anything, told you. Just let him have a go.'

Prue hesitated. Letting a seven-year-old boy tinker with a complicated piece of machinery would surely spell the end of it, but she didn't want to trigger the girl's defensive barriers now she seemed to be opening up again.

'Well . . . perhaps he might take a look,' she said cautiously. 'But eat up your pudding first, then you may leave the table.'

The children didn't need telling twice. They ate their way through two bowls of crumble and custard each before they were done, in half the time it took the adults around the table to finish one. The way they'd shovelled down their food, Prue was rather worried they were going to spend all night throwing it up again.

When they'd finished, Prue agreed that they could go look at the faulty gramophone. Jimmy still hadn't spoken a word but she could see that he was bouncing with excitement.

'I want to see this,' Jack said as Prue stood to accompany

them. He took his pewter pint pot of brown ale from the table and followed the three of them upstairs.

In Prue's bedroom, the two adults watched with amazement as the little boy deftly ran his hands over the old machine, peering inside, flipping open veneer panels, then tilting it so he could look underneath. He looked as if he'd been repairing gramophones from the cradle.

'What do you think of these two then?' Prue asked Jack under her breath. 'You haven't said a word through dinner. I know that means you've been making up your mind.'

'The girl pretends to be tough because she thinks she has to protect the boy,' he murmured back. 'Doesn't trust anyone, especially adults; a born survivor. The lad's haunted by something, or more likely several things. It's in his eyes, clear as day.'

Prue had come to the same conclusion herself. She saw something in Jimmy's eyes that she also recognised in Jack's. There was more that could scar a man – or a boy – than the battlefield.

Finally Jimmy let the gramophone alone and whispered something to his sister.

'Jimmy says the spring's snapped, that's why the motor ain't turning,' Aggie told them with the brazen self-confidence that no amount of hard treatment had been able to rob her of. 'You'll need to send off for a new one. No need to get a man in though, my brother can do it. Just give him a screwdriver, that's all.'

Jack glanced at Prue, eyebrows lifting. 'Well. We've got a junior Thomas Edison in our midst, Cheggy.'

'However did your brother learn so much about machinery?' Prue asked.

Aggie shrugged. 'Dunno, he just seems to know it. Gonna be a ginner when he's big, ain't you, Jim?'

The boy nodded enthusiastically.

Prue frowned. 'Ginner?'

'Engineer, I think.' Jack turned to Aggie. 'Don't he talk, your brother?'

'Nah.'

'Can't or won't?'

'Sometimes he will. Only not to just anyone, and not when he's scared.'

Jack smiled at Jimmy. 'Then we'll have to make sure he stops being scared quick sharp. You want to see something good, son?'

Jimmy cast an uncertain look at his sister.

'Depends what the something good is,' she said, with the wariness of one not accustomed to being given treats.

'You'll like it,' Jack said. 'Here, follow me.'

That Jimmy's vocal cords could work well enough was confirmed when Pepper swooped down over his head and he gave a shriek of delight.

'It's a bird!' Aggie said, clapping her hands as she watched Pepper settle on Jack's shoulder. 'Hey, I seen pigeons sit on people like that sometimes. Is it your bird, Mister?'

'She's her own bird, but she's tame,' Jack told her. 'Pepper's her name. She can talk too.'

Aggie shook her head. 'You can't kid us. Only birds can talk are parrots. That's a crow, that.'

'This crow can talk. Listen.' Jack bribed Pepper with a seed from his pocket. 'Say hello, Pep.'

'Hello!' she cawed.

Aggie's eyes widened. 'Blimey! Is she magic?'

'Not magic. Just very clever.'

'Nah, I don't believe it. It's you doing it, ain't it? Like one of them geezers with the dummies. Ventricolists.'

'Hello!' Pepper said again, in an affronted tone that suggested she resented this accusation of chicanery. As Jack was drinking from his pint pot, this seemed to satisfy Aggie.

'I s'pose she really can do it then,' she said in a hushed voice.

'Would you like to stroke her, Aggie?'

Aggie's eyes lit up. 'Blimey, wouldn't I! Yes please, Mister.' He bent his huge frame slightly and Aggie stood on tiptoes to run her hand over Pepper's feathers. The bird let out a soft caw.

'I like animals,' Aggie said. 'More than I like people, anyhow. People are only rotten to you, but animals are just your friend without any bother.'

'I think that depends on which people you know,' Jack said. 'Would you like to stroke her, son?'

Jimmy nodded vigorously, and Jack looked at Prue lingering in the doorframe. His odd pet frightened her, with its bright little eyes that seemed to know as much as a person's, and she always kept her distance when she had to come in here. Unlike Aggie and Jack, she wasn't a born animal-lover. She felt towards them the way she felt towards children: she charitably wished them well, but she was never quite sure what she was supposed to do with them.

'This little one will need a lift, I think, Cheg,' Jack said.

She shook her head. 'Oh no, Jack, I . . .'

'Come on. He won't weigh much, skinny little thing he is.'

Jimmy was looking at her, arms half raised, bashfulness forgotten in his anxiousness to get up to the bird. After a moment's hesitation, Prue lifted him up by his hips so he could run a finger over Pepper's head. He giggled with delight as the crow inclined her beak towards him.

'I thought you two might like to feed her sometimes,' Jack said as Prue put him down again.

Aggie stared at him. 'Really, can we?'

'Of course. I can see she likes you both already.' He smiled at Prue. 'Wouldn't you say so, Mrs Hewitt?'

Prue never could resist that grin of his. It belonged too much to the boy he'd once been; to the boy he still was, in his heart. What a marvel he was with the children! No wonder Bertie had always adored him.

'Yes,' she said, smiling too. 'I think we've all made some new friends today.'

Chapter 20

Over the next month, Edie settled into the routine of life as a Land Girl. Her body no longer hurt in every joint as she grew accustomed to manual work, and she rarely felt the tight pain in her chest that had been so constant a feature of her life in London. She even gained some weight, thanks largely to Tilly's cooking, and although she still didn't exactly have what you might call curves, she knew with all modesty that her looks were greatly improved. Boys stopped to look at her now when she visited the shops in Kirkton. Sometimes they even tried to make dates with her. She hadn't accepted any, but the attention was doing wonders for her confidence.

'Why, Edie, my dear, you're practically buxom,' Prue told her one evening over dinner. 'With that pinkness in your cheeks, you're a true English rose. I doubt your friends in London will know you.'

Edie had flushed with pleasure, noting how her landlady had chosen to use the shorter form of her name – the name her friends used.

The two women had grown closer since Aggie and Jimmy had joined the household. They seemed naturally to gravitate towards Edie, and Prue appeared grateful for the care the younger woman took of them: reading to them, playing with them, listening to their stories – or rather Aggie's stories, since Jimmy still refused to speak.

The boy seemed contented enough, though. Both he and his sister were blossoming under the kind treatment they'd received at Applefield Manor after a lifetime of hard knocks. Jimmy had formed a particularly close bond with Jack – Uncle Jack, as he had quickly become – who had endeared himself with piggy-back rides, games and tireless good humour. It was when he returned from a trip into town with the parts for the boy to build his own radio set, however, that he made a friend for life. Jimmy had thrown himself at Jack for a hug that Edie would swear had brought a tear to the grizzled ex-soldier's eye.

He really was a wonder with machines. Edie had gaped to see Jimmy deftly assemble the radio set, and he had fitted a new spring into Prue's old gramophone with the dexterity of a master craftsman. Aggie, meanwhile, had lost much of her defensive hardness, and spent long periods in the stables trying to teach Pepper new words.

Jack was such a natural father that Edie wondered why he'd never had a family of his own. Perhaps his experiences in the war had made it difficult for him to settle down.

Or perhaps there was something else. Edie couldn't help noticing the way his gaze followed Prue, with something in his eyes that spoke of more than brotherly affection. A certain wistfulness; even yearning . . .

Yes, the children had settled in well, but Edie did wish Prue would spend more time with them. While her reserve towards Edie had slowly melted, she just couldn't seem to show the same warmth to the two evacuees. She was kind to them, of course, going out of her way to ensure they had everything they needed; even giving up her own rations on occasion so the malnourished little souls could have a portion more. But she was always so stilted and formal in their company: awkwardly catechising them on what they'd learned at school or reminding them to wash some part of their anatomy like a staid Victorian governess. The children, likewise, regarded their landlady with a wary detachment, showing no desire to be in her presence unless they absolutely had to be.

By the time the apple blossom was starting to bud, the ground Edie and Jack had been clearing was ready for potato-planting, and the new lambs at Larkstone Farm were buxom and bouncy. Edie loved helping Jack on the estate, but it was her days working on the farm that she lived for.

Sam was still fond of keeping her by his side, and like Prue he had thawed considerably. These days he smiled, joked and talked: a far cry from the curmudgeonly farmer Edie had met on her first day. Over the weeks he taught her how to drive the farm's Fordson Thames truck, to repair the drystone walls that bordered his fields and deal with difficult births – Edie's slender arms and small hands were greatly prized by the farmer for groping around inside the sheep to get their infants in the right position for birthing. And despite Vinnie and Barbara's fears he never so much as flirted with her, let alone laid a hand on her. Edie would have thought of him as a friend, if it weren't for her lingering worry about Tilly.

That Tilly and Sam had what he'd referred to as 'an understanding' was obvious. Edie kept her eyes open, and she noticed the letters that passed between the two of them. She also noticed the visits Tilly occasionally paid to the farmhouse, always on the pretext of making some deal relating to game. And yet there didn't seem to be any romance between them: just a sort of jolly amiability that didn't fit their situation at all.

Edie couldn't work it out. Was Tilly in love with Sam? Was he in love with her? And whatever the feelings on both sides were, if Sam was responsible for Tilly's situation, why on earth didn't he do the decent thing and marry her? That he might be the sort to seduce and run was something Edie found hard to believe of him, and yet . . . what else could it be? A hundred times she'd been on the brink of asking Tilly about it, but she always stopped herself. Tilly would confide in her if she wanted to, and Edie shouldn't risk upsetting her friend just to satisfy her own curiosity.

It was about five weeks after his fight with Luca that Davy appeared back at Larkstone Farm. There was no warning; no fanfare. One of the Land Girls from the hostel had been helping with the lambing in Davy's place. Then one morning she was gone and there was Davy, in the farmhouse with the other workers as if he'd never left, with Sam barking out jobs for them in his usual way. The boy looked chastened since the last time Edie had seen him, some of the fight knocked out of him, and she noticed his arm was hanging limply at his side as if he'd been hurt.

'Don't say anything,' Vinnie whispered to Edie as she cast a puzzled look in Davy's direction. 'Failed his medical.'

It was the end of the day before Edie was able to get Vinnie and Barbara alone to find out more details.

'What happened?' she asked. 'I thought Sam was dead set against taking him back on.'

Barbara shrugged. 'Your guess is as good as ours. All we know is, Davy was turned down for the army and next day Sam offered him a job. Not his old one either.'

'How do you mean?'

'Davy was casual labour before,' Vinnie said. 'He was only supposed to be here for lambing. Now Sam's taken him on permanently, with lodging too. Davy's bedding down in one of the outbuildings Sam's fitted up.'

Edie could hardly believe it. What on earth could have brought about such a dramatic change of heart?

'What happened to Davy's arm?' she asked.

'He won't say, but I've got an idea,' Vinnie muttered darkly. 'That father of his. I suppose he wasn't too impressed at Davy failing to get into the army.'

'Why should Sam care about that?'

'Who knows?' Barbara said with a shrug. 'Still, it was damned decent of him.'

Edie was working with Davy and Luca in the infirmary around two weeks later when it happened.

She'd been worrying all morning that Davy might be about to dash all his newly realised good fortune in the same way as he'd thrown his job away before. He'd been casting ominous looks at Luca all the time they'd been working. The prisoner was whistling some pretty Italian tune as they cleaned out the pens. Eventually, Davy jumped to his feet.

'Davy, don't!' Edie whispered. 'You'll get yourself sacked again. Just let him alone.'

But the boy ignored her and strode determinedly towards Luca. Edie winced, convinced he was about to lunge at the man, but instead Davy stopped short and thrust his hands into his pockets.

'What's your camp like?' he demanded.

'Hm?' Luca looked up from his work. 'Our camp?'

'Aye, what's it like? Do they feed you proper and that?'

'We have no complaints,' Luca said, looking surprised. 'We have food to eat and pastimes to keep us occupied, and the guards are not unkind.'

'So they don't bray you or owt like that then?'

Luca looked helplessly at Edie. 'Bray? I do not know this word, I think.'

'He means, do they beat you?' Edie translated.

'Oh. No, certainly not. That would be against the law, Davy.'

Davy looked sceptical. 'What, thumping prisoners is against the law?'

'Yes, the Geneva Convention forbids it. Military prisoners must be humanely treated, or governments risk revenge attacks against their own men in enemy camps.'

Davy appeared to consider this.

'So . . . if we're nice to you, then the wo– the Italian guards will be nice to our soldiers?' he said in a hesitant voice.

'Exactly right.'

'That's really the law?'

'Certainly. You can make enquiries for yourself if you don't wish to take my word.' Luca regarded him. 'Why do you ask me this, Davy?'

He scuffed his foot against the straw-covered flagstones. 'Just wondering.'

'Your brother is a prisoner. Is that correct?' Luca said gently.

Davy nodded. 'In Italy.'

'And you are worried the guards there might hurt him?'

'I thought it might be like them concentration camps. I heard about them.'

'I promise you, there is no need to worry. Prisoners of war do not live in luxury, but they are treated well. Your brother is safe and will come home to you, healthy and happy, when the war is over.'

The following Thursday, Edie watched with interest as once again Davy edged closer to Luca.

'Luca.'

The Italian looked up. 'Hello, Davy. Can I do something for you?'

'I got a letter. From our Geordie, in that camp I said about.'

'What does he say?'

'Don't know. I only know a few of the words, and they don't make sense without the rest.' He looked puzzled. 'How'd he learn to write so fast? He never could before.'

'Do you have the letter?' Luca asked. 'Perhaps I might read it for you.'

Davy hesitated, then nodded. He took a grubby envelope from his pocket and handed it to Luca.

Luca skimmed the paper.

'Your brother is very well, Davy,' he said. 'He tells that he speaks his letter to a guard he has become friends with, Captain Massaro, who writes it down for him.'

'Can you read it me?'

'Very well.' Luca held the letter up in front of him. '"Davy, please do not worry, I'm safe and all that",' he read, the words sounding strange in his Italian accent. '"What an ass to get myself captured! Sorry to give you a fright. The other prisoners here are good lads, mostly English and Scots, and the Italians are decent once you understand them. Food's not like we're used to at home but there's enough of it to keep us from going hungry. The Red Cross send us parcels too – fags, chocolate, kippers, tins of Ovaltine and such. We'd rather the Ovaltine was beer but we mustn't complain!

We've got a wireless, a snooker table, and books too – no good to me, of course, but one of the guards, Captain Massaro, has been teaching me my letters. I might actually come home less of a dunce than when I shipped out! In the day we do work or exercise, so time passes quickly. The captain is a good man and is kind enough to write this for me. Hope you can get someone to read it to you. He says he will put the address for you to reply to, if you can get someone to write out your letters. Love always, your big brother Geordie.'"

'So one of the guards wrote for him?' Davy said.

'So it seems.'

'Why?'

'As a favour to a friend, I imagine.' Luca handed him back the letter. 'If you would like me to do the same, I am very happy.'

Davy blinked. 'You'd write to Geordie for me?'

'Of course.'

'Why?'

Luca smiled. 'Let us call it a favour to a friend.'

Davy stared at the ground, his cheeks bright red, as if trying to make up his mind about something.

'I'm sorry I blacked your eye, Luca,' he eventually blurted out.

'Davy, I have already forgotten it.'

Edie and Sam were working together one Friday afternoon, repairing a boundary wall that had been damaged, when Sam spotted Davy and Luca chummily sharing a cigarette some distance away.

'Heyup,' he said, raising an eyebrow. 'What's all this?'

Edie smiled. 'Didn't you know? They're great friends now. Luca's been helping Davy write to his brother over in Italy.'

'Has he indeed? Wonders never cease,' Sam said. 'That's what happens when you remove him from his father's influence. He starts to discover what human beings are.'

'Sam . . .'

He rolled his eyes. 'I know that tone, London. Am I wrong or are you about to poke your little button nose into my affairs again?'

'I'm curious, that's all. About Davy. He turned up back here like nothing had happened and you never said a word about it.'

'When do I ever?' he muttered as he selected a suitably sized stone.

'But there must be a reason you gave him his job back. You seemed dead set against it.'

Edie felt no embarrassment, now, in asking Sam questions. He was used to her curiosity, and although he often harumphed in his grumpy way, she knew that was just his way of teasing her.

'Discovering his father had half broken his arm is reason enough, isn't it?' he said.

'Is that all though? Fred must've hit him enough times before but you never offered him a permanent job.'

'Perhaps I felt sorry for him,' Sam said quietly. 'Being robbed of his future like that. All the lad ever dreamed of was serving his country, helping to win this blasted thing.'

Edie frowned. 'I never heard you talk about the war like that before.'

'You thought I didn't care, just because I'm stuck here?' Sam said. 'Then you don't know me as well as you think you do, London. If there's one thing I can't abide it's a bully, and that's all Hitler is. A power-mad little bully.'

'Then why aren't you –' She stopped.

'Why aren't I in uniform?'

'Um, yes.'

'Because people still have to eat. There's more than one way to win a war. I'm presuming you feel the same or you wouldn't be here.' He glanced at her. 'Or wasn't the Land Army your first choice?'

She flushed. How could he possibly know that? He seemed to have a knack for reading her mind.

'Actually . . . no,' she admitted. 'I wanted to be a Wren, but they wouldn't have me.'

'Why not?'

'I . . .' She hesitated. 'Some childhood health problems. I'm fine now,' she added quickly. 'But my doctor said they wouldn't take a risk on me.'

He sighed. 'Well, I know how you feel.'

'You?' she said, blinking.

He nodded. 'I tried to join up early in '39, when it'd become obvious to everyone but Chamberlain that war was inevitable. I'd made plans with a lad I know from a farming family in Kirkton who has a club foot to manage Larkstone, so they couldn't throw that "reserved man" nonsense at me. Made no difference though. The army don't want me.'

Edie looked over his solid frame. Not want him? How on earth could they not want someone like Sam? He was strong and athletic. He could run from one end of the farm to the other in no time, vaulting over stiles with his muscular arms. He could haul a full-grown sheep over his shoulders as if it barely weighed a thing. Edie couldn't imagine any medical reason for him being refused.

'Why?' she asked.

'Left ear didn't pass muster,' he muttered, unconsciously rubbing the afflicted organ. 'Problems as a lad left me deaf on that side, and apparently one working ear isn't good enough for His Majesty. Kick in the head, right?'

'But . . . everyone in the village thinks you dodged joining up. The feathers.. .' Now Edie had been at the farm a while, she knew that the white feathers and taunting graffiti of 'coward' and 'traitor' appeared semi-regularly around Sam's property.

'Let 'em think what they want,' Sam said, a fierce look in his eyes. 'I never asked for this bloody village's approval. They'd made up their minds to hate me long before this. It's a good way to get left alone, and I like being left alone.'

'I'm sorry,' Edie said quietly. 'Why didn't you tell me before?'

'What for? It wouldn't have made a difference.'

'It would have made a difference to me.'

'Huh.' He was quiet for a moment, glaring into the distance. Then his scowl lifted and he turned back to her. 'You still stepping out with Errol Flynn then, are you?'

'Who?'

'That pretty flyboy.'

'Oh.' Edie flushed. 'We were never . . . it was only a couple of dances.'

'Plenty of brass, I expect? Their lot always seem to come from some nobby school.'

'I really wouldn't know.'

Sam fell silent, then jumped suddenly to his feet.

'Come on, London,' he said, the old gruffness back in his tone.

Edie stood too. 'Where are we going?'

'Summat to show you.'

Puzzled, she followed him to the henhouse.

'Oh!' she said when he showed her what was in there. She clapped her hands. 'Oh, the loves!'

Sam laughed at the look of delight on her face as she examined the tiny yellow chicks.

'Hatched a couple of days ago,' he said. 'Take your pick, any two you fancy. They'll be ready to go home with you next week, I reckon.'

'We can really have them?'

'Promised, didn't I?'

'Thank you, Sam. That's very kind of you,' she said, beaming at him. 'I'll speak to Prue about getting a coop.'

Sam looked awkward under her effusive thanks.

'So, um . . . have you seen that new film then?' he said after a moment's silence. 'Supposed to be a masterpiece.'

'Hmm?' Edie was watching the chicks as they waddled about, looking like fluffy sherbet lemons on legs.

'This Orson Welles thing. I'd rather watch Stan and Ollie myself, but everyone seems to be raving about it.'

'*Citizen Kane*? No, not yet.'

'I, er . . . it's showing at the Empire in Kirkton.'

'Is it?' Edie was only half paying attention. 'Terrific, I can see if Vinnie and Barbara want to go. Tilly's too big now to be comfortable for a whole picture.'

Sam rubbed his neck. 'I did think . . . I wondered if you might like to go with me.'

She looked up, frowning. 'With you?'

'Yes, with me. Damn it, Edie, you know what I'm asking.'

'You're . . . you want me to go to the pictures with you?'

'Aye, well, you aren't forced to,' he said, retreating into surliness in his embarrassment.

'I can't . . . you're asking . . .' She stared at him. 'I don't bloody believe this!'

'All right, London, I get the idea,' he growled. 'Forget I asked.'

'You know, I'd actually started to think you might be a decent chap. Giving Davy his job back, letting us have the chicks, and then all those times it was only the two of us and you never . . . I'd begun to hope there might be more to what happened with Tilly than met the eye. But you're just another man, aren't you, Sam? Only after one thing.' She shook her head in disgust. 'The girls tried to warn me what you were up to. I should've listened.'

He frowned. 'What was that about Tilly?'

'You're responsible for her condition. You got her in the family way then you refused to marry her. You admitted as much to Vinnie.' She met his eyes with a glare of challenge. 'And I was going to be next, was I?'

'You weren't going to be anything,' he said in a low voice.

'Well, do you deny it?'

'That I refused to marry Tilly Liddell? Aye, I do deny it.'

Edie blinked. 'Pardon?'

'Suppose I offered and she said no? What then, London?'

'She . . . why would she do that?'

He turned away, his face red with anger and mortification. 'You'd have to take that up with her.'

Chapter 21

Edie rarely arrived home before seven when she was working at Larkstone Farm. As she had quickly learned, there were no short days in lambing season. Tilly was usually waiting for her in the kitchen, and the two girls enjoyed a gossip together while Edie ate her evening meal. Today, of course, she was particularly keen to get her friend alone. But when she got to the kitchen, she found not only Tilly but Jimmy and Aggie, beaming as if they had an especially good piece of news to share.

'Hullo,' Edie said as she eased her tired body into a chair. 'What're you two monkeys doing up?'

'We're allowed. Mrs Hewitt says,' Aggie told her. 'We got special permission to wait for you so's we can give you a surprise.'

Edie felt that she'd had enough of surprises today, but she could tell the two of them were bursting with excitement so she played along.

'Is it a nice surprise?'

'Oh, very,' Tilly told her, amusement sparkling behind her sober expression. 'Show her, Ag.'

'Right, this is my surprise,' Aggie said with an important

air. 'Jimmy's got a surprise too, but Tilly says I've to give you this one first because you'll be starved.'

Edie laughed. 'She's not wrong. Is it a food surprise then?'

Aggie nodded eagerly. She looked at Tilly, who put a plate of cheese pudding and spring greens down in front of Edie with a flourish.

Edie eyed the pudding warily. 'It hasn't got one of those snakes on a spring inside it, has it?'

'No,' Aggie said, bouncing on her heels. 'Eat it, Edie. I mean, eat it, please,' she said after a look from Tilly.

Edie swallowed a forkful.

'It's delicious,' she said, blinking. 'Should I be surprised by that?'

Aggie couldn't contain herself any longer.

'I made it!' she burst out. 'Jimmy helped too. Tilly let us make it for your dinner and she says it's betterer than anything she could make.'

'She's right,' Edie said, with an apologetic grimace for her friend. 'It's the best cheese pudding I've ever eaten, that's for sure. Thank you, both of you.'

Aggie beamed with pride.

'Jimmy's got something to show you too,' Tilly said. 'Haven't you, Jim?'

He answered with a shy nod.

'Go and get it then,' Tilly said.

The little boy bounded from the room and came back with his school exercise book, open at today's work. Several lines were filled with writing, each spelling out 'James Adam Cawthra' in letters that became steadily more legible as Edie looked down the page.

'Jimmy! Did you write this?' she said.

He nodded eagerly.

'All on his own,' Aggie said, glowing on her brother's

behalf. 'He said the teacher helped a bit with the first one – only a little bit – but all the others Jimmy done just himself. Ain't he clever?'

'I always knew he was,' Edie said, smiling at the pink-cheeked little lad. She ruffled his hair. 'Well done, Jimmy, I'm ever so proud of you. If you keep practising your letters with me and Uncle Jack, I bet you'll be ahead of everyone when you go into the big class.'

Aggie's brow darkened.

'What's the matter, sweetheart?' Edie said gently.

'Maybe he won't get to go into the big class. Maybe we'll get sent back to Bet.'

'Are you still worrying your daft little head about that?' Tilly said, flicking one of her pigtails. 'We told you: no one's going to send you away, not this time.'

'They will if the war finishes,' Aggie muttered. 'I hope it never, ever ends.'

'Ag, you oughn't to say that,' Edie said. 'The war's a terrible thing. People are dying because of it, all over the world.'

'If it's wicked to say, I don't care,' Aggie announced defiantly. 'I don't want the stupid war to end. I want to stay here, where there's food an' no one boxes your ears for talking too loud an' . . . an' . . .'

All of a sudden she burst into tears. Edie cast a worried look at Tilly before folding the little girl into a hug.

'Now, don't you worry,' she said softly as Aggie buried her face in Edie's shoulder. 'If you don't want to go back to Bet, you won't.'

'You mean we can stay here? Mrs Hewitt'll let us?'

'Well, I don't know about that. But you shan't go back to a home where you're starved and beaten. I'll make sure of it.' Edie's face knit into a determined frown. 'Whatever it takes, I will.'

'Promise?'

'Cross my heart.'

That seemed to satisfy Aggie. She sniffed and wiped her eyes, and the sight of Edie eating her cheese pudding – pausing after every mouthful to compliment Aggie on the texture, flavour and anything else she could think of – soon had the little girl smiling.

Edie had nearly finished when Prue put her head around the door.

'Children, you ought to be getting to bed,' she said in the stiff, formal voice she always used to address them. 'You may read a little before lights out if you wish, Aggie.'

Aggie cast an anxious look at Edie, who understood. She swallowed down the last mouthful of her cheese pudding with an appreciative 'mmm', and the girl broke into a grin.

'Scrumptious,' Edie said. 'Aggie, I need to have you make all my meals.'

Tilly laughed. 'Oh no, what have I done? I won't have a job by the end of the week.'

Aggie giggled.

'Here, can I have them?' she asked, pointing to the handful of crumbs on Edie's plate. 'I mean, please can I?'

'You're not still hungry, are you?' Tilly asked. 'You had three helpings at dinnertime.'

Edie smiled. 'I think I understand. They're not for you, are they, Aggie? You're saving them for Pepper.'

Aggie gave a shy nod.

'I'm not sure crows are supposed to eat cheese pudding but I expect a tiny bit won't hurt.' Tilly shook the leftovers on to a piece of brown paper and wrapped them up. 'There.'

'Thank you, Tilly.' Aggie graciously submitted to a kiss from both the women, as did Jimmy, then she took her brother's hand to take him up to bed. 'Night night.'

'They're really flourishing, aren't they?' Edie observed when she and Tilly were alone.

'I know. All it took was a bit of kindness.' Tilly glanced at the door. 'Jimmy still won't speak though.'

'He will when he's ready.' Edie smiled. 'So were they cooking with you all afternoon?'

'Yes, I told Jack to send them in when they got home from school. It keeps them out of Prue's hair, and they loved helping to make your dinner.'

'You see? You're a natural mum.'

'I certainly feel a lot less terrified by the prospect than I did before they came.' Tilly poured them both a mug of tea and heaved her huge body into the opposite chair. 'Oof,' she groaned. 'I've got at least another six weeks of this and already I'm the size of the Albert Hall. You don't suppose it's twins, do you?'

'God couldn't be so cruel.'

Edie stared down into her mug, wondering how to bring up what she wanted to discuss.

'So, good day at work?' Tilly asked, as if reading her mind.

'Yes and no.' Edie looked up. 'Sam tried to make a date with me today.'

Tilly frowned. 'What?'

'He asked me to go to the pictures with him.'

'What did you say?'

'I said . . .' She took a deep breath. 'I said I couldn't even think about walking out with a man who'd dealt so unfairly with someone I cared about.'

Tilly looked away. 'Edie, you shouldn't listen to idle gossip. I told you my story.'

'It's all right, Till. You don't need to lie any more.' Edie rested a hand on hers. 'I know.'

'How do you know?'

'Sam admitted it. To Vinnie, and to me when I confronted him today. Besides, it's all over the village.'

'Sam Nicholson . . . is a good man,' Tilly murmured, blinking back a tear.

'Are you in love with him?'

'With Sam?' She smiled. 'Now there's a thought.'

'He told me he asked you to marry him.'

'Yes,' Tilly whispered. 'That's true. He asked me to be his wife and I refused.'

'But why would you do that? If the two of you were married, that would solve all your problems, wouldn't it? The baby would have a father, you'd both be provided for . . .'

'It isn't that simple, Edie.'

'Why not? I know you like him. He's got his own liveli-hood, he's handsome, not to mention that you're having his baby. I can't understand why you wouldn't have him.'

'Perhaps I've got just enough romance left in me to think a man might want me for love rather than duty,' Tilly said in a quiet voice. 'Is that so strange?'

'What makes you think it isn't love?'

'A girl always knows.' Tilly pushed away her tea. 'I think I'll go up to my room. I'm not really in the mood to stay up late.'

Edie looked up at her. 'I upset you, didn't I? Till, I'm sorry. I just hate to think of you being badly used.'

Tilly summoned a smile. 'I'm not upset. Tired, that's all. I am very pregnant, you might have noticed.' She patted Edie's shoulder. 'Goodnight, Edie. And please, sweetheart, you must stop worrying about me. I know what I'm doing.'

Chapter 22

Edie was hoeing with Jack the following Wednesday afternoon when Jimmy and Aggie came running towards them, satchels and battered cardboard gas mask boxes banging against their sides. That meant it must be about quarter to four. Edie could set her watch by the children: every day, as soon as they arrived home from school, they came running to say hello.

She'd just been reflecting on her scene with Sam the week before, and worrying how the two of them would get along on the farm tomorrow. It had been Friday afternoon when she'd confronted him about Tilly, but she hadn't seen him since. When she'd arrived at work on Saturday morning she discovered Sam had gone rabbit-shooting, leaving a note allocating them their tasks. Clearly he was in no hurry to face her again.

Did she owe him an apology? It did seem that the situation between him and Tilly was more complicated than she had suspected, but that hardly absolved him of getting her friend pregnant in the first place.

The date he'd wanted to make with her though – what did that mean? Edie wasn't sure how she ought to feel about it. Her wariness of him as the seducer of her friend had prevented her thinking of Sam Nicholson as anything more than her boss before now.

Anyhow, it didn't make any difference. No matter how Edie felt about Sam, she couldn't walk out with the father of her friend's baby. Even if he wasn't a complete cad – even if he had wanted to do the right thing, and it had been Tilly's decision to refuse him – she couldn't do that. He was soon to become a father, and whether married to his child's mother or not, that came with certain responsibilities which she had no intention of interfering with.

She had been surprised, though, to discover Sam had tried to join up. Edie had never believed him to be a coward, but she had thought that like Prue, he saw the war as something foreign and far away; not his concern. It had come as a shock to learn he had been as adamant to fight the forces of evil as she had herself, and, like Edie, been robbed of his chance.

That he chose not to share this information but preferred to let the village believe the worst of him, just as he allowed people to think he had refused to marry the girl he'd got into trouble, was typical of Sam. Edie knew he didn't give a damn what anyone thought of him; in fact, he seemed to revel in being disliked. The irony was that he was actually rather easy to like once you got to know him – something Tilly had obviously discovered to her cost.

Yes, it was going to be an awkward working day at the farm tomorrow. Perhaps the best thing would be not to mention it at all and hope things could continue as normal.

Edie was glad to be pulled out of her thoughts by the arrival of the children. She stood up, groaning at the pain of straightening her back.

'Hullo, here's trouble,' Jack said, grinning at the evacuees. 'So you're back again, are you? Just my luck.'

Jimmy lifted his arms, and Jack swung the little boy effortlessly up on to his shoulders. Jimmy giggled with delight, holding on to tufts of Jack's thick, shaggy hair as if they were reins.

'How was school?' Edie asked Aggie.

She pulled a face. 'We did times tables. What are times tables for anyhow? I won't ever need them when I'm grown up.'

'You'll be surprised how often you do. I know they're boring to learn, but they can be very useful.'

Aggie looked as though she didn't believe a word of it. Edie wasn't sure she really did either.

Jimmy's arms had wrapped around Jack's neck, and the gardener frowned at an angry bruise on the boy's wrist.

'What's this, Jim?' he asked.

As usual Jimmy had no reply, but Aggie spoke up for him.

'It's that Charlie Armstrong,' she said, scowling. 'He pushed him. He teases Jimmy 'cause he's shy and don't fight, even though Charlie's in the big class with me. Calls him a coward.'

'Huh. There's no bigger coward than the one who hurts those weaker than him,' Jack muttered. 'He ought to be ashamed to push a smaller boy.'

'Did you tell the teacher, Aggie?' Edie asked.

'Nah, I pushed Charlie back,' Aggie said, looking pleased with herself. 'Told him if he picked on Jim again I'd thump him. That scared him. Didn't want his gang to know he'd been done by a girl.'

'Ag, you mustn't do that. It's not nice to hurt people.'

'Charlie hurt Jim, didn't he?'

'That doesn't make it all right to hurt him back. Otherwise everyone would be hurting each other all the time.'

'But it's not nice to tell tales either,' Aggie protested. 'That's right, ain't it?'

'If someone is hurting someone else then it's not telling tales,' Edie said. 'I'll tell you what: I'll talk to your teacher. Then you haven't told any tales. Will that be all right?'

Aggie cast a worried look at her brother's sore arm.

'S'pose that's OK,' she said cautiously.

'Good. I'll telephone Miss Padgett this evening.'

Aggie looked hopefully at Jack, always their favourite playmate. 'Hey, can we have a game, Uncle Jack?'

'Not while we're working, Ag, you know that. We can have a play before tea.' Jack swung a reluctant Jimmy to the ground again. 'Say hello to Pepper then go and change your clothes. We'll be finished in a couple of hours.'

The figure of Prue Hewitt strode into view, a look on her face that didn't bode well for someone.

'Agnes Cawthra, I want a word with you,' she said when she reached them.

The girl looked nervous. 'I ain't done nothing,' she mumbled, taking a step backwards towards the comforting bulk of Jack Graham.

'Haven't you indeed? That's not what Matilda tells me. I'm informed that in the past week she's lost half a loaf of bread, five slices of corned beef, a tin of ham, six biscuits and three carrots. Would you like to tell me where they could have gone?'

'Dunno,' Aggie muttered. 'I don't know nothing about no ham.'

She cast a worried look at Jimmy and Jack, and Edie noticed that it wasn't just the children who seemed nervous. Jack, too, had the look of a man hiding a guilty secret.

'Aggie, we've talked about how wrong it is to tell stories,' Prue said. 'Now, if you tell me the truth I won't be angry. Did you take the food?'

Aggie flushed. 'Yes,' she mumbled. 'I know it was naughty, but Jim gets hungry. He's growing, Mrs Hewitt.'

'Well, then why didn't you ask?'

'Because you might've said no.'

'No one will say no if you're as famished as all that.' Prue crouched down to bring herself level with the girl. 'Aggie, I know you understand what rationing is, and why we need to be careful with our food. Don't you?'

'Yes, Mrs Hewitt.'

'And I know you understand, now, that it's wrong to steal. Don't you?'

'Yes, Mrs Hewitt.'

Prue looked into the girl's wide brown eyes and sighed. 'Well, this once we'll say no more about it. But in future, Aggie, if you and your brother are hungry between meals, you must ask. If I find out again that you've been stealing, I'm afraid you will have to be punished. Do you understand?'

'Yes, Mrs Hewitt,' Aggie mumbled.

'Good.' There was an awkward silence as Prue fumbled for what to say next. 'Did you have a nice day at school?'

'Yes,' Aggie whispered, chastened by her reprimand.

'What did you learn?'

'Times tables.'

'And . . . did you enjoy learning them?'

'Yes, Mrs Hewitt,' Aggie chanted dutifully.

'Good. Good. Well, I'll see you at dinner, children.' Prue went back to the house.

When she was gone, Edie turned to Aggie.

'Did you and Jimmy really eat all that food?' she asked. 'It sounds like you half-inched a real feast, Ag.'

Aggie glanced enquiringly at Jack, who still wore the guilty look.

'What's going on, Jack?' Edie asked. 'Do you know something about this?'

'The food weren't for us,' Aggie blurted out.

Edie frowned. 'You haven't been feeding that stuff to Pepper? You could kill her with a diet like that.'

'No. Not Pep. Can we tell her, Uncle Jack?'

Jack sighed. 'I suppose we don't have any choice now. Miss Cartwright, would you come along to the stables?'

Aggie took Edie's hand as they followed Jack and Edie gave her fingers a squeeze. She was obviously about to be let into some great secret. What were the three of them hiding in here?

Pepper swooped to Aggie's shoulder as soon as they opened the door and gave her ear an affectionate nibble. The little girl had easily endeared herself to the bird through constant attention and scraps of food.

'Evenin'!' she cawed. With the combined efforts of Aggie and Jack she now had a vocabulary of three words, delivered in a comical mix of Cumberland and cockney.

Edie blinked into the shadows, wondering what else there was to see.

'In here.' Jack pushed open one of the half doors to the stalls, and was greeted by a delighted yelp. A second later a tiny chocolate Jack Russell had its paws on his calf, and Jack laughed as he crouched down to let the little chap lick his cheek.

'Coco!' Aggie and Jimmy dropped to their knees so they could make a fuss of the puppy. He wagged his tail ecstatically, bounding from one child to the other.

'Oh my goodness!' Edie said. 'Jack, what's this?'

Jack stepped back to let the children play with their pet.

Pepper had retreated to her perch in the rafters and was regarding this energetic intruder with a look of indulgent superiority.

'Aggie came home with him hidden in her satchel two weeks ago,' Jack told Edie. 'Found a lad trying to drown the poor little beggar in the beck.'

'I had to bring him, Edie,' Aggie said, looking up at her. 'The boy was going to kill him! Said his ma couldn't afford to keep pets no more since his dad got killed in the war. So I asked if I could have him and he said I could.'

'That's where the food's been going?' Edie said.

Aggie nodded. 'I give him a bit out of mine and Jim's food, but that ain't enough when he's growing. I thought no one would notice. There's always lots of food in the pantry.'

Edie plucked Jack's elbow and they retreated a little distance away.

'Why didn't you say anything to Prue?' she asked in a low voice.

'Missus isn't a fan of animals. It was a hard enough job to convince her not to chase Pepper out. She wouldn't be right happy if she knew there was a dog on the grounds.'

'Then why did you tell Aggie she could keep him?'

He smiled drily. 'I didn't. Not at first. Told her he could stay for a couple of days while he recovered, then she could take him back where she'd found him and leave him for one of the villagers to pick up. There're always homes on farms for ratters, even a runty one like Coco: he'd soon have been sorted out. Then she told me how she'd found him shivering, half-drowned, underfed . . .' He sighed. 'Well, I'm a soft old bugger. It's obvious the lass senses a kindred spirit. I thought it'd be good for her to have a pet. Not an independent thing like Pep, but one that needs some looking after.'

Coco was getting sleepy now – he was still a very little puppy, and a short play was enough to tire him out. Edie watched Aggie coo over him as she gently stroked his head, and realised Jack was right.

'She was such a hard little thing when she arrived, wasn't she?' Jack said quietly. 'That's what happens when someone spends their life getting knocked down. They put up a shell, and if it stays there long enough, no one's ever going to be able to break through it. This is just what she needs to bring out her softer side – something to love.'

'We can't keep him hidden though, feeding him on stolen food,' Edie said. 'Prue's bound to come in here sometime, and the longer it's kept from her, the angrier she'll be.'

'Aye, you're right,' Jack said with a sigh. 'Suppose I wanted to wait until the little feller was out of the woods before I told her, in case she slung him out.'

'You don't think she'd do that, do you? I know she doesn't care much for animals, but she's not cruel.'

'No, but she can be a stubborn old mare,' Jack said with the twitch of a smile.

'She'll listen to you, surely.'

'Aye, she might.' He looked at the children stroking the sleeping puppy. 'It'd be a right shame to take him off them.'

Edie sighed. 'We'd better do it now.'

'Suppose so,' Jack said soberly. 'I'll fetch her. You prepare the bairns.'

While he went to find Prue, Edie knelt down by Aggie. Coco blinked sleepily at her, his tail giving a few limp thumps of greeting.

'Aggie, sweetheart,' she said gently. 'I'm sorry, but we have to tell Mrs Hewitt about Coco.'

Aggie stared up at her with a look of hurt disbelief that cut right into Edie's heart.

'But she'll send him away!' She picked up the little dog and cuddled him to her chest. 'If she sends him away, he'll die! Get drownded or starved or eaten by a fox. He's too little to be on his own.'

'I hope she lets him stay but this is her home, Aggie. It's not right to keep things a secret from her, and steal her food, when she's kind enough to let us all live here.'

'But . . . but . . . it isn't fair!'

'I'm sorry, my love. We don't have any choice.'

The tears were welling up in Aggie's eyes, and little rivers had started to trickle down Jimmy's cheeks, when Prue arrived with Jack.

'Now what's all this about a dog?' she said, looking irritated.

'Mrs Hewitt, please don't send Coco away!' Aggie said, looking up at her with swimming eyes. 'He's only a baby. If you let him stay we'll be so good an' we'll do all our chores an' . . . an' anything you want, promise we will.'

Prue took a bewildered look at the puppy in Aggie's arms, then turned to Jack.

'How long has this been going on?'

'He's been here a fortnight,' Jack said with a guilty grimace.

Prue's face darkened. 'So that's where our precious rations have been going, is it? On some mangy stray you thought you'd conceal under my roof?'

'Cheggy, don't be like that. We thought –'

'You may address me as Mrs Hewitt during working hours, Mr Graham,' she told him stiffly. 'Perhaps you'd like to explain why you chose to aid and abet these acts of theft rather than bringing them to my attention?'

'I thought it would be good for the children to –'

'It's not your place to think anything,' she snapped.

229

'Sometimes I believe you forget you are a servant here and not the master of the house.'

Jack's face crumpled, and he turned away.

'I'm sorry, but the dog will have to go,' Prue said. 'We can barely feed ourselves, let alone every waif and stray that appears on the doorstep.'

'No!' Aggie jumped to her feet and tugged at Prue's skirts. 'Please, Mrs Hewitt, no! He'll *die* if you send him away. Please, I'll look after him. Clean after him and walk him, and let him share my food.'

'The dog will have to go,' Prue repeated. She looked down at the little girl, and her expression softened slightly. 'He may stay tonight, then tomorrow I shall make enquiries about finding him a home on one of the farms. I'm sure he'll be happy there.'

'But it's not fair!' Aggie's fierce scowl returned, and she glared up at Prue. 'You're . . . you're cruel, that's what you are! You don't want us here, you just put up with us because the war people make you. Coco was the only pet I ever had, the only thing what loved me my whole life apart from Jim, and now you're going to send him away. I . . . I hate you, Mrs Hewitt! I hate you!'

The girl burst into tears and ran, sobbing, from the stable.

Chapter 23

Dinner that evening was a sober affair. Jimmy and Aggie had shut themselves in their room and were refusing to speak to anyone, although their soft sobs were audible from out in the hall. Jack, too, declined to sit with the rest of the household in the dining room, choosing instead to eat in the kitchen. He delivered his apologies to Prue at the table.

She looked up at him. 'So you're sulking, are you?'

'Just thought it were best I remember my place,' he muttered.

Prue was silent as they ate their meal: an over-salted corned beef hash that wasn't up to Tilly's usual standards at all. Tilly, too, seemed morose, her face pale and rather pinched. Edie, assuming her friend must be suffering from another bout of pregnancy-related sickness, respected her desire for quiet and didn't try to draw her into conversation.

'Prue . . .' Edie began, wondering how to bring up the subject of Coco.

'Yes, Edith?' Prue's face was as dark as thunder.

'Nothing.' Edie knew when the fight was over before it had begun. Perhaps tomorrow Prue might have recovered her good humour enough for an appeal to her better nature, but all Edie was likely to do now was make things worse.

'Where are those children?' Prue said, frowning at the places that had been set for them.

'I don't think they're coming. Aggie's very upset. I'll take them some supper in a little while.'

'You will do no such thing. I refuse to pander to the child because she chooses to go into a pet. If she doesn't care to come to the table, she can go without until breakfast time.'

Again, Edie realised it was no good to argue.

Prue didn't speak again until the very end of their meal. 'Did you know?' she demanded of Edie.

'About the dog?' Edie shook her head. 'Not until today. I told the children it wasn't fair to keep secrets from someone who had been so kind to them, and they saw my point once I put it that way.'

Edie had hoped this might pour oil on troubled waters, but Prue's frown deepened.

'So it wasn't Jack's suggestion I be told,' she said.

Edie flinched, realising she'd put her foot in it again.

'Well, yes,' she said. 'That is to say, we both agreed you ought to be told at once. I suppose he wanted to give the children some time with the dog first. You know, it's done Aggie so much good. Really softened her hard edges.'

Prue barely seemed to be listening. She pushed away the remains of her salty meal.

'If you need me I shall be in my room,' she said, and disappeared upstairs without so much as a goodnight.

When she was sure the rest of the household were in their bedrooms, Edie sneaked to the kitchen and loaded a tray with bread and cheese from the pantry. She felt guilty for taking food without permission, but really, it was too bad to send the children to bed with empty bellies. They'd known too much of hunger already.

She added a couple of glasses of milk, then took the tray upstairs and knocked softly at the door of their bedroom.

'Can I come in?'

'No,' said a choked voice. 'We don't want to talk to no one.'

'Please. I brought you some supper.'

There was a pause, then the door opened a crack and a tear-stained little face peeped out.

'All right, you can come in,' Aggie said graciously. 'For Jim, not me. He's been hungry ages.'

Edie entered and put the tray down on top of their toybox. Jimmy started helping himself hungrily, and after a second's hesitation, Aggie joined him.

'Why didn't you come down to dinner, you two?' Edie asked.

'We didn't want to see *her*,' Aggie said with a deep scowl. The little girl might look almost comical, her furrowed brow not at all in keeping with a mouth full of bread and cheese, if it wasn't for the tragic look in her eyes.

'Mrs Hewitt was angry. This is her house, Aggie. You ought to have told her right away, you know.'

'Uncle Jack said to keep it secret a bit. Just till Coco was strong again, then he'd talk to Mrs Hewitt.' Aggie sniffed. 'I thought she wouldn't never send Coco away if Uncle Jack asked her.'

'Why do you say that, sweetheart?'

'She looks at him funny. Like grown-ups look when they're married, but pleased about being married, you know?' Aggie blinked innocent eyes at her. 'You know that way, like when they love each other?'

From the mouths of babes . . .

'She's angry right now,' Edie said, sitting down on Aggie's bed and putting an arm around her. 'You'd be angry too, wouldn't you, if you found out people you cared about had been lying to you?'

'She don't care about us,' Aggie muttered. 'All she ever says is don't do this, don't do that, speak proper, act lady-like and all that boring stuff.'

Jimmy finished his meal and came to sit by them, his mouth covered in milk. Edie took out her handkerchief to mop it for him.

'Mrs Hewitt says those things because she cares,' Edie told Aggie. 'She wants to teach you proper manners to help you in life.'

'If she cared about us she wouldn't send Coco away,' Aggie said fiercely.

'She promised to find him a good home. He'd be very happy on a farm, with all that space to run around.'

'But I don't want him to live on a farm.' The child's chin wobbled. 'I want him to stay with me. He's my dog, Miss.'

'I know,' Edie said, kissing the top of her head. 'Let Mrs Hewitt calm down a little, and perhaps by the morning she might reconsider.'

A low, droning sound came from outside and Edie frowned.

'That must be one of the planes from the airbase. It's flying low.'

Jimmy leaned over to whisper to his sister, and her eyes went wide.

'Miss,' she said in a low voice. 'That ain't one of ours.'

'What? But it has to –'

Suddenly there was a series of bangs, accompanied by bright flashes like lightning, and then, chillingly, an

ear-piercing scream. The bangs were outside, but the scream
. . . Edie drew the children against her, and they hid their
faces in her arms.

They all knew what those sounds meant. A bombing
raid! Here!

'They said the bombs couldn't get us here,' Aggie said in
a voice shaking with fear.

Edie could feel Jimmy trembling and squeezed him tight.
What should she do? What the hell should she *do*? There
were no dugouts here, no Underground stations: nowhere
they could hide if a stray bomber had decided to make
them a target.

She heard feet running down the hall, then, piercing the
air like a ghastly human siren, another shrill scream.

'What is that?' Aggie whispered. 'A ghost?'

'It's . . . it's Uncle Jack,' Edie told her, trying to keep her
voice calm and even, although she was sure the children
must be able to feel the pounding of her heart. 'He sometimes has nightmares, about the last war. The bombs must
have made him think he was back in the trenches.'

Aggie had looked frightened when she'd heard the
bombs. Now, discovering there was something ghoulish
actually in the house with them, she looked absolutely
terrified.

'Uncle Jack wouldn't hurt us, would he?' she asked,
looking up at Edie.

'No.' Edie forced a smile. 'Of course not, you know he
wouldn't. He'll be better just as soon as he wakes up
properly.'

There were sounds in the distance – more bombs,
followed by a volley of rapid machine gun fire. Edie held
the children tight against her until it had subsided, then
stood up. 'I'd better find out if there's shelter anywhere.'

'No!' Aggie clutched at her arm. 'Don't leave us on our own. Please don't.'

'I need to find somewhere to keep us safe, sweetheart.' She held out her hands to the two of them. 'Come on then. We'll all go.'

When she opened the door, she found Prue outside about to enter.

'Oh, thank God, you're safe,' she said, pulling Edie into a hug. 'Children, are you all right?'

'They're very frightened,' Edie said in a low voice. 'Where can we go, Prue? Is there a shelter anywhere?'

'No, we never had need of one. We're so far from the cities here, we've never been in the line of fire before.'

'What about a cellar?'

'Not any more. Albert had them boarded up for damp years ago,' Prue said. 'The dining table is the best we have – it's solid oak, and sturdy. Jack's underneath it already. Take the children and join him there, I'll go tell Matilda.'

'Is Jack . . .'

'He's awake and lucid. Although I think it will be some time before he stops shaking, the poor man.'

'All right, come on,' Edie said to the children as Prue went to knock on Tilly's door. She took their hands and the three of them hurried to the dining room, where Jack was on his knees under the table.

Prue was right, he was trembling all over, his face haggard and drawn. Although he was evidently now aware of where he was, his eyes still darted from side to side, as if he was under attack from invisible enemies.

'Oh God, children.' He pulled them to him for a tight hug. 'Are you all right, my pets?'

'They're frightened but unharmed,' Edie said. 'Are you?'

'I'll be fine.' But his unfixed gaze continued to stare into corners, and the two evacuees regarded Uncle Jack with a new fear in their eyes.

Prue returned a moment later and joined them under the table.

'Where's Tilly?' Edie asked.

'On her way.' Prue shook her head. 'Bombs, in Applefield! Whatever can it mean? Were they aiming for the aerodrome?'

'I expect it's a stray plane that decided to drop its load on the way home.' Edie had heard about such things. 'Or a damaged one jettisoning to gain altitude, possibly.'

Prue flinched as they heard the drone of the plane's engine close by, then another volley of machine gun fire. Jack started, almost banging his head on the table.

Jimmy whispered something to Aggie, who nodded.

'That's a flying pencil, Jim says,' she informed them. 'He can tell any plane just from the noise it makes.'

'It doesn't seem to be in any hurry to leave,' Prue muttered. 'I hope no one is hurt in the village, or on the farms. What a terrible thing for the animals! So many lambs aborted.'

She seemed to notice Jack then, trembling at her side, and laid a hand on his arm.

'Bearing up, old man?' she said softly.

He summoned a shaky smile. 'Well enough when I've you here to look after me.'

'Except when I'm a silly fool who doesn't appreciate how lucky she is to have you.' She gave his arm a squeeze. 'Forgive me, Jack. You know I didn't mean a word of it.'

'Already have, Cheg.'

There was another explosion outside, and Aggie looked up at Edie with wide, terrified eyes.

'Coco!' she whispered. 'Miss, he's out there! I have to get him before a bomb drops on him.'

'Don't be foolish, child. You can't go out there,' Prue said.

'But, Mrs Hewitt, he'll be so frightened! Please let him come in, just till the plane goes. I'll die if anything happens to him.'

'Aggie, it's dangerous outside,' Prue explained gently.

'I'll fetch him,' Jack said, squaring his shoulders. 'The dog's my responsibility.'

'Jack, don't be ridiculous. You can't go, the state you're in.' Prue crawled out from under the table. 'I shall go.'

'Cheggy, no!' Jack said. 'It's not safe.'

'We can't leave the little thing to be frightened to death, can we?' Refusing to listen to further protest, Prue went out.

She returned ten minutes later with Coco tucked under her arm, and Jack and Edie each breathed a sigh of relief. Coco leaped from Prue as soon as he caught sight of Aggie and bounded towards her.

'Coco!' Aggie pulled the little dog to her, beaming. He was trembling but otherwise seemed in rude health, wagging his tail at finding himself back among people he trusted.

'Poor thing was whimpering in a corner, scared out of his wits,' Prue said as she crawled back under the table.

'What did you see out there?' Edie asked in a low voice.

'Fires, down in the village. I couldn't tell what was burning. There's a lot of smoke and ash. I suppose we won't know all the damage until morning.'

Edie bowed her head. She'd been through this so many times before, but she never expected to be going through it here.

'I ought to be there,' she murmured. 'When the plane's gone, I'll cycle over and see what I can do to help.'

Jack shuffled closer to Prue as Aggie and Jimmy fussed over the puppy.

'Good with him, isn't she?' he said in a low voice.

'Yes, he really seems to bring out her motherly side. Something I would have sworn she didn't have the day she came to us.'

'She's a good lass really. All she needed was a bit of love.'

'Prue, won't you consider letting Coco stay?' Edie asked. 'Jack's right: it would do the children the world of good to have a pet.'

'Hmm. A conspiracy, is it?' But there was humour in Prue's eyes.

'Go on, Cheg,' Jack said, his previous chummy demeanour back now they were friends again. 'Let them keep the dog. I'll help them look after him, and he'll be a good little ratter for the gardens. You know the beggars had half our strawberries last year.'

'I'll think about it.' She shook her head. 'Where the devil is Matilda? She shouldn't stay in her room when for all we know chunks of the roof are about to start falling in.'

'I'll go see what's keeping her,' Edie said. The children didn't seem to need her quite so much now they had the dog to keep their attention. The comical chap was wobbling on his haunches like a furry Humpty Dumpty, making them laugh.

Edie headed to Tilly's room, flinching at the sound of another explosion from outside.

'Till?' she said, knocking on the door. 'You'd better come down. It's not safe in here.'

There was no answer so she peeped in.

'Oh my goodness,' she murmured.

Tilly was stretched out on the bed, her face pale and

drenched with sweat. Her breathing was ragged, and, as Edie entered, she let out a low moan.

'I'm so sorry, Edie,' she whispered, convulsing as birthing pains tore through her body. 'I hate to be a bother, but I think the baby's coming.'

Chapter 24

Edie stared for a moment, shock rendering her mute. But the pain etched on Tilly's face forced her to recover herself. She came forward to take her friend's hand.

'Oh, Till,' she whispered.

Tilly smiled feebly. 'I pick my moments, don't I?'

'I'll get Prue. She'll know what to do.'

Tilly grasped her hand as she turned to leave.

'Don't tell the little ones,' she whispered. 'They must be frightened to death already.'

Edie nodded, then hurried back downstairs.

'Mrs Hewitt, can you come upstairs for a moment?' she said with a falsely bright smile.

Prue frowned. 'Is there something wrong?'

'I need to show you something on the second floor.'

'The bombs didn't –'

'Just come, please,' Edie said, not entirely managing to keep the panic out of her voice.

Prue took one look at her face and got to her feet.

'Children, stay here with Coco and Uncle Jack,' Prue told them. 'Edie and I will be back shortly.'

Luckily Aggie and Jimmy were immersed in the all-consuming business of playing with their puppy, and they only nodded absently. Jack flashed her a worried look, but he didn't say anything.

'What is it?' Prue murmured when they reached the privacy of the hall.

'The baby's coming,' Edie whispered back.

'What? But she isn't due for six weeks!'

'Perhaps it was the bombs. That can happen, can't it? A sudden fright can bring it on early.' Edie didn't know where she'd heard that, but she was sure it was right.

'Right,' Prue said, recovering from her initial shock. 'I'll phone for Dr MacKenzie.'

There was a telephone in the hall. Prue consulted the little leather book beside it, then lifted the receiver and dialled.

She held it against her ear for a moment before hanging up, frowning.

'It's not ringing.'

'Do you think anyone was hurt in the raid?' Edie asked. 'He might be needed elsewhere.'

'It ought still to ring. I think it's more likely the bombs have damaged some of the telephone lines.'

'But what can we do?' Edie was feeling dizzy, and gripped the banister to steady herself. 'She's in so much pain, and if the baby's early they could both be in danger. Is there anyone else in the village who could help?'

'We don't even know what's left of the village,' Prue said in a low voice. 'The bombs could have hit anywhere.'

The notion that Applefield might have been half-flattened by an explosion, as so many areas of London had been, froze Edie to the marrow.

Prue stood in silence for a moment, her face working with worry. Then she drew herself up, and Edie saw her assume the no-nonsense expression that at first she'd feared, and then grown to trust.

'Let's go to Matilda,' Prue said.

Tilly was lying as Edie had left her, face white and drawn with pain.

'I think . . . the pains are getting closer together,' she panted. 'Is . . .' She paused to hiss through her teeth. 'Prue, is the doctor coming?'

Prue took her hand.

'Not yet,' she said gently. 'We can't reach him by telephone.' She cast a look at Edie. 'I'll have to walk into the village to fetch him.'

'Prue, no!' Edie whispered. 'It isn't safe.'

The bombs and machine gun fire had stopped now, and she was hopeful that the flying pencil, as Dornier Do 17s were nicknamed, was on its way back to the Fatherland. But there would be fires, falling rubble, perhaps unexploded bombs . . .

Tilly gripped Prue's hand tightly, and turned pain-filled eyes up to her.

'Luca,' she managed to gasp.

'Of course!' Edie said. 'Prue, Luca's a doctor. He can help us.'

Prue turned to look at her. 'But he's a prisoner. I doubt he'll be allowed to leave the farm at night.'

'This is an emergency though. Who else is there? Even if you find the doctor, he might have his hands full with injured people.'

Tilly seemed to be in a mild delirium now, twisting in pain as she repeated 'Luca, Luca' in a faint whisper.

'I'll go for him,' Edie said. 'If I take my bike I can be there in ten minutes, and I'm sure Sam would lend us the truck to get back.'

Prue shook her head. 'You mustn't, Edie! You said yourself it wasn't safe.'

243

'It has to be me. Jack's barely recovered from the shock of the attack, and I don't think you can ride a bike, can you?'

'Well, no, but . . .'

'Then it's settled. You take care of Tilly, I'll go for Luca.' She came forward to squeeze Tilly's hand. 'Hold on, sweetheart,' she said gently. 'I'll be back before you know it.'

The bomber had definitely gone when Edie mounted her bicycle and headed in the direction of Larkstone Farm. She could hear shouts in the distance though, and a couple of big fires blazed on the horizon. It sounded as though the villagers were trying to organise a chain to extinguish them. Edie felt a twinge of guilt that she was heading in the opposite direction, until she reminded herself she was on her own errand of mercy.

She reached the farmhouse in record time and was soon knocking, breathless, at Sam's door.

He blinked in surprise when he opened it.

'London! What the hell are you doing out in an air raid? Here, get inside.'

He tried to pull her into the comparative safety of the farmhouse, but she resisted.

'No . . . time,' she gasped. 'Need . . . Luca. Baby's coming.'

'Baby . . . baby!' His eyes widened. 'Tilly's baby is coming now?'

Your baby too, Edie found herself thinking, but this was no time for recriminations.

'Yes. We can't get through to the doctor – Prue thinks the phone lines are damaged. Please, Sam. She's six weeks early and the baby could be in danger. We need a doctor – we need Luca.'

'Right.' Suddenly he was all efficiency. 'He's down in the

cellar with Davy and Marco. Chuck your bike in the back of the truck and we'll be there in a minute.'

'There's no need for you to come. I can drive it.'

'You'll need me if you get stopped by police or military, unless you fancy explaining where you think you're driving to in the middle of the night with an Italian prisoner of war. Luca's my responsibility.'

That was true. She nodded agreement and went to wait by the truck while he explained the situation to Luca.

Luca was quiet during the drive to the manor – in shock, perhaps, from the bombs. Of course, he had some traumatic memories of his own to match Jack Graham's.

'Sam, you'd better wait in the library,' Edie said when she'd ushered the two men into Applefield Manor. 'Luca, I'll take you to Tilly.'

But Luca was already bounding up the stairs. Edie hurried to follow. He seemed to know where he was going, and she caught up with him just as he flung open the door to Tilly's room.

'Where is she?' he demanded. 'Where is my wife?'

His . . . Had she heard him correctly?

'Luca,' Tilly whispered, stretching out a weak hand to him. 'Here, love.'

He knelt down beside her, took her hand and kissed the fingers feverishly.

'My darling, does it hurt very much?' he asked softly.

'It hurts. My God, it hurts. But everything's all right now you're here.'

'Did he say his wife?' Edie whispered to Prue.

'Yes. But never mind about that,' Prue said. 'Dr Bianchi, what do you need from us?'

'Soap and hot water. And towels, as many towels as you can find – hot, if that is possible,' Luca said, throwing off his tunic and unbuttoning his shirt cuffs. 'If you have any brandy, that will be very welcome also.' He turned back to Tilly, gentling his voice. 'How long between your contractions, *cara mia*?'

'I'm . . . not sure. They've been getting closer.'

'I know,' Prue said. 'I've been timing them. There were five minutes between the last two.'

'And they lasted how long?' Luca asked.

'A minute, or perhaps a little less.'

'You would have made a splendid nurse, Mrs Hewitt,' Luca said, managing a smile even though his face was drawn with worry. 'Now. The towels, please.'

'I'll get them,' Edie said, pushing aside her shock at what now seemed so obvious: the true paternity of her friend's baby. Tilly hadn't asked for Luca because he was a doctor. She'd asked for him because he was the father . . . her lover. 'I can warm them in the oven. Prue, put the water on and I'll be down with all the towels I can find in a moment.'

'Keep one pan of water boiling,' Luca instructed. 'We shall need it for sterilisation.'

'I'm so glad they let you come,' Edie heard Tilly whisper to Luca as she left the room. 'I wanted you so.'

Edie collected up all the towels in the linen cupboard then grabbed two that were hanging on hooks in the bathroom, along with a bar of toilet soap. When she went downstairs, Prue had lit the oven and three saucepans filled with water were simmering on the cooker.

'Here, I'll take those,' Prue said, holding out her arms for the towels. 'I brought one of the old sheets I use to cover the furniture. If we wrap them in that, we can warm them inside the oven without them getting dirty.'

Jack peered around the door.

'How is she?' he asked.

246

'Better now she has a doctor,' Prue said. 'Are the bairns all right?'

'Aye, coping. Frightened, but they've the little pup to comfort them. I'm making up a bed for them under the table. They feel safer there, and they won't hear anything that might scare them.'

'Yes, you better had. If the baby . . . if there's bad news at the end of this, we don't want them witnessing anything that's likely to upset them.' She flashed him a wobbly smile. 'Thank you, Jack. You're such a help to me.'

Jack didn't have an answer to that, other than a 'humph' that sounded more pleased than annoyed. He nodded once and left.

Prue had a large, clean pail ready for the water. She poured in the contents of two of the saucepans, turning the third down to a low heat.

'Do you think you could carry that upstairs?' she asked Edie, nodding to the pail.

'Yes, I can manage. What about the brandy though?' Edie couldn't recall ever seeing spirits in Applefield Manor.

'I suspect you'll find a little whisky in Bertie's room if you hunt around. It's the second on the right.'

Edie nodded and went to the kitchen door with the pail handle gripped in both hands. She paused and looked back at Prue.

'Is she really his wife?'

'So I understand,' Prue said. 'Sanctioned by God if not by the law.'

'And you knew?'

'Yes. But never mind about that now.'

'You don't really think the baby could die, do you?'

Prue sighed. 'I dearly hope it won't, but it's a possibility. Get along with the water now, Edie.'

Edie headed upstairs, thankful for the little bit of muscle she'd managed to build as a Land Girl. Still, she had to stop a number of times while getting the heavy pail to Tilly's room.

She could hear her friend's groans echoing along the hallway as birthing pains ripped through her body. That must mean the baby was nearly here, surely.

Edie's thoughts were no longer dwelling on Luca and Tilly's relationship, or on anything else. All that was echoing in her brain was the same pleading prayer, over and over: *please let it live, please let it live, please let it live . . .*

She found her friend covered by a sheet, her knees up and spread wide with Luca kneeling between them. Edie felt embarrassed at the intimacy of the scene, as if she'd walked in on them on their wedding night.

Immediately she berated herself for being so foolish. She, who had delivered countless lambs over the past few months. She knew the facts of life well enough, so why did the schoolgirl blushes still come?

'I, um . . . here's the water,' she said, putting the pail down by Luca while trying to avert her eyes from her friend's immodest position. 'And the soap.' She handed it to him. 'The towels will be here in a moment. I might have to hunt for some whisky though – there isn't any brandy.'

'Yes, yes,' Luca said distractedly. 'Yes, whisky, as soon as you can.' He looked up over the sheet at Tilly's flushed, sweat-drenched face. 'You are doing wonderfully, brave girl. Keep pushing.'

Tilly moaned loudly as she strained, and Edie quietly made her exit.

Her next stop was Bertie's room. She'd never been in before, and cast a curious look around.

Edie's first thought was that it was the room of a boy

248

who was only just becoming a man: pictures of cowboys, Spitfires and pin-up girls adorned the walls, while cigarette cards and comics littered the dresser. And, yes: when she opened the wardrobe, she found a half-empty bottle of Scotch nestling inside one of his boots. Bertie had obviously thought it very slyly hidden from his mother. Edie snatched it up and dashed back to Tilly's room.

Prue was there, putting the towels down by Luca. Unlike Edie, she showed no embarrassment. She'd been through this herself, of course.

'I've got whisky,' Edie said, holding it up.

'There is a tablespoon on the dresser. Measure out two spoonfuls and give them to her,' Luca instructed. 'It is not an ideal anaesthetic but we are forced to make do with what we have. Mrs Hewitt, please take one of the towels and place under her body.'

With quiet calm, Prue did as she was asked. Edie measured out the whisky and gave it to Tilly. She had some trouble getting her friend to drink it, since her teeth were ground together in pain, and the first spoonful went mostly over the bedclothes. A second attempt was more successful, however.

'That ought to help a little with the pain,' Luca said. 'In twenty minutes, give her another two spoonfuls.' His face was intent with concentration. 'Another push, Matilda. I believe we will have the crown before long.'

Was the baby all right? Edie longed to ask if Luca could tell whether or not it lived, but she knew better than to do so in Tilly's hearing. Whatever the outcome, her friend needed to keep on fighting.

For the next hour Edie stood at the head of the bed, holding Tilly's hand while Prue mopped her brow. Occasionally, on Luca's instruction, Edie administered more whisky. It seemed to be a careful calculation, this method of killing pain: enough to ease Tilly's discomfort a little, but not so much that she ceased pushing as hard as she could.

The room was close and hot, filled with the fecund smells of blood, sweat and steaming flesh. A low-wattage lightbulb – dimmed further by a blackout-friendly paper lampshade – was the room's only illumination, creating a sense of pervading gloom. Edie dabbed her sweat-sodden face constantly until she found that her handkerchief was drenched, and her hair, stuffed into a snood, was a damp mass against the back of her neck. As they drew towards the finish, the only sounds were Tilly's pants and, every minute or so, a scream of raw pain.

And all the time, Edie's fervent prayer echoed in her head: *please let it live, please let it live, please let it live. Please, God, if I ever did anything good in my whole life, let Tilly and the baby both live.*

She had heard someone else make a bargain like that, once upon a time. He'd paid for it with his life. As Tilly's screams once again rent the air, Edie clenched her eyes shut, touched one finger to her watch chain and promised with all her heart that if that was what it took, she would gladly give her own life to save Tilly and the baby.

Finally the one sound she hadn't expected to hear cut through the silence. Laughter: the desperate, joyous, relieved sound of laughter. Luca's laughter.

'A little girl, by Jove!' he cried out in delight. 'One more push, Matilda, and we shall have all of her. Mrs Hewitt, I would be very grateful to borrow a pair of your scissors, if you are first able to sterilise them for me.'

Prue rushed to fetch the scissors and Edie gripped Tilly's hand for one final effort. Her last shout was filled with joyous triumph as the baby, finally, was pushed free of her body. Edie heard a slap as Luca smacked it on the bottom, and then the most wonderful sound in the world – the sound of a healthy baby screaming its head off – filled the room.

Tilly laughed then, and cried too: tears of sheer joy and relief. Wordlessly she held out her arms for her child.

Prue had slipped through the door with the sterilised scissors some half a minute earlier. Luca expertly cut the umbilical cord, then wrapped the baby – pink, wrinkled and beautiful – in a towel and placed it gently in its mother's arms. He knelt down at Tilly's side and rested his head against her, a picture of exhaustion and happiness.

'Oh, darling, look at her,' Tilly whispered, fixing a gaze of wondering adoration on the baby. 'Our little miracle.' She cuddled the child to her and pressed her lips to its head. Baby Bianchi, sensing this was where she was meant to be, stopped crying and gave an approving gurgle.

'Yes,' Luca whispered, blinking back tears. He took one of his little daughter's hands and gazed at the tiny but perfectly formed fingers that wrapped instinctively around one of his. 'I don't believe I ever saw anything more beautiful. Except her mother, of course.'

Tilly laughed, turning her face bashfully away. 'Give over. I've just had a baby, I must look like death.'

'You're more beautiful to me now than the day I saw you first,' he said, kissing her forehead. 'Yes, today I am the luckiest man in the world.'

Edie felt Prue pluck her elbow.

'Come on,' she whispered. 'We'll leave them alone.'

They slipped quietly out into the hall, the new mother and father so wrapped up in each other and their baby that they barely noticed them leave.

Edie wasn't sure what made her do it. The whole experience had been so frightening, so wonderful, so emotional and life-affirming and utterly terrifying, she couldn't help herself. She threw her arms around the older woman and hugged her tight, sobs of relief and happiness shaking her body.

Prue seemed taken aback for a moment, but she soon recovered and patted Edie on the shoulder.

'You were very brave, Edie. I was proud of you, dear.'

'Thank you.' Edie laughed wetly as she released Prue from the hug. 'Gosh, I'm sorry. I don't know what came over me. I . . . I was so afraid Tilly and the baby might die. She's such a tiny thing, isn't she?'

'With a hefty pair of lungs,' Prue said, laughing. 'I nearly went deaf when Luca gave her a smack. I ought to let the children know the baby arrived healthy. They had better take the day off school tomorrow, I think, after the night they've had.'

Edie's eyes widened. 'Oh my goodness, Sam!'

Prue frowned. 'Sam?'

'Yes, he's in the library. I'd better tell him the baby's here. And . . .' She winced. 'I owe him an apology.'

Chapter 25

Edie found Sam sitting in an armchair, staring at the *Picture Post*. It was open, but she could tell from the glazed look in his eyes that his mind was elsewhere – that and the fact he was holding it upside down. He looked up when she came in.

'Is it all right?' he demanded.

She nodded. 'A healthy baby girl. Mother and baby both doing well.'

He let out a low whistle of relief. 'Thank God. Luca would've been devastated.'

'Yes. I can only imagine how horrific it must be to lose your wife and child.'

He glanced at her in surprise. 'He told you?'

'It slipped out in the heat of the moment.' She shook her head. 'You knew. And yet you let me believe . . . why, Sam?'

'Here. Come outside where we won't be overheard, if you're going to start with your questions.'

She followed him out to the ornamental fountain. He took a seat on the stone circle that ran around the edge, and Edie sat down beside him.

'Why did you lie?' she asked.

He shrugged. 'I didn't really. People decided I was the father and I chose not to correct them.'

'Why did you choose not to?'

'I told you, they can think what they want for my money. People made up their minds about me the day I got here. Sixteen years old, and they had me branded from the outset. Doesn't bother me.'

He wasn't looking at her, but staring out over the grounds. Edie watched him, one eye narrowed.

'I don't believe you,' she said.

'Excuse me?'

She smiled. 'You're not so tough, Sam Nicholson. You did it for them, didn't you? Tilly and Luca.'

'Don't talk daft.'

'Why are you so friendly with the POWs, Sam? I'm guessing you're not really a fifth columnist.'

He turned to her, and something in her expression must have amused him. He broke into a smile.

'You know, London, I never knew a girl like you for asking questions.'

She grinned. 'If you answer them, maybe I'll stop.'

'Huh. Chance'd be a fine thing.' He looked at the house, shining silver under the light of a full moon. 'Perhaps I feel something kin to them. I know how it feels to be the outsider.'

'Luca obviously thinks a lot of you.'

'Aye, well, I think a lot of him. He's a good man.'

Edie waited in silence, sensing he'd confide in her of his own accord, and she was right. After a minute, he spoke again.

'I was angry when I found out what had been going on,' he told her. 'A prisoner of war carrying on with a Land Girl: it could have got Luca into a lot of trouble. He'd have lost his right to work outside the camp, that was certain. Then when Luca told me they'd fallen in love – well, they're sentimental buggers, these Italians, always making a bloody opera out of everything, but I could tell he meant it. So like the soft lad I am, I ended up promising I'd help them keep the secret.'

'That's why Tilly visits you at the farm.'

He laughed. 'She doesn't visit me at all. I'm just chaperone when she drops in to see her old man, and postmaster general when they want me to pass letters between them.'

'Are they really married?'

'After a fashion. Not in law, of course, and won't be unless they lift the ban on marrying enemy aliens. But they took communion together in the little chapel in one of my barns, and exchanged vows. Marco and I were witnesses. Married before God if not before Man, I suppose you could say.'

'That ring she wears . . .'

Sam smiled. 'Luca made it for her out of a two-bob bit. Not much of a wedding ring but she never takes it off.'

Edie fell silent. There was one thing that still bothered her.

'You said you asked Tilly to marry you and she refused.'

'Aye, that much was true. I did ask.'

'Were you in love with her?'

He laughed. 'Romantic soul, aren't you, London? No, course I wasn't in love with her. The girl was in trouble and . . . well, I'm not such a mean bastard that it didn't tug on the old heartstrings. I hated to think of a young lass and bairn all on their own in the world, sneered at by the sort of people who are always first in the queue to chuck a few stones. So I made her an offer.'

'But she turned it down.'

'That's right. She's already married, as far as she's

255

concerned, and she'd rather wait until Luca can legally make an honest woman of her than save face now with me. Can't say I blame her. I probably wouldn't have been much cop as a husband any road.'

Edie reached over to rest a hand on his.

'That was a very noble thing to do,' she said softly.

'Bloody stupid thing to do. But if I had it all to do over again, I'd not act any differently.'

She smiled. 'You know, the village is right about you, Sam: you are a coward. You're scared to death of them finding out what a decent chap you really are, aren't you?'

'All right, keep your voice down,' he said, with the hint of a grin. 'You'll ruin my reputation with that sort of talk.'

'Sam, I'm sorry. I shouldn't have been so quick to jump to conclusions about you.'

His mouth flickered. 'That makes two of us then, eh?'

He glanced down at her hand over his, then into her eyes.

'You look like hell, you know, London,' he said softly.

She flushed. It was funny: he'd just insulted her, but in a voice so laced with gentleness, with eyes so full of tender solicitude, that it had felt like the most beautiful compliment in the world.

'Well, I just helped to deliver a baby,' she said, attempting a lighthearted tone. 'It's not an experience designed to get you looking your best.'

'Oh, I don't know. I'd say it suits you.'

He ran one finger over her cheek, the skin of his fingertip rough but so, so gentle. She looked up to meet his gaze, and discovered his face close to hers.

He's going to kiss me, came the sudden realisation. And

Edie realised she wanted him to. That maybe she'd always wanted him to . . .

Her eyes had started to close when a voice pierced the air, calling her name. Prue's voice. The spell was broken, and hastily she turned her face away.

'We, um . . . they must be wondering where we are,' she said, feeling flustered. 'We'd better go back.'

'All right,' Sam said with a calm self-assurance that irritated her. Wasn't his heart hammering against his ribs the way hers was, damn him? 'I'm sure we can continue this another time.'

Prue was waiting for them at the door, looking younger and prettier than Edie had ever seen her. Her hair had come down while they'd been on nursing duty, and she seemed unconscious of the way it hung becomingly loose over her shoulders, or of the fresh pinkness in her cheeks. How different she was from the Prue of a few hours earlier, who'd so angrily demanded Coco be sent away and made little Aggie cry. Jack stood at her side with a sort of possessive pride, for all the world as if they were new grandparents.

Edie was worried Prue might demand to know what she and Sam had been doing outside, but her thoughts were occupied elsewhere.

'We just took the children to meet the baby,' she told Edie. 'They were so excited, the loves. They're back in bed in their room now, but I don't suppose there'll be much sleeping done tonight, especially not with the puppy running around. Tilly and Luca have asked for the two of you to go up. They've chosen a name.'

'What is it?' Edie asked.

'Don't tell them, Cheggy,' Jack said, laughing. 'We promised we'd keep it a secret.'

257

Prue smiled. 'Not a word.'

They found the new mother sitting serenely up in bed with her baby in her arms. Luca was in a chair by his wife, glowing with pride.

'Sam, my dear, dear friend!' He leaped from the chair to kiss Sam enthusiastically on each cheek in the continental fashion, then began pumping his hand vigorously. 'Now, come and look at my little girl, and try not to swoon at how beautiful she is. I am only sorry I have no cigars to give you.'

Sam laughed as he tried to flex some feeling back into his fingers.

'She's a real bobby-dazzler, Luca,' he said as he leaned over Tilly to look at the sleeping infant. 'We'll wet her head at the farmhouse tomorrow, if you promise not to tell your commandant I let you have a booze-up.'

Edie approached Tilly. She didn't say anything, but she gave her friend's shoulder a squeeze that she tried to fill with everything she was feeling. Tilly looked up with an expression of such joy that Edie felt tears pricking her eyes once again.

'Thank you,' Tilly mouthed, and Edie nodded.

'What's her name then, Luca?' Sam asked.

'For her middle names, we have chosen Edith and Prudence, after my two tireless nurses.' He slapped Sam on the back. 'And her first name shall be Samantha, after the kind friend who has done so much to help us. Samantha Edith Prudence Bianchi.'

'Or Liddell for now,' Tilly said. 'We still have a secret to keep, darling.'

'Ah, but not for long.' Luca snatched up her hand and pressed it to his lips. 'Soon, *bella*, the war will be over and we shall be married in law as we are in spirit.'

Sam had turned away when Luca had told him the baby's name, and Edie was sure his eyes were damp when he faced them again.

'Thank you,' he said. 'I only hope she grows up to be a better person than her namesake.'

'Well, we know that if she grows up to be even half as kind, selfless and humane as her namesake, she'll be a daughter we can be proud of,' Tilly said earnestly.

Sam laughed. 'I wish you wouldn't talk about me like that in front of Edie. You know how proud I am of my reputation as a miserable bastard.'

'Tsk. Such language,' Luca whispered to the baby. 'Now, Samantha, I hope you will not let your Uncle Sammy teach you any bad words.'

'I asked Prue and Jack to be godparents,' Tilly told them. 'We want Marco to make a third, but that will have to be unofficial. He won't be able to attend the christening.'

Sam had gravitated towards the bed again, and Edie smiled at the expression of curious wonderment on his face as he looked at the baby. Tentatively he ran his big, rough fingers over her head, and Samantha wriggled in her sleep.

'She's got your hair, Luca,' he said softly. The child did indeed have a thick mop of black hair, much like her father's dark curls.

'And my big mouth,' Tilly said, smiling. 'You should have heard her yell, Sam. We could use her as an air-raid siren.'

There was a knock at the door, and Prue popped her head around it.

'Sam, I've made up a bed for Luca in one of the empty rooms, if that's acceptable to you. You're welcome to stay as well.'

'No.' Reluctantly Sam turned away from the baby. 'I ought to go back. Marco and Davy will be worrying.' He clapped Luca on the back. 'You stay, old son, keep an eye on this little one. I can fetch you and Edie for work in the morning.'

'Thank you, boss. I do not deserve your kindness.'

'All right, that's enough of that. I'll see you tomorrow.' He cast a look at Edie. 'Both of you.'

Chapter 26

Baby Samantha acted as Edie's alarm clock the next morning, her shrill wails piercing the air a full half-hour before it was really time to get up. But, realising it was useless to go back to sleep, Edie got up anyway.

When she'd washed and dressed in her Land Girl uniform – now the summer costume of light fawn dungarees and linen shirt, far more becoming than the bloomer-like breeches she had worn in the colder weather – Edie knocked softly at the door of Tilly's room. When she entered, Tilly was sitting up with a now quiet Samantha snuggled against her.

'Morning, Mummy,' Edie said with a broad smile. 'I thought I'd see if you wanted any breakfast bringing up before I go to work.'

'A cuppa certainly wouldn't go amiss,' Tilly said. 'But sit down first, Aunty Edie, and have a cuddle.'

Edie took Luca's seat by the bed and Tilly put the little wriggling parcel into her arms. From the folds of towelling a tiny pink face looked up at her, the baby's expression a mixture of curiosity about this new creature who was holding her and resentment at being parted from her mother.

'Aww.' Edie touched her fingertip to Samantha's nose. 'Till, she's just . . . I don't have the words. Glorious. Well done, you clever lady.'

'Well, I can't say I'd recommend childbirth but the results make it worth it.' Tilly winced as she shifted her position. 'Oof. It's going to be a few weeks until I'm back on my feet, Luca tells me. I'm sorry to leave you fending for yourselves, but I'm sure between Prue and Aggie you'll be well provided for.'

'How are you feeling this morning? Are you very sore?'

'Horrendously. Every inch of me hurts.' She winced again. 'Some inches a lot more than others.'

'What did it feel like?'

'Well . . . have you ever sneezed up a football?'

Edie laughed. 'No, funnily enough.'

'Your time will come, young Edie.' Tilly smiled as Samantha shoved her chubby little fist into Edie's cheek. 'She's a madam, isn't she? I was really hoping she might take after her father rather than me but no such luck.'

Edie arrested the exploring baby fingers and pressed them to her lips.

'Why didn't you tell me, Till?' she said quietly.

Tilly sighed. 'I wanted to. Gosh, I've longed for someone to talk to – a friend my own age, not just Prue, although she's been lovely.'

'And yet you didn't tell me.'

'It was what you said that first week you worked at the farm,' Tilly murmured. 'About him being the enemy; that suspicion in your voice. You seemed so sort of . . . idealistic, Edie, about the importance of the war effort and all that stuff on the posters. You were such a new friend then, and I . . . I suppose I'm a coward really. I couldn't bear the idea you might think less of me.'

'Of course I wouldn't.' Edie reached out to take her hand. 'What I said about Luca, then . . . I was naive. Really, I was such a little girl when I came here. I didn't realise that things are always more complicated than just black and white.'

'Well, I'm glad you know finally. I think the worst thing was how unfair it felt on poor Sam, having you think he was the sort of bounder who'd do that to a girl. I know his manners can be abrupt, but he's really a lovely man.'

'I know,' Edie said, flushing slightly. 'We had a talk last night and he explained it all to me.'

Tilly smiled. 'Did he now?'

'So what do you and Luca have planned for after the war?' Edie asked, deciding that a swift change of subject was in order. 'Will he stay here with you, or will you go to live in Naples?'

'We haven't decided,' Tilly said. 'I do want to make a new start, but I expect where we eventually settle will depend on who wins the war.'

A few months ago, Edie might have been shocked at such an unorthodox statement. In London, none of her set had dared to question that anyone but the Allies would ultimately triumph – out loud, at any rate. But the older, wiser Edie of today only nodded.

'Where is Luca now?' she asked.

'He's been up all night, watching over us. The bed Prue made up for him never even got slept in. He only went out an hour ago, saying he had something he wanted to do before work.' Tilly sighed. 'You know, I used to dream of falling in love with a man in uniform. I must say, those horrible grey things the prisoners wear wasn't exactly what I had in mind, but I couldn't help it, Ede. Isn't he wonderful?'

Edie smiled. 'After last night, I'm not going to argue. He's certainly a wonderful doctor, and I already knew he was a wonderful man. A born father too, it seems to me.'

Samantha was starting to get restless now, and Tilly reached out to take her back.

'She wants her breakfast,' she said as the baby made greedy sucking noises at her mother's chest. 'I'd better give her a feed. Don't worry about that cup of tea, Edie. I can do without until Prue's awake.'

'No, I'll bring it. Sam won't be here to fetch us to work for a little while yet.'

She left Tilly unbuttoning her nightdress and was about to head downstairs when she noticed a little face peeping at her from behind the door of the children's room.

'Aggie. It's very early, dear. What are you doing awake?'

'The baby woke me up,' Aggie said in a low, reverent voice. 'Jimmy fell back to sleep but I couldn't. Edie, please may I help make them breakfast? Tilly and Baby Samantha?'

'Well, Samantha is having her breakfast now but you can help me make Tilly a cup of tea if you like.'

Aggie beamed and closed the door gently behind her. Tiny Coco, her new partner in crime, was bouncing at her feet.

'Oh, no,' Edie said, smiling as she picked the little dog up. 'Sorry, Aggie, but Coco will have to stay here with Jimmy. He's pushed his luck far enough without us letting him run riot in the kitchen.'

Luca's whereabouts were soon accounted for when Edie heard an Italian air ringing out in his familiar baritone from the direction of the kitchen.

'Who is it singing?' Aggie whispered.

'It's Luca – you remember him?'

She nodded. 'That prisoner. I seen him last night. Is he allowed to sleep here then?'

'Well, not usually, but this was a special circumstance. The doctor in the village couldn't come to bring the baby because of the bombs, so I went to fetch Luca from the farm. He's a doctor too.'

'So he brung the baby, the Italian man?'

'That's right. He's been up all night, taking care of Tilly and Samantha, so we must be very nice to him.'

That seemed to satisfy Aggie's curiosity, and Edie was relieved that she didn't ask any further questions about Luca's overnight stay.

Luca stopped his song when they entered the kitchen and looked up to smile at them. For a man who'd not slept a wink, he looked very fresh – buoyed up, perhaps, by the joy of new fatherhood.

'Ah, assistants. Just what I need.' He was putting rolled dough circles on to baking sheets while a pan of sieved tomatoes simmered on the cooker. 'Aggie, now you shall learn how to make real Italian food.'

'What are you making, Luca?' Edie asked.

'Lunch. I thought it would be helpful to Mrs Hewitt if I were to prepare it, now the house will be without its cook for a little while. I hope Mr Graham will not mind me purloining a few things from his gardens.'

'But what is it?'

'*Pizza*, a Neapolitan dish – a little like your Welsh rabbit, only a hundred times more delicious. Risen with yeast is best, but I lacked the time, sadly, so you must have your *pizze* unleavened today.'

'May I help make them please, Miss?' Aggie asked, looking hopefully up at Edie. Baking with Tilly was her favourite hobby, although the little girl always managed to mysteriously vanish when it came time to do the washing-up.

Edie smiled, noting how much improved the child's manners were. 'Yes, you may. Let Luca show you what to do while I make Tilly's tea.'

'The patient is awake then?' Luca said as he took the simmering mixture of tomatoes and herbs from the hotplate.

Edie nodded. 'Giving the baby her breakfast.'

'Ah, good. Samantha will soon grow big and strong with an appetite like she has.' He spooned a little of the tomato mixture on to one of the dough discs and spread it thin using the back of the spoon. 'This is how we do it, Aggie, and then we add sliced cheese. Do you think you can do that?'

Aggie nodded vigorously and started slopping the mixture on to one of the circles. Luca stood by, giving her instructions.

'No, not too much. A spoonful or so in the centre, then spread outwards. Be sure to leave half an inch for a crust – yes, so. Good, *patatina*! Aggie, you shall be a master chef one day.'

Aggie giggled, and Edie smiled to herself. She'd been right in what she'd said earlier: Luca was going to make a wonderful father. What a cruel business the war was, to keep the young family apart.

She was detained by Tilly for a few minutes when she took up the tea, and when she re-entered the kitchen she found that Luca and Aggie's conversation had moved on.

'No, Aggie, I do not believe there is anything I could do to help,' Luca was saying.

'Not with medicine or anything?'

Luca looked sober as the little girl blinked up at him with wide, trusting eyes.

'What's the matter, Ag?' Edie asked.

Aggie looked uncertain, as if she'd been caught talking about something she shouldn't, but Luca filled the silence.

'Aggie wonders if there is anything I can do to help your Mr Graham,' he said. 'I believe she greatly overestimates my skill as a doctor.'

'I didn't mean anything wrong, Miss,' Aggie said. 'I didn't like to think of Uncle Jack having them bad nightmares you said about. I wanted to help him.'

'That's OK,' Edie said gently. 'You won't ever get in trouble for trying to do a good deed, Aggie.'

'Doctors can help with nightmares sometimes, can't they?' Aggie said to Luca. 'Our dad used to get stuff to help him sleep better.'

'A sleeping powder can bring heavier sleep but it does not fix the problem.' Luca's eyes were far away, filled with a pain of their own. 'The nightmare is still there. It is only pushed deeper inside.'

'So there's not nothing you could do for Uncle Jack?' Aggie asked. 'I thought it'd be much more easy to fix bad dreams than bring a baby and you done that.'

'To bring a baby is a simple task compared to healing someone's memories.' Luca sounded as though he was talking to himself. 'That is not medicine. That is exorcism.'

The child looked puzzled, and Luca, remembering who he was talking to, summoned a smile.

'Well, I know one thing that can help with bad memories: lots of new, fresh good memories. The best thing you can do for your Uncle Jack, Aggie, is to help him make happy memories. You could do that better than any doctor, could you not?'

Aggie brightened. 'Oh, I reckon I can do that all right.'

'Then from now on he shall be your patient, my little

nurse. Mind you give your report to Edie every week so she can tell me how he gets along.'

'I will.'

'You are going to be needed a lot here now, Aggie. Matilda will be in bed for some weeks, and there is a new baby to take care of. Can Edie and Mrs Hewitt count on you to help them?'

Aggie nodded, her eyes sparkling. Coming from a home where she had been both unwanted and ignored, the idea of being needed – important – acted on the child like a tonic.

'I can do all the cooking,' she announced, puffing out her chest. 'I'm good at cooking, ain't I, Edie?'

Edie smiled. 'She is a brilliant cook,' she told Luca. 'Still, Ag, I think *all* the cooking will be a bit much with school too. We'll work together until Tilly feels well enough to go back to work.'

There was the sound of heavy tyres rolling up the gravel drive.

'Sam's truck.' Luca looked worried. 'I wonder what we will find at the farm today, Edie.'

So much had happened last night, Edie had almost forgotten about the bombing raid. How many of the ewes and their lambs had suffered? And what of the village: had it been badly damaged? With an unsettled feeling in the pit of her stomach, she followed Luca outside.

Chapter 27

'Get in,' Sam said with his usual lack of ceremony when they reached the battered truck. Luca jumped in the back and Edie climbed awkwardly into the front beside Sam. After what had happened – or at any rate, nearly happened – by the fountain, she was feeling oddly shy of him this morning. She wondered if they'd be working together today, and if so, what he might say . . . what he might do.

'How's the bairn?' he asked as he manoeuvred the vehicle out of the gates.

'As beautiful as her mother and as greedy as her father,' Luca said, smiling. 'She had the whole household awake at the break of morning, running around after her like the lady of the manor. She will become quite spoiled among the residents of Applefield Manor, I think.'

'And how are you, London?' Sam asked Edie quietly. He'd avoided looking at her so far, but he cast a quick glance in her direction before fixing his eyes back on the road.

'Tired but I expect I'll survive,' she said with a bashful smile. 'How's the farm, Sam?'

'Seems I got off lightly. Old Ted Cromwell on the

bordering heaf lost a score of his animals. Nine had their guts peppered with machine gun bullets, the rest just dropped of shock. And that's not counting the unborn lambs that died in their mothers.'

'Good God,' Edie muttered.

'What of our flock?' Luca asked. 'Did we lose many?'

'Eleven,' Sam said in a low voice. 'Five yows and six lambs, and I don't know how many abortions. It was a gruesome sight met me in the pens at sunrise.'

Edie tried not to imagine. The poor animals! No one thought how the war affected them.

'Good thing it wasn't earlier in the season,' Sam said. 'If this had happened in March we'd really be on our uppers. Unpredictable business at the best of times, lambing. One bad season can ruin you.'

Edie frowned as they took the road towards Kirkton.

'This isn't the way to the farm,' she said. 'Where are we going, Sam?'

'Where we're needed. Marco and Davy are going to have to manage on their own for a morning. I'm loaning us out to help with the clear-up at the Land Army hostel. They took a direct hit.'

'Oh my God! Are they . . . Vinnie and Barbara, are they . . .'

'Calm down, London,' he said in a soothing voice. 'No fatalities. Most of the girls were out at a dance, thank God. A couple who stayed behind suffered cuts and bruises, but nothing life-threatening. That's the report I got with my milk this morning.'

Applefield had a highly efficient method of news transmission. Sally Constance, the spinster daughter of the couple who owned the local dairy farm, stopped at every house she delivered milk to on the pretext of giving her ancient carthorse Betty a rest, but in reality to pick up all the gossip she could. This was then passed on to the next householder, who exchanged it for any news they might have, and so on.

'What of the village?' Luca asked. 'Was anyone hurt?'

'A few burned and bruised bodies, nowt that won't heal,' Sam answered. 'All the glass was blown out of Fred Braithwaite's shop when a bomb landed in the churchyard. Braithwaite was in the pub so he's all right, hangover aside.'

'Anything else?'

'There's a telegraph pole down, which accounts for the phones being out. The church had the worst of it though. Most of the roof's in.'

'Oh, poor Andrew,' Edie said feelingly. She couldn't help feeling that Tilly's kindly uncle really didn't deserve to have his church blown up when he already had the misfortune of sharing a home with Patricia. 'Is that all?'

'All the major damage. The church, the hostel and Cromwell's farm suffered most – the rest of the bombs fell in open country. We've been bloody lucky, considering.'

But it was hard to feel lucky when they arrived at the hostel and witnessed the devastation that had been wrought there. Edie's heart sank when she saw the mess of rafters and rubble where the dining room had once been, remembering how she'd enjoyed her first taste of grown-up flirtation right on this spot with Rob, so suave and handsome in his uniform.

Rob, too, was gone now. He'd been shot down on a mission the week before; Vinnie had broken the news the previous Saturday, the day after Sam had been probing Edie about her relationship with him. Edie, who had known the young flight lieutenant only fleetingly, had nevertheless shed many hot tears for a life so cruelly cut

271

short – nothing, of course, to the tears of his parents and loved ones.

This *bloody* war, where a few seconds could change someone's whole life – or take it from them. Dear God, would it ever end?

Two outbuildings that housed the girls' sleeping quarters looked to be mostly undamaged, although the glass in the windows had been shattered. But the farmhouse where they had eaten their meals and enjoyed their innocent revels was a mere shell now, destroyed by a crew who probably never spared a thought for the lives they might take when they dropped their bombs at random over the English countryside.

Gangs of Land Girls and villagers were picking through the detritus and putting out the small fires that still blazed in places, while members of the WVS served sandwiches and tea. Vinnie and Barbara, spotting Sam's truck, came to greet them.

'Oh good, it's you three.' Vinnie clapped Sam on the back. 'Thanks, boss, it was decent of you to spare us some manpower. We need all the help we can get here.'

'This is a rum do, isn't it, folks?' Barbara said with her usual unflappable good humour. 'I've just been hunting through the rubble for my last pair of silk stockings. I left them drying on the kitchen stove.'

'You girls all right, are you?' Sam asked in his gruff way, but Edie knew him well enough by now to sense the concern under his briskness.

'Yes, we always muddle through,' Vinnie said, with a fond look at Barbara.

Edie gave them each a hug. 'You must've been terrified.'

'We were at a dance in Kirkton with the other girls, but we came rushing back when we saw the fire and realised we'd been hit,' Barbara said. 'We've been lugging buckets of sand around all night.'

'Poor Dotty had a rough time,' Vinnie said. 'She was in bed with a cold when all the windows blew in. Got a few nasty bits of glass in the face.' She examined Edie. 'Are you all right, Ede? You look worn out. All three of you do.'

'Yes, it has been a busy night for us also,' Luca said. 'Matilda's baby decided she would join us during the raid. A most inconsiderate child. The doctor being unavailable, Edie asked if I might help.'

'The baby!' Barbara said. 'But it's early, isn't it? Is Tilly all right?'

'She is, and the proud mother of a healthy baby girl,' Edie said, smiling. 'Samantha.'

Barbara raised an eyebrow at Vinnie. It had occurred to Edie that the gossipmongers in the village would assume Samantha had been named after her father, but there was little to be done about that.

The warden came hurrying over, wearing a very different expression to that of the benevolent piano-playing matron Edie knew from the dances she'd attended here. Now she was all bustling efficiency.

'Ah, good. Men,' she said, nodding to Sam and Luca. 'I could do with a couple of those.'

Barbara sniggered, then hastily turned it into a cough.

'You boys, come with me,' the warden said. 'There are some heavy rafters you can help me shift, for a start.'

She clapped her hands and marched off, with Sam and Luca following like slightly bewildered puppies.

Vinnie laughed. 'Alison has quite an effect on men, doesn't she? She's a good sort. I hope they keep us all together when they find us another billet.'

'So what do we need to do here?' Edie asked.

'See what we can salvage from the rubble. Try to get the mess into neat piles for the powers that be to cart away. Put out the fires.' Barbara looked over the remains of the farmhouse and sighed. 'It's a shame, isn't it? We were happy here.'

Vinnie hooked her arm through her friend's. The two were silent for a moment, paying tribute to what they'd lost. Then they got to work.

After an hour's sifting through the rubble, Edie had managed to salvage a pile of hardback books – some fire-damaged and unreadable, but others worthy of a second life – a couple of chairs, a washboard, two gas masks and a print of the *Lusitania* in a cracked frame, plus a sizeable pile of scrap metal. The three of them then moved on to inspect the shed that housed the hostel's Austin Tilly, which had lost part of its roof.

'Oh no,' Barbara whispered when she went in.

'What is it?' Edie asked. The truck looked fine to her, other than a coating of thick dust from the fallen roof. But she soon spotted Barbara's grisly discovery.

It was Princess. The poor cat was on the floor, in a curled position as if asleep, but Edie didn't need to touch her to know she was dead. Her one eye was closed, never again to open.

'So there was a casualty after all,' Vinnie murmured.

Barbara knelt down by the dead cat and ran a hand gently over her fur.

'She doesn't look like she's been injured. It must've been the fright,' she whispered. 'Poor Princess, she was such a loving little thing. Vin, we'll have to bury her.'

Vinnie was standing by Edie, her head bowed. But she looked up as a strangled squeak emerged from somewhere.

'What is it?' Edie said. 'Rats?'

'I'm . . . not sure. Sounds like . . .'

Vinnie went to investigate the area behind the vehicle, poking about in the straw with the toe of her wellington.

'Oh crumbs. I thought so,' she said as another tiny squeak filled the air. 'Girls, come and see.'

Edie and Barbara went to join her, and Edie gasped. It was a nest of kittens – four tiny kittens, no more than a few weeks old, the same tabby colour as Princess. One little chap looked up at her with his big eyes and let out another squeaking mew.

'I thought Princess had been getting portly,' Barbara said. 'I assumed it was all the scraps she'd been scrounging.'

'Seems not.' Vinnie stretched out a finger to the crying kitten and he nibbled on the end, as if hoping it might produce milk. 'They're hungry. Whatever shall we do with them?'

'Poor darlings,' Edie murmured. 'The war must have orphaned so many animals. Do you think Sam might take them? Cats are always useful on farms.'

Vinnie shook her head. 'Too young. Their only chance of survival is regular bottle feeds, and Sam hasn't got time to play mother to a litter of kittens.'

'Could you take care of them?'

'We're getting moved on today,' Barbara said. 'They're putting us in an old Nissen hut out in the middle of nowhere, until a better billet can be arranged. I doubt they're going to let us bring pets.'

Edie looked at the kittens. They were old enough to have their eyes fully open and to stagger about on their drunken little legs, but they were really very tiny – four weeks at the most. So vulnerable and alone . . .

'I'll take them,' she said. 'We've got plenty of room at Applefield Manor.'

Barbara frowned. 'Will your landlady agree to that? I thought she was really strict.'

'I think I can talk her round,' Edie said, dearly hoping she was right.

Chapter 28

After a morning helping the Land Girls tidy up the remnants of their home, Sam, Edie and Luca returned to the farm. Vinnie and Barbara had remained behind to help with the relocation to their temporary billet, but the kittens came with them in the truck, mewling in a straw-filled box at Edie's feet.

'I don't know what you think you're going to do with those, London,' Sam said. 'They've got precious little chance of surviving, you know.'

'That's what you said about Wilf but he's still alive, isn't he?'

Wilf was the lamb Edie had discovered after her first day of work. Now two months old, he was as hardy a fellow as any of his mates, bounding around the fields with no memory of his early fight for life. He was a friendly little soul, too, after being hand-reared by Sam in the farmhouse. He would follow the farmer around like another sheepdog, taking Sadie's place at Sam's heel while she nursed her new puppies. Much to Sam's disapproval – or, as Edie suspected, his pretended disapproval – Edie had given the lamb a name, Wilfred, and the little chap's winning ways had made him a firm favourite among the farmhands. Edie had a strong suspicion that whatever happened to the other lambs born at Larkstone that spring, Wilf, at least, was safe from the butcher's block.

'Aye, and bloody hard work it was pulling him through,' Sam said gruffly. 'Constant feeds, all through the day and night. Who's going to do that for these noisy beggars? You?'

'Well . . . we can cross that bridge when we come to it.'

They were turning down the road that led to the farm now, and Edie put a hand on Sam's arm. As they were driving, a plan had been hatching – a plan to smuggle the orphaned kittens into Applefield Manor not only with Prue's consent, but with her whole-hearted approval. To convince her, in fact, that it had been her idea . . .

'Can you stop at the big house a moment?' Edie said.

'We've got work to do, in case you've forgotten, London,' Sam grunted. 'We've lost a morning already playing Good Samaritan, and we're two men down on top of that.'

'Please, I'll only be five minutes. I want to take the kittens inside. I don't suppose you want them at the farm, do you?'

Luca didn't say anything, but his face had lit up at the mention of a stop at Applefield Manor.

Sam sighed. 'All right, all right. If you're both going to be fluttering your eyelashes at me.'

Luca rested a hand on his shoulder. 'Thank you, boss.'

'I don't know what's up with me these days. Going soft in my old age.' But he was half smiling as he stopped the truck in front of the house. 'Hop out then, the pair of you. You've got five minutes to see to bairns, kittens and anything else, then it's heigh-ho and off to work we go.'

Edie picked up the boxful of kittens and entered the house by the back porch which led to the kitchen, while Luca went in through the front.

As Edie had suspected, Prue was in the kitchen, baking

the pancake-like things Luca had prepared for their lunch. They certainly smelled delicious while they cooked. The air was filled with the scent of baking bread, melting cheese and the aromatic tang of rosemary and ramsons, making Edie's mouth water.

Prue blinked. 'Edie. What are you doing home from work at this hour, child? I hope you're not sick.'

'No. I need to ask you for a favour.'

Prue eyed the box Edie was hugging suspiciously. 'All right, would you care to tell me why that box is meowing?'

Edie approached to let her see. Prue peered in, and four pairs of eyes looked back at her.

'Oh my goodness!'

'I found them,' Edie said. 'This morning, when Sam, Luca and I were helping to clean up the mess at the Land Army hostel. Their mother was killed in the air raid, the poor darlings.'

Prue's expression hardened as she deliberately turned her face away from the kittens and their little pleading eyes.

'Edith, in the past two months Applefield Manor has gained a Land Girl, two children, a puppy and a baby, all seemingly with me having little say in the matter,' she said. 'I'm not running a home for strays and orphans. I'm sorry, but the kittens will have to go elsewhere.'

'They will,' Edie said, wishing she had one hand free so she could cross her fingers behind her back. 'I just need someone to take care of them this afternoon. The Land Girls can't, they're moving to a new billet today, and I can't take them to work.'

'Edie –'

'Please, Prue. They'll die otherwise. Aggie and Jimmy can look after them, they'll enjoy that, and tomorrow I'll find new homes for them.'

Prue glanced into the box and Edie watched as her expression softened momentarily.

'Just today?' she said at last.

'Tomorrow at the latest.'

'And then they'll go to new homes?'

Edie nodded solemnly. 'Absolutely.'

Prue looked at the box of kittens in her arms, wondering how on earth she let herself be talked into these things.

When spring had arrived at Applefield Manor, all had been calm and serene: no outsiders, just herself, Jack and Matilda. Of course it wasn't perfect – there was still the war, and Bertie in danger out at sea. But it had been her little world, filled with people she knew and liked.

And now, as the spring became summer, Prue found her home bursting with life. First Edie had arrived, quickly disarming Prue with her girlish optimism, innocent soul and good sense. Then the children, so alien and hard at first, and now so very dear, although Prue hardly knew how to show it. Then last night the dog, and the new baby, and now . . .

One of the kittens, the tiniest one, met her eyes and let out a little mew. Prue absently tickled its ears.

The queer thing was, the unwelcome invasion was actually rather pleasant. The house had been full of joyous sounds this morning – the laughter of the children, the cries and gurgles of the baby, the playful yaps of Aggie's puppy – and Prue was filled with a warm goodwill towards her fellow man that she hadn't experienced in a long time.

The sound of the children playing reminded her of her own childhood here. She wouldn't have called it a happy one, exactly – there had never been any love lost between herself and her mother, and to the 'quality', as Mam had called Albert's parents, she was as good as invisible until the day their son had made his shocking announcement that he and Prue intended to be married. Nevertheless, her childhood had had its rays of sunshine. Albert . . . and Jack. What great friends they had been, and what adventures they'd had!

Prue remembered shinning to the top of the highest horse chestnut tree in the grounds the autumn Mam had first come to work here, shaking down conkers for the boys and teasing them for being too scared to follow. They'd had no time for her before that, a mere girl, but her guts and agility – not to mention the whipping she received for spoiling her dress and stockings – had earned their respect, and graciously they'd accepted her as a playmate. The three of them would spend hours together: taking turns to ride on Captain, Albert's grey pony; trying to tame the mice that lived in the stables; collecting frogspawn and climbing trees; swimming in the lake; being given piggy-back rides by old Mr Graham the gardener, Jack's father. The innocent, hardy fun of childhood, and the forging of an unbreakable friendship.

Prue could almost see the three of them as she looked out of the window across the grounds. In fact she thought for a moment she *could* see them. There was old Mr Graham, with little Albert riding on his shoulders and Prudence beside him, awaiting her turn. Then reality caught up with her and she realised it wasn't old but young Mr Graham – Jack, with Jimmy on his back while Aggie played with Coco by his side.

Yes, it was nice to have young people about the place, she reflected. Being with the young kept you young yourself. Perhaps that was why this morning Prue had paused when she'd gone to put on her grey stuff dress and instead donned a light summer frock with a floral pattern, the one she knew Jack admired. Perhaps, too, it was why she had chosen not to comb her hair into the usual tight bun but instead to leave it loose around her shoulders, as she had been accustomed to wear it when she was a girl. After all, she was lucky enough to have very little grey, even though she would be fifty this July. Why shouldn't she show off her one remaining beauty every once in a while?

'So you lost your mother, did you?' she said softly to the curious tom staring up at her.

The kitten continued to stare, unblinking, while its siblings played rough-and-tumble games around it.

Prue laughed. 'A cat may look at a king, I suppose. Well, come here and let me see you properly.'

She picked it up to examine it. It looked a healthy soul, although very young to be without its mother. She held it close to her chest and, seeming to appreciate the warmth, the tom snuggled against her. Prue felt its little body vibrate as it started to purr.

'Now, don't go getting too cosy, young man. You won't be able to stay, you know.' Still, she held the animal a little while longer, stroking its soft baby fur, before she put it back in its box.

'Well then, kitties, let's see what we can do for you,' she said.

She checked on Luca's cheese tarts, which appeared to be cooked, turned off the oven and put some milk on the hotplate to warm. Then she threw a tea towel over the box of kittens and carried them out to where Jimmy and Aggie were helping – or hindering – Jack to build a coop for the chicks that would soon be joining them.

Country air and outdoor life were working wonders for the children, just as they had for Edie. The evacuees no longer resembled the shoeless, malnourished urchins whose appearance had so shocked Prue when they'd shown up on her doorstep. There was colour in their cheeks now, and a full, healthy plumpness in their little limbs that made her glow to see. Really, the city was no place for children. The country was where they ought to be: wide open spaces where they could enjoy their innocent games and adventures, and be ruddy and healthy and free.

It broke Prue's heart to think of them going back to London and the dreadful so-called stepmother, Bet. She fully intended to see if anything could be done about that. This woman wasn't a relative by blood or law, so she surely had no right to keep them. And if she was regularly hurting and starving them . . . it made Prue's blood boil. Cruelty to children and animals was indefensible. Jimmy and Aggie would be far better in a children's home, where they'd be fed and cared for, and where there was a chance for them to be adopted by a family who'd love them as children ought to be loved.

Prue smiled as she watched Jack show Jimmy how to hammer in a nail, then handed the hammer to the boy so he could try it for himself. Jimmy's tongue protruded from the corner of his mouth as he focused all his concentration on tapping it in.

Jack, too, had been looking younger and healthier since the bairns had come. They did him good, and he them. What a wonderful father that man would have made!

Life hadn't worked out that way though. Prue had often wondered why. Why there'd never been any sweetheart, even before the last war when Jack was a young man with a healthy mind to go with what had undeniably been a healthy, handsome body – and was still, for a man of his years. Yes, Jack Graham could still turn female heads if he

283

fancied sampling the delights of matrimony. But the gardener had always seemed satisfied with his lot here, working for his two old friends and playing uncle to Bertie, who of course adored him. He'd never expressed a wish to be anywhere else, and Prue, selfish as she knew it was, secretly harboured relief in her soul that no one had ever come along to tempt Jack away from the estate – away from her. She really couldn't imagine life without him here. The day Jack wasn't at Applefield Manor was the day it would stop feeling like her home.

She watched Aggie go running up to him, Coco at her feet. Jack picked her up and swung her around in his arms, to the girl's shrieking delight.

Edie still kept on at Prue about reviving the treat days. She had resisted so far – the idea of filling the grounds with those sneering, snobbish folks from the village appalled her. But she had to admit, it would be a splendid thing for the children. She'd looked forward to the treats herself when she was their age. Perhaps . . . perhaps it might not be so bad if they planned it together, as a household. A family.

Jack smiled at her as she approached, casting an approving glance at her dress and the way her hair fell in shining curls over her shoulders. 'Well, and who's this pretty young lady? I didn't know we had any film stars visiting.'

'Oh, give up, you daft old man,' she said, blushing slightly.

She turned to the children, and felt a jolt of pain when she noticed how they recoiled; the wariness they displayed only to her. They loved Jack, and Edie, and Matilda, but they were afraid of her. Perhaps what hurt most of all was that Prue knew it was her own fault, with the ridiculous stiff manners she couldn't help resorting to whenever she addressed them. She just wasn't one of those people who was naturally good with children – she never would be.

But Aggie's wariness was only momentary. After hanging back a second, Prue was amazed when the child hurtled forward and hugged her around her middle.

'Well! Whatever is this for, Aggie?'

'For Coco,' Aggie said. 'Thank you, Mrs Hewitt, for letting him stay, and for saving his life when the bombs come.'

'Oh, well . . . I should hate to see anything unpleasant happen to him.' Prue tucked the box she was holding under one arm so she could awkwardly pat the girl's head. 'Now, now, get along with you. You're a good child.'

Aggie let her go and nodded to the box. 'What's that then? I mean, please what's that then?'

Prue put it down on the ground and removed the tea towel from the top. Aggie and Jimmy dropped to their knees so they could peer in.

'Blimey, kittens!' Aggie said in a hushed voice. 'Are they coming to live here too?'

'No, they're just our guests for today until Edie finds a new home for them. Their mother was killed in the air raid last night.'

'Aww, poor babies,' Aggie whispered. Within seconds she and Jimmy both had a couple of kittens cuddled to their chests and were cooing over them while Coco eyed these new rivals for his humans' affections resentfully.

'Oh, don't look at me like that,' Prue said in an undertone to Jack as he smiled at her. 'All right, so I'm a soft old lady who can't learn how to say no. You knew that already.'

'That's our Cheggy.' He squeezed her arm.

'They're hungry,' Aggie said, looking up at her. 'How do we feed 'em, Missus? I never fed a kitten before.'

'I've some milk warming in the kitchen. Do you and

Jimmy want to come in and help me give it to them? Your lunch is ready too. I'm sure Uncle Jack can finish building the coop without you.'

Aggie glanced at Jack, who nodded his consent, and the two children skipped back to the house with their arms full of kittens.

Chapter 29

Edie knew as soon as she arrived home that her plan had worked. On entering the sitting room, she discovered the cosiest of scenes.

Jack was dozing in one of the armchairs with Jimmy asleep in the crook of his arm. Coco, likewise asleep, was lying on the little boy's chest. Open on his knee Jack had the *Arabian Nights*, which he'd been reading with Jimmy in an effort to help the boy learn his letters.

On the floor in front of the blazing hearth were Prue, Aggie and the kittens. The humans had made a comfortable nest for them out of a soapbox and some tattered blankets. Aggie had a mug of warm milk by her, into which she was dipping the dropper from an old medicine bottle to feed the kittens. Soft chamber music played on the wireless. It was the perfect picture of a happy little family.

Aggie looked up in delight as the kitten she was attending to finished his meal then rubbed his ears against her hand, purring loudly.

'Aunty Prue, look!' she said. 'He knows I'm his mum now, don't he?'

Prue smiled. 'Yes indeed. I think we ought to give him a name, oughtn't we?'

Aggie thought for a moment.

'Felix,' she said at last. 'Like the cartoon.'

'Yes, that's a good name. Felix means lucky, which is appropriate when he was lucky enough to find us to take care of him. You and Jimmy had better think about names for his sisters too.' It seemed to have been established that Felix was the only tom in the litter.

In celebration of his new name, Felix pounced on one of his siblings and started tugging on her ear with his baby teeth.

Prue glanced up when she became aware of Edie in the doorway.

'Oh, Edie, you're home,' she said, smiling warmly. 'Come in, dear. You'll catch cold standing in the draught like that.'

'No, I'd better change before I get comfy. I just wanted to let you know I was back.'

'Well, there's food in the pantry: I kept some of Luca's cheese tart for you, and there are cold boiled potatoes to have with it. I must say, the tarts tasted a lot better than I'd feared. One hears such dire things about foreign food.' She gave one of Aggie's pigtails an affectionate flick. 'I only barely saved your portion from The Human Dustbin here.'

Aggie giggled.

Jack blinked himself awake.

'Time for ye two to be in bed,' he said with a yawn. 'Jimmy's fast asleep already, look.'

'Just quarter of an hour more while we finish giving the kitties their supper,' Prue said as Aggie filled the dropper. She glanced at Edie. 'I suppose we ought to take it in turns to do the night feeds. They can sleep in my room tonight.'

Edie nodded. 'If you don't mind. I can have them tomorrow.'

Nothing was said about finding new homes for the kittens, and Edie knew nothing ever would be said about it. She had been banking on the fact that Prue was too soft-hearted to spend all day with the animals without succumbing to those big, pleading eyes, and she'd been right. Princess's kittens were here to stay.

Edie was glad. There must be so many homeless animals in need of sanctuary. Applefield Manor could be that sanctuary, if Prue could only be persuaded to open her heart to them, and it looked as though Princess's babies had managed to break through the widening chink in her armour.

The kittens had achieved something else too, something that neither Edie, Tilly nor Jack had been able to do – finally breaking down the awkward reserve Prue always displayed with the children. She and Aggie looked for all the world like grandmother and granddaughter as they sat by the fire, feeding the new arrivals. Edie had always suspected the problem wasn't that Prue disliked children, or animals either: only that she had too little experience of both to behave naturally around them. All it had taken was something to bind them together.

In her bedroom, Edie began the painful process of changing out of her dungarees and into her civilian clothes. It had been an even busier afternoon than usual at the farm, with a morning's work to catch up on and two farmhands missing, not to mention dealing with the aftermath of the air raid. Sam said they had got off lightly, but many of the sheep were suffering with their own ovine version of shellshock. Several were off their food and there had been a number of early births, with, sadly, more than the usual number of dead lambs. Edie suspected that at Larkstone Farm they would be feeling the effects of the lone plane

289

that had wrought havoc on Applefield for many weeks to come.

They had been so busy that she'd barely seen anything of Sam: it had been every man for himself as they'd dashed around tending to the distressed sheep. Edie didn't know if she felt relieved or disappointed. If he tried to kiss her again, or asked her for a date . . . what would she say, now she knew all that she knew? Every time she reflected on his kindness to Tilly and Luca, she found herself smiling.

Not being all that hungry – they'd barely had time to breathe on the farm today, let alone eat, and it had been after five when she'd finally caught a minute to bolt down her sandwiches – Edie went back to the sitting room to say goodnight to the children before Prue took them off to bed.

'Have you had your food, dear?' Prue asked.

'No, I'll have it as a supper with my cocoa later,' Edie said as she claimed a chair. 'I only had my sandwiches a few hours ago. It's been a demon of a day.'

Prue got to her feet. 'Come on then, children, to bed with you. It's back to school tomorrow, I'm sorry to say.'

'Aww,' Aggie groaned. 'But we need to stay and look after the kittens.'

Prue smiled. 'Nice try, young lady. Jack and I can take care of the kittens until you come home. It would be a shame for Jimmy to fall behind on his reading and writing when he's been doing so well, wouldn't it?'

'S'pose,' Aggie muttered. 'Come on, Coco.'

Coco, immediately alert at the sound of his mistress's voice, leaped off Jimmy's chest. Jack lowered the little boy, blinking with sleep, to the floor.

'Bedtime now, son,' he said in the gentlest of tones,

ruffling his hair. 'You'll find a softer mattress than me waiting for you upstairs.'

Aggie ran over and flung herself at Jack for a goodnight hug.

'Night night, Uncle Jack.' She picked up a kitten and put it on his lap. 'Here you are. Felix can play with you till it's your bedtime too.'

Edie smiled, remembering how Luca had earnestly entrusted Jack to the girl's care and she'd sworn to make him well again with happy memories.

Jack laughed. 'Well, thank you. Go with Cheggy now, child, or you'll be grumpy in the morning.'

Edie submitted to a kiss from each of the children, then Prue took them up to bed. All was quiet apart from the music on the wireless, the crackle of the fire and the soft purrs of fed kittens.

'Little hurricanes,' Jack said, slumping back in his chair. 'They've tired me out today. Until the kittens turned up to distract her, I had Aggie following me all over the grounds. I'll be glad when they're back at school tomorrow.'

'She's been worrying about you,' Edie said softly. 'She heard, you know. Last night, when you . . . when the bombs started falling.'

Jack looked down at Felix trying to climb up his shirt front and lowered him gently to the floor. 'Well. She's a grand little lass.'

'Jack, can I ask you a question?'

'Depends what it is, don't it?'

'What does Cheggy mean? Is it short for something?'

He laughed. 'Is that all? Round these parts it's an old word for a horse chestnut. That's a conker to you.'

'What have conkers got to do with Prue?'

'Oh, something from when we were nippers.' His eyes

clouded with memories. 'Soon as autumn came round she had the glossiest, plumpest beast of a cheggy you ever saw on the end of a string. She was like a monkey, shinning up trees for the best ones, and she managed to lick me and Bert every bloody year. Embarrassing, it was. Mind you, she was gracious enough not to tell the village lads we'd had our cheggies smashed to pieces by a girl.'

'You're in love with her.'

Edie bit her tongue almost as the words left her lips. Good heavens, what had possessed her to say that? Jack didn't look offended, however. He just smiled sadly and stared into the fire.

'That obvious, is it?' he said. 'Aye. Thirty-five years and still going strong.'

'Jack, I'm so sorry. I don't know what made me say that.'

'Well, it's not much of a secret, I reckon. I never was any good at hiding it.'

'That's why you never married.'

'Suppose it is. Never had much interest in women, since I couldn't have the one I wanted.'

'Prue doesn't know though, does she?'

'No.' He sighed. 'Sometimes I think she don't see it because she don't want to.'

'Why don't you tell her?'

'Edie, Bert Hewitt was about the best friend I ever had. But when he came to me one day and told me his great secret – that he'd made up his mind he was going to marry our Cheggy – well, I could've thumped him. Eighteen, we were: me apprentice to my old dad in the gardens here and Bert getting ready to go up to Oxford. I knew that meant the end of any hope I might've had with her.'

'Did you thump him?'

'Course I didn't, we were pals. Anyhow, he didn't know

how I felt – no one did.' His brow knit into a fierce frown. 'But I couldn't help resenting him for it. She never was meant for him! He was the squire's boy, he could've chosen anyone. When it comes to marriage, people are better off keeping to their own kind.'

'That's rather an old-fashioned notion, isn't it?'

'Oh, I don't mean they should know their place,' Jack said. 'If I ever believed there was some sort of God-given social order, the war cured me of it – the last war, I mean. We had some proper posh lads in our platoon, heirs to castles and titles, fighting shoulder to shoulder with dustmen and miners, and all of them the same sacks of meat and bone at the end of the day. Fodder for Jerry's machine guns, as we all were.'

His eyes once again held the haunted look that made Edie shudder.

'Well, what do you mean?' she asked.

He shrugged. 'It only brings pain when we try to change how things are. People don't like it, and they won't accept it. Prudence would've been happier with her own sort: them that could see her for who she was and not what she was.'

'People like you,' Edie said softly.

Jack stared gloomily into the fire. 'Once. Not now.'

'Why not?'

'Because she's mistress and I'm the sodding gardener, aren't I?' he burst out, slamming his fist down on the arm of the chair. 'I couldn't compete with Bert when we were boys, with all that he had to offer her – his house and his money and his place in society – so I never spoke up. And now . . . he didn't just beat me to her; he went and bloody *elevated* her. Took her out of my class so even after he's dead I've got no hope.'

'I don't believe that's true, Jack.'

He went on as if he hadn't heard her. 'I thought I'd learned to live with it, but it's as if Fate's been mocking me since the little ones came. Cosy evenings by the fire, with the missus I never had and the children I always wanted. Visions of the life I might've led, if things had gone my way instead of Bert's.' He sighed. 'Feels real, but it's a mirage. No more substance than a dream.'

'But it is real,' Edie said earnestly. 'Or it could be, if you just told Prue how you felt.'

He smiled sadly, glancing down at the *Arabian Nights* on the chair arm. 'You've read too many storybooks, child. Prudence don't even talk like she used to. She's too much the lady now.' He held up a hand and watched it shake. 'And me, what the hell am I? A trembling, broken-spirited wreck who screams like a bairn every time he has a bad dream. If I was a carthorse they'd have taken me out and shot me by now.'

'Prue doesn't think you're a wreck.'

'Huh.' He was silent for a long moment, brooding darkly as the fire cast flickering shadows over his hunched body. But eventually he looked up, with just the glimmer of something like hope in his eye. 'What makes you say that, lass?'

'The way she looks at you. Even little Aggie sees it. Haven't you ever noticed how she –' Edie began, but they were interrupted by the arrival of Prue herself. Jack gave a guilty start.

'All tucked up,' Prue said, beaming at them. 'I told Aggie she may read Jimmy a story before they go to sleep. It helps with her vocabulary, and it does them good to have happy thoughts in their little heads at bedtime.' She frowned as she looked from Edie to Jack. 'I didn't interrupt a conspiracy, did I? You look as guilty as Guy Fawkes, Jack.'

'We, er . . . we were just talking about the treat day again,' Edie said, fabricating wildly. 'I know you said you wouldn't consider holding it here, but I wondered if there might be space in one of the fields, if the farmer was amenable. Sorry, I know you're sick of me wittering on about it.'

'Oh, yes, I've been meaning to talk to you about that.' Almost unconsciously, Prue dropped to her knees and made a soft cooing noise that instantly brought the four kittens purring and rubbing at her legs. 'You know, Edie, I'm rather coming around to the idea. You're right, it would be an excellent thing for the children.' She smiled at the kittens. 'And since my home seems destined to be the victim of invasion by stealth . . . what do the Americans say? If you can't beat them, join them?'

Edie blinked. She hadn't been expecting that. Prue had been so vehemently against the treat day, Edie had just about given up on the idea. The only reason she'd brought it up again was that it was all she could think of to cover for Jack's embarrassment.

'Really?' She glanced at Jack, who also looked surprised at Prue's sudden change of heart. 'Well, that's . . . thank you.'

'I'll speak to Patricia and Andrew about it. It always used to be planned with the Sunday School.' Prue reached out to tickle one of the kittens, her face seeming to glow in the warmth of the fire. Edie had never seen her looking so blissfully content and at peace with the world. 'Wouldn't it be splendid, Jack, if we could arrange it for when Bertie will be home on leave? You know the boy adores any kind of fair.'

Jack smiled. 'Aye, that he does. He'll be the biggest child of the lot.'

He watched her fondly as she played with the kittens.

295

Clad in a becoming cotton dress, her hair loose down her back, Prue, Edie thought, must look once again like the girl Jack had fallen in love with all those decades ago. Nevertheless, she could see that there was pain as well as affection in his eyes.

Chapter 30

A fortnight passed, and Applefield prepared to don the mantle of summer as May edged towards June. Prue sang as she worked in the kitchen one Tuesday, occasionally patting her apron pocket to remind herself of what she had stored there.

It was the start of jamming and pickling season at Applefield Manor. Prue had considered delaying it until Matilda was sufficiently recovered to go back to work, but they had had a bumper crop of strawberries this year – largely thanks to Coco's efforts in keeping down the Applefield Manor rat population – so it really couldn't be put off any longer. Besides, Prue loved making jam, and she had never been in a better mood for indulging in it.

She had received two pieces of good news that day. The first, announced on the wireless earlier, was that the fearsome battleship *Bismarck* – the pride of the German navy, deemed unsinkable – had been despatched to the depths by Allied forces. Prue knew this meant an end to a reign of terror that had cost many lives, and that the seas were now safer for the one sailor in whose welfare she had a particular interest. However, she couldn't help feeling sadness, too, when she thought of the men aboard who had been injured or killed. Every one of them was some-body's son, after all.

The second piece of good news was of no significance to the course of the war but of great significance to her. It had arrived by letter that morning – a letter currently tucked safely in Prue's apron pocket while she stirred the pan of delicious-smelling syrup simmering on the cooker.

She looked around when she heard a noise, and saw a twitching canine nose poking around the kitchen door.

'Oho. An intruder,' she said, smiling. 'Coco, you needn't think that as saviour of the strawberry crop you're entitled to any of this jam. I'm saving it for a special guest.'

The dog looked up at her, tail wagging hopefully, and Prue went to pick him up. She sat down with him on her lap, and he rested his front paws against her arm while he licked her cheek.

'Look, Coco,' she said, taking the letter from her apron and showing it to him. 'Do you see what this says? It says that my son Bertie will be coming home on leave in July. What do you think of that?'

The little dog blinked puzzled brown eyes at her. Laughing, Prue put him on the floor.

'Well, a mouthful of bread won't do you any harm, I expect,' she said. 'But that's all until your dinner, pup.'

Aggie stuck her head round the door as Prue was slicing a bit of crust from yesterday's loaf. It was around quarter to four and she and Jimmy were just home from school.

'Is Coco here, Aunty Prue?'

'Yes, begging bowl in hand as usual. Or in paw, I should say,' Prue said. 'Come in, children. I want you to taste something for me.'

The evacuees entered the kitchen and Prue dipped a teaspoon into the jam mixture for them to taste.

'Be careful now, it's very hot,' she said. Aggie blew on the liquid then put it in her mouth.

'Mmm!' She smacked her lips. 'That's sweet. Is it to drink?'

'No, it's strawberry jam,' Prue said as she spooned out a little for Jimmy to try too. 'Once it's hot enough, it can go into jars to set and we'll be able to eat it on our bread and butter. Well worth the investment of our precious sugar, I think – we shall be glad of it now preserves have been added to the ration. Would you two like to help me finish making it?'

'Ooh, yes please!'

'All right, but go wash and change out of your uniforms first.'

The children didn't need telling twice. Somehow the two of them managed to get changed and back to the kitchen in under five minutes. Cooking – and especially cooking sweet things – was a favourite hobby for them both, second only to licking the bowl afterwards.

'Now,' Prue said when they'd rejoined her. 'You see all those jars on the kitchen table? When the liquid is at the right temperature, we'll leave it to settle and warm the jars in the oven. Then we can ladle the jam into them. But first they need to be thoroughly washed – can you do that, Aggie?'

Aggie nodded. She didn't object to washing-up when it was done in the name of cookery. She went to the sink and turned on the tap to fill it.

'You look happy, Aunty Prue,' she observed artlessly.

'I am happy,' Prue said. 'I had some good news this morning. My son is going to be coming to visit.'

'Your son what's in the navy?'

'That's right: Bertie. You'll like him, he knows lots of fun games.' She glanced from Aggie to Jimmy. 'Have you two ever been to a fair?'

'You mean like with games and rides and things?' Aggie said.

'Yes, that's right.'

'No, but we seen one once. It come near our house.' Aggie's eyes glazed. 'They had all these brilliant things, I could see 'em through the gate. There was a gypsy man with an accordion and a little monkey, and for a tanner you could hold it. And there was a helter-skelter, and a merry-go-round, and a big coloured organ, and a fortune teller, and candy floss and toffee apples and ginger beer and . . . and everything good you can think of, Aunty Prue, honest there was.' Her face darkened. 'But then Bet come and give us a clip round the ear for looking. She wouldn't never let us go to nothing like that.'

'Well, I don't know if we can get a monkey or a helter-skelter, but I'm certain we could have candy floss and toffee apples, and swingboats and a coconut shy and other good things,' Prue said, giving the little girl a fond squeeze. 'Should you like that, my dears?'

Aggie's eyes went round. 'You mean you'd take us?'

'I mean we could have a fair here at Applefield Manor, in the gardens. We used to have them every year, until . . . well, until they stopped.' Prue rested a hand on Jimmy's head. 'I think now that we have young people living here again, it's high time we brought them back.'

Aggie didn't seem to know what to say. She just stared at Prue for a moment, her mouth open, before her feelings exploded in the single word 'Blimey!'

'Now, Aggie, language,' Prue said, frowning.

'Sorry, Aunty. I didn't mean to, it just popped out.'

'That's all right, but be more careful in future.'

300

Prue was turning back to stir the jam when she felt it. A little hand slipping into hers, and the whispered words, quiet as a summer breeze, 'Thank you'.

She looked down. Jimmy was holding her hand as he looked up at her with shining eyes.

'What did you say, Jimmy?'

'Thank you, I says,' he murmured. 'No one ever done anything that nice for us before.'

Prue cast a surprised look at Aggie, who shrugged.

'I told him he better start talking but he said he was scared to,' she said. 'Changed your mind, did you, Jim?'

He nodded shyly. Prue, realising that making a fuss might well cause the boy to retreat back into himself again, just gave his hand a squeeze and let it drop.

'You're welcome, Jimmy,' she said. 'Now, can I give you a very important job?'

'Yes, please,' Jimmy whispered.

'Are you sure? This is actually the most important job, so I wouldn't want to give it to you unless you were positive you could do it properly.'

Jimmy puffed himself up. 'I can do it.'

He had the same East End accent as his sister, of course, but Jimmy's tone was softer: less bold, more hesitant. It was a strange novelty, hearing the little boy speak. Prue felt as though she was at the picture house and Harpo Marx had turned to deliver a lengthy monologue to the audience.

'Good.' Prue pulled a chair over to the cooker and hoisted Jimmy on to it, then handed over her preserving thermometer with some ceremony. 'Now, Jimmy, when this says 220°F, the jam will be ready. The mercury must go up to exactly that number, do you understand? If the jam isn't hot enough then it won't set.'

Jimmy nodded.

'In two more minutes, put the bulb end of the thermometer into the jam, hold it there for a moment and read the number. Be very careful not to scald yourself, dear. If the number is less than 220, then wait a while and try again. Can you do that?'

Jimmy nodded again, then turned to watch the bubbling liquid intently, as if afraid it might try to escape.

The doorbell rang, and Prue wiped her hands on her apron.

'That will be the Reverend and Mrs Featherstone, come to talk about plans for the fair,' she said. 'Just a moment, children, and I'll ask Edie to come in from the gardens to mind you.'

'We're all right,' Aggie said. 'We can do it on our own, can't we, Jim?' Jimmy nodded enthusiastically.

Prue could only imagine. The cooker on fire, the kitchen covered in liquid jam, little Coco doggy-paddling through it while the kittens floated along on top . . .

'I'm sure you can, but you might need help . . . reaching things from the shelves,' Prue said diplomatically. 'I think you'd better have an adult here.'

Edie was harvesting rhubarb in one of the greenhouses. Prue went to fetch her, explained briefly what was needed, then left her with the children while she went to answer the door.

'Good day, Andrew. Patty,' Prue said, beaming at them. She was in such a good mood, she even had smiles for Patricia. 'Oh, and little Edgar is with you too. How lovely.'

Patricia looked taken aback by the warmth of the greeting. 'Why, yes. Good afternoon, Prue.'

'Come in, please,' Prue said, ushering the three of them into the hallway. 'We'll go into the sitting room.'

'The sitting room?' Patricia knew that Prue very rarely

received visitors anywhere other than Applefield Manor's austere library since Albert had passed.

'Yes, I've become used to spending time in there since the young people came. We've been having some jolly evenings – well, children do tend to make a house a home, don't they?'

Patricia looked rather lost for words. 'Um, yes.'

'Go on through, please.' Prue smiled at Edgar. 'Unless you'd be interested in something more interesting than sitting with the old folk, young man? Jimmy and Aggie are making jam with Edie if you would like to join them.'

'Oh, no,' Patricia said, curling her lip. 'I couldn't have Edgar playing with those comm– with those London children. Goodness knows what words he might pick up.'

That was typical of Patricia. When she had wanted Prue to take the evacuees in, she'd waxed lyrical about the innocence of childhood and the horror of the bombings, as if to underline the contrast between her own public-spiritedness and Prue's selfish isolationism. Now Jimmy and Aggie were no longer her problem, the snobbish side of her personality came to the fore. But Prue had promised herself that nothing was going to ruin her happiness today, not even Patricia, and she managed to keep smiling.

'I'm sure it wouldn't do the boy any harm to play with the evacuees, my dear,' Andrew said to his wife. 'I believe it does children good to make friends outside their own circle.'

'I said no, Andrew,' Patricia told him shortly. She grabbed Edgar's hand and swept him into the sitting room.

The kittens were in there, sleeping in a little furry huddle on one of the armchairs. Edgar let out a squeak when he laid eyes on them, clapping his hands together.

'Grandmother, please may I?' he whispered, bouncing a little in his anxiousness.

'Absolutely not. Who knows what diseases they might be carrying? Nasty, smelly things.' Patricia turned a look of disgust on Prue. 'Wherever did they come from?'

'They were orphaned in the air raid,' Prue told her. 'Somehow we ended up adopting them.'

'And those?' Patricia nodded to a pair of canaries clucking happily at each other in a birdcage.

'Ah, those are Jimmy's little pets. A boy in his class needed to find a new home for them.' Prue moved the kittens from the armchair to their soapbox bed so she could sit down. 'We've got quite the menagerie here now. So far, I seem to have gained four cats, two canaries, two chicks, a dog, a crow, two children, a baby and a Land Girl.'

'I thought you couldn't abide animals.'

'I think it's unfair to say I couldn't abide them. I was always a little nervous around them.' Prue leaned down to stroke a kitten, which rubbed its face against her fingers. 'But you do grow fond of them in time.'

'Why take them in though?'

'Because they had nowhere else to go, I suppose. Perhaps they are only animals, but they can still suffer; feel sadness and pain. I hate to think of them dying alone out there.' She lowered her eyes. 'There's far too much of that going on as it is.'

'That's a very charitable attitude, Prudence,' Andrew said. 'We're all God's creatures, after all.'

'Yes, that's how I think of it.'

Patricia pursed her lips. 'I'd have thought that with a war on, one would have more important things to do than shelter a lot of mangy animals. I can think of a hundred useful purposes a house this size could be put to.'

Prue frowned at her. 'I'm sure you can, Patty, but this is the useful purpose I've chosen for it. Now, can I offer you both something to drink? We're on the last of our tea ration, I'm afraid, but we do have some Camp Coffee.'

'Oh, no, thank you,' Patricia said. 'Andrew and I can't stand chicory.'

Edgar was still gazing longingly at the kittens. Andrew rested a hand on the child's shoulder.

'I don't see why you shouldn't play with the kittens, my lad,' he said. 'These aren't strays but pets. I'm sure Mrs Hewitt sees to it that they have no fleas or diseases.'

'Really, Grandpa?' Edgar whispered.

'Andrew, I do wish you would tell him not to call you "Grandpa" in that common way. "Grandfather" is the proper term,' Patricia said with a click of irritation. 'And you heard me say no, quite clearly.'

'And you heard me say yes,' Andrew said mildly, meeting her eyes.

Patricia looked at him for a moment, noting the steely spark in his usually placid expression. She turned to Edgar.

'I suppose five minutes won't do any harm,' she said with a magnanimous nod.

Edgar gave another excited squeak and dropped to his knees by the kittens, who immediately began exploring him. Princess's babies had been far too thoroughly spoiled at Applefield Manor to have any fear of humans.

Andrew took a seat on the couch opposite Prue with a satisfied smile. His wife sat down beside him, her expression black at having lost a battle of wills with her mild-mannered husband.

'Why on earth have you started wearing your hair in that juvenile manner, Prue?' Patricia demanded waspishly.

Prue knew her so-called friend was trying to provoke her and refused to take the bait. She reached up to pat her hair.

'The children have forbidden me from having it any

other way since they saw it loose. They say it makes me look less stern.'

'I think it's very becoming,' Andrew said gallantly. 'You look ten years younger, Prudence.' His wife shot him a disgusted look.

Prue smiled at him. 'Thank you, Andrew. You're always such a gentleman. Were you able to make those enquiries for me?'

'I was.' Andrew took a piece of paper from his pocket. 'I have a letter here from a clergyman friend who works with the Waifs and Strays Society in London. He paid a visit to the Cawthras' home at my request and it seems the children haven't exaggerated, although the lady in question denied any mistreatment, of course.'

Prue nodded soberly. She knew that as a clergyman, Andrew would be able to get the facts with greater ease than if she made enquiries herself. That was why she had asked him to look into Aggie and Jimmy's situation, and to find out what could be done on their behalf.

'She couldn't deny having starved them, surely,' Prue said. 'They were like scarecrows when they arrived here.'

'She defends herself with the usual excuses – poverty, time of war, very little to go around, et cetera. However, my friend seems to suggest the woman is an incurable drunk, frittering away what little money she receives on black-market whisky. She appeared to be mostly skin and bones.' He sighed as he put the letter away. 'She is to be pitied too, I suppose. The poor wretch sounds to have been in a very sorry state. There was a man present who may have . . . some rough handling, I believe.'

'What of Jimmy and Aggie?' Prue said. 'I couldn't bear to send them back there to be beaten and brutalised by these people.'

306

'It sounds as though they couldn't go back even if they wanted to. Their, er . . . their stepmother's gentleman friend was adamant they wouldn't be allowed to return.'

'Have they no other relatives?'

'None who could afford to provide for them.'

'Then it would have to be an orphanage,' Prue said, bowing her head. 'The poor loves. Still, they'd be fed and cared for, at least.'

Andrew nodded. 'I'm hopeful places can be found at one of the institutions in their local area. I'm going to write to the authorities and ask what arrangements could be made. Hopefully there'll be no need for them to be separated.'

Prue frowned. 'That isn't a possibility, is it?'

'I'm afraid so. Places are scarce these days – the war has made too many orphans.'

'Oh, no.' Prue thought of Jimmy, shy and silent, clutching his sister's hand. Aggie, fiercely protective, determined to keep her little brother safe at all costs . . . 'No, Andrew, that can't be allowed to happen. The children would be devastated. You must tell the authorities it shouldn't be considered.'

'I don't think I have any say in the matter,' Andrew said. 'Nevertheless, I'll make your views clear.'

'Thank you. And please inform them that there's no hurry. The children are welcome to stay here for as long as they have nowhere else to go, war or not.'

Andrew smiled warmly. 'You're a good woman, Prudence. We could do with a few more like you in Applefield.'

Patricia cleared her throat. 'Can we please discuss the treat day now? I don't want to be late for this evening's WI meeting.'

'There's plenty of time yet, my dear,' Andrew said in his tranquil way, and Prue wondered again however two such opposite characters managed to rub along together.

'I'd like to arrange it for Sunday, 13 July if possible,' Prue said. 'My boy will be home on leave then.'

'Oh, how lovely. Well, I think that will be enough time to plan, don't you, Patricia?'

Patricia looked as though she was straining to think of some sort of objection, but, unable to do so, she nodded grudgingly.

'What will we have on the day?' Andrew said.

'The Women's Institute must do something,' Patricia said. 'Clara Jenkins suggested we sell cakes and run a ring-toss game for the children.'

'I'd like to have some fairground rides,' Prue said. 'A merry-go-round and swingboats, and perhaps a helter-skelter. I'll cover the costs involved myself. Edie suggests we ask the Kirkton Town Band to play for us. And I should like a coconut shy, and tin can alley, and hook-a-duck. They were great favourites in years gone by. There must be a tombola and a raffle of some sort for the adults, and I shall have a stall to sell some of our jams and pickles.'

Patricia nodded, scribbling in her notebook. This sort of planning was what she excelled at, and she looked almost happy at the prospect of organising everything. 'I'll appeal for volunteers at tonight's WI meeting, and Andrew, I'm sure you can make an announcement in church on Sunday.'

Andrew laughed. 'You make our temporary chapel in the Boy Scouts' hut sound very grand when you call it a church, my dear. Yes, of course.'

'Oh yes, that's the other matter I wanted to bring up,' Prue said. 'I hope we shall raise a little money for good causes. Edie suggested the Spitfire Fund, and I agree we ought to make some donation to the war effort, but I'd like a portion of the profits to go to the church roof repair fund. Charity begins at home, after all.'

Andrew smiled. 'That's very kind. Thank you.'

'I don't know when you became so public-spirited, Prue,' Patricia said.

Prue shrugged. 'It felt like time I started.'

There was a tentative knock at the sitting room door, and Prue called for whoever it was to come in. Tilly appeared, Baby Samantha in her arms.

'I thought I heard Uncle Andrew,' she said. 'Sorry to interrupt, Prue. I wanted to bring Sammie to meet the family while they were here.'

She was smiling, but she looked nervous. Prue knew this was the first time she had seen her aunt and uncle since the baby had been born.

'Are you sure you ought to be up, Matilda?' she asked.

'I'm perfectly all right. Dr MacKenzie fusses too much.'

She looked pale, however, and Andrew stood up to offer her his seat. Patricia curled her lip at the baby and shuffled along the couch.

'So this is our little grand-niece,' Andrew said softly, leaning over Tilly to look at the baby. 'May I, Matilda?'

She smiled. 'Be my guest.'

Patricia's face was like thunder.

'Andrew, you will not hold that baby,' she snapped. 'That . . . that *illegitimate* baby.'

Andrew frowned at her. 'You forget, Patricia, that I will shortly be baptising this baby. No child is illegitimate in the eyes of the heavenly father – or in mine.' He smiled at Samantha. 'Besides which, she's family.'

'I forbid it, Andrew. I absolutely forbid it. Do you hear me?'

'Yes, Patricia. I hear you perfectly well.' He took the child from Tilly and touched a finger to her nose. She opened her gummy little mouth and gurgled happily.

'Well if that's how you feel, then I shall wait outside. With your *grandson*,' Patricia snapped. She dragged Edgar reluctantly away from the kittens, and, without a backwards glance, marched out of the room.

'Well done, Andrew,' Prue said quietly.

'I let her have her way most of the time, but very occasionally I have to put my foot down.' He turned to Tilly. 'You must forgive your aunt, my dear. She was raised in a time when things were . . . well, rather different. She does care for you and the baby.'

Tilly sighed. 'I wish I could believe that, Uncle.'

'Well, well, she'll come around. Patricia's a good woman – too good, I think, sometimes.' He looked down at Samantha. 'My word, what a fine complexion she has! And all that dark hair. What did you say her name was, Matilda?'

'Samantha.'

'Ah.' Andrew looked embarrassed, but he quickly recovered. He planted a kiss on the baby's head and handed her back. 'Well, Samantha Liddell, welcome to the family. I hope I'll be seeing you in church soon.'

'Hopefully in one with a roof,' Prue said with a smile.

Chapter 31

Edie was ladling the jam into jars when Prue joined her in the kitchen.

'Are the children not here?' Prue asked.

'No, I sent them out to feed the chicks. There'd be as much jam on the table as in the jars if I let Aggie loose with the ladle.' Edie looked up from what she was doing. 'You'll never guess what happened.'

'Did Jimmy speak to you?'

Edie blinked in surprise. 'Well, yes, he did. How did you know?'

'He spoke to me too.' Prue smiled. 'I believe it was excitement about the treat day that finally broke through. He must have decided he could trust us at last.'

'I thought I had such a lovely surprise for you,' Edie said, smiling too. 'Still, I suppose it would be you he spoke to first.'

'Why do you say that, dear?'

'Just something I've noticed when the two of them are around you,' Edie said, continuing her ladling. 'I don't know how to describe it. It's as if when they're with you, they feel sort of . . . protected. Ever since the air raid.'

Prue blinked. 'Do you really think so?'

Edie nodded. 'Coco has something to do with it, I think. The way you put yourself in danger to save him from the bombs, just as you kept the children safe, and Tilly and Samantha – well, all of us, really.' She looked up to smile. 'You're the heart of Applefield Manor to us, Prue. I hope you know that.'

Prue didn't know what to say. She turned away to hide her emotion. For so long she'd thought of Applefield Manor as belonging to Albert and his parents, even now when all three were long dead. Somehow, hearing those words brought a tear to her eye.

'I . . . thank you,' she murmured. 'That's very kind.'

Edie, seeming to sense Prue's embarrassment, merely nodded before changing the subject. 'Are Mr and Mrs Featherstone gone?'

'Yes. There was a rather unpleasant scene actually.'

Edie looked alarmed. 'Why, what happened?'

'Patricia happened, as usual,' Prue said, sinking into a seat. 'She marched out when Andrew insisted on holding the baby. Poor Matilda was so upset.'

'I don't wonder.'

'Andrew was lovely, of course, like the good Christian he is. But Patty wouldn't even look at Samantha.' She shook her head darkly. 'How anyone can sit in judgement on a blameless little baby I have no idea.'

'Honestly, that woman!' Edie said, scowling. 'I don't think she has an ounce of compassion in her, for all her so-called good works. I'm jolly glad she isn't my aunt.'

Prue sighed. 'Goodness knows how she's going to react when she discovers the truth. She'll never recognise Matilda's marriage, of course. And when she knows Samantha's father is an enemy prisoner . . .'

'I'd say it was none of her business.'

'But Matilda will be hurt by it. For her sake, I do wish Patricia didn't have to be quite so . . . Patricia.'

'She didn't try to throw cold water on the treat day, I hope.'

'Oh no, she was all for it,' Prue said, smiling. 'Patty may be difficult, but she's a born organiser. In that respect alone, the village is lucky to have her.'

'Hmm.' Edie wasn't convinced Patricia Featherstone's skill as an event organiser made up for her shortcomings as a human being, but at least the treat day was still going ahead. 'What about the children? Was Andrew able to find out more about this Bet person?'

'Yes, and it seems she's quite as bad as Aggie described,' Prue said, curling her lip. 'What's more, she's taken up with a man who knocks her about. I'm sorry, but I refuse to send the children back to a household like that. Andrew is going to find out if an institution would have places for them.'

'Institution?' Edie said, frowning. 'You mean an orphanage?'

'Yes, that's right.'

'Oh.'

'I don't think you need be concerned, Edie,' Prue said. 'I know the word "orphanage" tends to conjure images of brutal Victorian workhouses, but in this day and age the reality is far removed from that. The children will be fed and cared for, and provided with a good education, in much better conditions than before.'

Edie thought of the evacuees, each their own unique little self. They'd blossomed under the care and attention they'd been shown at Applefield Manor. Perhaps an orphanage might provide for their bodily needs, but what of their emotional ones? Children needed love to grow, just as much as food and drink.

'Still, to be one face among many. It's no way to grow up,' Edie said. 'I wish there was another way, Prue.'

'No. It isn't ideal, is it?' Prue said, sighing. 'Andrew believes the authorities might try to separate them. If there aren't enough places to keep them together.'

'What? No! They couldn't do that, could they?'

'I presume they could, if they had to. Let's hope it won't be necessary.' She frowned as the doorbell sounded. 'Now, who can that be? Surely Patricia hasn't left something behind.'

She went to answer it. Edie, curious as to who was calling – unexpected visitors were a rarity at Applefield Manor – put down her ladle and followed.

'Hello,' she heard a jolly, familiar voice saying as Prue opened the door. 'I hope I'm in the right place. I'm looking for Edie Cartwright.'

'Oh my goodness!' Edie said. Prue stood aside, looking puzzled, as Edie launched herself at the visitor for a hug. 'Sue! What on earth are you doing here?'

'Darling, didn't you get my letter?' Susan said, laughing as she squeezed her friend tight. 'I got a spot of leave and thought I'd pay you a visit.'

'No, I never had a word! I suppose it's at the bottom of a mail sack somewhere. The post here isn't the most reliable.'

Edie stood back to look at her friend. She was as beautiful as ever, clad in her ATS jacket and breeches. An army motorcycle was parked on the gravel behind her.

'Oh gosh, I'm sorry,' Edie said, turning to Prue. 'Prue, this is Susan Hume, my oldest friend. We grew up together in London. Sue, this is my landlady, Mrs Prudence Hewitt.'

'It's a pleasure to meet you, Mrs Hewitt,' Susan said, holding out her hand. 'Edie talks about you all the time in her letters.'

'She doesn't tell you anything too awful, I hope,' Prue said, smiling as she shook the proffered hand. 'Do come in, dear. Edie, I think you've earned an hour's holiday if you'd like to finish work early today. Why don't you and your friend go into the sitting room? I'll just finish ladling out the jam then I'll bring you in some tea. I managed to save the last of the leaves from Patricia.'

'Thank you, that's very kind,' Edie said, pressing Prue's shoulder.

She hooked her arm through her friend's and guided her to the sitting room.

'So that's the terrifying old dragon you wrote me about, is it?' Susan said in a low voice when they were both seated on the couch. 'Edie, she's adorable.'

Edie smiled. 'Well, I'm not too proud to admit that I was wrong about her. She is a dear, once you break through her reserve.' She glanced at the kittens play-fighting by the fire. 'Mind you, you have to know how to handle her. One wrong move and she can close up like an oyster.'

Susan reached down to pick up a kitten. 'And I suppose these are poor Princess's babies.' She held the kitten up to her face and it blinked at her comically. 'Well, hello there, little one. I've heard all about *you*.'

Edie laughed as Susan rubbed noses with the kitten and put it back with its siblings. Susan and Alfie had been told so much about Applefield Manor and its residents, they were almost as familiar with the place as Edie herself.

Prue came in with the tea – she'd used the nice cups they saved for company, Edie noticed – and put the tray down on the table.

'Will you join us?' Edie asked.

'Oh, no, you don't want me eavesdropping on your

gossip,' Prue said. 'You girls have a good natter. I'll keep the children out of your way.'

'She's a lot younger and prettier than I expected,' Susan whispered when Prue had gone. 'From your letters, I was picturing someone like your Aunt Caroline.'

'She seems younger nowadays,' Edie said as she poured their tea. 'I thought it was just that she'd changed her hairstyle, but generally she seems fresher, somehow.' She paused, trying to put her finger on what was different about Prue. 'I think it's because she's happier.'

'She seems fond of you.'

'Well, I've grown fond of her too – of all of them, here and at the farm.' Edie handed Susan a teacup on a delicate china saucer. 'You know, I wasn't sure when I arrived if I was going to fit in here. I was dreadfully homesick the first week or so. If it hadn't been for Tilly, I'm not sure I wouldn't have been on the train back to London after a fortnight.'

'Ah, yes. Your new best friend,' Susan said, pursing her lips.

Edie smiled. 'Come on, don't be daft. You'll love her, and the baby's just darling. We'll go up and see them after our tea. And you must meet Jack and the children too, and all the animals.' She gave her friend's arm a squeeze. 'Honestly, you're a sight for sore eyes. I've missed you to pieces.'

'I've missed you too,' Susan said, smiling. 'I'd love to meet them all, Edie. Even though I do feel like I know them already.' Edie knew her friend was too good-natured to ever be truly jealous.

'How much leave have you got?' Edie asked.

'Six whole days, isn't it wonderful? And I'm giving them all to you, darling. I've taken a room at the YWCA hostel in Kirkton. You'll never guess what else too.'

'What?'

'Go on, guess.'

Edie laughed. 'Sue, you know I'm frightful at guessing games. Tell me.'

'Alfie's coming,' Susan said, beaming. 'This Friday: he's coming here for the weekend before he goes to Mum and Dad. He's going to stay at the pub in your village.'

'Oh, wonderful!' Edie said, clapping her hands. 'It'll be just like old times. We can take a picnic down to the lake, oh, and I'll show you the woods where the deer are, and the lambs on the farm I delivered myself, and we can –'

Susan laughed. 'All right, darling, calm down. One thing at a time.' She put down her teacup and helped herself to a thin finger of bread and butter. 'So, any new beaus I should know about? I notice you've been very quiet on the subject in your letters.'

'I . . . no. I don't think so.'

'What, don't you know?'

Edie paused, feeling awkward. She hadn't wanted to say anything in her letters about Sam and the kiss that never was. She knew she could tell her friend anything, but what she felt for Sam . . . Edie didn't know what she felt, but she knew it wasn't some girlish flirtation to gossip and giggle about. It was more important than that. Except these last couple of weeks, she'd wondered if it was anything at all . . . if she might not have imagined the almost-kiss, the lingering looks; everything.

'There was someone who I thought might be keen on me,' she admitted.

'Who? Not that handsome flight lieutenant?'

'No.' Edie bowed her head. 'Rob's . . . gone, Sue. His Spit was shot down over the Channel three weeks ago.'

'Oh. I am sorry to hear that.'

They were silent for a moment. Both women knew boys

who hadn't come home – old friends, cousins, suitors – but no matter how often it happened, loss and grief never could become commonplace.

'So who is he, this new man of yours?' Susan said at last. 'The gardener? He's good-looking, isn't he?'

Edie laughed. 'Jack? Don't be daft, he's old enough to be my dad. Besides –' She stopped herself. 'No, it's not him. It's . . . it's Sam.'

Susan frowned. 'What, that grumpy farmer? I thought you hated him.'

'I didn't hate him. I did believe he . . . well, I made a wrong judgement about him early on in our acquaintance. I seem to have made a hobby out of jumping to conclusions ever since I arrived here.'

'What happened, Ede?'

'We'd been getting closer, working on the farm. I'd say we'd become friends. Then a few weeks ago he asked if I'd go to the pictures with him.'

'What did you say?'

'I said no, quite abruptly. I thought I had reason to, then – I thought he was involved with someone else and just wanted to have a bit of fun with me. I was wrong though. Then he brought the doctor over to deliver the baby, and while he was here, we . . . almost kissed. Outside, in the moonlight.'

'That sounds suspiciously romantic,' Susan said. 'Why almost? Did you stop it?'

'No, we were interrupted. Since then, there's been nothing. I'm starting to wonder if I imagined the whole thing.'

'You mean he hasn't tried to make another date with you?'

Edie shook her head. 'I haven't seen much of him since that night. He always used to pick me to work with him on the farm, but now he chooses one of the others, every time. I don't know if he's angry with me or if I misread the whole situation.'

'Hmm. He sounds like the type of man who enjoys stringing girls along to me.'

'I . . . don't know. I wouldn't have thought so, but . . .' She sighed. 'I feel a complete fool, Sue. Really, I'm such a clueless schoolgirl when it comes to these things. I wish I had you here to advise me.'

'Sam's the fool if he can't see what's right under his nose. The best girl in the whole world, that's all.' She turned to cast an approving look over Edie. 'You look wonderful, my darling. Positively blooming with health. Do you cough much these days?'

'Hardly at all, now. Dr Grant was right: it's done me the world of good being out in the open air.'

'Oh, bless you. In that case I'm glad you had to take the Land Army over the Wrens.' Sue finished her tea. 'Do you think you might go back home this year?'

'Home?'

'Yes. Haven't you been listening to the wireless? The raids have really eased up these past few weeks.'

'Only because of the bad weather. The Luftwaffe will be back once the skies clear; they always are.'

'That's what the powers that be are telling us, but at work people are whispering that the Blitz might finally be done with. A major I'm friendly with thinks old Adolf is saving his bombers for the Ruskies now. Alice told me in her last letter that she and Joan are planning to go back to London in autumn if it seems like the worst is over.' Alice and Joan Wilson were old schoolfriends, sisters who had evacuated to relatives in the countryside.

Edie shook her head. 'I can't go back, can I? Not to sound

too much like Lord Kitchener about it, but the Land Army needs me. Besides, what is there for me in London now? You and Alfie aren't there, or Aunt Caroline. She's actually talking about selling the house in Pimlico and retiring to the Cotswolds permanently.'

'Would you go with her?'

'I shouldn't think so. Not unless I had to.' Edie gazed out of the window, watching the swallows swoop and dive against the glorious backdrop of the fells. 'I have been thinking lately . . . I'd like to stay. Not just while the war's on. Forever.'

Susan blinked. 'Stay here? It's the middle of nowhere, Ede.'

'Maybe that's why I like it,' Edie said with a half-smile. 'I feel I belong here, Sue. The air agrees with me wonderfully: I've never been happier, or healthier. I adore my work, and since the evacuees came to live here, and the animals . . . I really feel like I have a purpose now. That at Applefield Manor, I'm part of something important.'

'Well, perhaps, but –'

'I dreamed of being a Wren because I wanted to make a difference to the course of the war – to save lives. The Land Army felt like a disappointing substitute at the time. But since coming to Applefield – planning the fete, taking care of the children and animals, working on the farm – I've realised that making a difference in lots of small ways is just as important as the big stuff. At any rate, it is to those you're able to help.'

Susan was staring at her. 'You'd really leave London for good?'

'Yes, I believe I would.'

'What about when the war ends though? There won't be a Land Army then, or farm work. Not for women.'

'No.' Edie was silent for a moment. 'I suppose not.'

Susan was regarding her curiously, as if seeing her for the first time.

'What?' Edie said, smiling.

'Nothing.' Susan shook her head. 'You just seem so . . . different, Ede. I mean, still the same lovely you, always trying to save everyone, but sort of grown-up and confident. What happened to you?'

'Applefield did, I think. Don't you approve?'

'No, I do.' Susan patted her hand. 'In fact, my little butterfly, I'd say it's been the making of you.'

Chapter 32

It was a warm, fragrant Thursday evening at Larkstone Farm, the air rich with the scents of summer. Edie was stretched out under a tree with her hands pillowed behind her head, enjoying the feel of the sunshine on her skin.

There was no one else there. Edie had been on her own for most of the afternoon, clearing away the heather and gorse that, if left unchecked, had a tendency to encroach on the farmland from the surrounding fells. She had actually finished work half an hour ago, but the farm was peaceful and pleasant and she was in no hurry to leave. Days felt long since the Government had introduced double summertime earlier that month, and although there were the same number of hours in a day as there always had been, they seemed to pass more slowly, somehow.

Little Wilf the pet lamb had settled at her side. Edie reached out lazily to tickle his ears. There was no sound but the soft bleating of the animals and the sleepy buzz of insects in the hawthorn blossoms and clover that perfumed the air.

Still, it was time she thought about stirring herself. She was due to meet Susan at the Golden Fleece in Applefield for a bite of supper in a little while.

Back in Edie's part of London, public houses were the preserve of working men: places she would never have dreamed of setting foot. Things were different here though. Along with St Mark's Church, the pub was at the heart of village life in Applefield, and it wasn't unusual to see people from all backgrounds spending their leisure hours there: ladies and couples retreating to the snug while gentlemen played darts in the public bar. Edie had been on a few occasions with Vinnie and Barbara. Strangely enough, though, news of her visits to the Fleece never seemed to make it into her letters to her aunt.

It was payday and, as she was stony broke, she needed to collect her money from Sam or she wouldn't be able to treat Sue to the meal as she wanted to. With an effort, she pushed herself to her feet and bade Wilf goodbye until the next day.

Alfie was arriving tomorrow too. Edie couldn't wait to show her friends all the beauty spots of the area. Sam had agreed to grant her a holiday on Saturday morning: the three of them would have the whole weekend to explore. Perhaps they might take the children out to the lake, and little Coco –

The farmhouse came into focus, and Edie noticed Sam mounting the old bicycle he kept for his own occasional visits to the pub. Had he forgotten he still needed to pay her?

'Sam, wait!' she called, but whether because of his bad ear or because he was too far away, he didn't hear her.

'Bugger it!' she muttered: a phrase new to her vocabulary, and one which she'd taken to using far too often since starting work at the farm. She ran the rest of the way to the farmhouse, swung one leg over her own bike and started pedalling furiously after Sam.

Ten minutes later, Edie still hadn't managed to catch him up. Clearly she couldn't compete with those long, muscular legs, and was panting some distance behind as she followed the Sam-shaped speck.

He hadn't taken the road that led to Applefield Manor, or headed in the direction of the village. Where on earth could he be going? It couldn't be anywhere too far away or he'd surely have taken the truck.

He'd soon sailed past the shell of the old Land Girls' hostel on the Kirkton road. After half a mile he took a sharp right down the track that led to Carnmere Reservoir.

What in heaven's name could he be going to the reservoir for: an evening dip? Dearly hoping Sam would stop when he got there – and that she wasn't about to find him preparing to dive naked into the water – Edie swung her bike down the track.

When she reached the bottom, she dismounted and propped her bike against a tree, panting heavily.

She knew Sam must be around somewhere. She could see his bike, lying on its side at the water's edge. Edie shielded her eyes from the sun and peered into the distance, soon spotting Sam sitting on the grass with his back against a tree trunk as he gazed pensively over the water.

'London,' he said when she'd approached him, lifting his eyebrows. 'What the devil are you doing here? Did you follow me?'

She was silent for a moment while she got her breath back.

'I'm trying to get paid so I can take my friend to the pub,' she panted. 'It's Thursday, Sam. You owe me sixteen bob.'

He grimaced. 'Oh hell. Sorry, I forgot. Why didn't you call in for it before you left?'

'Because I didn't leave. I stayed a bit later than usual, clearing that bracken.' She followed his gaze to the water. 'What are you doing all the way out here?'

He smiled, a little sadly. 'Being a sentimental old bugger, mostly. I don't know if it's your influence or Luca's but I do find I'm more prone to it these days.'

'Pardon?'

'Oh, nothing.' He patted the grass beside him. 'Here, sit down a minute. You're making me nervous hovering about like that.'

She hesitated. 'I need to meet my friend in an hour.'

'And it's half an hour's ride back to Applefield so you can afford to get your breath back first.' He took a note from his pocket and handed it to her. 'Here's ten bob. All I've got on me, I'm afraid. We can settle the difference tomorrow.'

'Well . . . I suppose there's time to sit down.' She pocketed the money and sat by him, feeling awkward.

They were silent for a while, watching the dragonflies dip and scoot over the water. It was a secluded little place, as beautiful as any lake, for all that it had been fashioned by Man and not nature. The water shone a sparkling blue-green, surrounded by a ring of pine trees that made it feel quite cut off from the rest of the world.

'I'm told you've got quite a zoo at your place now,' Sam said after a little while. 'What was the latest addition? Canaries?'

'No, a rabbit. Jimmy found a little one with an injured back leg on his way home from school yesterday and brought it home to nurse – a white one, not wild. I suppose it escaped and was attacked by a fox or something. Jack's making a hutch for it today.'

'How did you end up with them all? I never thought I'd

see old Mother Hewitt with a house full of kiddies and animals.'

'Oh, Prue's a big softy really. She can't resist helping something when it's . . .' Edie laughed softly. ' . . .when it's a lost cause.'

'And neither can you.'

'No.' She didn't look at him, her eyes fixed on the water as the sound of buzzing insects and birdsong lulled her senses. 'My friend Susan always teases me about that. She says I'm addicted to trying to save things.'

'She's right.'

He put a finger under her chin and turned her face towards his. Edie looked at him, feeling as if she was in a sort of trance. Sam seemed different in the golden evening sunlight. Softer, but sort of intense, his eyes darting over her face. It felt dreamlike . . . and . . . and he was holding her now, wasn't he? His large arms had enfolded her body, as if it was the most natural thing in the world that they should. Edie felt she should probably tell him to let her go, but she didn't. She didn't want him to, so why should she?

She was wearing her watch around her neck, as she always did. Sam hooked the chain with one finger and drew out the ornate silver timepiece on the end.

'You touch this when you're upset,' he said softly. 'Tell me why.'

'You noticed that?'

'I notice a lot of things.'

She took it from him and pressed the catch to open it.

'It was my mother's,' she said quietly. 'She died having me so I never knew her. One of my last memories of my dad was him giving this to me. He said that as long as I wore it, they'd both be with me.'

'How did he die?'

She swallowed. 'Consumption. When I was six.'

'That's rotten luck, London. I'm sorry.'

'The worst thing was he . . . that it was my fault.' She wasn't sure why she was telling him all this, but now she'd begun, she felt as though she wouldn't be able to stop until the whole story had come spilling out.

'Your fault? I don't see how.' He frowned. 'You told me you couldn't join the Wrens because you'd been sickly as a child, didn't you?'

'Yes,' she whispered. 'I was five when I got it. Dad took it from me.'

'You know that wasn't really your fault, don't you? That's just how those lung illnesses work.'

'No, Sam, you don't understand.' She turned her head away sharply, feeling tears prick her eyes. 'It *was* my fault. Not just because he caught it from me. He . . . he made a bargain.'

Edie could still hear him, her father, offering payment for his little girl's life. It was one of her earliest, most excruciatingly painful memories.

They'd been in Brighton. Daddy had packed the two of them off there for a seaside holiday, only it hadn't been much fun. Little Edie just couldn't understand why they'd gone all the way to the seaside only for her to be told she couldn't go to the beach or play with the other children, but that she had to stay inside until her silly old cough got better. She'd had coughs lots of times, but all that usually happened was that she got made to take nasty-tasting medicine by Dr Grant. She didn't know why this time Daddy looked so white and afraid; why he'd suddenly announced they were going to Brighton as if it was the most important thing in the world.

One day Edie had sneaked out of bed to the parlour of the hotel they were staying in and climbed up on the window seat, pulling the curtains to behind her. From there she could watch the other children playing on the seafront, and dream about the time when she would be well enough to join them.

Edie started when she heard the door open. She shrank back, knowing she would get into trouble if Daddy found out she had crept out of bed.

'Damn it, Dick, I've not slept in weeks. I can't lose both of them.' The voice she could hear cracked with a sob. 'What sort of God would take the very things a man lives for, and yet insist he keeps on living?'

Edie knew her father's voice immediately: those deep, broad North Country vowels that had never softened in all the years he'd lived in London. She loved to hear them; to pick his tones out of a crowd. But she didn't like the way he sounded to her then – afraid; frantic.

'Now, Seth, calm yourself,' came a soothing voice. It was Dr Grant, Daddy's friend, who sometimes came to visit from London to see if her cough was better yet. Edie peeped through the curtain and watched her father sink brokenly into a chair.

'Dick, I've seen this before. I know what the shadow of death looks like.' Her father looked up at his friend, eyes filled with desperate tears. 'Good God, but if He would only take me instead!'

'A lot of stuff and nonsense,' Dr Grant said stoutly, clapping him on the shoulder. 'There's no need for anyone to be taken. Consumption isn't the certain death it used to be. The child improves every time I see her. You keep on saying your prayers, and trust little Edie to me.'

Consumption. Edie knew that word. That was the name for her cough. Was it . . . did Daddy mean he thought she would die?

Cold fingers gripped at her heart. Unable to hold it back any more, her little body trembled as it was racked by a fit of painful coughing. The velvet of the curtain grew mottled with bloody spittle.

Dr Grant glanced at his friend. 'I believe we've a spy in our midst, Seth.'

A second later, the curtains were pulled apart and Edie found herself being swung into her father's bear-like arms.

'Edie, what are you doing out of bed? And in your night-dress and bare feet, child!'

'I'm sorry, Daddy,' she whispered in her croaking, cough-rattled little voice. 'I only wanted to look at the seaside.'

She expected her father to be angry, but he just smiled and kissed her hair.

'Well, my pet, never mind this once. But you must go back to bed now.'

'Daddy, am I going to die?' she asked as he carried her to her room. There was pleading in the crack of her voice; the desperate need for the answer to be a firm, strong 'no' from the person who was, then, her god, sun and stars.

'Not this time, sweetheart.' He held her tightly to him, his face buried in her hair. 'Please God, whatever it takes, not this time,' she heard him whisper.

Less than a year later, he was dead.

Chapter 33

Edie blinked back a tear as she lived, again, one of her most painful memories.

'You don't understand, Sam,' she whispered. 'My father made a trade. I heard him do it.'

'What trade?'

'My life for his. He prayed that I'd be spared and God would take him instead. Then I started to get better, and he . . .' Unable to help herself, she started weeping softly.

'Hey.' Sam gently guided her head to his shoulder and rested his cheek against her hair. 'Edie, you can't torture yourself with thinking that way. It was coincidence. God doesn't bargain with people's lives like that – only the old bastard downstairs makes those sorts of deals. Some people get better and some people don't, that's all.'

'I know.' She mopped her eyes with her handkerchief. 'But, Sam, I didn't know that when I was six. I grew up thinking it was my fault, and I still . . . I can't just stop feeling that way, even though I know it isn't true.' She laughed. 'I must sound like such a silly, superstitious little girl to you.'

Sam didn't answer. He just gazed across the water.

'You couldn't save your dad so you try to save everyone else, don't you?' he said at last.

'I suppose I do. I always felt I had to make my life . . . worth it, somehow. Worth the price he'd paid for it.' She smiled wanly. 'I'm not doing a very good job, am I?'

'We'll see,' Sam said enigmatically.

She looked up at him. 'What about you? I don't know anything about your family, except that your great-uncle had Larkstone before you. I'll trade you my story for yours.'

He nodded to the water. 'My story's out there.'

She frowned. 'In the reservoir?'

'It wasn't always a reservoir. Here, I'll show you.' He stood up and stretched out his hand to help Edie to her feet. Puzzled, she let him lead her a little way along the track that circled the water.

'There, look,' he said when they reached a certain point. 'About half a mile in, I reckon.'

'I don't understand, Sam.'

'There used to be a farmhouse just there: a whitewashed, storybook sort of place with a millstone against the wall and a gang of fat white chickens by a red pump in the yard. I was born in it. In fact there was a whole settlement here, until the late twenties – Carndale. The villagers were evicted and buildings demolished, then they submerged the ruins.'

'Good God,' Edie muttered. 'But . . . then where are your family?'

He pointed to a different part of the water. 'That was the churchyard. You can still see the remains of the spire sometimes, when it's been dry for a spell. My mam and little brother are in there. I don't know where my dad is, he was off long before.'

'Oh, Sam, I'm so sorry.'

She looked up at him, and was surprised to see that his eyes were wet.

'It's not like me to be such a sentimental old bugger,' he

said in a choked voice. 'I don't come down here much, but our Jacob would've had his birthday today. He'd be twenty-three, if he'd lived. He was only a bairn when we lost him.'

'Tell me about him,' Edie said quietly.

'Oh, bright: bright as they come,' he said with a faraway smile. 'Shy, sensitive, studious: nothing like his dull-witted oaf of a big brother, but for some reason he still thought the world of me. Mam talked about scholarships, trying to get him into some posh school so he could join one of the professions. But scarlet fever carried him off before he turned ten, and Mam was right behind him. Losing Jacob broke her.' He sighed. 'And you know, London, some days I'm glad. It would've killed her all over again if she'd had to see her home destroyed as well.'

'What happened to you after she died?'

'I was fifteen. That's a man, round these parts, and I made a decent job of managing our little plot on my own for a while. Then when they announced Carndale was due to be flattened, my dad's uncle offered me a job at his place. I'd only met the old boy once.'

'Why?'

'Suppose he must've felt responsible for me. He was a nice old lad, was Pete: a real gentle giant. He had no children of his own, and I reckon he got fond of me over the years – God only knows why, mardy little sod that I was. When he shuffled off, I found out he'd left me Larkstone.' He picked up a stone and skimmed it across the water. 'So, there I am still: doomed to the life of a small farmer for evermore, since the army won't have me.'

'How come the village never warmed to you? You were only a boy. It doesn't seem fair they took against you from the start.'

He shrugged. 'Well, that was my fault. I wasn't much different from Davy Braithwaite at that age – angry at the world, after what happened to my family and my home, and hardened from struggling by alone. A tough little sod to like, in other words. I never went out of my way to make friends in Applefield, and they were naturally suspicious of someone who appeared in their midst without roots or relatives in the sort of place where families had been established for generations. Always ready to believe the worst of me. But I'm content enough, long as I've got a book to read and a bottle of stout to wash my bread and butter down with.'

'Sounds like a lonely life,' Edie said quietly.

'For some it would be. But you know I'm not much for company, London.' He looked down into her upturned face, and his voice softened. 'Sometimes, though, I could wish . . .'

'What?'

'Sometimes, at night in the farmhouse, I think it would be pleasant . . .' He trailed off, holding her gaze for a moment. Before she knew what was happening, he'd leaned forward and pressed his lips to hers.

He drew back almost immediately. Edie could feel her lips tingling from the brief, unexpected kiss.

'Sorry,' he said, looking as though he'd surprised himself as well as her. 'I didn't mean to do that.'

'Um, that's all right,' Edie said, colouring deeply. 'You . . . you were saying something about the farmhouse?'

'Yes. I was thinking . . . I was thinking it might be nice to have some company of an evening. If I could find someone who wanted to keep company with me.'

'Davy and the POWs could sit with you.'

'Not the sort of company I had in mind, London.' He

333

drew her into his arms and planted a soft, lingering kiss, quite deliberately this time, on her lips. Edie's eyes closed as his mouth caressed her.

'What sort did you have in mind?' she asked breathlessly when he drew away.

'The sort that keeps you warm at night,' he whispered as he pressed her close. 'To have and to hold, you know? The sort that might eventually result in new, smaller company.'

Edie felt light-headed, and sagged limply in his arms. 'I . . . Sam, I . .'

'No need to give me an answer now. We've got all the time in the world, sweetheart.'

The endearment sounded strange on those eternally gruff, teasing lips of his, but Edie's tummy jumped to hear it. Sam kissed her again – once, twice, three times, each touch of his lips so gentle and tender, yet simmering with barely suppressed desire. Then, to her great disappointment, he let her go.

'We'll discuss this further tomorrow,' he said, stroking soft fingertips over her cheek. 'It's getting late. You ought to go meet your friend.'

Susan spluttered on her shandy. 'He did *what*?'

'All right, keep your voice down,' Edie hissed. She glanced around the Golden Fleece's cosy snug, which was filled with farmers and their wives enjoying an evening pint of bitter after their hard day's work. 'He proposed. At least, I think he did. The word "marriage" never actually cropped up.'

'You didn't say yes, did you?'

'Well, no, but I didn't say no either. Sam told me I didn't need to give him an answer right away.'

Susan shook her head. 'This is all very sudden, Ede. Yesterday you weren't even sure he was interested in you, then tonight . . . How did it happen?'

'I'm not entirely sure myself.' Edie paused to take a sip of the sherry Susan had insisted she have to help her recover. She'd still been in a daze when she arrived. 'I chased him to the reservoir because he'd forgotten to pay me. The next thing I know, we're sharing all these personal things – I mean, Sam Nicholson, never known to use one word when none will do, crying in front of me and telling me all about how his brother . . .' She trailed off. 'I don't think he meant to ask me, really. We were sharing a moment and he got carried away.'

'I thought he'd been giving you the cold shoulder.'

'Not quite, but he's avoided being alone with me since we almost kissed, definitely.'

'And yet all the time he must have been pining away for you,' Susan said in a low voice. 'Did he tell you why he'd been avoiding you?'

'No, he never brought it up.'

'Well? What answer will you give?'

'I'm . . . not sure.' Edie swallowed another mouthful of her drink, enjoying the sensation of the sherry warming her right to her toes. 'When he kissed me – Sue, it felt wonderful. I didn't want him to stop, at the time. But . . .'

' . . . but you're still unsure whether to accept him.'

Edie blinked into her glass. 'I've really fallen in love with this place. The people, the countryside, the animals – this whole part of the world. I love Larkstone Farm, and the work I do there. If it was possible for me to stay forever, I would.'

'Have you fallen in love with Sam though? That's the important question.'

'I think . . . I think I might have,' Edie murmured. 'I'm just not sure he loves me.'

'You mean he didn't tell you he did?'

Edie shook her head. 'He was ever so sweet when I told him about my dad, and when he held me, it felt like what I always thought love must feel like. But the word itself never crossed his lips. He isn't the sort of man who'd find it easy to talk about feelings, I know that.' She sighed. 'I've just always had this idea of the perfect proposal in my head, you know? Ever since I was a little girl.'

'Darling, we all do. What was yours?'

'Oh, nothing very original. The man I love on one knee, telling me I'm the only woman for him and he can't live without me. In my daydreams he tends to be in uniform – since the war started, at any rate.'

'Well, how did Sam ask you?'

Edie scoffed. 'Not like that. He told me he got lonely in the farmhouse and wouldn't mind a bit of company, if I fancied it. No telling me he loved me, no down on one knee, no ring; not even so much as a "Darling, will you marry me?"'

Susan pursed her lips. 'Mmm. Very romantic.'

'That's Sam all over: just a rough-around-the-edges Northern farmer, more used to talking about treatments for ovine foot rot than love. And I wouldn't mind him asking me the way he did at all, if I really believed he did love me. I'm just not sure if it's really me he wants or any old wife – someone to share the evenings with, and help shoulder the burden at the farm. He knows I'm a hard worker; that comes in handy in a farmer's wife.'

'You don't think he asked you for that reason, do you?' Susan scanned her friend's slight figure. 'You're hardly a beast of burden, Ede.'

Edie sighed. 'No, I suppose not. Sam's a difficult one to read, but I do believe he's . . . attached to me. But however much I like the idea of staying in Applefield as his wife, that isn't enough for me. I need to know his feelings are strong enough for us to make a life together. Marriage must be a miserable affair when one side loves more than the other.'

'Of course you need that,' Susan said, squeezing her hand. 'After all the affection you missed out on growing up, the least you deserve is a husband who adores you.'

'What shall I do?'

'Well . . . he said he was in no hurry for your answer. Take some time to think it over. I'm sure your heart will guide you down the right path.'

Chapter 34

It was the next morning when Edie saw Sam again. When she arrived at work he was there in the farmhouse, barking out jobs in his usual manner. She tried not to blush as she took her place in line.

Lambing season had drawn to a close now. Edie had worried that might mean the War Ag would move her on, but she'd heard nothing so she assumed she'd be remaining at Larkstone for the time being.

She was glad. She'd grown fond of her fellow workers, and she dearly wanted to see what she thought of as 'her' lambs growing up. Luca had told her Larkstone would be a paradise in the summer, and Edie longed to experience it.

Then, of course, there was Sam. Edie was prepared to admit, if only to herself, that he was the main reason she didn't want to go anywhere else. She hadn't realised how precious her teasing, kind, curmudgeonly boss had become until he'd held her in his arms and planted those too-fleeting butterfly kisses on her lips.

She could still hardly believe he'd made her an offer of marriage, out of the blue like that – an offer which, if she accepted it, meant she could remain on the farm she'd grown to love forever. If she could only be sure of his feelings . . .

Edie felt a stab of disappointment when Sam put her on hoof-cleaning duty with Davy instead of choosing her to help him muck out the chickens. He was back in business-like mode, barely registering her presence, and for a moment she wondered if she'd dreamed the kisses, the proposal: everything. But as she went to follow Davy out, he put a hand on her shoulder.

'Hold on, London. I owe you six bob. You'd better take it now or no doubt I'll have you chasing me halfway round the county for it this weekend.'

'Oh. Yes.' She hung back while the other workers went to their jobs, watching him open his cashbox.

'The farmhouse is looking nice,' she said, to fill the awkward silence as much as anything.

He glanced around at the fresh paint, the new carpet, and the watercolour prints that now adorned the walls. 'Aye, thought I'd get it looking a bit more homely. You like it, do you?'

'I do. Very cosy.'

'I'm glad to hear it.'

He handed her six shillings and she put the coins in her dungaree pocket.

'Busy tonight?' he asked as he closed up the cashbox again. 'Wondered if you fancied going to the pictures with me.' He looked up. 'Nothing funny. Thought it'd be nice to spend some time together away from this place, that's all.'

Edie thought so too, and she was about to agree when she remembered she already had plans.

'I wish I could,' she said with an apologetic grimace. 'I'm going to the Palais in town.'

'What, out again? Never knew you were such a social butterfly, London.'

She laughed. 'I'm not usually, but some friends from home are here on leave. That's why I asked for a holiday tomorrow.'

'Right. Well, another time then.'

'Definitely.'

He hesitated, hovering over her, and Edie thought for a moment he might be about to kiss her again. Her stomach leaped in anticipation, but then he seemed to change his mind and only nodded briefly.

'Better get to work,' he said.

At the end of the day, Edie was preparing to mount her bicycle when she heard a familiar voice call her name. She broke into a smile of delight when she spotted a long-legged figure in army uniform striding towards her, waving.

'Alfie!' She beamed at her friend, who, as he got closer, she could see was handsomer than ever. He was sporting a deep tan, and his light brown hair had been bleached pure blond by the sun. 'Darling, you didn't need to meet me from work. I'll be seeing you tonight.'

'How could I keep away, knowing my best girl was so close by?' He picked her up and swung her around in his arms, then planted a hearty kiss on her forehead.

She giggled. 'Put me down, you daft so-and-so. When did you arrive?'

He looked at his wristwatch. 'About half an hour ago. I dropped my bags at the pub and dashed straight here.' He cast an approving glance over her figure. 'Ede, you look like a million quid.'

'I'm hot, dirty and covered in sheep muck, Alfie Hume,'

she said, laughing. 'I appreciate the compliment, but you're not fooling anyone.'

'Well, maybe it's just that I'm viewing you through the eyes of true love.' He crooked his arm for her to slip hers through. 'Come on, I'll walk you home.'

'I've got my bike.'

'All right, then you can ride home and I'll sit in the basket.'

Edie smiled and stood on tiptoes to kiss his cheek. 'Alf, I've missed you to bits. You and your daft bloody jokes.'

'The feeling's mutual, sweetheart.'

'Come on then. I'll push the thing home and we can have a nice stroll.'

She wheeled her bike along, Alfie walking at her side.

'I mean it, Ede,' he said as they walked. 'You look like a film star. You always did to me, of course, but now you're all rosy and plump.'

She raised an eyebrow. 'Plump?'

'Oh, in all of the right places, believe me,' he said, giving her bottom a cheeky pat.

'Will you ever stop being such an incorrigible flirt?'

'Course I will. When I get married, I promise I'll retire.'

Edie smiled. 'And until then no girl is safe from your charms.'

'Well, you certainly aren't.' He cast another sly sideways look at her. 'I like you in uniform. I bet you've got loads of lads after you here, haven't you?'

'Don't be daft, Alf,' she said, blushing as she thought about Sam.

'Well, have you?'

'Now, you mustn't tease me this weekend. I've been dying to see you both for ages.'

'All right, for you I'll behave.'

Applefield Manor was coming into focus and Edie pointed it out to him.

'That's where I live,' she said. 'What do you think?'

Alfie blinked. 'Bloody hell! You didn't tell me you'd moved into a castle.'

'I know, I feel like Rapunzel. Here, come back with me and I'll make you a cuppa.'

The rag and bone man was approaching on his cart, and Alfie took Edie's arm to guide her to the side of the road. When the cart had passed she was about to set off walking again, but Alfie held her back.

'Hang on, Ede. Before you go home, there's something important I want to talk to you about.'

He looked serious, which was a novelty in itself, and she frowned. 'What is it?'

'Here. Come down this road a bit.' He took her bike and rested it against a wall, then guided her a little way down the leafy, secluded lane that led into Applefield. When they reached the old packhorse bridge, he stopped.

'What's the matter, love?' she asked. 'Nothing's wrong, is it?'

'Don't know yet.' He took a deep breath. 'Ede, there was another reason I came to meet you. I wanted to see you alone before we met up with Sue.'

'Why?'

'Well, I've got something I need to ask you.'

'All right, go ahead,' she said, blinking.

He took something from his tunic pocket, and the next thing she knew he was down on one knee in the mud, holding it up to her.

'I told you it was important,' he said quietly.

Edie stared at the ring, glinting in the sunshine. It was

a real engagement ring, with a diamond in the middle and everything.

This wasn't the first time Alfie had asked her to marry him – he'd been throwing joke proposals at her since he was fourteen years old, and Edie had been laughing them off for just as long. But he'd never had a ring before, nor that earnest expression on his face . . .

'Not again, Alf?' she said with a smile, hoping she could make a joke of it. But her friend shook his head.

'I mean it this time, Edie,' he said softly. 'Thing about going to war: it makes you realise what's really important. Hang it, I'll be kicking myself for evermore if I don't ask you properly before someone else does. You're too smashing a girl to be single long.'

'Alfie, please don't –' Edie began, but he held up a hand to silence her.

'Let me say what I've got to say before you make up your mind.' He took another deep breath. 'Edie Cartwright, I love you to bits. I've loved you since I was in short trousers, and now I'm risking my life every day in long ones I think it's about time I finally stopped making a game out of it and told you how I really feel. There's no other girl for me, Ede – there never has been. And if you'd do me the honour of becoming Mrs Hume, I'd count myself the luckiest lad who ever drew breath. That's all.'

'Alfie, love, do please stand up.'

'Give me an answer first.'

His face, so dear to her always, was filled with earnestness and love. Edie couldn't help hesitating, even though she knew perfectly well what answer she had to give.

'You know I love you, Alf,' she said gently. 'Always have, always will.'

'Oh . . . God.' He groaned, pressing his eyes closed. 'The

words "like a brother" aren't about to follow that sentence, are they?'

'Please stand up.'

He sighed and got to his feet. A damp patch of mud stained one knee of his uniform, but he didn't seem to notice.

Edie put her arms around him. She felt him convulse with a sob as she held him.

'Won't you, Ede?' he whispered. 'I'd make you so happy, sweetheart, if you'd let me.'

'I wish I could.' Edie felt a tear escape and slide down her cheek. 'You know you're every girl's dream man. You're handsome and charming and funny and . . . and just perfect, really you are, Alf. You could sweep any woman off her feet.'

'Except the one I want,' he said in a toneless voice. 'Because I'm not your dream man, am I?'

'We've just been brother and sister for too long. I'm sorry, but I can't change one kind of love into another. It isn't possible.' She let him go. 'Alfie, darling, I never believed you really . . . that you had those feelings for me. If I caused you pain, I'm sorry.'

Alfie scuffed at the ground with his boot. 'I don't think I realised it fully myself, until my call-up papers dropped through the letterbox. Makes you think about things, Ede, knowing your days might be numbered.' He looked up at her with damp eyes. 'Couldn't you perhaps learn to love me, in time?' he asked quietly. 'I can wait.'

That tone of tender entreaty, those irresistible green eyes . . . if Edie had been any other woman, she knew she'd be melting into Alfie's arms now. The pain in her old friend's face was like a knife in her chest. But she couldn't. She couldn't love Alfie, not in that way . . . and not when she'd already given her heart to someone else.

'I'm so sorry,' she whispered. 'You know I'll love you forever, as a friend and brother. But I can't love you the way you want me to, no matter how long you wait.'

'Is there someone else you care for, is that it?'

'That . . . wouldn't matter. I couldn't love you as a wife ought to love a husband, not if I tried for twenty years. I love you far too much in the other way.' She took his hands. 'Do you hate me very much, darling?' she asked softly.

He summoned a wan smile and kissed her cheek. 'You know I could never do that. You'll always be my best girl, Ede. No matter what.'

Prue hummed to herself as she got the evening meal ready. Tilly had prepared lunch, determined she was ready to start earning her keep again, but she had looked tired this evening so Prue had sent her into the sitting room with Samantha to be fussed over by the children while Jack kept order. She well remembered how exhausted she had felt nursing Bertie twenty years ago.

She was looking forward to joining the little group after dinner for a night at the fireside. The evenings they spent together as a family – reading to the children, playing with the kittens, helping Jimmy try to teach his little birds to speak – had become the high point of her days. Prue couldn't bear to remember, now, all the time she had spent alone in her room before the young people had come. All it wanted was for Bertie to be at home and everything would be perfect.

They wouldn't have Edie with them tonight, of course. She was going out to the dance hall with that pretty ATS friend of hers, Susan, and her soldier brother. Prue had given Edie special permission to stay out until midnight if she liked. The child so rarely got to see her friends, she ought to make the most of it.

'Oh, Edie,' she said when that young woman herself came in through the porch door. 'You're just in time to join us for dinner. I must say, it's nice having you home earlier now the lambing is done.'

Edie didn't say anything. She just stood there, looking pale.

'Is anything the matter, dear?' Prue asked, frowning.

To her great surprise, the girl burst into tears.

'Why, Edie!' Prue came forward to embrace her. 'What on earth is wrong, my love?'

'I've . . . broken the heart of one of the people I love most in the world, that's all,' she sobbed. 'Prue, I feel just awful. I am awful – I'm an awful, awful person.'

'Now, now. Come and sit down.' Prue guided Edie into a chair and pulled up one beside her. 'I can't believe the big-hearted girl who managed to get through even my thick old hide could have done anything so very terrible. Why don't you tell me all about it?'

Edie took out her handkerchief to blow her nose.

'I'm in such a deal of trouble, Prue,' she whispered.

'Trouble?' Prue felt a stab of worry. 'You haven't done anything foolish, I hope. You've always been such a sensible girl.'

'No, nothing of that nature.' Edie laughed through her tears. 'It seems that sometime in my sleep on Wednesday night, I became the most desirable woman in Cumberland. I'm really not sure how, since I'm positive I'm exactly the same scarecrow I was before. I've had two proposals in two days.'

'Proposals! Goodness me! I didn't know you had a young man.'

'Nor did I.' She dabbed at her eyes. 'Yesterday Sam Nicholson managed to ask me for my hand without ever so much as mentioning the word marriage.'

'Did you accept?'

'I told him I'd think it over, but then I must have conjured up some sort of curse. Afterwards, in the pub, I was telling Sue about my dream proposal – a man in uniform, on one knee with a diamond ring, telling me I was the only girl for him. The very next day, the last person I could ever marry was doing exactly that.'

'Your friend who's here on leave,' Prue said slowly. 'The soldier you knit socks for.'

Edie nodded miserably. 'Alfie Hume, the best man I know. And I had to be the one to break his dear little heart.'

She gave in to another wave of tears, and Prue stretched an arm around her.

'Edie, I never had a daughter,' she said softly. 'When Bertie was born, I was almost grateful he was a boy and not a girl, knowing how hard it would have been to guide her through the tricky business of love affairs. But if I had been blessed with a daughter, I would have told her she was under no obligation to marry any man, no matter how strong his attachment or how much she might admire him. I would have advised her, with the strongest language I could summon, never to give her hand where she couldn't give her heart.'

Edie smiled weakly. 'Thank you.' She sighed. 'Still, Prue, if you'd seen his face . . .'

'He's hurt now, but think how much more pain it would have caused him – caused both of you – if you had married him without love.'

'Yes. Yes, I know. I just feel so guilty.'

'You will for a while, I suppose. But I firmly believe you

did the right thing, Edie. I think this friend of yours will realise that too, eventually.'

'I do hope so. He wasn't very happy when I told him he was like a brother to me, but he really is as precious as any brother. I'd be devastated if this drove a wedge between us.'

'Well, well, let us hope it won't come to that,' Prue said, giving her a squeeze.

Edie smiled. 'Prue, if you'd had a daughter, she'd have been very lucky to have you as her mother.'

'If I'd had a daughter, Edie, I hope I'd have raised her to care as much for people's feelings as you do.' Prue waited for Edie to blow her nose again. 'Now, tell me about young Sam. I didn't know he'd been courting you.'

'He hadn't, really. He asked me to go to the pictures with him once and for a silly reason of my own I said no – that was all the hint of romance there had ever been between us. Then yesterday we were talking and . . . there it was. I think he was as surprised by his proposal as I was, to be honest.' She looked up. 'Would you approve?'

Prue blinked. 'Why, would you like me to?'

'I'd like to know you'd be happy to see me with him. I know he's not well thought of around here, and . . . well, it matters to me what you think.'

'He's not liked down in the village, perhaps.' Prue scowled. 'A bunch of idle gossips with nothing better to do than paint their neighbours' souls black. But Applefield's opinions have never been any rule for mine. I've usually been on the wrong side of them myself.'

'So you approve of him?'

'Yes, I've always liked Sam. He's done me and mine a few kindnesses over the years.' She leaned around to look into Edie's face. 'But it's not me he wants to marry, is it? What are your feelings towards him, Edie?'

'It's his feelings towards me that I'm worried about,' Edie murmured. 'When he asked me to marry him, he said he wanted a companion; he never mentioned anything about love.'

'Well, never mind his feelings for the moment. Let's work out what yours are first.'

'I think . . .' Edie took a deep breath. 'No. No, I don't think, I know. I've fallen in love with him.'

Chapter 35

It was Wednesday evening and Sam was in the farmhouse, trying to read. But he couldn't concentrate. His mind was too full of dark thoughts.

She'd be here again tomorrow, and he didn't know how he was going to react when he saw her. A lifetime of keeping his cards close to his chest hadn't prepared him for the moment he'd have to see the woman he loved again when he knew she'd given her heart to someone else.

One of the framed watercolours he'd bought last market day caught his eye. He jumped to his feet and ripped it from the wall.

God, but he'd been a fool! Of course Edie would have a sweetheart. Of course she could never be interested in having someone like him for a husband: a rough country farmer who could barely keep up a conversation if it wasn't about sodding sheep. A man reviled as a scrimshank and a seducer by his neighbours, emasculated by rejection for war service, who spent his evenings reading alone by the light of a paraffin lamp and got his water from a pump in the yard. What could he have to offer a bonny, glittering thing like Edie Cartwright?

Not as much as her handsome soldier, clearly. Nothing

in his life had prepared Sam for the pain of seeing her in another man's arms – nothing. When he'd kissed her at the reservoir, when she'd cried on his shoulder and he'd confided in her things not even his few friends knew, he'd honestly believed there was something between them – that his attentions at least weren't unwanted. The deluded ass that he was!

That had all been shattered when he'd glanced out of the farmhouse window on Friday and seen Edie there with her lover. Sam wasn't given to violence, but he had only barely restrained himself from running out and swinging his fist into the young soldier's face.

All these weeks he'd been preparing to make Edie what he hoped was an attractive offer of marriage; keeping her at a distance so he wouldn't be tempted to speak before everything was ready. He'd done his best to transform the farmhouse from a crude bachelor dwelling into the sort of nest a young lady might like to call home, investing a portion of his small savings on home comforts – chintz covers for the furniture, a carpet, fresh paint, pictures for the walls. Sam hadn't believed he had much vanity, but what little he had must have been whispering treacherously in his ear these last few months, abusing him into thinking that a bright, sophisticated woman like Edie might actually consider throwing her lot in with someone like him.

The only bit of advice he could remember his Uncle Pete ever giving him that wasn't about sheep had been about women. 'Don't fall for girls, son,' the old man had grunted. 'They'll make a chump of you in the end.'

And yet Sam hadn't been able to help himself. Edie had walked into his life, and suddenly his world was a different place; a place that shone and sparkled like the noon sun on the lake. No longer had he seen every day as a burden.

The days when Edie worked at Larkstone were his favourite of the week, even if he only saw her for ten minutes. Just knowing she was here on the farm filled him with a sense of warm contentment, as if God was in his heaven and all was right with the world.

Lord help him, he thought with a wry smile. It's a sorry state of affairs when a woman has a man quoting Robert bloody Browning to himself.

When the girl had first arrived – this skinny, Walt Disney-eyed slip of a townie, with her posh way of talking, her soft heart and her lily-white skin – she'd ended up costing Sam half a crown. He'd made a bet with Luca that the new Land Girl would be on a train back to London within the month. But the tiny redhead from down south, it turned out, had a fighting Spitfire spirit he'd never have suspected. Sam had never seen such a grand little worker, and she'd soon earned his respect – and his liking, too. Edie seemed to him to be the perfect blend of toughness and tenderness: skilled with the animals, intelligent, kind, courageous, yet with a disarming innocence that made Sam feel he wanted to protect her.

New, unfamiliar, at first unwelcome feelings had stirred in his breast: feelings strange to him, that he had no idea how to put into words. After a lifetime of pushing people away, refusing to allow himself to get close to anyone after the losses of his early youth, Sam had found that here, at last, was someone he longed to keep by his side.

Then Luca's baby had arrived, that little, gurgling miracle, and Sam had started to ponder . . . to dream.

Sam's only experience of marriage had been witnessing his parents' disaster of one in the days before his father had walked out. Dad had been a vicious, brutal bully in the Fred Braithwaite mould, not averse to knocking his wife and sons about when he was in his cups. But a marriage like Tilly and Luca's, where there was love, respect, companionship . . . suddenly a whole new world had opened up in Sam's imagination, a world with a cosy fireside, a bouncing bairn or three, and a loved and loving wife he could share it all with.

And then, just like that, the dream was gone: snatched from under his nose by this boy soldier who'd stolen his Edie's heart.

He could hardly blame her. Young girls wanted romance, didn't they? Dashing acts of heroism, passionate speeches, moonlight serenades; all that Clark Gable business. They didn't want scruffy farmers with the smell of a hard day's work on them, mumbling some unromantic nonsense about a bit of company. Christ, he hadn't even had a ring to give her! Why hadn't he done things properly? He'd promised himself he was going to wait until he had everything ready before he spoke up. Not that it really mattered, when he was obviously too late.

Sam unlocked the cashbox where he kept the farm kitty. He took out a small box, flicked it open and sighed. The gold of the ring looked tarnished now; the diamond that had seemed so lustrous in the jeweller's cabinet, cheap and dull.

He hastily put it away when a knock sounded at the door.

'Come in!' he called out.

Young Davy entered, dressed in the khaki denims of his Home Guard uniform.

'Sam, I'm going to parade now,' he said. 'Need any errands running while I'm in town?'

'No, we're fine. But thanks for offering, lad.'

'Is it all right if I borrow the truck?'

'Can't you take the bike?' Sam asked. 'We need to be watching our coupons.'

'It won't use much petrol. You can take it out of my wages.'

'Why so keen to drive tonight?'

Davy flushed. 'Well . . . it's just that I'm going to the pictures with Ivy Constance afterwards. Can't take her home on the back of a bike, can I?'

Sam smiled. 'Ah, I see. Go on then.'

'You OK, are you, boss? You look a bit funny.'

'I'm all right.' Sam roused himself and pulled his gaze from the cashbox. 'What're you up to tonight then?'

'Lieutenant Bradley's giving us a talk on aircraft recognition.' Davy scuffed at the floor with a sort of bashful pride. 'He says I might be NCO material once I've learned to read.'

'Luca's making progress with your lessons, is he?'

'Aye, does his best. I've a long way to go but he says he won't give up on me.'

'Well, keep working hard and you'll be a lance-corporal before you know it. Ta-ra then.'

'You sure you won't come with me, Sam? The platoon could do with young blood.'

'Nay, they won't want me there playing at soldiers,' Sam muttered. 'You know what high regard folk round here hold me in. I don't suppose they keep places open for cowards and traitors, do they?'

Davy scowled. 'But you're not those things, any more than I am. Why don't you tell them you couldn't join the regular army? I hate people saying that stuff about you now I know.'

'They'd only find something else to gripe about. Hating me's too popular a pastime in Applefield for them to just give it up.'

Davy shot him a crafty look. 'I reckon Miss Cartwright would like it if you joined the Home Guard.'

'All right, son, don't push your luck. Just because you've got a girl now, it doesn't make you an expert on women,' Sam said, smiling. 'Go on, go enjoy your parade. If Hitler invades while you're out, I'll hold him off.'

They were interrupted by loud barks from outside, and the sound of yells and scuffling.

'What the hell is that?' Sam jumped to his feet, and they both ran out.

Two small boys were engaged in a fight in front of the farmhouse door, which Sam saw immediately had been chalked with the familiar word 'coward'. Another lad, slightly younger, was standing to one side, holding his arm as if it had been hurt. A tiny dog tugged at the trousers of one of the scuffling boys, growling.

'Right, pack it in!' Sam shouted.

Davy strode into the fray and pulled the fighting boys apart. Both wriggled fiercely, trying to get free with no success, until one hit on the bright idea of sinking his teeth into Davy's arm. Davy yelped, and the boy used his advantage to make a break for freedom. Sam tried to tackle him, but the child dodged and was soon running away over the fields.

'Leave him,' Sam said as Davy prepared to give chase. 'I know who he is: Jenny Armstrong's boy. We can have words with him later. Get these two into the house and let's see if we can get a story out of them.'

'It weren't our fault,' the bigger boy said when Davy had pushed them roughly inside the farmhouse.

'Now why do I find that hard to believe?' Sam said. 'So you're the little buggers who've been vandalising my place, are you? Davy, go into the village and fetch a policeman.'

'No! Don't,' the smaller boy whispered. 'We didn't do nothing, Mister, promise. Charlie Armstrong done it. He's always sneaking up here to write on stuff, we hear him showing off about it at school.'

Sam frowned. 'That accent's not local. Where've you come from, lad?'

The child glanced at the other boy, who shook his head.

'Nowhere,' he muttered.

'I've seen you two before.' Sam turned to the older boy, the one wearing clothes he looked to have long since grown out of. 'You're Prue Hewitt's kids. The evacuees. Take that cap off.'

Aggie hesitated, then removed the hat she was wearing to let her pigtails tumble free.

'Jimmy's tellin' the truth. We didn't do nothing,' she said, sticking out her chin. 'We just come to hide a letter somewhere for Edie.'

'Edie? What for?'

'Because if we leave it at home and she finds it, she'll know we're gone and come after us. But if we leave it here, she won't see it till tomorrow morning when she comes to work.'

'I see. Very clever.'

'Charlie were already writing on the door when we got here, we had nothin' to do with it. Then he hurt Jim's arm, so I had to thump him to teach him a lesson.' Aggie cocked her head. 'Why's Charlie always call you a coward, Mister? Are you one?'

'I don't believe so. No more than anybody else.'

'He calls our Jim that too, 'cause he's quiet and he don't like to fight.'

'Well, I think your definition of cowardice depends on your definition of bravery. Charlie probably believes a brave

356

man is one who never feels afraid. I believe it's one who feels afraid but keeps his head and does what he needs to do anyway.' Sam glanced at Jimmy. 'But a boy who hurts those smaller than him, and who's happy to call a man names behind his back but runs off when confronted, certainly has no right to throw accusations of cowardice at anyone else. You tell him that if he comes near you again, Jimmy.'

Jimmy nodded, smiling for the first time since Sam had caught the pair of them.

'Now tell me why you were writing to Edie,' he said, sensing they were starting to relax.

'We're running away,' Jimmy blurted out, before immediately covering his mouth with his hands.

'Running away!'

'Um, Sam,' Davy said in a low voice.

'Aye, go on, son,' Sam said. 'You don't want to be late for parade.'

Davy opened the door to leave. Sam followed him out.

'Call in at Applefield Manor, speak to the old lady,' he muttered. 'Tell her we've got her kiddies here. I'll get the whole story out of them. Reckon I'll have them talked out of it by the time she comes to fetch them.'

Davy nodded and headed for the truck. Sam went back into the farmhouse, closing the door behind him.

'Now then, does one of you want to tell me why you're running away?' he asked. 'Mrs Hewitt will be very worried when she finds you gone.'

'You shouldn't ought to of told him,' Aggie hissed to her brother.

The little terrier they'd brought with them had crept over to the fireplace, where Sadie and Shep were sitting with their remaining puppy, Meg – Sam had been too soft to sell them all in the end. The dog started sniffing Meg, and she wagged her tail in greeting.

'Looks like someone's making new friends,' Sam said. 'What's your dog called?'

'Coco,' Jimmy whispered.

'Is Coco running away too?'

Jimmy hesitated, and Sam smiled as he took a seat in the armchair.

'Here, sit down,' he said, gesturing to the old couch near the fireplace. 'Just tell me, were you running from something or to something?'

'From something,' Aggie muttered.

'Can you tell me what? I thought you were happy at Applefield Manor. Mrs Hewitt's been kind to you, hasn't she?'

Aggie nodded. 'We love it there. But I heard Edie's friend say that now the bombs've stopped a bit, it'll be safe to go back to London. An' . . .' She swallowed. 'An' then Jimmy heard Aunty Prue say that they'll put us in orphanages. Into different ones, so we wouldn't never see each other again.'

'So we had to run away, see, Mister?' Jimmy said, blinking wide eyes at him. 'We can't let them break us up.'

Edie answered the front door to find Davy Braithwaite on the doorstep, wearing the uniform of the Kirkton Home Guard.

'How do, Miss Cartwright?' he said, taking off his cap. She'd told him a dozen times he could call her Edie, but the boy couldn't seem to bring himself to do it.

'Davy. Is everything all right?'

'Sam asked me to call on my way to parade with a message for that Mrs Hewitt. Is she in?'

358

'No, she's walking over to the Constances' farm for our milk. Sally forgot us on her round today.' Edie smiled. 'A dicky bird tells me you've been walking out with Sally's little sister.'

Davy blushed crimson, but he was smiling. 'Might've been.'

'So do you have to speak to Prue, or might I be able to help?'

'I reckon you'll have to do. It's them two bairns of yourn, the little lass and her brother. Sam's got them and he wants someone to fetch them back.'

She frowned. 'What? Sam's got our evacuees?'

'Aye, trying to run away from home or summat.'

'Hold on a moment.'

Edie ran up to the children's room. Sure enough, it was empty and the window gaping open, with a rope made of knotted sheets tied to one of the bedposts.

'Whatever could have possessed them to do that?' she said to Davy when she went back downstairs.

'I don't know, I went before they said. Can you go for them then, Miss? I'm going to be late for parade if I don't get going.'

'Yes, I'll cycle over now. Thanks, Davy.'

When he'd gone, Edie called into the kitchen to let Tilly know she was going out. She didn't say why – she wanted to get the full story about why the children had run away first. At least they were safe with Sam and hadn't managed to get any further than Larkstone Farm. If they'd fallen into the hands of the sort of people who might do them harm . . . it didn't bear thinking about.

What could have made them want to run away? Edie had noticed they'd seemed quiet when she, Susan and Alfie had taken them out for a picnic on Sunday, but not to the

359

extent that it had concerned her. Baby Samantha had had an unsettled night, so Edie had assumed the children were just tired.

She felt a surge of guilt as she mounted her bike. It was her fault. She'd been so distracted by developments in her own life, wondering what answer she ought to give Sam, that she'd probably missed the signs Jimmy and Aggie were worrying about something.

Her friends had gone now: Susan back to her billet in Hull, Alfie down to London to visit his parents. It had been lovely to see them both, but Edie was forced to admit it hadn't been quite like old times. Alfie's proposal had cast a shadow over the weekend – not that he mentioned it again after that Friday evening, but there was a sadness behind the familiar roguish grin, and in Sue's eyes too. He must have shared what had happened with his sister. Edie knew it had always been Susan's dearest wish that the two of them would make a match one day, and the fist of guilt in her stomach had given her another wrench.

It wasn't until Alfie was due to leave on Sunday evening that he made any reference to what had happened, when he stopped at Applefield Manor to say goodbye.

'Couldn't you, Ede?' he'd whispered as he'd embraced her.

'Alf, dear, I'm sorry.'

And so he'd gone, with tears swimming in his eyes.

Edie had made up her mind on one point, at least: she needed an answer from Sam before she could decide what hers ought to be. Immodest and unmaidenly it may be – that's what Aunt Caroline would no doubt say – but she needed to ask Sam if he loved her.

The farm soon came into view. Edie could see the children outside the farmhouse with Sam: Jimmy sitting on

Sam's old Fordson tractor and Aggie playing with Coco and Meg. She wondered again what could have made the pair of them want to run away, when they'd shown every sign of loving their new life. Prue and Jack had fallen naturally into the role of parents and the children, as far as she could see, had never been healthier, happier or better cared for in their lives. Hopefully there would be some answers waiting for her.

'Children!' she gasped when she reached the little group. She threw down her bike and pulled Aggie to her for a hug. 'Aggie, sweetheart, what on earth did you think you were doing? I was worried to death!'

'Are we in trouble, Edie?' Aggie whispered.

'You're not in trouble, but it was very naughty to give me such a fright. Now, you must come home and we'll have no more talk of running away.' She looked up at Sam. 'Thanks for looking after them, Sam.'

He grunted, but he didn't say anything.

Edie glanced at Jimmy on the tractor. His eyes sparkled as he turned the steering wheel around in his hands.

'Is it safe for him to be messing about in that thing?' she asked Sam, straightening up. Aggie squealed as Meg jumped up at her leg, and turned to chase her around the yard.

'Engine's off. It can't do him any harm,' Sam said. 'Where's the old lady? The message was meant to be for her.'

'She had to go out.'

Something was wrong. He was refusing to meet her eye, and his face looked like thunder.

'Sam, what's the matter?' she asked, frowning. 'The children didn't misbehave, did they?'

'Nay, they're good kids.'

She shook her head. 'Whyever would they run away? I can't understand it.'

361

'Here.' He handed her an envelope. 'This'll answer a few questions.'

Edie's own name was written on the front, in an unformed, childish scrawl she recognised as belonging to Jimmy.

Deer eedy, the letter read. *We av ran away and we are sorry becus we reely like you and evryone at the howse and we wull mis yu and arnty prew and uncul jack and tilli and samanfer and the kitens and chics and canirees and bugs and pepa. We wish we cud stay for ever and ever, but soon they wull take us to a orfanidge and split us up becus the boms av stopt. We no becus we erd arnty prew say so. Sorry for lisnin, we dint meen to. I leev my best marbels to yu and the souljers wot uncul jack made me to baby samanfer and my canirees to arnty prew and my radio wot i made and bugs my rabit to uncul jack, to remeber me. Aggie givs er book wot she wun as a prize to tilli and er best dol to baby samanfer, and she says yu and arnty prew and uncul jack mus share er kitens and to giv em all a kis from us. We will mis yu lodes and we luv yu for ever. Fanks for takin care of us. James Adam Cawthra (and Aggie and Coco too)*

'What do you think?' Sam said quietly.

'Well his vocabulary's coming on but his spelling needs work.' She sighed. 'Poor lambs, so this is what's been on their minds. I had no idea they'd heard us talking.'

'Is it true? Are they going into an orphanage?'

'They might have to go into some sort of institution eventually,' she admitted. 'It's better than sending them back to a stepmother who beats and starves them. But Prue and the vicar are fighting to make sure they won't be split up.'

'I think they could do with a dose of reassurance when you get them home.'

'Yes. Thank you.'

Sam glanced at Jimmy, who'd hopped down from the tractor seat and was running his fingers lovingly over the engine. 'Bright lad, that, spelling aside. He was showing me the book where he draws designs for inventions. They looked like summat out of Flash Gordon.'

Edie laughed. 'Yes, his patented Jimmy Cawthra Shrink-o-matic Ray Gun is going to revolutionise human life as we know it.'

'Reminds me of our Jacob. He was just like that: magic with any sort of machinery. You should've seen his face light up when he got near a steam engine.'

Sam's scowl had lifted and for a moment it almost looked as though he might smile, but as his gaze fell on Edie, he seemed to remember something and the black look descended again.

'Sam, is something wrong?' she asked.

'Nowt new, no.'

'Then why are you . . . are you angry with me?'

'Why, have I any reason to be? Or any right, for that matter?'

'Well, no.' She paused, wondering how best to bring up the subject she wanted to discuss. 'I, um . . . there was a question I needed to ask you.'

'Make it quick then, London. I've got things to do.'

She looked at him for a moment. He was still glowering, his eyes turned down so he wouldn't meet her gaze.

'So? What is it then?' he demanded. 'Ask if you're going to, I've not got all night.'

Edie hesitated, then shook her head.

'It's nothing,' she said. 'Never mind.'

It felt as though, in his furrowed brow and cold manners, Sam had already given her all the answer she needed.

363

Chapter 36

Sally Constance was in the stable when Prue arrived to fetch the milk that hadn't been delivered that morning. From the way the girl turned away and wiped her eyes with her sleeve, Prue would swear she had just been crying.

'Oh. Mrs Hewitt,' Sally said, smiling weakly. 'I'm sorry, you've caught me here with my curlers in and housecoat on, all at sixes and sevens. We weren't expecting no one to call round.'

'That's all right, Sally.' Prue held up her milk jug. 'I think you forgot us today, didn't you?'

Sally groaned. 'Oh gracious, however did I manage to do that? I'm sorry, Mrs Hewitt. I've been having one of them days.'

'Don't worry about it, dear.' Prue handed over the jug and went to stroke Betty, the Constances' ancient shire horse. 'And how are you, old girl? The children missed giving you your handful of oats this morning.'

'Sorry, Mrs Hewitt,' Sally said again. 'That's how come you got missed off. You see, Betty, she . . . she had a bit of a turn this morning and couldn't finish her round. I had to do the rest on foot.'

To Prue's amazement, Sally burst into tears.

'My dear, what on earth is the matter?'

'Miss, I been making my rounds with Betty for twenty-five year, ever since I were a little lass. I never thought I'd see the day she'd have to give it up, but vet says she mun. He says she's too old now to be in harness.'

'We all have to retire sometime,' Prue said gently. 'Perhaps at her age, it is best that Betty be put out to pasture.'

'You don't understand, Mrs Hewitt.' Sally mopped her eyes. 'She isn't being put out to pasture. Dad says . . . he says he can't afford to give board to an animal that can't earn its keep, not when there's a war on, and Betty'll have to go to make way for a new horse.'

'Sally, what are you saying?'

'She . . . she . . . the knacker man's coming for her tomorrow,' Sally managed to say through choking sobs. 'They're going to shoot our Betty, Mrs Hewitt.'

'Oh, my love. Come here.'

Prue pulled Sally into a hug.

'You know, I used to think you was such a scary lady,' Sally said with a wet laugh. 'Sorry, I don't mean no offence by that. I just mean, you're not scary at all really, are you? You're lovely. Everyone's talking about how kind you've been to them little mites from London.'

Prue didn't quite know what to say to that, so she only patted Sally's back in what she hoped was a comforting manner.

Betty surveyed the devastating scene calmly, her wise old eyes seeming to accept her inevitable fate. She let out a low whinny as Prue met her gaze.

'Sally . . .' She let the girl go. 'Suppose another home could be found for Betty? Would your father agree to that?'

'I reckon so, long as her board wasn't coming out of his

pocket.' Sally's eyes lit up. 'Mrs Hewitt, you aren't saying you know someone who'd take my Betty, are you?'

'Yes, I believe I am.'

'Oh, Mrs Hewitt, if you knew someone who'd do that, I'd think they were sent from Heaven! But who round here wants a horse that can't work? Betty's no good to anyone now, she's too old.'

'Well, I know of a place where she can live out her last years in peace, and you'd be welcome to visit her anytime, Sally.'

'Do not say a word,' Prue muttered as she led the old horse through the gardens while Jack looked on in amazement.

'I see you forgot the milk, Cheg.'

'Yes, yes, all right, I'm as soft as the young ones. But we had the stables sitting empty, and . . . well, it seemed rather hard on the old girl to get a bullet in the head as a reward for a lifetime of service.'

Jack threw down his pitchfork and followed her to the stables. 'The Constances weren't going to shoot old Betty?'

'They were, and break poor Sally's heart into the bargain. Not only that, they had the cheek to demand five pounds from me to "buy" her. Compensation for what they would've got from the knacker man for her remains.' Prue shook her head darkly. 'It makes for some hard people, this war.'

'Evenin'!' Pepper greeted them. She swooped down to Jack's shoulder and nibbled his ear, then cocked her head to appraise her new stablemate. Prue guided the old horse backwards into one of the stalls, and Betty surveyed them calmly over her half-door.

'Dignified old lady, aren't you?' Prue said, stroking the horse's nose. 'Deserving of a dignified end. You'll be happy

366

here, sweetheart, and your friend Sally can come to visit whenever she wants.'

'She'll earn her keep, any road.' Jack gave the horse a pat. 'Between us we'll have them roses looking lovely, eh, old girl?' He turned to smile at Prue. 'You've a golden heart, Cheg, for all that you try to hide it.'

'We'll need fodder for her, and grooming equipment. I'll go into town tomorrow. It's so long since we kept a horse, I can't remember what they need.'

Prue fell silent, looking around the stables. She so rarely came in here. The building contained too many memories, both happy and painful – or perhaps not painful but bitter-sweet, since the good Lord had seen fit to take Albert from her.

'You're thinking about Captain, aren't you?' Jack said softly.

'Yes,' she whispered. 'This was his stall, next to Betty's. Dear little beast. Albert loved him so.'

Captain, a grey pony just the perfect height for a nine-year-old boy to ride, was the only horse who had ever lived at Applefield Manor in Prue's time. He had been given to Albert by a kindly uncle who was fond of him – Albert's parents, practising the parsimony of the truly rich, very rarely bought the boy presents.

As with everything he had, Albert had generously shared Captain with his two best friends, and the little horse had bounced these inexpert cavaliers merrily along without complaint until they were too big to ride him comfortably. He had lived long enough to bounce an infant Bertie too, but eventually the placid little animal had died in his sleep at the ripe old age of twenty-five. It was one of only two occasions when Prue could remember seeing her husband cry. The other was the day the armistice had been signed.

'That's how an animal like Betty ought to die, Jack,' she murmured. 'Painlessly, after a lifetime of being useful and loved, as our Captain did.'

'Aye, you're right. You've done a good turn today, Cheggy. I'm proud of you.'

Prue wasn't sure what made her do it – the shadow, perhaps, of the boy who had been her childhood friend in his eyes. Suddenly she was seized with the desire to give Jack a hug, so she did.

'Well!' Jack said, blinking at the arms he found around him. 'I wasn't expecting that.'

'You mean a lot to me, old man. You know that, don't you?'

'Reckon so.' Jack took off his cap and rubbed his hair awkwardly. 'You're in a queer sort of mood today, lass.'

'I suppose I've been letting myself get sentimental. Remembering the old days.'

'You miss Bert,' he said softly. 'Well, I do too.'

'Every day.' Prue gave him a squeeze before she let him go. 'But at least I've still got you.'

'Cheg, I . . . there's something I've been meaning to talk to you about. I wasn't going to, but since the bairns have come, I reckon it's now or never for me.'

He twisted his cloth cap in his hands, his cheeks flushed.

'What is it?' Prue asked.

'Well, you know I never got around to the fathering business. I'd have liked children of my own, but . . . I mean, you need a wife for that, and I hadn't got one. I wanted one, but she . . . but I . . .' He trailed off.

'Jack, what are you on about?'

'Give us a clue here, Pep,' he said to the crow on his shoulder.

'Blimey!'

'Aye, very helpful. Useless ruddy bird. Go on, bugger off then.'

Prue could swear the animal grinned before she sailed back to the rafters.

'Cheg, what I'm trying to say . . . what I want to tell you . . .' Jack groaned. 'You know, I'm starting to understand how it is I never married.'

'What did you mean about the bairns?'

'Well, you did say they had no home to go back to, and it'd be a crying shame, if you ask me, to pack a couple of little smashers like them off to some orphanage. As to breaking them up, it can't be allowed to happen. So I was wondering if, um . . . if I could keep them.'

'Keep them?' Prue said, blinking. 'Jack, these are children, not kittens or orphaned crows. You can't make pets of them.'

He smiled. 'I don't mean that. We'd do it all official, like. Adopt them, properly, with all the right legal papers. I've come to care for them as if they were my own, these few months. Life's been a different beast since they've lived here – I've been a different man.'

Prue had noticed that too: the change in Jack since the children had arrived. His nightmares were less frequent now, and his eyes had lost a little of their hunted look.

'Any road, I don't think we're too old to start again, me and thee, are we, lass?' Jack said with a nervous smile.

'We?'

'Aye, well, I do think it's best for bairns if they've got a mam and a dad. And I suppose the authorities expect you to have a wife to do an adoption, don't they, so I wondered . . . I did think . . .'

'You're not talking about me?'

He twisted his cap awkwardly. 'If you've got room for

one more broken old shire horse in your stables, Cheg, I'd be honoured to set up home in them. Would you have me, love?'

Prue felt as if she was in a bizarre dream. 'Jack, are you saying you want me to *marry* you so we can adopt Aggie and Jimmy?'

'No.' He stepped forward so he could cup her cheek. 'I want you to marry me because I've been in love with you since bloody 1906, you daft mare.'

Prue gripped the door of Betty's stall.

'But Jack, this is . . . I never had any idea that you . . .'

He silenced her fumbling speech with a kiss, and Prue's eyes widened before falling closed. What a revelation there was in that kiss! What a world of feelings – unexpressed, unexplored and unacknowledged, but simmering, always, just below the surface. Had she really not realised what he felt – what she felt herself, all this time?

'Well!' she gasped when he drew back. 'There really is no fool like an old fool. Or a pair of them, in this case.'

They sprang apart as the stable door opened and Edie came in with the children.

'Ah, there you are,' she said. 'Prue, I've been looking all over the house for you.' She frowned at the horse. 'Surely that isn't Betty?'

'Er, yes,' Prue said, feeling horribly flustered. 'She's going to be spending her retirement with us.'

'Oh.' Edie blinked at the old horse for a moment, then drew the two children forward. 'Aggie and Jimmy have something they need to say to you.'

It was only then that Prue noticed how dirty they were, and that Aggie appeared to be wearing her brother's clothes. What had they been up to? They'd been clean enough when they'd arrived home from school.

'We're sorry, Aunty Prue, that we tried to run away,' Aggie whispered. 'We didn't mean to frighten you after you been so nice to us. We was scared, that's all.'

Jack frowned. 'Run away?'

Edie nodded. 'Sam found them at the farm, trying to hide a letter for me.'

'But, my dears, whyever would you do that?' Prue said. 'You're not unhappy at Applefield Manor, are you?'

Aggie shook her head, her eyes fixed on the ground.

'Here,' Edie said, handing Prue a letter. 'This explains everything.'

Prue read it through, feeling a tear rise in her eye when she reached the end. She handed it to Jack.

'Aggie. Jimmy,' she said earnestly. 'I'm sorry you had to hear us talking. But if you'd come to me, we could have discussed it instead of you running away and putting yourselves in all sorts of danger. We don't want you to be sent to separate orphanages any more than you do.'

'You couldn't stop them though,' Jimmy muttered. 'If they said we had to, you couldn't do nothing about it.'

Prue drew them to her, one in the crook of each arm.

'There is one thing I could do,' she said softly. 'Children, how would you like to stay at Applefield Manor? Not just while the war's on. Forever.'

Aggie stared at her. 'You really mean it, Aunty Prue?'

'I do.' She glanced up at Jack. 'Your Uncle Jack and I have been talking and we've agreed we'd like to adopt you, legally. Then you could live at Applefield Manor forever and no one could take you away.'

'And you'd be like . . . our mum and dad then?'

'That's right.'

Aggie threw her arms around Prue with a squeal of joy, and Jimmy ran to Jack to be swung up into his arms.

371

'We'd like that the best of everything in the world, wouldn't we, Jim?' Aggie said breathlessly. 'Thank you, Aunty Prue. We'll be so good forever, promise we will.'

Prue laughed. 'Knowing children as I do, I suspect that will turn out to be a bare-faced fib, but never mind.' She hugged the little girl tightly. 'I'm glad you're safe, sweetheart. Now no more running away, please. This is your home and there'll never be any reason for you to have to leave it.'

Edie looked at Jack, who had tears in his eyes as he hugged Jimmy to him.

'I told you so,' she whispered, and he smiled.

Chapter 37

Edie pushed her bike across the gardens, heading for the stables. There was something in her basket she needed to deposit there.

Inside she cast a quick look around to make sure she was alone, then took her bundled headscarf from the basket.

A little black face blinked up at her, trembling with fear, and Edie made soft cooing noises over it as she stroked its fur. Pepper looked on curiously from the top of Betty's head, her new favourite perch. The mild-mannered old carthorse didn't seem to mind the crow taking up residence between her ears – in fact, she seemed to enjoy the company.

'Poor pup,' Edie whispered to the tiny mongrel. 'Where's your master, eh? Did you ever have one?'

Edie had found the ragamuffin little stray peeping at her with hungry eyes from behind a dustbin down in the village. The poor thing looked to be half-starved. She was tame enough, though, and hadn't objected to Edie picking her up.

She was very tiny, and Edie suspected she couldn't have been weaned for long. Perhaps her mother had been a stray too, and the puppy orphaned before she was really old enough to care for herself – another victim, perhaps, of the recent air raid.

Edie took the dog into the stall next to Betty's and settled her in one corner.

'Here you are, my love.' She unwrapped a corned beef sandwich she hadn't eaten at lunchtime and put it down in front of the puppy, who fell on it gratefully. 'It's all I've got for now, but I'll bring you more in a little while. I just need to prepare the ground with Prue before I break the news you'll be joining the menagerie.' She fancied she saw a worried look in the dog's eye and smiled. 'Oh, don't worry, she's an old softy. She wouldn't throw you out.'

Once she'd put away her bike, Edie headed for the kitchen. Tilly was in there, cooking dinner while Samantha watched from her baby basket.

'Hello, beautiful,' Edie said, leaning down to give Samantha a kiss. 'Have you been good for your mummy today?'

'She's been a little monkey,' Tilly said. 'You'd think butter wouldn't melt in her mouth, wouldn't you? This is the first time she's been quiet since she woke up.' She gestured to a chair. 'Sit down and I'll fetch you a tea. There's a pot just mashed.'

'Thanks.'

'So?' Tilly said as Edie sat down. 'How was Sam today?'

Edie sighed. 'Cold again. He barely speaks to me now except about work. Till, I just don't know what's going on.'

'Did you talk to him about it?'

'I didn't get the chance. He's going out of his way to avoid me. The only time I see him is in the morning when he gives us our jobs.' She shook her head angrily. 'Honestly, is this some sort of game? He nearly kisses me, then spends weeks avoiding me. He asks me to marry him, then glowers at me whenever he sees me. I was an ass to ever let myself fall for him.'

'There must be something behind his behaviour. He's a good man, Edie. He wouldn't toy with you.'

'Then why is he acting this way? I'm sure I did nothing to deserve it.'

'Can't you find an opportunity to speak to him?'

She sighed. 'I don't know whether I want to, now. I just feel so humiliated by the whole affair.'

Tilly put a cup of tea down in front of her. 'Don't give up on him. Perhaps he's had some bad news or something.'

'Perhaps,' Edie said non-committally. 'Where's Prue?'

'In the sitting room with Jack and the little ones, listening to *Children's Hour*. They're practising happy families for after the wedding.'

Edie smiled. 'At least that's one piece of good news. Imagine Jack speaking up after all this time. She'll have written to Bertie, I suppose.'

'I should think so.'

'How will he take it? Do you think he'll object to his mum marrying the gardener?'

'Oh, he'll be delighted, I'm sure. Bertie's no snob, and he adores Jack. He's been the closest thing the lad's had to a father since his own passed away.'

'I'm glad. Everything's worked out wonderfully, hasn't it?'

'Thanks to you,' Tilly said, smiling.

'Me?'

'I don't think you realise what a difference you've made here, Edie. I never would've believed crumbling old Applefield Manor could be like this, bursting with life and happiness. Prue's a new woman.'

'I didn't do anything.'

'Rubbish. You made her care again – about people, and about life. And just look what an effect that's had on everyone around her. Jack's happy for perhaps the first time in his life, Aggie and Jimmy are part of a loving family, the village has its treat day back. Not to mention all the animals who have a home now.'

'Prue should take the credit for that. I just gave her a nudge.'

'You did, and in such a gentle way that you opened her heart again,' Tilly said earnestly. 'I don't believe anyone else could have done what you did, Edie.'

Edie blushed at the praise. 'Well, thank you. I hope you're right.'

'It would have made your parents very proud.' Tilly squeezed her shoulder. 'I'm proud of you.'

Edie glanced out of the window at a sound from outside. Johnny Metcalfe, who was employed as a sort of general errand boy by a couple of the village shops, had just skidded to a halt on his bike. A moment later, the doorbell sounded.

'I wonder what he wants,' Tilly said.

'Bit late to be bringing anything over.' Edie sipped her tea. 'What sort of mood is Prue in today, Till?'

'Floating on air,' Tilly said with a smile. 'I caught her arranging fresh roses in the dining room earlier, humming "Oh Here is Love" from *The Pirates of Penzance*. Why?'

'I've got a surprise in the stable.'

Tilly shook her head. 'Not another animal?'

'Yes, a stray bitch pup. I hope she –'

Suddenly, the calm was broken by a heartrending wail. Edie jumped to her feet. 'Oh my God! What is it?'

At first she thought it was Jack, but this hadn't been a man's voice. A sense of horror settled on her heart, and as she met Tilly's eyes, she realised her friend was thinking the same thing. Because one of Johnny Metcalfe's jobs in the village was telegraph boy for the post office – or, as they were often nicknamed nowadays, an angel of death . . .

'Edie,' Tilly whispered. 'You don't think Johnny was here to . . ?'

'We'd better go to her.'

In the hall, Edie's worst fears were realised. Prue had sunk on to the bottom step, her face deathly white as she clutched a telegram. Edie felt the blood draining from her face too. Everyone lived in fear of telegrams these days – with good reason.

'Prue, not . . . not Bertie?' she whispered.

Jack and the children had appeared now. Prue didn't look at any of them; she only stared blankly ahead with unseeing eyes.

'Jack,' Prue whispered. 'My boy, Jack.'

She held out the telegram to him, and Edie watched the same deathly pallor creep into his face.

'Jack, what does it say? Tell us,' Tilly said. 'Bertie isn't . . . dead, is he?'

'Missing in action,' Jack whispered.

He choked back a sob and grasped at the banister for support. Edie took the telegram from him so she and Tilly could read it too.

Deeply regret to inform you your son 32819 Midn. A J Hewitt has been reported missing. Letter follows.

Just a few cold, formal words to deliver such complete devastation . . .

Coco, seeming to sense that Prue was in pain, pressed his nose against her hand. Coming to her senses, she pulled the hand sharply away.

'What . . . what is this?' she demanded, looking round at them as if newly awake. 'What are you all gawping at?'

'We're not,' Edie said gently. 'We just want to help, Prue.'

'Help!' Prue said, rising to her feet. A desperate, angry grief had replaced the blank look in her eyes. 'Can you bring back my boy? No one has that sort of black magic.' Her brow knit into a hard frown as she looked down at Coco. 'Why must this creature keep badgering me?'

'He's only being nice, Aunty Prue,' Aggie whispered in a tremulous voice. 'He don't like to see you sad.'

'Why is my home overrun with these things? This . . . this damned invasion!' Prue's voice was becoming shrill now.

'Please calm down,' Edie said. 'I know you're upset, but –'

Prue spun to fix her with an angry glare. 'This is your doing. All these animals, these children: every time I turn a corner I trip over one of them. Everything was peaceful until you came.'

'Prue, please. We all want to help you. Don't be angry with us.'

'I knew you were going to bring trouble, with your flag-waving nonsense about the war and these animals you insisted on bringing into my home. I should have trusted my gut and put you back on the train to London.'

'You're not making sense,' Jack said, putting a hand on her shoulder. 'Edie's not done anything wrong. Why don't you come with me?'

'Go with *you*!' She spun to face him. 'This is a judgement on me, that's what it is. God's punishing me for betraying Albert's memory. And you, his best friend, trying to take his place in my affections! How . . . how dare you!'

'I've never tried to take anyone's place,' Jack said quietly. 'I'm in love with you, Cheg. That's all.'

She pushed his hand away from her shoulder. 'For God's

sake, will you please stop addressing me by that silly childish name? You seem to make a habit of forgetting who's mistress here, Jack Graham.' She glared round at them. 'All of you. You treat this place as though you own it, filling it with every mangy stray you come across without so much as a by-your-leave. This is my home, damn you all! Mine and Albert's and . . .' She choked on a sob. ' . . .and Bertie's.'

The evacuees looked terrified now, and Tilly rested her hands on their shoulders.

'Prue, please,' she said in a low voice. 'You're upsetting the children.'

Prue looked down at them, and suddenly her fierce glare disappeared, replaced with a crumpled look of pain that was quite horrible to witness.

'I want them all out,' she said in a hoarse whisper.

Edie frowned. 'What?'

'I want every single one of these cursed animals out of my home, immediately. And the rest of you . . .' She swallowed hard. 'Stay out of my sight. We're not a family, we never were. We're just a group of people living under one roof because we're not wanted anywhere else. I never want to see anyone, human or animal, again as long as I live.'

She brushed Jack aside and swept upstairs to her room. The hurt expression on the gardener's face as he watched her go was heartbreaking.

Edie put a hand on his arm.

'You know she doesn't mean any of that, Jack,' she said quietly. 'She's grieving and she lashed out. At all of us, not just you.'

'Sounded like she meant it to me,' he muttered. He took the telegram from Edie and stared at it with blank eyes. 'That's what war does to people. Tears their hearts out. Makes them cruel.'

'We won't never be adopted now,' Aggie whispered to Jimmy. 'Aunty Prue don't want no one here now.'

'That isn't true, Aggie,' Tilly said in a soothing voice. 'Aunty Prue is upset, that's all.' She glanced at Edie. 'I think I ought to take the little ones to their room.'

Aggie went to pick up Coco, but Edie shook her head.

'Coco had better sleep out in the stables tonight, Ag. We don't want to risk upsetting Aunty Prue any more than she already is. We'll put the animals out of sight until she's had a chance to calm down.'

'She wouldn't really send them away, would she?' Jimmy whispered tremulously. 'Not Felix an' Coco an' Pepper an' all of them? They'll die, Miss.'

'I don't believe she will. When she's had time to recover from the shock . . . well, let's see where we stand in the morning.'

Jack, still reeling from the hurt caused by Prue's hard words, retired to his room while Edie and Tilly made the animals comfortable in the stables. It was a tricky business, trying to ensure that canaries were kept out of reach of kittens and there was enough bedding for them all to stay warm overnight, but with the aid of old blankets and weighted vegetable crates to block off the bottom part of the stalls' half-doors, the girls were able to create a dormitory of sorts.

'Well, it's all right for one night but it won't do for long,' Tilly said. 'Do you think Prue will change her mind about the animals, Edie? She sounded awfully certain.'

'She's in pain. Of course she is, her only son is most likely dead. I can't even imagine how much that must hurt, can you?'

Tilly shook her head soberly. 'It's every mother's

380

nightmare.' She glanced up. 'It's not without hope though. Perhaps he was captured.'

'It's possible, I suppose,' Edie said, but she could hear the doubt in her voice.

'He was due home on leave in a fortnight too.' Tilly sighed. 'What a horribly cruel thing to happen.'

'Poor Prue,' Edie said softly. 'And poor Jack. I felt like I could see his heart breaking when she accused him of trying to take Albert's place.'

'And he's been so happy since the engagement,' Tilly murmured.

'Prue's still got the same good heart though. We just need to find some way to get through to her again.'

'How? She seemed determined to shut us all out, along with the rest of the world. We're right back to where we started with her when you got here.'

'Except that even then, she couldn't resist a lost cause. You told me so yourself.' Edie glanced at the stray pup she'd brought home that evening, who was sharing a meal of horse meat with Coco. 'Till, I think I have an idea.'

'Are you sure about this?' Tilly hissed as Edie smuggled the little pup into the stone porch that led to the kitchen. 'She'll freeze to death out here if no one finds her.'

'Trust me,' Edie whispered back. 'Prue always checks front and back doors are locked before she retires. The puppy might be cold for a short while, but she'll be found within the hour. This is for the greater good.'

'What if Prue doesn't find her? What if she stays shut up in her room? Don't forget she's grieving.'

'She checks the doors every night, always at the same time. We just have to trust she's too much a creature of habit to change her routine.' Edie picked up one of the plant pots that sat in the nooks either side of the porch. 'This'll give our pup a cover story. It's important Prue thinks she's the one to have discovered her.'

She smashed the thing as quietly as she could, crouching down and cracking it against the flags like an egg.

'What if she throws the dog out?' Tilly whispered. 'She was adamant she never wanted to see another animal again.'

'She won't.' Edie glanced at the shaggy-haired puppy, which was looking up at her with big, puzzled eyes. 'She couldn't.'

Chapter 38

Prue was sitting on the end of her bed, hands folded in her lap, staring at the white-faced old lady in her dressing table mirror.

It was funny how she hadn't managed to shed a tear. Her eyes were as dry as they had been when the telegram arrived. She didn't feel anything now her anger had subsided: just numbness.

There was a photo of Bertie in uniform on the dresser, looking at her with his father's eyes and the boyish grin that had always been so effective at getting him out of scrapes. He couldn't be dead, could he? He was too much a living presence in her life: her brave young son of whom she'd always been so proud.

Prue's brain was filled with memories, flickering across it like a magic lantern show. Bertie, a babe in arms, while his father stood proudly over his wife and child. Bertie, giggling with delight as old Captain trotted around the gardens with the toddler on his back. Bertie in his school uniform, playing cricket with Jack in the grounds just as his father had once done – just as Jimmy did now. Each generation following the one before . . . until today.

There would be no grandchildren playing cricket in the

grounds of Applefield Manor to brighten Prue's old age. Bertie would never know, now, the heady joy of falling in love, or the blissful serenity of marriage with a kindred spirit. All of these pleasures would be denied to him by this war, this *damned* war, that stole young men's futures from them. Thousands of them slaughtered every day, ending not only their lives but the lives in potential: the children and grandchildren who would never be.

Suddenly, Prue was overwhelmed with anger. Anger at the war, and the men who sat behind their desks sending children to be butchered. Anger at God, for allowing something so utterly monstrous. Anger at the unfairness of it, that it had to be *her* boy who was taken, her only child – all she had in the world. She snatched up the mirror and hurled it at the wall, feeling a satisfaction that was all too fleeting as she watched it shatter.

Seven years' bad luck, wasn't that what the old superstition said? Prue gave a hard laugh. Well, Fate could do its worst, now. With Bertie gone, she had nothing else left to lose.

And yet still the tears wouldn't come.

Through the wall she could hear Samantha's soft wails. Matilda sang a lullaby as she rocked the child to sleep, just as Prue had once done for her own little baby.

Why had she ever opened her home to these people? It only brought pain when you let yourself care. First you trusted people, then you learned to love them, then . . . then they left you, and broke your heart. She had been right to close the doors when Albert died, to her home and her soul. The more people you let in, the more they'd end up hurting you, until your heart had been shattered over and over, like the shards of mirror on her bedroom carpet, and no amount of glue could . . .

But she was rambling, and it was nine o'clock. She still had enough concern for those under her roof to ensure they weren't all murdered in their beds. Throwing on her dressing gown, she crept downstairs to lock the front door, then went into the kitchen to check the back.

She frowned when she opened the door that separated the kitchen from the porch and discovered a pair of little eyes staring up at her.

Another damn animal! Hadn't she said she wanted them all out of her sight? Which one was it: that terrier of Aggie's?

The thing let out a small whimper, and Prue bent to look at it.

No, it wasn't Coco. This was a dog she'd never seen before, a mongrel of very uncertain heritage with shaggy black fur. It was small, very small; too small to be away from its mother, Prue was sure, and skinny to the point of starvation. What was more, it was shivering all over. The porch was solid stone, and it wasn't a warm night.

'Now, how on earth did you get in here?' she said to it.

There were two arch-shaped holes just above ground level on either side of the porch: a decorative feature that Prue liked to fill with pots of flowering shrubs in the summertime. One of the pots, she could see, had been shattered on the porch floor, soil and flowers spilling out everywhere.

'So that's it, is it?' she muttered. 'You broke in. It seems even now I'm not safe from invasion.'

She picked up the dog, opened the porch's back door and put it out, trying to ignore the way its little frozen body cuddled into her.

'Go on now, go,' she told it firmly, pointing out into the night. A cold drizzle misted the air. 'Go find somewhere else. We're not open to strays, not any more.'

The dog looked up at her with pleading eyes.

'No. I said no.'

Prue resolutely turned her back and went into the house. She locked both outer and inner doors and went up to bed.

But she couldn't fall asleep. Her mind was still full of thoughts of what she'd lost. Fragmented images of Bertie, as a boy and a young man; of the pain on the faces of the people she loved as her anger had exploded; and of a malnourished little puppy, shivering with cold and fear.

'Oh . . . damn it.' Prue got out of bed again, went downstairs and unlocked the porch doors.

The dog was still there, curled in a shivering, wet ball by the back step, seemingly unsure what to do with itself.

'All right, dog, come on. I won't see another life lost, not today.' Prue picked up the dog and took it into the house.

Prue carried the puppy to the sitting room, where she stoked up the embers of the fire until it was blazing again. She wrapped the dog – a little girl – in a couple of old blankets and put her in front of the blaze to warm up, then went to make her a dish of bread and milk.

'I could be arrested for giving you this, you know,' Prue said as she put down the dish. 'It's against the law to give milk to dogs these days.'

The puppy seemed suitably grateful, licking Prue's hand before she fell on her meal, and Prue tickled her between the ears.

What a cruel world this was, Prue reflected as she watched the dog lap hungrily at the concoction. She remembered how Jack had once saved a stray like this from a gang of lads who had been throwing stones at the poor thing, many years ago when they were children. Jack had seen them off with his fists – a gentle boy by nature, he could nevertheless fight well enough when he set his mind to it, and he never could abide cruelty to animals. Nor could Prue. How could anyone derive pleasure from causing pain to a defenceless creature? There must surely be a special place in hell for those who mistreated animals and children.

And she had put the starving little thing out into the cold and rain, to die perhaps! What had she become? She was sure she never used to be hard, or cruel. And yet tonight, in the rawness of her grief . . . she could see their faces now, how they had looked when she said those awful things. The children, Edie, Matilda . . . Jack.

Then the tears came at last. Suddenly Prue was overwhelmed by breathless, hacking sobs, choking her so she could hardly draw breath. Her heart hurt as she thought not only of what she'd lost but what she'd thrown away. Who was she? When she heard again the hurtful things she'd said, she didn't know herself. If Albert could see her from Heaven, if – God forbid – Bertie could, how ashamed they must be. To the children too! And to Jack, her dearest friend; the only man besides Albert she had ever loved in her life. What had she said to him? To throw his position in his face like that, and accuse him of betraying Albert when for years he had stayed silent out of respect for his old friend. She doubted he would ever forgive her. She didn't deserve him to.

Not knowing what else to do, Prue fell to her knees beside the little puppy and offered up a desperate prayer.

'Please, if Bertie is alive, keep him safe for me,' she whispered. 'Please, God, keep them all safe.'

When Edie came downstairs early the following morning, she found Prue on the couch with the little puppy sleeping in her arms, and she knew her plan had worked.

'Edie,' Prue whispered as she awoke. 'Oh, my dear, I'm so sorry. So sorry.'

Edie went to sit beside her.

'Where did this little chap come from?' she asked, reaching over to stroke the puppy. It wagged its tail sleepily.

'I found her in the porch half frozen, the poor thing.' Prue took Edie's hand. 'Sweetheart, please forgive me. I didn't mean a word of those dreadful things I said to you.'

'I know you didn't. You were grieving. Please, Prue, don't think any more about it.'

'I was so angry,' Prue murmured. 'Angry at the unfairness of it all, and I took it all out on you and the children. And poor, poor Jack, who's never said a hard word to me in forty years. I'm a bitter, ungrateful old lady and I don't deserve any of you.'

'Don't say that. People do and say things they don't mean when they're in pain. I know that's not who you are.' Edie took the puppy on to her own lap and tickled her between her ears. 'And so does this little lady.'

A couple of pale faces peeped around the door.

'Oh, children,' Prue said, summoning a weak smile for them. 'Now, come here and hug your Aunty Prue, if you still care to after she was such a crotchety old thing.'

Aggie hesitated, but Jimmy ran straight to Prue and threw himself into her arms. A tear slid down her cheek.

'I've lost one little boy, but I still have this one,' she whispered. 'I'm sorry, my darling. You must have been so frightened and upset.'

'I was upset 'cause you were sad,' Jimmy muttered. 'I didn't like you being sad.'

Overcoming her initial wariness, Aggie tiptoed in too and climbed on to Prue's knee beside her brother.

'Do you hate me very much, Aggie?' Prue asked softly, stroking the little girl's hair.

'No. I know when you feel like that. When our dad died, I was always getting done for fighting. I suppose this is a bit sort of the same.' Aggie snuggled into her. 'I'm sorry your son's missing, Aunty Prue. You won't send us away, will you?'

'No, my dear. I told you before, Applefield Manor is your home, always. No matter how much of a crosspatch I might be sometimes, nothing will ever change that.' She glanced at Edie. 'For any of my children.'

Edie smiled and patted her shoulder.

'An' Coco can stay, can't he?' Jimmy asked, looking up at Prue. 'An' the kittens an' Betty an' all the other animals?'

'Yes, dear, everyone can stay. I'm not going to lose anyone else I care about; I'm keeping them all right here, safe with me.' She looked at Edie. 'Where are the animals?'

'In the stables,' Edie said. 'We thought we'd better put them out of sight until you felt better.'

Prue gave the two children a big squeeze. 'Oh, you wonderful little darlings. I believe you've saved me, all of you. I feel I'd be quite desperate now without you. I'm so sorry I shouted.'

'Have you seen Jack yet?' Edie asked. 'He looked ever so hurt, Prue.'

Prue bowed her head. 'Not yet. I hope he can forgive me. I said some awful things to him, didn't I?'

'Why don't you go to him now?'

'Yes.' Prue took a deep breath. 'Yes, I must. Excuse me, children.'

As Prue climbed the stairs to Jack's room, she wondered what she would say to him. Could he forgive her for her cruel words? She needed him now . . . oh, so badly. She'd been a fool to push him away at a time like this. And of course, he would be grieving too. He had been almost a second father to Bertie. Wrapped up in her own pain, Prue had never spared a thought for how he must be suffering.

'Jack?' she whispered, knocking gently on his bedroom door.

There was no reply, so she tried again, a little louder.

'Jack? It's Cheggy, dear. Please let me in so we can talk.'

Again, no answer. Hesitantly, Prue pushed open the door.

The cupboard was open, ransacked of clothes. The leather case Jack used on the rare occasions he went travelling, which usually sat at the foot of the bed, was gone.

And so was Jack.

Chapter 39

'Ladies, see to the chickens, please. Make sure you bait the rat traps.'

Vinnie nodded. 'Yes, boss.'

'Marco, you can do the feeds. Davy, you're with me fixing that top wall,' Sam said. 'Luca, you and London take the truck down to Kirkton. The feed needs picking up, and there's a couple of bottles of foot rot ointment to be fetched from the veterinary's.'

Luca saluted. 'Yes, Sam.'

'London?' Sam said when Edie didn't acknowledge him. 'Did you hear that?'

'Oh.' Edie summoned a wan smile. 'Yes. Sorry.'

He frowned. 'You all right, are you? You're white as a corpse.'

'I've not been getting much sleep.'

'Then go to bed earlier. I expect you to be ready to do a day's work when you get here.' He regarded her, and his expression softened. 'Not ailing for owt, are you, lass?'

'I'll be OK.'

He was silent for a moment, looking into her face.

'Well, perhaps you'd better stay here if you're badly,' he said. 'Davy, you go with Luca.'

That was the first time Sam had picked her to work alone with him since before his proposal, over a month ago now, but it wasn't like it had been before. He showed no sign of wanting to make conversation while they worked, which suited Edie fine. She was in no mood for small talk.

After working in silence for over an hour, Sam spoke.

'All right up at yours, are you?' he demanded gruffly. 'I heard about Prue's boy.'

'She's been very upset, but the children are a comfort to her.'

'Well, it's a shame. Bertie Hewitt was a grand lad. Tell her I'm sorry, and if she needs owt she only has to ask.'

'Thank you. I'm sure she'll appreciate that.'

'Is there any hope?'

Edie bowed her head. 'It doesn't look that way. The letter Prue got said his ship went down. Some men were rescued, but the missing crew are feared drowned.' Her eyes started to fill. 'Poor Prue. She . . . she's really been having a difficult time.'

Unable to hold it back, she burst into tears.

'Hey,' Sam said gently. 'What's this?'

'Sam, it's horrible,' she whispered. 'Everything's just awful. Prue's in so much pain, and Jack's gone –'

'Jack Graham? Where's he gone?'

'That's just it: no one knows. Andrew Featherstone heard he was seen boarding the early train from Kirkton to London, and we haven't had a word since. Prue's worried sick about him.'

'Why would he just go like that? Last I heard, the pair of them were planning on getting hitched up.'

'They had an argument. She was upset when she got the telegram, and she . . . said some hurtful things to him. Now Prue's lost the two people she loves most, the children are

392

in tears all the time for worrying about Jack . . . I don't know what to do, Sam. I feel utterly helpless.'

'Sometimes there isn't anything you can do.' His face relaxed into a smile. 'Still trying to save everyone, eh, London?'

She smiled through her tears. 'I know, I can't help myself. I just wish there was some way I could help.'

'Well, you won't be much use to them if you're making yourself ill with worry.'

'I suppose not.' She looked up, and, in spite of everything, felt a surge of happiness at seeing the black scowl that had become his habitual expression in her presence lift.

'Sam . . .' she whispered. 'Will you hold me? I'd really like to be held, just for a moment.'

'I don't think that's a good idea, do you?' he said, and the scowl reappeared.

'Don't you want to?'

'Maybe I do, but I'm assuming your fiancé won't be keen.'

She frowned. 'My what?'

'Or your sweetheart then. The young soldier.'

'I don't know any . . .' She blinked. 'You can't mean Alfie?'

'Tanned bloke, blond hair, handsome?'

'Yes, that's him.' She stared at him. 'So *that's* why! All this time, you've been sulking because you thought Alfie and I were lovers?'

'You expect me to believe you're just good friends, do you? I saw you two kissing and cuddling outside the farmhouse.' He turned away. 'Well, I've no right to be jealous. You were never my girl. I was a fool to think you might want to be when you had so many better offers.'

Edie laughed, shaking her head. 'Sam, you . . . you ridiculous bloody man!'

'Look, let's just get back to work.'

She reached out to turn his face back towards her.

'Sam, Alfie Hume is one of my oldest, dearest friends,' she said gently. 'And that, I promise you, is all.'

'Come on, Edie. I might not have much experience of love, but I do know what it looks like. You're not seriously telling me he doesn't have those feelings for you?'

She bowed her head. 'No, he does. He asked me to be his wife, in fact, that same day. But I said no.'

'You what?'

'I said no because Alfie was too much like a brother to me for me to ever see him as anything else. And because . . .' She looked up at him. ' . . . because I was in love with someone else.'

Sam stared at her.

'Edie,' he whispered. 'Is that really how things are?'

'It is. So you see, you've been stomping about in a foul temper all these weeks for no reason at all, you big idiot. Now are you going to hold me or aren't you?'

Laughing, he folded his arms around her and planted a soft kiss on her lips.

'You know, London, you were right about me. I am an arse.'

Edie smiled. 'I'd forgotten about that. You were right too though. I was a bit of a prig back then, wasn't I?'

'I'm not sure that isn't the moment I fell in love with you. I'd never been insulted so sweetly before.'

Edie stared up at him.

'Sam,' she whispered. 'What did you say?'

'I reckon you heard me well enough, but since there's no one to hear me making a fool of myself but you and the Herdies then I don't mind repeating it.' He planted another gentle kiss on her lips. 'I love you, and I'm sorry. Sorry I nearly sabotaged my own happiness and yours by being a jealous pig. Can you forgive me?'

She stroked gentle fingertips over his cheek. 'Oh, I think I can, in time. Certainly before the wedding.'

'Sweetheart, really?' he whispered. 'You'll have me then?'

'I will.' She kissed him again. 'I tried my best, but you're a hard man to stop being in love with, Sam Nicholson.'

Prue was washing dishes when Edie arrived home. Molly, the orphan pup she'd nursed, was sitting at her heel. Since the night Prue had saved her from the porch, the little dog had refused to leave her side.

'I gave Tilly the afternoon off to take the children to the lake,' Prue said. 'They can play at catching minnows with those nets Jack made for them. The poor loves need some fun.'

'Any news?' It was a ritual, now, that Edie would ask this question whenever she arrived home.

Prue shook her head. 'No word from Jack, or anything more about Bertie.'

She burst into tears, and Edie wrapped her in a hug. The tears seemed to come at the strangest times. Just when Prue thought she was starting to adjust to this new world without Bertie or Jack, the truth would hit her again like a great, crashing wave, and there was no holding back the flood.

'We'll find Jack,' Edie whispered. 'He must be somewhere.'

'But there's no guarantee he'll come home if we do find him. I must have hurt him terribly for him to leave like that without a word.' Prue sighed as she sank into a chair. 'Edie, what if he has one of his attacks, out there alone? He might hurt someone . . . or himself.'

'Have you any idea who he might go to? Family or friends?'

'No family he's close to. Some old army friends, but I don't know their names.'

'You must know his regiment, though, and the dates and places he served. Do you?'

'I could find out. The details are all in the letters he wrote to Albert and me.' She wiped her eyes, feeling the kindling of something like hope. 'Do you think we might be able to find him that way?'

'It's worth a try.' The girl blushed. 'Perhaps Sam might be able to help. He's clever about finding out things like that.'

Prue raised her eyebrows. 'You're not telling me you spoke to that boy at last?'

Edie smiled shyly. 'Yes, we made it up. He'd got the wrong idea about Alfie and me, the silly man.'

'Are you engaged then?'

'We seem to be. Although I still don't have a ring, and there was no actual proposal as such.' She laughed. 'I think Sam must be an expert in proposing all the wrong way. But I don't care. He loves me, Prue; he told me so.'

'Oh, I am glad, dear. I've hated seeing you unhappy. I knew there'd be some foolish misunderstanding behind him withdrawing his attentions.'

'I ought to have known it would be something like that. He never was one for talking about things.' Edie sighed. 'It would all be perfect if things weren't so awful here. I'm sorry, Prue. It feels horribly selfish of me to be happy about anything right now, with Jack goodness knows where and Bertie –'

The doorbell rang. Prue dabbed her eyes dry and stood up to answer it.

'Are you expecting anyone?' Edie asked.

'Yes, Patricia. I asked to speak with her about the treat day. She's assuming I'll want to cancel, but it seems a shame when everyone's worked so hard. I won't be in any sort of mood for attending a party, but there's no reason it can't still be held in the grounds.'

But when Prue opened the door, she discovered it wasn't Patricia standing on the step. She nearly fainted when she saw who was filling the doorframe: his face rough with a full beard, looking tired and careworn, but with a smile on his face.

'Well, I'm home,' Jack said. 'Always seem to find myself back here, don't I?'

'Jack!' she gasped, falling on his neck. 'Oh, you stupid, stupid, wonderful man, where on earth have you been? I thought . . . I thought you'd left me.'

He wrapped his arms around her. 'Couldn't keep away, Cheg.'

'Do you know how worried I've been? What possessed you to disappear without a word like that?'

'Seemed you didn't want me here no more.'

'Oh, I said some awful things, I know, but I didn't mean them. I love you, you silly old man. Everything I said that night . . . I was so upset about Bertie, I didn't know what I was saying. When I thought I'd driven you away, do you know how that tore me apart? Where did you go?'

'To visit an old comrade. He was our chaplain – good man, and a good friend. He's attached to a military hospital down on the south-east coast now.' He freed himself from her arms. 'Which reminds me. Picked you up a little souvenir from the seaside.'

Prue frowned. 'A souvenir?'

'Just a moment and I'll fetch it. Better than a stick of rock, I promise.'

There was a long black car parked behind him on the drive. Jack opened the back door and gave his hand to a thin young man in a naval officer's uniform, who walked with the aid of a crutch. His left trouser leg was pinned up: empty below the knee.

Prue gripped the doorframe.

'Oh,' she whispered. 'Oh my goodness. Oh my *goodness*!'

Bertie smiled shyly as Jack supported him to the door. 'Hello, Mother.'

'But, Jack, wherever did you find him?' Prue asked when the tears and embraces had subsided – not before some time had elapsed – and Edie had brought the reunited family a pot of tea. There was no time of triumph or tribulation that the British didn't face with a hot cup of tea in their hands.

Bertie was sitting at his mother's side with little Molly on his lap. Every once in a while Prue reached out to press his shoulder, as if to reassure herself he was really there.

'Like I said, I went to stay with an old army friend, Tom Little, in Brighton,' Jack said as he lit his pipe. 'He was our chaplain, and I knew there was no better man to go to when you had a bit of soul-ache.'

Prue winced. 'I really am so sorry, Jack.'

'Well, mappen it was divine providence in the end,' he said, smiling at Bertie. 'Tom's chaplain at a field hospital there, and he asked me to go along with him to see a lad who's been suffering from the night terrors since Dunkirk. Thought it might do him some good to talk to an old soldier who understood what he was going through. And who should I spot further down the ward but young Bertie?'

'I was still unconscious then, an anonymous casualty fished out of the drink by a trawler,' Bertie told his mother. 'When I came round, the nurses told me Uncle Jack had been in every day, watching over me. Well, he always did, you know, Mother. I didn't know it was him, of course, till he came again – the nurses said there was an old soldier who liked to sit by me, but I had no idea it was my old soldier.'

Jack reached over to pat the boy fondly on the shoulder.

'I'm sorry, Cheg,' he said softly. 'I would have written, but the doctor told me . . . it wasn't certain, then, that he'd wake up. I didn't want to give you any false hopes.'

'But it's all right now,' Bertie said, putting an arm around Prue's shoulders. 'The quacks say I'm out of the woods and safe to come home. The war's over for Midshipman Albert John Hewitt, I'm afraid to say.'

'Darling, I'm so . . . it's just the most wonderful thing. God must have heard my prayer that night, after I got that dreadful telegram.' She glanced down. 'Oh, but Bertie, your leg.'

'Yes.' He gave the pinned-up part of his trouser leg a morose glance. 'I suppose I ought to be grateful to have escaped with my life. Still, I must admit that the future looks rather different than I expected it to.'

'Anything you need, darling, you'll have it. The best doctors, everything.' She looked again at the maimed limb. 'My poor boy,' she whispered. 'It must have hurt terribly when it happened.'

'I don't remember much apart from an explosion, then everything going dark. I suppose a magnetic mine got us, or one of those blasted U-boats.' He bowed his head. 'I don't know what happened to the other chaps. If they're dead or alive.'

Jack stood up and rested a hand on Bertie's shoulder. Prue saw a look pass between them, one she had no share in: a bond of distinctly male understanding, forged by love and by war.

'It's good to have you back where you belong, son,' Jack said in his quiet way. 'I'll leave you and your mam to have a talk.'

'Well, this place certainly looks different,' Bertie said when Jack had gone, glancing around the room. Jimmy's canaries were chattering in their cage while the kittens engaged in rough-and-tumble under the piano.

'A lot of things are different,' Prue said.

'So I see.' He turned to her. 'Mother, you look quite young and pretty again. Almost as you did when Father was alive.'

'Oh, don't be silly, Bertie. I'm an old lady now.'

He smiled. 'Uncle Jack doesn't think so, does he? He told me the two of you were planning on a wedding soon.'

Prue flushed. 'Yes. I wrote to you, but I suppose you would have been in the hospital. Do you mind, dear?'

'Nothing would make me happier. I always hoped he'd ask you one day.' He squeezed her hand. 'You know, Mother, if I'd bought it out there, and if I'd had a girl back home, I'd have wanted her to meet someone else. I wouldn't want her to feel guilty if she fell in love again.'

'Do you have a girl?'

He smiled. 'You know perfectly well I'm talking about you and Father. You don't need to feel guilty, you know. He'd want you to be happy.'

'Yes, I believe he would, the generous old soul.' Prue looked up at him. 'You're rather different yourself, Bertie. Ever so grown up. What happened to that boy I waved goodbye to?'

'The war did, I suppose.' He was silent for a moment. Then he roused himself and broke into a smile. 'Anyhow, Mother, I'm jolly glad to be home.'

Epilogue

The day of the village treat was everything a fete day ought to be: a cloudless sky, the grass stirred only by a gentle summer breeze, the air filled with the sound of laughing children and the delicious scents of popcorn and candy floss. Edie was surveying the scene complacently when someone tapped her on the shoulder.

She turned to find Sam behind her, dressed in the denims of his new Home Guard uniform.

'Well, doesn't somebody look dapper?' she said. 'I'm glad you decided to join, darling.'

He grunted. 'I'm only doing it so we can have a guard of honour at the wedding.'

'No, you're not, you big storyteller.' She stood on tiptoes to give him a kiss. 'A man in uniform. I always wanted one of my very own.'

He smiled as he put his arms around her. 'Whatever do you see in a grumpy old sod like me, eh?'

She shrugged. 'Mainly, I just wanted to get my hands on your sheep farm. But your rugged good looks have a certain charm.'

'You're a minx, London.'

'That's why you love me.'

'I do. And on that note, I want to ask you something. Again.'

She stared as he got down on one knee and produced a gorgeous diamond ring.

'Now then,' he said. 'I never quite seem to get this right, but I will this time because I'm not doing it again. Edie Cartwright, I've been desperately in love with you since the day you stood over me and told me what an arse you thought I was. And I know I'm only a rough country farmer, with nothing much to offer but a broken-down old farmhouse and an even more broken-down old heart, but if you'll have me, sweetheart, then I promise I'll do my best to make you happy, every day we spend together. So, would you please do me the honour of becoming my wife?'

'Hmm, I don't know. Can I have some time to think it over?'

'No, you can bloody well say yes before my knee gives way.'

'Well . . . all right, go on then.'

He stood up and slid the ring on, and she rewarded him with a kiss.

'Thank you, Sam,' she whispered. 'That was just how I always imagined it. Perfect.'

Their tender moment was interrupted by Aggie and Jimmy, who came running over and crashed into Edie's legs.

'I won a peashooter on the tin can alley!' Jimmy told her excitedly.

'I went on the merry-go-round three times in a row and I wasn't even sick!' Aggie announced proudly.

Edie laughed. 'It sounds as though you're having an eventful afternoon.'

'Edie, can we have a penny for a toffee apple?'

other toffee apple? You've already had one each, not to mention all the candy floss and lemonade.'

'It's not for us, it's for Bertie,' Jimmy said. 'We want to get him one 'cause he's going to be sort of our brother soon, ain't he? When we're adopted.'

'Ah, I see. It's a gift toffee apple. In that case, I think I can spare the money.'

'Here,' Sam said, taking a couple of two-shilling pieces from his pocket and handing them one each. 'This ought to buy a toffee apple and let you enjoy yourselves for a bit.'

'Blimey!' Aggie said, blinking at such unimagined riches. 'Thanks a lot, Mister!'

'And that's how you deal with children,' he said to Edie when they'd run away again. 'Good old-fashioned bribery. Never fails when you want to get your girl all to yourself.'

'I can see you're going to be a wonderful father.' Edie spotted Vinnie and Barbara a little way away near the brass band, talking to Prue and Jack. 'Oh look, it's those two. Come on, let's go say hello.'

Sam sighed. 'I'm never going to get you alone today, am I?'

'No, sorry.' She lowered her voice. 'But I might be available for a kiss and a cuddle in the blackout later, if you're a good boy all day.'

'Then I suppose I'll just have to bide my time and hope for better things to come.'

He followed her to the little group by the band tent.

'Hello, ladies,' she said, beaming at her Land Girl friends. 'I didn't know you were coming. What are you all talking about?'

'Mrs Hewitt was just telling us the good news,' Vinnie said.

Edie frowned. 'Good news?'

403

'Well, now you've ruined my surprise,' Prue
laughing. 'Edie, I've offered the house to the Land Army.
We have all those empty rooms, and of course after the
wedding . . .' She looked at Jack and blushed. 'Well, there'll
be another one spare soon. I think we can accommodate
all the girls and their warden, with a little shuffling and
rearranging. A house this size really ought to be helping
the war effort.'

Edie smiled. 'I can recall saying something like that
myself, once upon a time.'

Prue cast an affectionate glance at Bertie in the distance,
clutching a toffee apple as he instructed Aggie and Jimmy
in how to work the swingboats. 'And you were absolutely
right. Perhaps I only realised the importance of everything
we're fighting for after Bertie was injured. If my boy can
sacrifice his leg and almost his life fighting the good fight,
giving up a few spare rooms feels like the least I can do.' She
pressed Edie's shoulder. 'Of course you're welcome to stay
as long as you wish, dear, with the other girls. You'll always
have a home at Applefield Manor, whether single or married.'

Sam laughed. 'Try not to talk her out of it, Prue. I still
need to get her to the altar.'

'I suspect that once you've been introduced to my Aunt
Caroline, I'm going to be the one fighting to get you there,'
Edie said, grinning at him. 'Don't forget your tin hat when
we visit her, will you?'

'She doesn't frighten me. I'm still going to be the happiest
man in the country the day I get you up that aisle.'

'That reminds me.' She looked at Jack. 'Jack, I wondered,
um . . . would you give me away?'

Jack blinked. 'Me?'

Edie nodded shyly. 'I think my dad would approve, and
I can't think of anyone I'd rather have.'

̱ looked pleased. 'I'd be honoured, lass.'

'What about all your animals, Mrs Hewitt?' Barbara asked. 'Edie tells me you've got quite a houseful. Will there be room for us Land Girls too?'

'That's our other piece of news,' Jack said, smiling fondly at his future bride. 'Do you want to tell them, Cheg?'

'Jack and I have decided to modernise and expand the old stable building,' Prue told them. 'We want to turn the place into a sort of sanctuary, for animals made homeless by the war. I'm sure there are hundreds who need a home, and we have the land, of course.'

'Oh, Prue, it's a wonderful idea!' Edie gave her a hug. 'That's the perfect thing to do with Applefield Manor. It's been a sanctuary for so many of us already.'

'I should thank you, Edie,' Prue said as she returned the hug. 'If it hadn't been for you, I'd never have opened myself up to happiness a second time. Life has meaning and sweetness now in a way I never believed it could again. God bless you, dear. I hope you won't ever forget us.'

Edie blinked away a tear.

'Of course not,' she whispered. 'I don't believe I ever had a home, a true home, until I came here.' She glanced at Sam. 'And thanks to Mr Nicholson's generous offer, now I'll always be near the people I love the most.'

She turned to look over the grounds as the band struck up the stirring notes of 'Nimrod'. It felt like the whole village was there: Andrew and Patricia, the tweedy vicar's wife smiling serenely for a change as she looked after the WI cake stall; Marco and Luca, given special permission to attend by their camp commandant so they could run the stall selling Applefield Manor's jams and chutneys; Tilly with Baby Samantha in her arms, pretending to browse the jams so she could have a surreptitious conversation with

her husband; Davy Braithwaite and the young lady ı
courting, Ivy Constance, walking old Betty round as s
gave sedate rides to some of the little ones; Bertie, leaning
on his crutch as he watched his new siblings on the swingboats; Vinnie and Barbara, inseparable as ever, discussing
their new lodgings; Prue and Jack, eyes for no one but each
other and their little family, glowing with love and pride.
And Sam, her Sam, tall and beautiful in his new uniform,
smiling alongside her with his arm curled lovingly around
her waist.

Since she'd been a little girl, Edie had wanted to do
something great; something that would justify the life she
felt her father had bargained so dearly for, like joining the
Wrens and helping to win the war. But as she looked around
the bustling, lively, joy-filled grounds of Applefield Manor
and thought about how different it was, now, from the
dismal place it had been when she arrived, she realised that
it wasn't the scale of your actions that mattered; it was the
lives you changed along the way – and those you saved.

Edie experienced a warm glow of satisfaction as she
looked around her at the sea of happy, laughing faces. It
felt as though her work here, at last, was done.

CRIMINOLOGY SKILLS